Her hands squeez
unbearable. "I wouldn'

Parker ran a hand through his hair. "Argh! Don't you understand? She'd take one look at your face and know the truth. Don't forget, you're the one who wanted us to protect him."

She stood. "Well, you did a hell of a fine job, didn't you? You divorced Grace and deserted him. Parenting takes sacrifice, Parker. You were too busy changing careers, and now he's messed up with drugs. How did that protect him?"

Standing, he reached for her.

"No. You stay away from me." She extended her hands and backed up a step. "Justin's dying! Dying, Parker! And I don't know him...You won't let me see my own son."

He wrapped his arms around her.

She pushed him, pummeling her fists against his chest with all her strength.

He silently took his beating.

"Why did I do it? Why did I ever give him up?" She searched his face. Finding no answers, she rested her head against him and let him hold her. A dozen daggers stabbed her core. "Oh, Parker. It hurts so much. I missed his whole life. What if I lose him forever?" With as much force as she could muster, she scraped her nails deep across her hands.

Finding Euphoria

by

Caroline,
Find your joy!

C. Becker

C. Becker
2019

Euphoria, Book One

Finding Euphoria

Cover Art by *R.J. Morris*

The Wild Rose Press, Inc.
PO Box 708
Adams Basin, NY 14410-0708
Visit us at www.thewildrosepress.com

Publishing History
First Mainstream Thriller Rose Edition, 2019
Print ISBN 978-1-5092-2491-3
Digital ISBN 978-1-5092-2492-0

Euphoria, Book One
Published in the United States of America

Dedication

To Bub

~*~

Acknowledgments

Deepest thanks to all the people who helped make this book possible.

First, an enormous thank you to Rhonda Penders and the amazing team at The Wild Rose Press. RJ Morris used my input and created an intriguing masterpiece, designing the best cover I could have asked for. A huge thank you goes to my extraordinary editor ELF, who believed in my story and pushed me to make it better. Her feedback, advice, and edits shaped *Finding Euphoria* into a compelling thriller.

My dedicated writers' group who spent endless hours, providing comments and edits, especially Gene Turchin, Lindsey Minardi, Ron Knoblock, Sandra Woods, and Diane Davis. We had many laughs and lengthy discussions during our meetings at the bakery-café (and a few odd stares when we discussed murders). They stuck with me through the end. I can never thank them enough.

A special thank you to my loving husband, Paul. When I began writing this novel, he humored me but always remained my number one supporter in this crazy venture. Thank you for putting up with my ridiculous schedule of going to bed at 3 a.m. I love that we muse over who will star in the roles when this story becomes a movie.

To my children: Kevin, Ashley, Brian, and Brooke, who believed in me. Their patience during the past years has been amazing. Whether it was through encouraging words, or washing dishes, making dinner, and cleaning the house when writing preoccupied my time, their support truly inspired me. I love you all.

Finally, thank you to my community of beta readers who read the story: Melissa, Suzanne, Mitzi, Lois, Lauya, Barbara, Rose, Debbie, Brianna, Maria, Kent, Antoinette, Kelsey, Sharon, Holly, James, Mary Jo, and a special unnamed supporter. They are my cheerleaders, and I couldn't ask for better friends.

This story is the result of all of you.

Chapter One

January 1998, California

Hailey Robinson stared at the masked man slouched on the tattered recliner. She shivered and huddled deeper in her jacket. A sharp pain stabbed her in the lower ribs, and she gasped. She turned her head away from the warm fireplace and glanced out the cabin window at the light fluffy snow. Daylight was creeping in. This man had better drift off soon. All night he had sat in his clown disguise and ogled her. The shotgun cradled across his bulging belly moved with each breath. Another batch of goose bumps spread across her arms.

Finally, his head drooped. Just a few more minutes. Let him fall into a deep sleep. Then she could escape. A heavy weight pushed on her stomach. What if the plan didn't work? No. she couldn't go there. It *had* to work. She glanced out the window again. The snow came down faster, heavier. The kidnappers had arranged a ransom pickup later in the afternoon. She had nothing to lose. How could her parents come up with the ransom when they couldn't afford a cell phone? At last, the man snored.

"Psst. Hailey, you awake?"

She turned her head to look at the boy lying next to her on the stone floor. The fire illuminated Sam's handsome face. "Yeah." The smoke strangled her voice to a whisper. "I can't sleep."

"Me, too." His voice was hoarse. "How bad are you hurt?"

Tears burned her eyes. Her sides throbbed as if a wild horse had trampled her. She'd do anything to feel her mother's comforting arms around her. "It could be worse."

"Are you able to run?"

She inhaled, and a streak of pain ran across her back. She closed her eyes. Papa would expect her to stay strong. "Yeah. I think so."

"Why did Madge kick you last night?"

"You stupid bitch. Your parents have no money." An ember popped in the fireplace. She wrapped her arms around herself, unable to stop her lip from quivering. "I don't know."

"Did you give Ken the key?"

She nodded. "I palmed it to him after I swiped it from Madge's purse."

"Good. He's the fastest runner. He'll start the van."

Hailey pictured the evil battle-ax yelling with a cigarette dangling from her mouth.

Sam leaned closer. "Sounds like this guy's out for the night. We should go before Madge and the other guy wake up. It's starting to snow. If we don't leave now, we're stuck."

The wind whistled outside. Getting off this mountain would be tricky. She started imagining a reunion with her parents and stopped. With her luck, something would still spoil the plan.

Sam nudged her shoulder, and she gritted her teeth from her arm's tenderness. "Are you sure you're okay?"

"Yeah, I'm good." She forced a smile and shivered. What was the point in telling him everything ached? "Wake Ken and Victoria." Rubbing her arms against the chill, she prayed for a miracle.

The four teens pulled on their shoes and zipped up the jackets they had worn while lying on the cold floor. Hailey hurried and finished putting on her gear first. Turning to the kidnapper, she knotted the laces of his snow boots together. That would slow him down.

Sam motioned toward the door, but Hailey pointed to the shotgun. "It'll protect us. Madge and the other guy have a gun. This dude's not waking anytime soon." Trembling, she held her hand on the stock and nudged the metal part around the trigger from his clutch. She held her breath and slid the barrel across his lap.

He grabbed her arm, and she jumped, dropping the gun on his lap. She jerked away, but he yanked her back. The clown mask, with unnatural red lips and wild orange hair attached on the sides, seemed to jeer at her. Chills raced through her body. Ken and Victoria pulled on her arm. Sam stepped forward and punched the man's face, once, twice, three times, until he slumped back in the chair.

Hailey quivered as she led the others in the race to the door. When she opened it, the frigid air snapped at her face. The cold gusts shocked her lungs, but she continued trudging as quickly as she could through the deep snow. The van was a distance ahead next to a dilapidated shed. Ken pulled ahead with Sam and Victoria following three steps behind. She couldn't keep up. Her ribs screamed, and she gasped for air. How much time did she have? She looked back. The two men stood outside the cabin, and Madge screeched at them. Hailey turned her head forward. Her foot banged against a snow-covered rock. Crying out, she fell forward in the snow.

She looked up as Sam spun around from a distance ahead. "Are you all right?" he shouted.

Pain bit through her leg, and she lifted her head. Behind her, a gun fired, and she turned. The kidnappers were running toward her. She twisted back again toward Sam. "My ankle." She struggled to her feet, but the heavy snow weighed her down. "I'll never make it."

The van's engine turned over. From inside the van, Ken yelled, "They're coming."

Sam took a tentative step closer. Too much space was between them.

A few yards ahead of Sam, Victoria turned. "Come on. Don't waste time on her." She raced forward.

Voices cursed behind Hailey in the distance. She was on her knees, but the pain in her ankle increased when she added weight. *Don't leave. God, please don't leave.* She turned her head once more. The kidnappers were getting closer. A thickness formed in her throat. "Go without me."

"No." Sam took another step toward her and glanced behind her.

"Go! Get help!" A chill spread through her body.

Victoria climbed in the van's front seat. Hailey shut her eyes. "Go!" Tears flowed as the wind whipped her cheeks. She tried lifting her knee and screamed.

A second shot fired, and the van's horn blared. The van propelled forward, fishtailing through the snow, finally hitting solid ground. "Okay, we'll find help. I promise." Sam darted to the vehicle and dove through the door that Victoria held open. Another bullet ripped through the air, pellets spraying the side door as it closed. A hint of gunpowder permeated the air. The van disappeared down the lane as one more blast echoed.

The shaking wouldn't stop. Her teeth chattered against the wintry air. Images of the bus driver and math teacher lying in a pool of blood at the gas station flashed through her mind. She visualized herself bleeding to death in the snow, her parents sobbing next to her body. Footfalls crunched behind her, and she twisted her torso. The dark muzzle of a shotgun pointed in front of her eyes.

Chapter Two

March 1998, Austin, Texas

"Aargh! Agh!" Hailey jumped off the bed, pushing into the darkness, thrashing at someone poking her arms.

"Honey, we're trying to help you," a soft female voice spoke.

She squirmed as someone gripped her arm. Why was the voice muffled? She tugged at her ears and sat back on the mattress, rocking herself. *Momma. Papa. Where are you?*

"Tie her to the bedrail."

"No." *Whose gruff voice was that?*

"But Dr. Hanover, we have to examine her."

She clawed the hand pressing on her shoulder. Lifting her other arm, she scratched the covering over her eyes.

"She's ripping off the bandage again!"

"Ouch, she's a fiery one!"

"Let her alone. You'll traumatize her even more."

Hailey pressed her palms against her ears at their intermittent babble. Why were they whispering?

"What if she hurts herself again?"

"I'll stay with her." Another man's deep gentle voice was clearer. Was he standing closer to her?

"It's settled." Dr. Hanover's rough voice was the easiest to differentiate. "Dr. Parker will stay. I'll check on you both later."

The room quieted and the unfamiliar pawing over her body ended. Next to her, the mattress sank. "Hailey. I'm Parker. I know this is hard on you, but we're trying to help you see and hear again. We need you to cooperate. Please don't be scared."

Her body trembled, and she sat rocking herself, concentrating on his voice. Something heavy covered her legs. She tugged at it—a soft blanket. When she pulled it over her chest, her body relaxed.

"You were hurt, but we're taking care of you. You're at the clinic of the Special Crimes Agency in Austin, Texas. The FBI brought you here after your rescue."

She scrunched her face as he spoke. Rescue?

"You were kidnapped. There was trauma to your entire body. Broken bones. Lacerations. Bruising. Burns on your back and face. But you're safe now. The whole team has been working hard to help you."

She lifted her hand and touched the smooth bandage wrapped around her eyes.

"The swelling should lessen over the next few days, and we'll remove the bandage. Dr. Hanover is designing another ear implant. Besides being a doctor, he works in the Research and Development complex. He makes gadgets to treat special cases like yours."

She gripped the velvety blanket and drew it to her neck. Where were her parents? Why were these people keeping them away? She lay down and rested her head on a pillow, mashing her hands against her cheeks. Would the nightmares come back tonight?

7

"Try to sleep. I'll stay for a while." Something about his voice soothed her, and her body relaxed. She would let herself nap for a few minutes.

****

Knock. Knock. "Hi. Hailey. It's Dr. Parker. Are you ready for your big day?"

She rocked back and forth on the bed. He had talked about this day for a while. The days blurred together. What if she couldn't see after Dr. Hanover removed the bandages? She tilted her head as his heavy soles clacked against the floor.

A thud bumped against the bedside tray. "Looks like you didn't eat anything."

She remained silent and wiped her sweaty palms on her cotton nightgown.

He held her hand. "Nervous?" Why did he ask her silly questions when she didn't speak? "Dr. Hanover should be here any minute. He's been busy designing another implant for your ear—one that will give you more hearing."

Shaking, she gripped the crisp sheet with her other hand. Was she selfish to want both sight and hearing returned?

Another hard knock sounded. "Good morning, Hailey."

She stopped rocking. At last, Dr. Hanover was here.

He stepped closer. "I brought one of your nurses with me."

"Hi, Hailey. It's Jan." The woman's feminine flowery scent reminded Hailey of her mother.

"Let's begin." Dr. Hanover coughed. "It's important for you to understand that if your vision doesn't return today, your eyes may need more time to heal. Don't get discouraged. This is like the ear implants. We'll keep trying different approaches."

She straightened her shoulders. *Please begin already.*

Dr. Hanover's spicy aftershave took hold of her senses as he came closer. "I'll keep the lights dim when I remove the patches."

She waited, biting her bottom lip. The bandages pulled on her hair as Dr. Hanover unwound them.

Parker tightened his grip on her sweaty hand and gave her a reassuring squeeze.

"Okay, now open your eyes." Dr. Hanover's words emboldened her.

Her heart pounded against her chest as she drew in a breath and exhaled. She raised her eyelids. Everything around her was gray. A lump lodged in her throat. She tried to swallow it down.

Parker squeezed her hand. "Give it a minute."

She blinked a few more times. Blurry figures stood around her. She blinked again, letting her eyes adjust. Beside her, Parker held her hand. Dr. Hanover and Jan stood next to him. They looked different than she imagined. Dr. Hanover was middle-aged, with dark-blond hair. And glasses. She never picked up on the glasses. Parker was more muscular. Athletic and handsome. Very cute. Dark eyes. Maybe in his late twenties. He was younger than she'd envisioned, and definitely taller than Dr. Hanover. Dressed in a white nurse's uniform, Jan smiled, watching. Was this friendly woman the monster touching her arm during blood pressure readings? The room behind them was fuzzy.

"Hailey?" Dr. Hanover stared.

She couldn't hold back her smile. Her eyes blurred with dampness. Blinking back the tears, she lowered her head in her hands and sobbed.

****

As the days passed, hope filled Hailey's soul. The soreness in her body lessened. She no longer screamed when the therapists stretched her arms and legs. The mauve bruises on her arms had faded into light shades of green. The nightmares diminished. Parker beamed as he checked on her each day. Dr. Hanover often visited, giving updates on the new ear implant he was inventing.

One morning, a phone rang and woke her. She concentrated on the hushed voice that answered the call.

"I can't have this conversation now. You knew about my intense workload when I took this internship. A baby will have to wait." Parker. She'd recognize his smooth, deep voice anywhere. "I'm not moving back to Chicago. Why won't you listen to me? I don't care if your parents can help with a baby. This is a once-in-a-lifetime opportunity."

How long had she slept? She had drifted in and out of sleep countless times during these past weeks. She opened her eyes and focused on the doctor wearing a white lab coat. Thankfully, her sight was almost back to normal.

Parker stood with his back to the window and held a phone to his ear. "Don't call me selfish. I'm not ruining our marriage." The irritation in his voice was evident. "Why do you always argue about this? I'm keeping my options open. Can't you realize the benefits of splitting research and patient care? I'm still unsure what route I want to take with my career."

She rolled on her side and turned her head. His private conversation was none of her business. She pressed her ear against the pillow. It was useless. Her hearing was improving, especially in the lower range. The latest implant worked better than Dr. Hanover had expected. She scanned the room. *Concentrate on something else.* The vase next to her bed was different today. The nurses must have taken out the lilies and filled it with pink daisies while she slept.

Parker paused. "Grace, I have to go. I'll see you tonight." Soft footsteps tapped behind her. "Hailey?"

She closed her eyes and faked a soft snore.

A light tap knocked on the door. "I got your message. Any change?"

Dr. Hanover! She covered her long bangs over her face and peered at him.

Parker walked to the door and lowered his voice. "No. She's been asleep since I came on this afternoon."

"She needs her rest."

"She still doesn't talk. It's time to consider transferring her."

Hailey tensed her muscles. Transfer?

"What are you talking about?" Dr. Hanover spoke in a sharp tone.

"Her physical bruises are healing, but she has too many psychological wounds."

"She's not ready yet. She just had eye surgery a few weeks ago. And she's only regained partial hearing on her left side."

Parker looked at her and turned. "She doesn't even look at us. It's disheartening, watching her stare straight ahead, not registering her surroundings. It's like a solar eclipse has darkened her soul. I think she should stay at a psychiatric hospital."

Papa, no. Help!

"Absolutely not."

"Why keep the girl here if she won't speak?" Parker raked a hand through his hair. "We can't do anything else. Her physical injuries are healed."

"Keep your voice down. Don't let her hear you talk like that." Dr. Hanover shook his hand at him. "My, God! Just because a chicken has wings doesn't mean it can fly. You've read her blood tests. There are issues we haven't addressed yet. Why are you quitting on her?"

"I'm not. Someone experienced in psychology should work with her."

The nails in her fists dug into her skin.

"Bullshit! You're running away! You want to pass her off to the next doctor who will spend months medicating her, drowning out her emotions." Dr. Hanover lifted his hand and massaged his chest. "Why do so many doctors forget a living, breathing soul exists inside the body?"

"I'm not doing that."

"Like hell you're not. We may never realize the trauma this girl endured. She's paralyzed. Her recovery is only beginning, and she needs to make some big decisions soon. I won't turn my back on her. Besides, I'm still fine-tuning another device to restore the rest of her hearing. I say she stays."

Parker sighed. "I don't understand why you're adamant about keeping her when we can't give her the specialized care she needs."

A knife stabbed her heart at his betrayal.

"I'll bring in specialists. It's the least I can do for her." Dr. Hanover inhaled loud breaths and continued massaging his chest.

"What are you talking about?"

Dr. Hanover glanced at her, and she shut her eyes. She didn't dare move a muscle.

"Nothing. Please respect my decision. I intend to help her as long as it takes."

"But—"

"But nothing. I'll stay with her for a while. You have rotations to finish."

The room quieted, and she raised her eyelids. Near her bed, Dr. Hanover sat on a chair with his head lowered in his palms.

She bit her lip and remained silent.

Dr. Hanover raised his chin and brushed the bangs covering her face. His gaze met hers. "Don't worry. I won't abandon you." His voice was brittle. He pulled out a handkerchief and dabbed sweat from his forehead. He clutched his chest, his arms trembling. "After twenty-six years, I thought the torment would've faded. Forgetting my past is like trying to bag some flies."

She tilted her head and stared. He talked in strange riddles.

****

Each day Parker came to her room carrying snacks, offering them to her. He always sat on her left side, as if he knew she could hear better in that ear. His cheerful attitude encouraged her.

Hailey spent time exploring the room. She hadn't noticed the colorful artwork hanging on the walls until now. Parker demonstrated how to operate the nurse's call button—in case she needed it. She opened the music box that Dr. Hanover had bought her and listened to "Amazing Grace." The nurses even filled a crystal vase with fragrant flowers. But she refused to speak.

Parker's monologue was always the same. "Hello, Hailey. I'm Dr. Tom Parker. You can call me Parker if you prefer. Everyone does."

She remained quiet. Why would he show kindness if he wanted to send her away?

"I'm making you my personal mission. I want to crack the armor you're hiding under so you can live again."

She considered his goal. No, she wouldn't let him in. He was a part of humanity that had betrayed her. She couldn't trust him. Besides, he hadn't let her parents visit, and she ached for them. They had to be worried out of their minds.

Despite her silence, he persisted. "I'll stay and keep you company." Parker sat in the visitor chair near the bed and read her novels, magazines, and newspapers. He talked about the drought in Texas and his work in the research lab.

She breathed easy with his continued presence.

More weeks passed, and one day she woke, more aware of her surroundings. She sat in a chair and stared out the window, trying to make sense of her dream. Papa and Momma had appeared the night before. Papa held her and brushed a finger across her cheek. *Be brave, little Hailey.* Momma kissed her. *We want you to get better. Trust Parker.*

The door creaked and footsteps tapped behind her. "Hello, Hailey. I'm Dr. Tom Parker."

A single tear trickled from her eye. Her face scrunched as she tried to form a sound. "P...P...Parker," she whispered.

****

Hailey sat on her bed and stared at the peculiar paintings on the wall. She grabbed the sheets as the room spun around her. The pictures looked like the inkblot tests used in one of her gifted classes. Vibrant paint splotches were spattered on the canvas. Were the pictures supposed to brighten her day or make her dizzy? Was there a deeper meaning to uncover? The small vase of lilacs on the bedside dresser offered more significance. The soft colors and sweet fragrance warmed her senses, transcending hope.

Despite the contrived comforts in the room, she was a prisoner. Other than Parker, the nurses, and Dr. Hanover, no one came. Not even her parents. She swept the brush down her hair, untangling the knots. Was today the day her parents would visit? Another clump of brunette hair caught in the bristles. She should ask the nurse for a trim. Lifting her hand, she explored her face. Bumps and scabs dotted her cheeks and jawline. Uneven thicker textures adhered to her smooth, soft skin. Dr. Hanover refused to give her a mirror. How many blemishes did she have?

A gray-haired nurse entered the room and set a dinner tray on the over-bed table. Parker would stop by soon. He came each evening and chatted before he drove home.

A warm glow flowed through her as she awaited the visit. She put on a new blouse and ran the brush through her mane once more.

A knock thumped on the door, and Parker strode in the room. "Look who I bumped into."

Dr. Hanover followed, a bright smile across his face. "How's our patient today?"

She gave a small wave. "I'm okay."

Parker stepped closer and sat in the chair beside her bed. His fresh scent gave her security. "The audiologist reviewed your tests." He leaned back and propped his hands behind his head. "Your hearing is close to one hundred percent with the new implants."

Joy sang in her soul. "That's great news."

"The therapist told us you're getting stronger. We'll increase your rehab time if you're up to the longer workout."

Hailey nodded. All the rehab exercises were becoming easier. She had walked down the corridor eight times today. She wanted to keep walking, but the therapist had insisted she take a break.

Dr. Hanover peeked under the dinner tray cover. "Looks like you're having chicken and rice tonight." He touched her hand, and his smile faded. "Dr. Parker and I want you to see another doctor."

A chill ran through her. "Why?"

The two men exchanged glances. Dr. Hanover rubbed a hand along his jaw; the stubble scratched against his hand. "Dr. Singh is a psychiatrist."

Her gaze shifted to Parker. "You want me to see a shrink?"

Parker pressed his lips together in a tight line. "We prefer to use the term psychiatrist. Dr. Singh is from Boston. She's helped many trauma victims and comes highly recommended."

"But why?"

He sighed. "You're dealing with a lot of issues. She can help you."

She crossed her arms over her chest. "I don't want her help."

"You need to talk to someone." Dr. Hanover's tone was reassuring. "You're not opening up about the kidnapping."

Staring at them, Hailey narrowed her eyes. There was no way in the world she would talk about that horrible time with a stranger. "I'll talk to my parents when you let them come."

"Ahem." Dr. Hanover sat straighter in his seat. "We can't do that."

"You say that all the time," she snapped.

Parker scratched his head. "It's not that easy."

"Sure it is. I know they'll come. They love me." She swallowed hard. Were they embarrassed by what had happened to her?

Parker stared at the older doctor and waited. At last Dr. Hanover spoke. "They can't come."

"Why not?" Hailey touched her face. "Am I so grotesque you're afraid they won't visit me?"

"Of course not." Dr. Hanover sounded subdued.

"Then why can't I see them?"

Dr. Hanover nodded to Parker. "Go ahead. Tell her."

"Tell me what?"

Parker squirmed in the chair. His wood-scented cologne brought back memories of the cabin. "We've been trying to protect you."

She swallowed hard. "From what?"

Parker sighed. "There's no easy way to tell you. Your parents both died the day of your rescue."

17

Bile surged at the back of her throat and her hand flew to her mouth. "What?"

His face paled. "There was a car accident. The snowy roads at the top of the mountain were slick. As they followed behind the rescue vehicles, they skidded on an icy patch and went over a cliff."

In a panic, she leaned forward and retched.

Parker grabbed the wastebasket next to the bed and held it under her chin.

Finally, she wiped her mouth with her sleeve. "You're lying."

"We're so sorry." He reached out and gathered the loose hair away from her face. "We wanted to wait until you were stronger."

The room spun as she stared at them. "No!" Holding her side, she heaved again. She swayed and pressed her hand on the mattress, steadying herself.

Parker leaped from his chair and held her. "We'll help you through this."

Dr. Hanover grabbed a tissue from the dresser and handed it to her. "You won't go through this alone."

She raised her head, their sympathetic faces swimming around her. She didn't need their pity. Her bottom lip jutted out. "Get out."

"Hailey." Parker put his hand on her shoulder.

She flung her arm across the bed table, and the food spilled on the floor. "I said, 'Get out!' "

Dr. Hanover opened his mouth, but Parker stood and motioned him to the door.

Trembling, she waited as they stepped toward the door. The two morons stuck together like magnets. When the door closed, she yanked her hair. "Nooo!" She shoved the table into the bedside dresser. The vase crashed on the floor, and the color in her world faded. She buried her face in the pillow and screamed.

****

Hailey cried most of the night. The nurses hovered around until she implored them to leave her alone. Sadness eroded her inside until hollowness echoed through her body. She pressed a hand over her mouth and stifled her sobs. "Momma. Papa. No!" Why didn't someone tell her sooner? She exhaled a long sigh and hiccupped back a sob. She had no one left in the world. Another wave of tears crested, and she wailed again.

Furious, she wiped her eyes. *Stop crying.* She wrenched a handful of tissues from the box on the nightstand and dried the stray tears on her face. *Pull yourself together.* Dammit! Why couldn't she stop the damn tears? She lifted her right arm and dug her nails deep into her skin, scraping a long mark down her arm. Stop crying! Stop crying... Stop... Crying! She scratched three times, as hard as she could, and paused. Ouch.

She lay on the bed and blinked. For a moment, the sadness and heartache disappeared though her inflamed arm hurt. Using lighter pressure, she scraped her hand instead of her arm. She grinned at the faint imprint. The nurses would never notice these marks. She spent the morning hours curled up in bed, scratching.

A knock tapped on her door and Dr. Hanover stepped in the room. "Mind if I come in?"

She stiffened and dropped her hands. *Go away.*

He slid a chair closer to her bed. "I'll take that as a yes."

She straightened her shoulders and stared at the inkblot hanging behind him. Two inverted tarantulas with giant fangs eating a grasshopper. Maybe the figures were Dr. Hanover and Parker.

Dr. Hanover made a poor attempt at a cough and leaned forward. "I can wait all day until you're ready to look at me."

She scowled and met his eyes. His blank expression made it hard to read his mind.

"Did you sleep last night?"

She sighed. "I'm sure the nurses already told you about my night." She lowered her eyelids. "Now, will you please leave? I'm tired."

"I'm sorry about your parents. We didn't want to hurt you."

She pursed her lips. "I had a right to know. I loved them. They meant everything to me." Her voice quivered. "Do you know what it's like to have no one left in the world that cares about you?"

He flinched. His face mirrored her pain. "I reckon that's where you're wrong. I care about you. Parker cares. The staff cares."

"It's not the same."

"From what I learned, you were part of a wonderful, loving family. Hang on to those memories."

She clenched her hands, letting the nails dig into her skin. "They were the best. We never had a lot of money, but they worked hard. Somehow, we always had enough. They sacrificed everything for me. Even their lives." She wrapped her arms around herself and rocked. "My heart hurts. How do I deal with this ache?"

His voice wavered. "The scars are the stories of our souls. They never disappear, but the pain fades over time."

"How?" She searched his face.

"Trust me." The lines across his forehead softened. "One day when you're ready, you'll feel happiness again. You'll think back on your losses and realize the joys you hold. Then you'll move on. Remember, a dry well teaches us the value of water."

She stared. What in the world was he talking about?

A light knock tapped on the door. Carrying a tray, Parker peeked through the doorway. "I thought I heard voices."

Dr. Hanover winked. "It's just me. I decided to give Hailey some company since your morning was busy."

"I finished rounds a couple of minutes ago." Parker's dark solemn eyes stared at her. "I brought breakfast."

Dr. Hanover rose from the chair. "I'll let you visit. I'm meeting Stefan this morning."

Parker laid the food on the over-bed table, his eyes widening. "The SCA director is coming to the research lab?"

"He wants information on the ear implant. He'll skip around the lab when he learns the agency is still the forerunner in developing new gadgets." Dr. Hanover walked to the door and turned. "I expect you in the lab later this morning, Parker. Hailey, I'll check in on you later."

She shook her head and propped pillows behind her back. "He says the strangest things."

Parker sat in the chair and laughed. "Bruce is eccentric. The man has no life. Rumor is he sleeps in his office." He leaned closer. "How are you doing? For real?"

She pulled a sheet over her tender hands and scratched. "I didn't sleep at all. My head's pounding."

"Maybe food will help. If the headache doesn't go away, I'll have the nurse give you something."

She gave him a half-hearted smile. "Thanks, but I'm not hungry."

He handed her a fork. "Eat."

The aroma of bacon drifted through the air. Her stomach rumbled. She took the utensil and ate a tiny bite of scrambled egg, conscious of him studying her.

"I hope you realize we didn't intend to hurt you."

"Dr. Hanover said the same thing." She sniffled.

"I guess in hindsight we should've told you sooner." His tone was apologetic.

She laid down her fork. "So they're really gone?"

"I'm afraid so."

"I loved them so much." She stifled a sob. "Where are they buried?"

"In your hometown."

"Can I go there?" She waited for his reaction. His cloudy gray eyes were sedatives for her nerves.

"When you're stronger. You can't make the trip to California yet."

She covered her mouth, her hands trembling. "I can't believe they're gone. I never said good-bye."

"They knew you loved them. They'd want the best for you." He patted her hand. "Do you remember discussing Dr. Singh last night?"

She nodded.

"You should talk to her."

A chill ran through Hailey as she gripped the bedsheet. "I don't want another doctor."

"She'll help. She has a lot of experience in helping kids through traumas."

"No." She should have died with her parents.

"Please consider going one time."

"Will you come with me?"

He hesitated. "You should meet alone first. After you talk to her, if you still want me to come, I could join you. What do you say?"

She choked up. "On two conditions. First, I want to wait a few weeks. I need time to adjust to my parents' death."

He shook his head. "Non-negotiable. Dr. Singh can help you now. What's the second condition?"

"I want a mirror."

His face turned white. "Not a good idea. Bruce restricted them. "

"Then I won't see Dr. Singh."

Parker looked at the ceiling and sighed. "You are so stubborn. You still have bruises and marks from the stitches. It would only upset you."

"Do you think not knowing how I look is easier? I envision myself as some hideous monster trapped in a prison who you're embarrassed to let out. You should start calling me Quasimodo."

"You're being ridiculous."

"Then give me a mirror."

He tapped his foot.

That was a good sign. "Do you know how many times I gaze at the window trying to see my reflection?" She held up a spoon. "I even stare into the silverware. Sometimes I sit close to Dr. Hanover to see my reflection on his glasses."

Parker chuckled. "Now that's a scary thought." He rose from his chair. "Okay. You win. I'll find you a mirror."

A mini victory. Her heart leapt. "To keep."

"Maybe." He stepped toward the door and turned. "Depending on your reaction."

He came back holding a handheld mirror. He sat next to her on the bed, nudged her table aside, and placed the mirror on her lap.

She gripped the mirror and slowly raised it in front of her. A stranger marked with scars, bruises, and thick scabs stared at her. She caught her breath. This was far worse than she imagined. She tried not to tremble. Lifting her fingers to her cheek, she touched a scar and moaned.

Parker pointed to a scab near her ear. "This should go away in time." He shifted his finger higher near her temple. "But these two marks are from the cigarette burns. The plastic surgeon expects some minor scarring."

She outlined her nose profile. This wasn't her.

"Your nose was broken, and the surgeon reshaped it. You'll need some time to adjust."

She peered closer and touched the bone under her eye. The tender skin was a mixture of pale yellow and olive.

"The scars are still healing."

Hailey squeezed her eyes and threw the mirror on the bed. She choked back a sob and gagged.

Parker raised the wastebasket under her chin until she finished vomiting.

She wiped her mouth. "I'm sorry."

"I expected it." He smoothed her hair. "I'll ask Bruce for some extra time this morning. I'll stay as long as you need me. We can talk about whatever you want."

"I'd like that." She met his attentive eyes. "Can you also ask him to schedule Dr. Singh for my first session?"

A smile spread across his face. "Of course."

Chapter Three

August 29, 2002, College Park, Maryland

Hailey stepped into the campus bookstore at the University of Maryland and halted. *Come on. If she could travel around the world, this place shouldn't intimidate her.* Students scurried, pulling textbooks off shelves and sorting through supplies. The queue at the cash registers flowed past the posts guiding the stations.

"That will be \$482.63. Cash or charge?" A ruggedly handsome man wriggled books into a plastic bag and then handed it to the student. He appeared older than the other students—maybe her age. He was clean-shaven, but with rumpled russet hair. A loose tie hung around his neck, and his rolled-up sleeves ended at his elbows. What color eyes did he have? The man glanced up, making eye contact for a fleeting moment.

She turned away, flustered, and hustled down the science aisle. It took a few minutes, but she figured out the system of matching the course and section number to the required texts. All sections of cell biology required new books for the current semester. She grabbed one from the shelf and shifted to the chemistry texts. There was a used one, half the price of a new textbook, and she added it to her stack. Her pile grew heavier. She should have driven her car into campus.

On the other side of the store, she scratched her head and considered the English books. Each professor specified different works. Should she buy the recommended novels or only the required texts? She skimmed the room, but the staff assisted other students. *Just take a breath. You're the one who wanted to start a new life.*

"Can I help you?" a deep voice asked.

The tall guy from the checkout station stared down at her. His eyes were blue.

"Dreamy blue," she whispered.

"Pardon?" He tilted his head, studying her.

Her heart raced. She needed plenty of help. "No, thank you. I'm good." Good? Why did she say that?

He nodded his head at the sales counter. "Do you see the cranky old lady standing over there by the registers?"

He waited as she found the woman, and he made a silly face. "She's my supervisor. If she catches me chitchatting with a pretty girl and not helping her, she'll dock my pay for goofing off. So pretend you need me."

Hailey suppressed a giggle. "Well, since your job is on the line, I could use some help." She handed him the schedule. "The price of these books is shameful."

His eyes sparkled as he grinned. "All newcomers have sticker shock. The books cost as much as tuition."

"How could you tell I was new?"

His cheeks dimpled, sending her pulse twitching. "The confused look on your face when you walked in gave you away." He extended his arm. "I'm Mark. Mark Langley."

She adjusted her books and shook his hand. "Hailey Robinson."

27

"What year are you?"

"I'm a freshman."

His eyebrows lifted. "You seem older. Are you a transfer student?"

"No. I'm starting college later than usual."

He stroked his chin. "Let me guess, you spent the past three years traveling around the world finding yourself."

She laughed. He was cute *and* witty. "Not quite. What year are you?"

He held his head high and flashed an infectious grin. "I'm a senior."

"I bet you're eager to finish." She studied him closer; his facial expressions entranced her.

Mark chuckled. "Time to move on and find a job. I have to pay off these student loans." He eyed the small stack in her hands. "Looks like you collected some material. I'll help you find the English texts. They can get tricky." He led Hailey around the store, helping her select books, lab goggles, graph paper, and supplies. At the checkout line, he waited with her. "This is the end of my shift. If you want, I can carry your books. They get heavy."

She raised her eyebrows. "Does your supervisor make you do this, too?"

There was a faint glint of humor in his eyes. "No, but I get a bonus if I do. What do you say? I'd like to get to know you better."

Her cheeks warmed. "I'm quite capable of carrying my own books—" The memory of Bruce Hanover's voice interrupted her. *A new life won't begin unless you embrace it.* She shut her eyes. Let go of the past. And Parker, too. And all the painful memories. She opened her eyes and smiled. "That's kind of you, thanks. I live off campus. My apartment is four blocks away."

He slanted his brow. "I assumed you lived in a dorm, but I don't mind walking."

She waited as he clocked out. The day had been long already, though it was early afternoon. It was time to start life on the East Coast. A new life. Without any heartache.

Swiftly, he grabbed the heavy bag, and they strolled out of the bookstore. "Where are you from? I can't quite place the accent."

She hadn't expected this question so soon. Startled, she dropped a bag of supplies. Bam! Pencils, pens, and highlighters scattered across the sidewalk. "Gosh, I'm a klutz today." She bent and picked up a pen.

"Let me help." He leaned down, touching her hand as they collected the same pack of highlighters.

A shock whizzed through her body. She jerked her hand away and stuffed the supplies back into the bag, then peered up at him.

He was studying her.

They continued walking along the path. Hailey struggled to control the butterflies fluttering in her stomach. "What's your major?"

"Criminology. What's yours?"

"Biochemistry."

Mark stopped walking. "Biochemistry? Don't tell me you're one of those science geeks who sits with their friends on the grass and memorizes the Krebs Cycle."

She laughed. It felt good. "Gosh, I hope not."

"You never answered my question. Where are you from?"

Something in his voice made her trust him. After all, she couldn't avoid the subject forever. "California, but I lived in Texas the past four years."

He gave a quick laugh. "So that explains your tan. Why did you come *here*? Are you mad?"

The innocent bantering was refreshing. She giggled. "No, I wanted to see the East Coast."

He tilted his head. "How do you like it so far?"

Her pulse raced as he gazed at her. "This place is amazing. I only moved here last week, but I think I'm going to like living here. There's so much to see."

The two chatted until they arrived at her apartment. The old brick building had two mailboxes for the lower level and second floor apartments. Rusted nails braced the weathered wooden stairs leading to the upper unit. *Don't ask to come inside. Not yet.* She unlocked the door and exaggerated a yawn. "Well, this is my place."

He stared for a moment. "I should go. I'm sure you're tired, with classes starting tomorrow."

Part of her didn't want him to leave. "Thank you for carrying my books—and helping me. I was too embarrassed to ask for help."

"I figured as much." A mischievous look came into his eyes. "I have a confession to make."

"What?"

"The old lady at the bookstore wasn't my supervisor." She covered her mouth with her hands, and he gave a boyish grin. "I wanted an excuse to talk more."

A soft gasp escaped her, and she struggled to contain her smile. "Shame on you. One day a grumpy old woman will torment you. Just wait."

He cleared his throat. "Would you like to go out for pizza sometime? Or coffee?"

As he waited for her decision, he tilted his head in that enchanting way again—a definite turn-on. He seemed like a good man. One time wouldn't hurt her. "Sure. That would be nice."

His face brightened, and he pulled out his cell phone from his pants. "I'll give you a call. What's your number?"

"Uh…" She scratched her neck.

Mark raised his hands in front of his chest. "I'm an honest guy. No criminal records. You can trust me."

She burst out laughing. "A second ago you admitted lying about your supervisor. I should do a risk analysis on you." Hailey gave him the information, said goodbye, and stepped inside. Out of habit, she locked, unlocked, and then relocked the deadbolt. She leaned her back against the door. Giggling, she peeped through her curtains and glanced at him again. He jumped, clicking his heels in the air, and meandered down the sidewalk. School hadn't started yet, and she was starting a social life. She grinned. Who'd have thought college life would be so entertaining?

****

Hailey strolled home after her first day of college classes and collapsed on the sofa. A lot had happened since the previous day. Meeting Mark. Going to class. Meeting Mark. She chuckled. She was being childish. Last night, she lay in bed, unable to stop thinking about their encounter at the bookstore. She had promised herself she'd stay away from men. Parker had hurt her deeply. Trusting someone again was difficult. Wasn't that part of starting over? Meeting new people? Making new memories?

Her cell phone rang, and she stretched her arm over the coffee table. "Hello?"

"Hi, Hailey. This is Mark Langley. How are you?"

He didn't need to identify himself. His deep voice was distinctive, husky. "Mark. This is a surprise. I'm doing well."

"I was wondering if you'd like to go out to eat and talk about our first day of classes."

He was moving too fast, but if she turned him down, she might regret it. "Thanks. I haven't cooked dinner yet. When do you want to meet?"

"How about now?"

She peered out the window and stifled a laugh. Dressed in khaki shorts and a white T-shirt, he stood on the sidewalk, facing her apartment, waving. "Give me three minutes." She combed her hair, put on her sneakers, and locked the front door.

She was conscious of his broad shoulders and muscular arms when she greeted him. Her heart danced at the tenderness of his gaze.

When she neared, he straightened. "So? How did it go?"

His interest was flattering. "Fantastic. The labs will be intense, but as long as the room doesn't get too hot, I'll handle the pressure."

He grinned. "Assuming the room's volume stays the same, which is an *ideal* situation."

She laughed. "Someone remembers the gas laws."

Mark pointed to the far end of the street. "The pizza place is down here. Do you think your classes will be hard?"

She shook her head and smiled. "They won't be if I study and keep up with the reading. Luckily, I'm not too far from campus. Where do you live?"

"I have a small apartment about fifteen minutes across town."

"Do you have any roommates?"

He nodded as they stepped on the street. "One. I've roomed with my friend David since freshman year. He's doing an internship now. I'll introduce you next semester."

"I can't wait."

"We've been friends since grade school. He gives me a hard time about some of the girls I hang out with. Not that I date a lot. My social life isn't anything to write home about."

Mark was cute when he was flustered. She tried not to stare, but couldn't resist. His tousled hair gave him a sexy appearance, and he radiated a mysterious quality about him. What drew her in the most? Was it the defined lines around his mouth when he grinned? His captivating eyes? Or his gregarious personality? Hmmm.

"So, why did you choose this campus?"

She raked her fingers through her hair. The question was inevitable, but she was safe from her former life. Mark couldn't discover it. No one could. "I wanted to experience a new place. One with seasons. I hear you get snow."

"You'll see plenty. Believe me." He slowed his pace. "Ah, here's the place." Putting his arm around her waist, he led her into the café.

She stiffened, and he withdrew his arm. *What was wrong with her? He was being polite.* The smell of warm, homemade bread and pizza drifted from Pappy's Pizzeria. Her mouth watered from the scent of sausage, tomatoes, and onions.

The host seated them right away in an empty corner of the room.

Mark skimmed through the menu. "The pizza with everything is delicious here."

"Sounds fine. Pizza it is."

The server came to their table and asked for their order.

Hailey considered the different drinks. "Water's fine, thanks."

Mark nodded. "I'll have a coke. And we'd like a large Pappy's special." He waited until the server collected the menus and left. "What do your parents think of you moving away?"

She lowered her face. The pain of losing them still stung.

Mark must have sensed her sadness. "What's wrong?"

She choked out the words. "My parents are dead."

"Hailey, I'm sorry." He placed his hand over hers. "I had no idea."

"I try not to dwell on it." She pulled her hand back and wrung her hands on her lap. "But it still hurts."

"Do you want to talk about it?" His gentle eyes cushioned the pain.

"There's nothing much to say. They died in a car accident when I was seventeen."

"I'm so sorry. Do you have any other family? Any brothers or sisters?"

"No. I'm an only child. My dad had a brother, but he died when my dad was a teenager. The only family I ever knew was my dad's father. Grandpa had a lot of health issues and died when I was ten."

"Who watched over you?"

"I had a guardian. The family was a blessing, but when I turned eighteen, I lived on my own."

"How are you supporting yourself?"

"I work odd jobs. You know. Babysitting. Waitressing. Wherever I can find something. Now I'm taking out school loans."

"Gosh. You've had to handle a lot."

She nodded, but said nothing.

The server returned carrying their drinks and a basket of breadsticks.

Mark stared at Hailey with a feeble smile.

She could get lost in the way he gazed at her.

"Are you okay? We can leave."

Shaking her head, she reached for a breadstick. As she bit into the warm, buttery bread, a stomach pang reminded her that she hadn't eaten since early morning. "I'm fine. I don't like to talk about my past. Why dwell on yesterday when your future is unchartered territory?"

"I suppose you have something there." He studied her. "Did anyone ever tell you your eyes glimmer?"

Her cheeks warmed. "No one's ever pointed that out before."

"Well, they do. It's like watching fireworks."

"Now you're making me blush. Tell me. What are *your* parents like?"

"My parents? Dad's an auto mechanic. He works in his garage. My mom's a teacher." A flash of humor crossed his face. "They're pretty typical. They worry too much, give outdated advice, spoil my two older sisters, and never have money left for me. Which is why I have to work."

"How adorable. You're lucky."

He leaned forward and slid his elbows on the table. "Hey, what are you doing this weekend?"

She shrugged. "Probably catching up on some laundry. I'm new in town. I don't have a social life. Why?"

"A couple of us are taking a bus into Baltimore for a day trip Saturday. We want one last outing before the studying and homework begin. Would you like to come? It's an opportunity to meet people."

"That sounds fun. I'd love to tour some of the sites."

"Great. I'll meet you around nine."

****

A warm glow expanded through Hailey as she walked to the rec center parking lot. Mark was talking with a group of students toting backpacks. She waved. "I hope I'm not too late. I wasn't sure what to wear today." She lowered her head and frowned at the navy denim jacket she had pulled from her closet. If she was overdressed, she could leave it on the bus.

Mark pointed at the street next to the engineering building. "You're good. The bus is pulling up." His eyes widened as she removed her jacket. "You look really pretty."

"Thanks. I'm excited about coming." She chose a seat on the bus, and they chatted during the entire ride into Inner Harbor.

They started the morning at the Maryland Science Center. As they strolled around the Chesapeake Bay, they watched the pigeons fight for crumbs. In the late afternoon, Mark led her down a narrow street lined with whimsical restaurants. He stopped at the street corner and turned. "Are you hungry?"

She nodded. "I could eat. This breeze is building my appetite."

He pointed to a one-story building across the street with white siding, blue shutters, and a giant red lobster sculpture by the entrance. "Do you want to try that restaurant?"

Seagulls flocked the sign in front of the building. Hailey squinted her eyes. "The Captain's Crew—Seafood & Burgers. It looks charming." Spending the day talking to Mark seemed natural. Had she met him only two days ago?

When evening came, they strolled beside the harbor and listened to the entertainment. The sea breeze smelled of fish. Just like San Francisco.

They stopped at a street vendor selling ice cream. Mark paid the woman and grabbed some napkins. He handed Hailey the ice-cream cone. "What was your favorite place today?"

The commotion of people bustling around them dazzled her. "I don't know. Everything was great. I liked touring the submarine and the warship by the docks. What was your favorite?"

"I thought the aquarium was fun."

She smiled and tasted the ice cream. "Even the part when the dolphins flicked their tails and soaked us?"

He laughed. "We *were* sitting in the Splash Zone."

"Yeah, but I didn't actually think we would get wet. You made a wise suggestion with the paddleboats afterward. We got to dry off and see the spectacular view of the harbor."

He nodded and licked the ice cream. "I'm glad you came today."

"Me, too. Thanks for inviting me." She pinched herself. Uh-huh. She was here, enjoying this perfect day without any worries. Mark had acted like a total gentleman, and he grasped she needed to take things slowly.

He guided her to a nearby park bench. "We have fifteen minutes until we board the bus. Let's sit here and eat our ice cream before it melts."

As they ate, a thin dark-haired man with a trimmed goatee and mustache approached. "*Bonjour Jacqueline! Quelle charmante surprise*!" He bent down and leaned his lips toward her cheek.

She jumped and shoved him away. Ice cream spilled on her blouse. "What are you doing?"

Mark stood and set himself between Hailey and the middle-aged man. "Pardon me, sir, but you must have the wrong woman."

"*Non*. Jacqueline, don't you remember me?"

A sudden coldness flowed through her. "No, I don't."

"We met in Strasbourg at the American consulate. The night of the assassination attempt on Monsieur Moreau."

Her heart raced as she stared at him.

"A gentleman suitor accompanied you. I was shot in the leg and you protected me during the commotion as people tramped over each other."

She grabbed a napkin beside her and wiped her blouse. "You have the wrong person."

He shook his head. "No. You were there. Surely, you remember. I never forget a face, especially one as lovely as yours."

"I'm sorry. I don't know you." She looked down. How had he recognized her?

Mark shifted his shoulders back. "Sir, the lady doesn't know who you are. You don't even have her name right." Turning to Hailey, he offered his hand and helped her off the bench. "Let's get out of here."

He tightened his grip around her hand as they hurried to the bus. She laced her fingers with his, moving through the crowds and bumping into tourists.

The fellow called after her, but his voice disappeared in the distance.

Mark didn't speak until they sat in their seats. "Crazy Frenchman." His brows knitted when she scratched her hand. "Did a mosquito bite you?"

"No. I'm just itchy." Hailey stopped scratching and shifted the hand under her thigh.

"You must be spooked. That man seemed infatuated with you."

She shrugged. "A case of mistaken identity. It could've happened to anyone. Thanks for getting us out of there." Inside Hailey trembled. She had used all her self-control to refrain from shaking on the outside. The bus drove away, and she exhaled, relieved the man hadn't said more. She'd recognized the man the moment he had called her name. He wasn't the only one who never forgot a face. How long would her past haunt her? When she moved away from Texas, Bruce had warned she couldn't lie low forever.

Chapter Four

Mark couldn't stop smiling. He tossed a worn plaid blanket over the grass and inhaled slow breaths. He tried to stay calm, but inside he jumped up and down. Hailey would come any minute now. He had almost let the news slip. The pressure to find a job was over. School was almost finished and a new phase would begin. Yahoo!

He frowned. Graduating might cripple his relationship with Hailey. They hadn't even slept together yet. She had taken two months to hold his hand, and their first kiss happened much later. Whatever normal etiquette was, she wasn't rushing into romance.

The break-up with Colleen still evoked painful memories. He never thought he'd love a girl again. And then he met Hailey. A gem—unearthed. Everything about her was perfect. Her looks. Her personality. Her honesty. Her sense of humor. Her fresh outlook on life. Her… he could go on forever.

He sat waiting on the blanket, flinging sunflower seeds at the squirrels. The year had been a blur. Who would have dreamed he and Hailey would have so much fun? She cheered like a true fan after the football team had scored a touchdown. When the basketball team pulled off a shot as the buzzer rang, she high-fived the whole row of fans. In the evenings, they attended the university band and orchestra concerts at the Performing Arts Center. And he actually enjoyed the music. He didn't understand *The Taming of the Shrew* until she took him to a theater performance. Many nights, they studied in the library. He didn't study as much as Hailey, but it was fun watching her pore over her notes and learn her material. She always found the funniest allusions to work science into her conversation. How ironic that she was actually a real science geek. During spring break, he introduced her to his parents, and she helped him change a car battery in his dad's garage. She had beamed. "The battery's electrical charge is like the mitochondria fueling a cell." She didn't even complain about his greasy hands. Yep, she was definitely the *one.*

But Hailey had trust issues—that was obvious. Why did she keep her past a secret? Even his mother couldn't pry out information. Maybe Hailey had a bad breakup with a boyfriend the way he had with his former girlfriend Colleen. Whatever the reason, he'd give her time to build that trust.

Spotting her climbing the hill, he waved. He fidgeted with the velvety box in his pocket.

She neared him and pointed at the basket. "Mark, this is so sweet. A picnic in the park!"

He wrapped his arms around her midriff and leaned in, brushing her cheek with a kiss. "I missed you. How did genetics go?"

The freckles on her nose danced in the sunlight. "Good. The fruit fly experiment is officially complete. I have three generations of wing shapes and eye colors to plot on a Punnett square. Then I have to map out the crossbreeding results." She shrugged out of her green sweater and tossed it on the blanket. "How was your day?"

"Terrific, actually. I got a surprising phone call earlier. Wait a second." He sank his hands in the basket and lifted two fluted plastic glasses and a bottle of champagne. "Hold these, please."

She giggled as she took the glasses. "What's going on?"

"We're celebrating. I got a job working as a crime statistics analyst in Virginia."

"That's awesome news." Hailey laid the glasses on the blanket and leapt up, throwing her arms around him. "Congratulations! I'm so happy for you." They settled back on the blanket, and he opened the bottle and poured the bubbly wine.

"To you and your new job." She clicked her glass against his. "Cheers."

"I'm blown away. Nervous. I hope I can handle a real job once I graduate."

Hailey's smile turned upside down. "I try not to think about graduation."

He set down his glass. "We need to talk."

"About what?"

Her nearness made his pulse race. Hailey's lush hair flowed down on her shoulders, and her sheer blouse screamed at him to stare at her breasts. Yep, he wanted to spend the rest of his life with her. The small box in his pocket urged him to forge ahead. Didn't she realize they would discuss this?

"Hailey, it's no secret that I'm enamored with you." He took a deep breath, gathering courage, capturing her lovely eyes with his. "My life changed when I met you. I wake each morning longing to see your smile. You cheer me up after a tough day. I can't wait until you finish school so we can be together. I love you." He pulled out the black box and shifted to one knee. Holding her hand, he gazed at her hazel eyes shimmering in the sunlight. "Hailey Robinson, will you marry me?"

She gasped and covered her mouth with her hand. "Mark. I...I...I can't."

The air deflated from his lungs, and he sat down. "What? Why?"

"We're not ready. I want to finish school."

He tilted his head. He hadn't prepared for this response. "But don't you want to get married?"

Her expression softened. "Someday—yes. But not now. We can't plan our life like it's a schedule. Big changes are coming in your life. I have goals, too."

"But I want to be with you."

"I do, too. We can still visit each other on weekends until I finish school. Virginia's not too far from here."

He turned his face away and blinked away his tears. Why was life so complicated?

She placed a hand on his shoulder. "Hon, Look at me."

He turned back and sighed. "What?"

"I love you."

"Then why won't you marry me?"

She reached over and touched his hand. "If our relationship is meant to last, we have to trust things will work out." She opened her lips and kissed him. "We can make this happen, but I'm not ready to get married yet."

He lay down and shook his head. Maybe she had a point. "I guess I jumped the gun."

Hailey leaned closer and lifted wisps of hair from his forehead. "Are you upset?"

"I'll survive." He pulled her into his arms and crushed his body against her. His finger brushed over her chin, and he kissed her. "I'm giving you advance notice, though. Over the next three years, I'm going to flood you with TLC. And when you graduate, I'm marrying you."

Chapter Five

June 3, 2016, Fairfax, Virginia

Hailey stood by the stove and poured the remaining batter on the sizzling griddle. She flipped the amoeba-shaped pancake and dumped the empty bowl into the sink. "Anna! Ethan! Turn the TV off. Breakfast is ready. The bus comes in twenty minutes. You'll need your umbrellas from the closet."

The two children raced into the kitchen and claimed their seats around the table. Anna raised her arm and flashed a ponytail holder. "Mom, can you braid my hair?"

Hailey smiled. Anna had inherited her hair color *and* hazel eyes. "We don't have much time. I'll do it while you eat." She stood behind Anna and sectioned her daughter's brown hair into three strands. "Don't forget. I'm coming to your classroom later this morning for story time."

Anna plopped two hotcakes onto her plate. "Mrs. Dawson said this is the last day you're reading."

She nodded. "School's over soon. I scheduled lots of fun activities for us this summer."

Ethan stuffed a huge helping of hotcakes in his mouth and gulped his orange juice. "Can I sleep at Nate's house tonight?"

She tied the elastic band around Anna's braid. "You can play for an hour after school, but you have soccer practice this evening."

Frowning, he transferred another hotcake onto his plate and poured the syrup. "Can I sleep over tomorrow night?"

Shaking her head, she started the second braid. "I'm afraid no sleepovers this weekend. Tomorrow's your soccer tournament, and Sunday we're visiting Grandma and Grandpa."

"Are Kayla, Eric, and Sammy still there?"

She nodded. "Aunt Laura and your cousins are flying home Sunday evening. We'll have lunch at Grandpa's place and see everyone before they leave town. Then Daddy and I are celebrating our anniversary with a nice dinner."

The eight-year-old wiped the crumbs from his mouth with his sleeve. "Is Daddy still mad at us?"

She paused from plaiting Anna's hair. "He's not mad at you." Her voice cracked as she spoke.

Anna's eyes widened as she shook her head emphatically. "Yes, he is. You yelled at him last night."

Hailey lowered her head and continued braiding. She shouldn't have chastised him in front of the kids. She, of all people, understood the stress his career entailed. "Daddy was preoccupied. Sometimes he has a bad day. He still loves you."

Standing, Ethan pushed in his chair and yanked one of Anna's braids. "It's your fault. Next time, don't ask him to feed your stupid baby doll."

"Ethan! Be nice." Hailey twisted the rubber hairband around the second braid. "All done." She collected the dirty plates and lowered them into the sink. "Daddy was tired last night. He'll play this evening when he gets home. Now put on your shoes. We're running late."

The rain reduced to a sprinkle as they walked to the bus stop. The bus came a few minutes late. Hailey looked to make sure she knew the driver and let the children step on the vehicle. She waited until the bus left her sight.

"Yoo-hoo! Hailey!"

She turned toward the silvery voice calling her from across the street. "Morning, Katherine."

"Would you like to stop in for a cup of coffee this morning?"

She considered the woman who had moved into the neighborhood a few months ago. They had chatted a few mornings at the bus stop on Katherine's days off from the hospital. "I'm sorry, I can't today. I'm going into Anna's classroom, and then I need to pick up Mark's suits at the dry cleaner's and go grocery shopping. Ethan's complaining there are no snacks left in the cupboard."

Katherine laughed. "I can't keep Nate out of the pantry either."

Hailey waved good-bye and walked down the street. The ache in her heart was more noticeable than other days. She locked, unlocked, and relocked the front door, and she moseyed into the kitchen. On the counter, a brown paper bag leaned against the toaster. Mark's lunch. She sighed. He forgot a lot lately. Work consumed him, even at home.

This weekend she and Mark would celebrate ten years of marriage. *I hope he feels like celebrating after last night's argument.* Guilt gnawed at her as she picked up her cell phone. Maybe she could convince him to see a doctor for his stress.

****

Mark leaned back in his seat and groaned. "Third accident this week." Why couldn't drivers be more vigilant? Now he was late for work again. The slick roads from the rain didn't help his morning commute either. His phone dinged. The screen displayed Owen Kaln, his supervisor at the Drug Trafficking Agency. "Can this day get any worse?" He punched the button on the steering wheel. "Yes?"

"Mark, where the hell are you? I've been stopping by your office all morning. I need to speak to you and Greg ASAP."

The car behind him honked, and he glared in the rearview mirror. "I'm stuck in traffic. There's a three-car collision on the Beltway. Vehicles are backed up for a mile. I'll come as soon as I start moving again."

"When you get here, I want an update on the Sherman case. I have a meeting with the assistant director this afternoon."

Mark sighed. It was a wonder he didn't have an ulcer. "Greg and I are working on it. We've gone through Sherman's paperwork, emails, and old files for weeks. We keep hitting dead ends."

"Elliot Sherman isn't just any missing person. Have you contacted the DEA? They're storing the old files for the NNIC."

He gripped his fingers tighter around the steering wheel. He had contacted the DEA to access the National Narcotics Intelligence Center records the day before. "More files are due to arrive later this morning, sir."

"What am I supposed to tell the assistant director? He's not going to be happy when he hears one of our agents disappeared and no one knows his whereabouts."

"I don't know what else to say, sir. We've been working on this case twenty-four seven."

"No excuses. I think you're breathing in too many damn exhaust fumes. Stop idling in your car and get your ass in gear. I want a status update by noon." The screen blanked abruptly.

Mark cursed and slammed his hand on the horn. Not that it made the traffic move, but it helped him blow off some of his frustration. How could someone working in the division for two years pick up and disappear?

When the phone dinged a second time, he cringed. He didn't need Owen issuing more orders for his already jam-packed workload. This time, Hailey's name appeared on the display. "Hi." He tapped his fingers on the steering wheel. *Here comes the lecture.*

"Hey, hon. Your lunch is here." Hailey sounded subdued.

He sighed. "I knew I forgot something when I rushed out this morning. I'll pick up a sandwich somewhere. Thanks for telling me."

"And I wanted to say I'm sorry about last night."

His mood softened. She wasn't the one who should apologize. "Don't worry about it."

"I didn't mean to jump all over you, but you've been pretty grumpy. Ethan and Anna waited all day for you to play, and when you came home, you couldn't run to bed fast enough."

A lump formed in his throat. He swallowed it down. "There's a lot going on at work."

"Are you sure that's all?"

Mark closed his eyes. He couldn't hide much from her. "Yes. I'm just distracted...Is there anything else going on?"

"Ethan's coach rescheduled practice for tonight at six. Don't forget, his tournament's tomorrow. If you're not home in time tonight, I'll take him when I pick up Anna from dance...I love you."

He glanced again in his rearview mirror. "I love you, too. I'll text when I leave work."

Her voice sounded happier. "I'll save dinner for you. Bye."

Mark groaned. Hailey wanted him home more, but she was moody at the house. His best bet was to stay away. No, that wasn't the entire truth. She was right. He was grouchy, too. Why did her secrets bother him so much? He dodged the issue by focusing on work, which equally exasperated him.

The traffic began moving, and Mark arrived in the District an hour later than usual. The rain poured as he walked from the city garage toward his office. He wrestled with his umbrella, finding minimal shelter under the flimsy dome. A strong gust of wind flipped the umbrella inside out. He trudged the last two blocks struggling to see through the torrential rain. His right leg began aching. The impromptu football game with Ethan's friends the past weekend was a bad idea. He limped into the federal building and showed his badge to the guard.

Mark hung his drenched topcoat on the hook behind the office door. A knock sounded, and the heavy door pushed into him, throwing him off-balance. "Watch it!"

Greg Tremblay walked in the room eating a donut. "Oh, sorry. I didn't see you back there."

"Can't you wait for me to say 'Come in' before barging in here?"

Greg gave him a dejected look. "Sorry. I didn't realize you got up on the wrong side of the bed this morning." He dropped in one of the chairs by Mark's desk and handed him a paper bag. "Do you want a donut?"

He tightened his lips together at Greg's carefree mood and considered the offer. Naturally, he would love to eat a donut, but he had already tagged on an extra twenty pounds over the years. "No, thanks. Hailey's been after me about my cholesterol."

Greg patted his hefty midsection. "My doctor says the same thing."

Mark sat in his chair and grinned for the first time that morning. Greg had a way of trivializing serious concerns. He never watched what he ate, despite being overweight. He was six years older than Mark, with a receding hairline to go with his advancing age.

Greg wiped his fingers on his pants and pointed to the corner of the room. "More boxes on the Sherman case arrived this morning."

Mark launched a pencil from his desk and followed its trajectory as it bounced against the wall. "It amazes me Congress voted to defund the NNIC with all these cases."

Greg grabbed another donut from the bag. "You're telling me. Shutting down the agency was national suicide. When I worked there, we had a backlog of several months probing networks of drug operations. There are too many people buying drugs, and not enough resources to stop them. It's a shame. Damn the politics."

Mark walked over to the corner and selected a report from the box. "The NNIC's loss is our gain."

Greg nodded. "I'm glad the DTA hired me, but my home in Pennsylvania was hard to leave."

At eleven o'clock, Owen knocked on the door and barged in. The odd-looking man stood around five feet tall, and his heavy build accentuated his short stature. Although only in his mid-fifties, his hair was completely gray. He wore it slicked to the side, hiding his hair loss on top with a classic comb-over. Working as a supervisor must have accelerated the aging process. If that was the case, Mark could do without the catalyst.

"I'm glad you finally made it to work. What's the progress of the Sherman case?"

Greg flashed a smile at his boss. "Well, good afternoon to you, too. As you can see, we're swamped. We've been searching records and computer files all morning."

Owen ignored the retort. "Have you found anything to link Sherman's disappearance with his past drug cases?"

Mark picked up the report on his desk and handed it to Owen. "We were heading to your office with our progress. We've reviewed his former cases. Greg and I checked with the parole officers assigned to the dealers Sherman sent to prison. We thought someone might have wanted revenge. So far, nothing has flagged."

"What about his more recent cases?"

"Those came up empty." Greg lowered the file he was reading and leaned back in the chair. "We concentrated on those cases at the beginning."

Owen scratched his chin. "Is it possible he was working on something and didn't document it?"

"Greg and I discussed the possibility. We've sorted through files for weeks. We haven't found anything suspicious." Mark pointed to the stack of boxes. "After we finish reviewing these, we'll reexamine the interviews."

Owen paced the floor. "It won't hurt to question his wife again. I need something to tell the assistant director."

Mark frowned. "We're doing the best we can with our resources." He walked over to the boxes and retrieved another folder.

"Keep working." Owen rubbed this forehead. "Sherman maintained contacts with other agencies. They might be able to give us some insight on his disappearance."

Yawning, Greg stretched his arms over his head. "I'll work on that when I interview his family again. Mark's busy finishing paperwork on some other cases."

Mark stared at his supervisor for empathy, but Owen only widened his smile and chuckled. He sounded like a pig snorting.

"That reminds me. I almost forgot my other reason for coming in here. The paperwork for your five-year reinvestigation is due Monday. I'm not accepting any excuses, Mark."

He rubbed his neck; he could almost feel the albatross tightening its grip. "I'm trying to get to it. If I could take time off from my other assignments, I could complete it."

"Those cases are important, too. Work Sunday if you have to." Owen walked to the door and turned. "I want the report on my desk Monday morning. I'm beginning to wonder if you're hiding something."

Mark's muscles tightened. He had ignored Hailey's past for too long. Her secrets complicated the reinvestigation. Completing her paperwork was more daunting than the Sherman case.

Chapter Six

Washington, D.C.

Grrr. Bella pressed her hand against her abdomen and peered over the top of the computer screen. If Manuel and Antonio heard her stomach rumbling, they didn't show it. No doubt, they were being polite. Oh, good—they were too preoccupied with other problems. She finished ordering the project supplies and gazed out the tinted office window. Tourists converged on the National Mall below. It was the perfect sunny day to dine at her favorite café and shop at the high-fashion boutiques. She sighed. There was no time for such frivolous indulgences.

Standing at an angle across from her, Manuel grimaced as he stared out at the crowd. He often brooded with his shoulders slumped and hands thrust into his pocket, acting as if he were responsible for solving the world's problems. "Look at those commoners below. They're tiny ants scurrying for food."

Antonio rose from a chair beside Manuel's desk. "The weather's getting warmer. This time of year always drags out tourists and kids on field trips."

"They're hyenas. Listen to their annoying laughter." Manuel turned from the window. "The crowd behaves as if they don't have a care in the world. I envy them. My life is…"

Bella nodded at Antonio. The bodyguard strode to the wet bar and raised a tumbler from the counter. "Are you ready for your Scotch?"

Manuel nodded. "Yes, I could use it."

Antonio poured the drink and handed him the glass.

She waited until Manuel took a swig. "Did you receive any reports yet?"

Manuel clenched his teeth. "No."

She sighed. "They're two months overdue. How am I supposed to finish my part of the project?"

He finished the drink in a long gulp. "I hate delays." He gave the glass to Antonio. "I want another one."

Glancing at Bella, Antonio dutifully took the glass and frowned. "They're slowing everything down. Can Cerdo put pressure on them for you?" He returned to the bar and poured another drink.

"Cerdo?" Manuel scoffed. "What an idiotic buffoon. Coming and going as if he's the one in charge. He's nothing but a pretentious asshole."

Antonio handed him the refill. "Too bad you need his contacts for the project."

"It's easier to let him think he's essential." Manuel nimbly raised the glass in the air and gulped the drink. "Working with Bella is easy, but the other two researchers and this idiot are impossible. They each have a massive ego to stroke. Unfortunately, I need them." He handed Antonio his empty glass.

Cerdo. Bella cringed at the name. Pushing the chair away from the desk, she stepped to Manuel and began massaging his shoulders. "You're tense today. Did you remind them the results were due weeks ago?"

Manuel shrugged. "It doesn't make a difference. Their replies are always the same. How many times can I listen to the dangers of rushing research? Bruce Hanover is the worst offender. His nervousness annoys me. Four years and nothing to show for it."

Bella shifted her hands upward and rubbed his neck. "We're doing everything we can."

Manuel's shoulders tensed again. "You devised this plan. Can't you tell me how close we are? Aren't you monitoring the computers?"

"I linked our network to the other computers, but if the researchers don't add the data, I can't spy on them."

"We needed their information a month ago. All I get is excuses."

"You knew from the beginning this operation would take a considerable amount of time." Bella grimaced. Even she hadn't expected these delays.

Manuel pointed to his left shoulder, and she adjusted her massage, gently kneading a tight muscle. "I never imagined the project would take this long. Even my father is pressuring me."

Antonio's expression grew somber. "Is the admirable José de Mendoza still threatening to fly in if you can't carry out the operation?"

"Yes." Manuel sneered. "A knot tightens in my gut when I think about it. These delays are sabotaging my dreams."

The phone rang, and Bella lowered her hands. Manuel stretched his arm across the desk and picked up the handset. "Yes? Excellent. Set up the meeting at the old warehouse on Sunday. Tell him to bring his data."

He cradled the phone. "That was Cerdo. Charles Moulin finished his report."

Bella's heartbeat quickened. Finally, some good news. She wrapped her arms around his waist and kissed him. "See? Life is beginning to look brighter already."

Chapter Seven

Hailey lay on the lush lawn, escaping her children's view in a game of hide and seek. The birdcalls from the trees above soothed her. She felt like a cell in interphase, its resting phase before cell division. Seeming to sleep, waiting until her world burst in pandemonium.

Ethan and Anna piled on top of her.

"You're it." Ethan poked her.

"We found you, Mommy!" Anna tumbled on the grass.

"You are both good hide-and-seekers." She gave them a tight squeeze.

Anna pointed at the small clump of dried twigs in the maple tree above. "Did you see the nest? The momma bird is feeding worms to her babies."

"Let me see." Ethan stood closer and peered.

She smiled at the similarities Ethan shared with Mark. He was even born with Mark's tousled hair. What did the other boy look like? He would be almost grown now. Hopefully, he inherited her father's features, not those of his biological father.

The mother bird fed the smaller birds and flew away. Ethan wrinkled his brow. "Where did she go?"

She must have a lost bird somewhere. "Hmm. I suppose she has things to do for her babies…like I take care of you." She tickled the squealing children, and they jumped up and ran toward the center of the yard.

Ethan turned his head. "Let's play another game." He tugged on her shirt and then dashed. "Tag. You're It."

"Okay, one game before Daddy comes back from the gym." She chased them to the front of the house, enjoying the mild weather.

Mark steered his SUV into the driveway and greeted them with a bright smile. Sweat soaked his old T-shirt and basketball shorts. His hair was matted down around his head with beads of sweat still dripping from his forehead.

She flushed at his dishevelment. He was adorable. She should make a better effort to have more alone time. When she first married him, they made love any time of day. It was too bad how life and kids got in the way of intimacy.

The kids raced to his vehicle, and Anna reached him first. "We're playing tag, Daddy. Betcha can't catch us." She and Ethan sprinted across the yard toward the swing set.

Hailey welcomed Mark with a kiss, but quickly put her arm out. "Hon, you better shower before we leave for your parents'. Laura's heading back to New Jersey this afternoon with her kids."

He grimaced. "I can't go today."

"Why not?" She didn't care that she sounded bitter. "Every time your sister's in town, you're busy."

He groaned. "I'm busy all the time. I have to go to the office."

"Again?" She stiffened. "You need to get your priorities straight and concentrate on your family. The kids are growing up, and we have to spend time with them while we can. One morning you'll wake up and they'll be gone."

He let out a heavy sigh. "I know. I'm just under a lot of stress."

"Work isn't the solution. You need rest. You're never home anymore. It's like you're leading a double life." Her mouth tasted sour as soon as she spoke. That was *her* MO.

He scowled and raised his shirt, wiping his sweaty forehead. The scowl disappeared as fast as it had appeared. He ran a finger across her cheek and his voice softened. "I'm sorry. Today's our special day. I don't want to upset you. Tell Laura I'll see her next time. Ethan and Anna will have fun playing with their cousins."

He was right. They shouldn't argue over something trivial. She squeezed his hand and smiled. "Can you at least promise to come home at six? I planned a special dinner."

He wrapped his arms around her. "Count me in." His mouth claimed her lips, and she melted beneath his touch. "Umm. Your kisses are addicting."

She sighed. Not addicting enough.

The kids ran from the backyard. Anna squealed and stretched her fingers, tagging Mark. "Daddy. You're It."

His hands tightened around Hailey, and he swung her around. The kids giggled.

"Mark, put me down!"

"If you insist." He lowered her to the ground and kissed her. "You're It."

****

At noon, Hailey drove the kids five miles to her in-law's small three-bedroom Cape Cod home. Peggy Langley opened the door, and Hailey breathed in the aroma of the country kitchen—apple pie and cinnamon. She and her mother had baked and talked for hours at the kitchen table after school. "Wow, Mom. Cookies *and* pie."

The kids dashed past her into the house and greeted Peggy. "Hi, Grandma!"

Peggy wrapped her arms around Ethan and Anna. She lifted her head and peered out the open door. "Mark's not coming?"

Hailey flashed a smile. "I'm afraid not. He's working again."

Laura stood from her chair at the wooden farmhouse table and hugged her. Anna and Ethan gave Laura a high five and each swiped a chocolate chip cookie from a plate on the counter.

Kayla, Eric, and Sammy rushed in from the living room, giggling. Kayla grabbed Anna's hand. "Let's wake Grandpa. He's sleeping on the couch."

The children headed into the living room and pounced on Adam, waking him.

"Help! I'm under attack!" He chased the kids upstairs as they shouted hysterically.

Hailey turned to Laura. "It's a shame you live so far away. The kids have so much fun together."

"That's why we try to visit often." Laura sat down and patted a chair next to her. "Have a seat. So why's Mark working on a Sunday?"

Hailey slid a chair from the table and sat. "He's working on a big case. His supervisor wants some paperwork finished before the weekend is over." With an effort, she put on a cheerful face. "Mark couldn't go in yesterday because of Ethan's soccer tournament."

Peggy frowned and untied her apron. "But today's your tenth anniversary, sweetie."

"I know. He promised to drive home in time for dinner, so we'll still celebrate."

Peggy rested her arm around Hailey's shoulder. "You're good for him. The best thing Mark ever did was marry you." She donned her oven mitts and removed a pie from the oven. "Someday he'll appreciate how lucky he is. Now he's preoccupied with his family responsibilities and work. Adam was the same way."

"I'm at my wit's end. How did you handle the obsession?"

Laura sat back in her seat and chuckled. "Mom needed plenty of patience. Dad and Mark have intense personalities."

"It wasn't easy being married to a workaholic. When Adam retired, he was finally able to enjoy life. That's why we love spending so much time with our grandkids." Peggy lifted the plate of cookies from the counter and moved it to the table. "Hang in there, sweetie. He needs you—more than he realizes."

Laura grabbed a cookie and passed the plate to Hailey. "It's true. Mark's changed a lot since he met you. He was really awkward around girls. Do you remember his first girlfriend, Mom?"

Peggy groaned. "That relationship ended in catastrophe."

Laura bit into the cookie and brushed the crumbs onto a napkin. "Francine and I doubted our baby brother would ever date again."

Peggy shook her head. "I never found out what happened."

Laura grinned. "I did."

Peggy's face reddened, and she gave Hailey an uneasy look. "Maybe we shouldn't talk about this."

Hailey squirmed in her chair. Naturally, she was curious. "Mark never discusses his old girlfriends with me."

Laura grabbed another cookie and snapped it in half. "He was only serious about one girl that we know of. Hearing about her would give you some insight into what Mark's been through." She tasted a piece. "Mmmm. These are delicious, Mom."

Hailey sampled a warm cookie and nodded. "How long did he date the girl?"

Laura leaned forward as if she held the biggest secret. "Over a year. From the end of his junior year until the beginning of college. He fell in love with her, but from what I heard, Colleen Toole used him."

Peggy's eyes narrowed. "How do you know what happened between them?"

Laura straightened and lifted her chin. "Mark's friend David told me. The guy who used to hang out at the garage. I taught him how to French kiss in exchange for the information."

Peggy gasped. "Laura!"

"What?" She laughed. "Sisters are supposed to snoop. It was a small price to pay. I got the lowdown on Colleen, and David turned out to be a decent kisser."

Peggy leaned in closer. "So what happened with them?"

Laura's smile turned upside down. "When Mark moved away to college, Colleen conned him into buying alcohol with a fake ID. She planned a huge back-to-school blowout at her new apartment. The one she convinced her father to lease after she flunked her classes. She *said* the dorms were too noisy."

Tilting her head to the side, Hailey rested her cheek in her palm. "But Mark rarely drinks."

Laura nodded. "I know, but he went along with it. They purchased enough beer, wine coolers, and hard liquor to sustain half the campus."

"What happened after they bought the alcohol?"

"Mark and David walked over to her swanky apartment the night of the party. When they arrived, she was already drunk, schmoozing with an older college boy. Hands all over each other. Whispering in his ear." Peggy gasped, but Laura continued. "She didn't even notice when Mark entered the room."

Hailey sighed. "Poor Mark!"

Laura put up her hand. "Wait. I didn't even get to the best part. As the frat boy pawed her, the doorbell rang. Someone opened the door and the room got quiet. Colleen's parents had come to surprise her with flowers and a bag of groceries."

Hailey covered a hand over her mouth. "Oh, no."

Laura nodded and continued speaking. "They stood at the door, staring with their jaws dropped, while she made out with the guy. Can you imagine how uncomfortable everyone must have felt? Finally, the silence interrupted Colleen's deep kiss. She turned her head to see the entire room staring. Her father's face was so red David thought the man would suffer a heart attack right there in the room."

Hailey closed her eyes, taking in the scene.

"She was quite the operator." Laura grinned.

Drawing her lips together, Peggy frowned. "Why didn't you tell me sooner?"

Laura bit into the last cookie. "You would've fussed over him. That would only have made Mark feel worse. You can't deny it, Mom. She was a spoiled manipulator. Once she started college, she didn't need a high school boyfriend."

Peggy nodded. "I remember Mark calling her, begging her to come home and go to the senior prom."

"David had a gut feeling she'd drop Mark like a bad habit once someone better came along—and he was right."

Hailey choked back a cry. "That's horrible."

"He felt like a fool. Colleen Toole was a pathological liar. Just between us, the girl was crazy."

"How did she explain everything to Mark?"

Laura shrugged. "She refused to answer his calls. He never heard from her. Mark didn't date much after that. He didn't want to get hurt again. The two things he wanted in a relationship were honesty and trust. When you came along, he took a chance that he could finally have that relationship." She glanced at the empty cookie plate. "Where'd the cookies go?"

Peggy squeezed Hailey's hands. "We're happy you're the one Mark chose, dear."

Hailey forced a smile. Trust and honesty. Two virtues she couldn't give him. With her mother gone, she craved the nurturing Mark's family gave her. She lowered her hands below the table and scratched them. Would they look at her differently if they knew about her past? She loved the girl talks, but how could she ever let them know who she really was? "Thanks. I'm lucky to have you in my life."

Chapter Eight

Bella glanced at her watch and paced by the smoke-stained warehouse window. What was taking so long? Cerdo hovered near her, but she waved him away. "Stand back by Manuel and Antonio. I don't want anyone to see us." She lifted the slats on the blind, peeking down at the parking lot. "Charles should arrive any minute. His flight landed almost an hour ago."

The ride wouldn't take long. Sunday afternoon traffic didn't compare to the crazy bedlam of the weekday gridlock. She had met Charles Moulin three times and understood his quirks. He would hail a cab outside the terminal, unwilling to risk the paper trail of renting a car. After all, Charles had a medical practice in Chicago. Any appearance of impropriety would hurt his career, especially a deal as shady as this. But despite his professional reputation, the guy had guts.

She peeped through the blinds again.

A yellow cab from the city crept into the parking lot. Charles got out, carrying an attaché case. He handed the driver some money and the cabby sped off, squealing his tires.

She smirked as Charles surveyed the area. Junk cars lined the streets with trash strewn around the decrepit buildings. He should feel at home in this city. Chicago wasn't the only tough place. Manuel's rundown warehouse was the perfect hideout. But she could do without the mildew stench.

Below, Charles placed his hand on the knob and opened the steel door.

She turned and faced the others. "He's here."

They moved into position. Manuel sat on a chair at the dilapidated desk in the far corner of the dim room. Cerdo walked over and stood next to him. Bella hurried to the opposite corner and hid in the shadows with Antonio.

A knock tapped at the door.

Manuel spoke in a deep voice. "Come in."

The door opened and Charles stepped through the doorway, carrying his bag. He was a tall man, about the same height as Manuel, and his gray hair and beard were neatly trimmed. With his free arm, he wiped the beads of perspiration from his forehead.

Manuel motioned him closer. A faint glow from the banker's lamp on the desk lit the room. The shadows magnified the men's shapes.

With an arrogant grin, Cerdo prodded the visitor. "Yes?"

"Sir, I finished the job." Charles moved a step forward, squinting at them in the dim light. "The final notes and structural formulas are in my briefcase."

Manuel held out his arm. "Pass them here."

Charles removed the documents, stepped toward Manuel, and handed him the papers.

Even from his chair, Manuel was an authoritative man; his broad shoulders and dark features gave him an imposing quality.

While Manuel devoured the contents, Charles surveyed the room.

Bella shifted, scraping her heels against the floor. She scowled at her blunder.

Charles turned toward her and peered into the darkness.

A smile grew on Manuel's face. "Outstanding work. This is what I had hoped to see."

Charles nodded. "I've worked nonstop to complete everything. You wanted the formula ASAP."

Cerdo flashed a roguish grin. Even from where Bella stood, Cerdo's cold eyes revealed his empty soul. Charles was foolish to make excuses for his recurrent tardiness.

Manuel lowered the documents to the desk. "Are you sure you and your father are the only people who have these plants?"

Charles nodded. "Yes. We smuggled the two plants back to the States when we went to the Amazon. No one knows they exist."

"How long have you had them?"

"Since the 60s—before I went to med school. My father still grows his shrub at his house in Detroit. But I germinated many saplings."

"Where do you keep yours?"

"At my house. I can't risk my patients touching the oil from the flowers."

"How many do you have?"

"Over a dozen. My living room looks like a greenhouse. My father always said whoever cultivated the plant could control the world."

Manuel's jet-black eyes sparkled. "I want the plants."

Charles jutted his chin and stretched his shoulders back. "But that will end my research."

"I'm sure you could think of others ways to live out your days." Manuel raised the papers in his hand. "You are getting paid handsomely for this work."

"I planned on using the money to build a drug rehab clinic."

Cerdo laughed. "A clinic?"

Charles nodded. "Yes. In my friend's memory— The Robinson Rehab Center."

Manuel snickered. "How ironic."

Charles scratched his head. "The plants weren't part of the original deal. I could sell them for the right price. Say another $100,000?"

Bella chewed on her lip.

Manuel tapped his fingers on the desk and frowned.

Cerdo stepped forward. "No." He nodded at Antonio.

Charles turned and squinted into the shadows. His eyes widened. "Noo—"

Crack!

Squealing, Bella jumped at the sound.

The bullet struck Charles between his eyes. His body stumbled backward, falling to the floor. Blood seeped from the small hole on his forehead.

Cerdo stared at the body, a grin forming on his face. "What a shame. What a damn shame."

Manuel shot from his chair and met Antonio as he emerged from the shadows, striking him in the face. "What the hell did you do? You blazing idiot! I needed him. Why the hell did you shoot him?"

"I thought you wanted him dead." Antonio's gaze shifted to Cerdo.

"You have no brain sometimes." Manuel snarled. "I never told you to kill him. I intended to send the bastard away empty-handed. I didn't need the worthless plants. I already collected the formula. You stupid moron."

The room became silent again.

Cerdo stepped closer to the dead body and raised his stare to Antonio. "I trust you will dispose of Dr. Moulin."

Antonio nodded, but his gaze was fixed on Manuel, who gave him a harsh look. No doubt, he'd suffer strong repercussions for the wrongdoing.

Bella followed Manuel out the door and a chill ran down her spine. Cerdo posed a bigger headache in this venture than the researchers did.

Chapter Nine

Mark stared at the untouched pile of reports, and his chest tightened. His two objectives at work that day weighed on his mind. The Sherman case and his five-year reinvestigation paperwork. Neither was an easy task. The case would be the easiest to address. Walking to the elevator, he pressed the button to the sixth floor. Maybe he'd missed some clues in Elliot Sherman's office. He swiped his badge across the sensor and opened the lock to the sealed room.

The material on the desk was in a tidy layout. Pencils and pens filled the cup holder at the corner. A schedule and small stack of technical books were near the phone. Paper clips, a brown notebook, and a daily planner filled the top drawer. Mark had searched the room so often he could see the items with his eyes closed.

He leafed through the notebook again. Dates for the Washington Nationals games. Did he really think he would find something new after searching five times? The appointment planner showed no new information, either. Sighing, he leaned back in the seat. Wait, there was a small notepad pushed to the back of the drawer. His hands shook as he drew it out and scoured the pages. Why hadn't he seen this notepad before? The

pages were blank except for a scrawl on one sheet—
Look into Euphoria

He copied the note onto a piece of scrap paper and tucked it in his wallet. Removing the drawer from the glide, he searched behind the compartment. His wristwatch beeped, and he replaced the drawer. Time to start the next paperwork. He rode the elevator back to his office.

The hours passed. Mark looked down at the blank spaces on the reinvestigation forms. He raked a hand through his hair. How could a simple task drain so much time? The phone buzzed.

"Hello?"

"Hey, Mark. I missed you today at Mom's."

He straightened in his chair. "Laura? Are you back home yet?"

"No. We're at the airport. The kids are watching the planes take off before we start boarding."

"What's going on?"

"I wanted to tell you happy anniversary before you left for your romantic night with Hailey. She said you were working this afternoon. She's worried about you."

Mark frowned. "I know. Work has been pretty demanding."

"It sounds like it. I hear the stress in your voice. What's going on?"

He sighed. "It's my five-year reinvestigation paperwork."

She laughed. "That shouldn't be a problem for you. You do everything by the book."

"Yeah. I finished my part in ten minutes."

"Then what's the problem?"

He tapped his fingers on the desk. He could use someone to bounce his frustration off of. "Promise you won't say anything to anybody. Not to Jack and especially not to Mom and Dad."

"I swear. Scout's Honor."

"Hailey's hiding something, and her paperwork is hard to fill out."

"What do you mean she's hiding something?"

He exhaled a long sigh. "You remember when I started working at the DTA?"

"Yes. After you got married. So?"

"The agency did a polygraph and background check on me, and ran a routine check on Hailey. I thought everything was fine, but one afternoon I used the copier while the secretary was at lunch. I saw a report left on the tray. It stated Hailey's classified file with the Special Crimes Agency had passed review."

"The Special Crimes Agency? What's that?"

"I'd never heard of it, either. But I did some research. The SCA is a small, top-secret organization that focuses on counterterrorism. It's located in Austin, Texas, but there are satellite offices in Washington, D.C. and San Francisco."

"How did Hailey get involved in something like that?"

"I don't know. She would have only been in her late teens or early twenties when she worked there. I tried to get her personnel file, but it's sealed."

"How frustrating."

"Tell me about it."

"Did you ask her about it?"

"No. She doesn't talk much about her past." He rubbed his forehead. "I knew when we dated that she had secrets, but I never imagined this. I always assumed she would tell me when she was ready."

"Obviously, she never did."

He stared at the incomplete form. The papers mocked him. "Five years ago I went through the same thing, but for some reason this time it's bothering me."

"Can you call anyone and ask them what happened?"

"I called one of my contacts from another department this evening. I'm waiting for him to call me back with more info, but he emailed me a list of the staff during the time Hailey worked." He looked at the names on the printout. Stefan Bruno, the SCA director, was first on the list. "Looks like the director during Hailey's tenure still runs the agency. I also got the names of other agents employed during that time. When I get the chance, I'll look them up."

"I hope you find your answers. Do you want me to talk to her?"

"No. You promised not to say anything."

"Okay. I won't, but if you need me to do some digging, I can be pretty sneaky."

He smiled. "Thanks. I'll talk to you later. I still have work to finish. Tell Jack and the kids hello."

He tore off the list of Hailey's former contacts and placed it in his wallet next to Sherman's scribbled note. His to-do list was growing longer. He picked up his pen and continued working. His heart squeezed. Trust her. If he didn't have trust in his marriage, he didn't have a marriage worth keeping.

****

Hailey sat at the dining room table set for two and tapped her fingers on the tablecloth. She had spent the latter part of the afternoon creating a romantic anniversary meal for Mark. She even splurged on a bottle of Cabernet Sauvignon. Earlier, she'd fed the children pepperoni pizza and then tucked them in bed.

After she had showered, she put on her favorite outfit. The purple cinched dress accentuated her narrow waist and flattered her curves. She blow-dried her hair and put on make-up to cover up some barely visible scars. Cruel reminders of her past. Green eye shadow and brown eyeliner highlighted her hazel eyes. Mark always commented on her hypnotic eyes. She applied her lipstick and used a flat iron to tame her natural curls. Standing in front of the mirror, she'd admired her reflection. Not bad. Hopefully, Mark would notice and say she looked pretty.

Dusk was creeping in as she dimmed the lights and lit two tapered candles on the dining room table. The clock hands inched around the dial as the flames on the candles flickered, creating shadows in the darkened room. Checking her phone, she read the text Mark had sent two hours earlier.

I need another hour. Looking forward to tonight.

She replied: *Where are u?*

She stepped to the bookcase and pulled out their wedding album. A loose photo of her and Mark standing in front of a marina fell on the floor. Inner Harbor. That trip was such a long time ago. She frowned. The Frenchman had almost blown her cover.

For seventeen years, she had kept her secrets. Hands shaking, she opened the wedding album cover. Reminiscing over the bridal party photos calmed her nerves.

Mark's friend David had been the best man, while one of her college girlfriends stood as her maid-of-honor. Mark's family and a few other friends helped celebrate the intimate affair. The honey fragrance of the peonies, clematises, and sweet peas in her bouquet provided the proper ambience of a summer garden.

She sighed. She had been naïve to think their lives would stay as carefree as that perfect day. Encouraged, she turned the page.

At ten o'clock, she snuffed out the candles. The food was cold and so was her dream of celebrating their anniversary. She scratched her hands; it was less painful than crying. Changing into her nightgown, she climbed into bed and drifted to an uneasy sleep.

Chapter Ten

Mark's fingers fumbled as he buttoned his dress shirt and looped the tie around his collar. Watching Hailey from the corner of his eye, he banged the dresser drawer shut. Still no movement. He braced himself for another horrible day. "Honey, do you want me to make the kids breakfast today?"

She seemed to be sleeping, but no one could sleep through his terrible singing in the shower. Sooner or later she'd have to get the kids ready for school.

He had called the office and rearranged his work schedule to go in late. He was running out of ideas.

"Hailey? The bus comes in forty minutes." He finished adjusting his tie and pulled the quilted bedspread over her. Still no movement. Yep. Another terrible day. He walked down the stairs into the kitchen.

The previous day, Owen reprimanded him for his lack of progress on the Sherman case. But that was the least of Mark's concerns. How could he be such a jerk? His eyes squeezed shut. The wine bottle and dishes on the dining room table were etched in his mind. Monday morning, he tried to apologize, but Hailey had taken the kids to the bus stop and started her daily run. When he left for work, she still hadn't returned. At night, she helped the kids with their homework and went upstairs to bed, refusing to look at him. When he apologized, she ignored him and walked away.

He had been so inconsiderate. His anniversary of all things! Forgotten. He tossed cereal in a bowl and poured a glass of grape juice. A vase of twelve pink roses decorated the table, filling the room with a sweet floral scent. At least this bouquet hadn't landed in the garbage can yet. The florist was delivering a different bouquet to the house each day. Unfortunately, the peace offering hadn't softened Hailey's mood. The only person happy about the daily order was the florist padding his pockets.

Mark walked into the living room and switched on the TV. The commentator spoke:

And now for the top story in the news this morning: Authorities are investigating three separate drug overdose incidents around the Chicago area. Twenty people are dead and one teenager is hospitalized. In the Lincoln Square region, six male teens died last night in what appears to be a drug suicide. Authorities say the teens, ranging in age from fifteen through nineteen, ingested an unidentified drug. The teens reportedly experienced cognitive problems and hallucinations. Witnesses report teens running in the streets, in front of passing cars. Two of the teenagers jumped from a six-foot wall. One male teenager was admitted to Chicago General Hospital. Doctors are performing toxicology tests, but so far, the lab tests are inconclusive.

At the South Side Park, another group, five boys and two girls, ages sixteen through twenty, died in a similar manner. And on the west side of town, in what appears to be a related incident, three teen girls and four teenage boys were pronounced dead. We will update you with more details as this story develops.

He turned off the TV. "Damn drugs." The Chicago PD would have one hell of a time investigating the case. No doubt, they'd call for help. Twenty deaths. *Shit.*

Laughter came from the stairway. "Daddy, Daddy!" Anna raced into the room, her fair hair lifting from her angelic face.

Ethan zoomed past and grabbed the remote on the end table.

"Morning!" Mark put on his brightest face and hugged his little girl. He turned to Hailey as she walked past and lowered his head to kiss her, but she brushed by, hurrying into the kitchen. He glanced at Anna and Ethan and exhaled relief. Thank goodness the sitcom distracted them.

He walked into the kitchen and stopped beside Hailey. The kids' cereal bowls were on the counter, and she stood by the sink, idly scratching her hands. "Honey, can we at least discuss this? I was a jerk. I'm sorry about Sunday night." How could he sound any more sincere? "I don't have any other excuse. Work's been crazy, and I lost track of time."

He circled his arms around her waist and pulled her toward him. He expected her resistance. Drawing her closer, he kissed her. "Come on. I don't know what else I can do to make it up to you. Can't we get past this?" he whispered in her ear. "I love you." Mark kissed her again, a slow drugging kiss. Then he caressed her shoulders, trying to erase the pain in her face. Her body relaxed. As a last resort, he scrunched his face and made sad puppy-dog eyes. If that expression didn't work, nothing would.

She shook her head and let out a small laugh. "I can't stay mad at you for long."

"Thank you." Mark breathed out the words.

She narrowed her eyes. "You've got to stop being so stressed. It weighs you down."

"I know."

"It's not fair to us."

"I'm sorry." He rubbed his hand on her back.

"I'm not going to sit around feeling miserable anymore."

He hugged her tighter. "I'll make it up to you. Let's go out to dinner tonight, anywhere you want. I'll make the reservations."

A tenuous smile flitted across her mouth. "Okay, I'll ask if your parents can babysit the kids. But you'd better not cancel. I might not forgive you next time."

He traced a finger under her jaw and kissed her. A jolt rushed through his body. "There won't be a next time."

Chapter Eleven

Bella lay in bed, her skin tingling from Manuel's warm, muscular arm around her as he slept. The previous night had been incredible. Almost like the first time they had made love. She closed her eyes, reliving their first tryst. She had attended a cocktail party of Washington elites four years past. As she spoke to a Pennsylvania senator, she eyed the attractive man next to him. When the congressman introduced him, she questioned Manuel about his country. They ended up chatting for hours.

When he asked her to dance, his six-foot stature towered above her by five inches. The royal-blue satin evening gown she wore framed the four-carat sapphire necklace adorning her neck. Her golden hair swept up in a chignon highlighted her long neckline. She bubbled inside that this handsome man had shown an ardent interest in her. When he called her Bella, she felt like a princess.

During the party, she had engaged him in sophisticated conversation. Her poise seemed to enchant him. When she recounted her research under a renowned biochemist, he stilled her lips. He claimed they distracted him. He admitted later that he longed to kiss them. At the end of the night, Manuel proclaimed her lips were as sweet and luscious as he imagined. He made love to her afterward.

He satisfied all her needs. She didn't demand anything in return, even when he asked her to work for him. There was no talk of a long-term commitment. Manuel's family expected him to marry someone from Colombia. As time passed, his attention toward her grew more intense. The chemistry between them was unmistakable, especially when they danced the salsa. He added spark to her life, an excitement she hadn't felt in a long time.

Smiling, she reached her arm across the pillow and touched his thick coarse hair. Her worries disappeared when she was with Manuel. She loved him. Loved how her body reacted when he breathed in her jasmine-and-magnolia perfume. Wow, the chills she got when he whispered endearing comments in her ear. Her insides fluttered thinking about how special he made her feel. She had been alone for too long. Far too long.

She glanced at the antique carriage clock on the nightstand. Regrettably, she didn't have time for lovemaking. Stretching her arm, she picked up the remote next to the clock and kissed him. "Babe, it's time to get up. I'll turn on the news."

****

Bella's stomach squeezed in a tight knot as the news reporter conveyed the top stories. She should have known Sunday's meeting wouldn't end without repercussions. The newscast ended, and she grabbed Manuel's cell phone from the nightstand. She pressed her lips together and handed the phone to Manuel. Never had she seen his face so flushed.

He dialed and put the call on speaker.

Cerdo answered on the second ring. "Yes?"

Manuel gnashed his teeth. "Did you see the news?"

"I wasn't expecting that."

The veins protruded from Manuel's face. "Did you ever stop to think Moulin might set up a contingency plan to double-cross us?"

"I guess he planned to blow the lid off the entire project if we didn't pay him his money."

"The bastard was a loaded cannon and you lit the fuse. Now the authorities are investigating twenty deaths. If someone identifies this drug before we're ready to ship, the whole project will explode in our faces."

"I get it. I'll check how I can delay any investigations on my front." Cerdo paused. "We didn't know Moulin would do this."

Bella shook her head in disgust. Leave it to Cerdo to make excuses.

"Hell, is that supposed to make me feel better?" Manuel clenched the phone as if he were strangling it. "I pay you the big money. You need to keep one step ahead of these scientists. Now we have to destroy the evidence. Light a match and burn down his house. Ransack his medical office. Find out where he keeps his safe deposit boxes. Send Antonio to help wipe out any connections to us."

"I'm on it."

"Keep me posted…and this time, no screwups." Manuel slammed the phone on the nightstand and looked at her. "What an arrogant prick. Why the hell did he order Moulin's death? I'm the one in control. Not Cerdo."

She wrapped her arms around him; his body was hard as granite. "I can't believe Moulin double-crossed us."

Manuel threw the covers off his chest and sat up. "Dammit! Moulin must have shipped Euphoria to his dealers before he met us the other day. Twenty teenagers dead. And one in a coma." He gripped a goose down pillow and threw it on the floor. "Damn. Something's wrong with the drug. Moulin guaranteed he could process his plant into a synthetic chemical."

She rolled on her back and sighed. Manuel always expected her to fix the problems. Luckily, even though Moulin had more experience, she was smarter. "I'll run some tests to see what I can find out."

"You've got to find the error," he snapped. "We can't sell a drug that wipes out the buyers."

Nodding, she sat next to him and raked a hand through her hair. "I'll get right on it. But this could get complicated."

"The authorities are involved now. Once they ID the drug, they'll notify the agencies and add it on the Schedule I list for illegal drugs. Inspectors will open our shipments." Manuel banged his fist into the mattress. "Moulin sabotaged this entire operation. We're so close to having the drug shipped to our suppliers. We're set to make billions off this venture!"

Bella leaned over and gave him a quick kiss. "I have an idea. Let me take a shower before breakfast, and then I'll start working on it. Don't worry. Our plan will work. It has to work." She stood and sauntered to the bathroom.

When she stepped out of the shower, he was gone. She walked downstairs to the kitchen where the housekeeper was unloading the dishwasher. "Good morning, Lola. Is Manuel eating on the patio?"

Lola shook her head and placed two tumblers in the cupboard. "No, *Señorita*. Mr. Mendoza stormed out with Antonio. He didn't want any breakfast today." She poured a cup of coffee and passed it to her. "Can I make you a hot breakfast, *Señorita* Bella? Maybe some bacon and eggs?"

Bella slid on a barstool at the kitchen island. "No, thank you. Yogurt is fine."

The housekeeper set a variety of yogurt containers on the granite counter. "I'll be in the laundry room if you need me, *Señorita*."

"Thank you, Lola." She read the Chicago news report on her cell phone as she ate. When she finished, she bumped into Cerdo in the hallway behind the catering kitchen. "Manuel's not here."

"I know." His eyebrows narrowed. "Why are you still here?"

"I got a late start." She folded her arms. "I have a lot to do today, thanks to you." Her flesh crawled when she stood near him. She pointed to a small bag of chicken nuggets and the bottle of water in his hand. "Why are you bringing food?"

Cerdo looked around then waited as Lola climbed the stairs with a basket of clothes. Flashing an arrogant grin, he opened the mahogany door to the back stairwell. "I'll show you."

She followed him down the steps past the wine cellar. The fieldstone walls reminded her of an old castle. Why hadn't Manuel ever shown her this place? Raising her arm, she covered her nose and blocked the musty air. They walked in silence through the narrow dark hall, Cerdo's cell phone light guiding them. Her hand brushed against a spider web, and she wriggled. "Yecchh!"

Cerdo turned and his eyes narrowed. "Shhh! We're almost there."

Goosebumps prickled her arm. Manuel didn't even know where she was. She could use self-defense moves in case Cerdo tried anything funny. Pulling out her phone, she groaned silently. There was no cell service.

As she began to turn back, Cerdo stopped. "Here we are." He lit an old-fashioned oil lamp on the wall and the flame illuminated an arched entrance. The wooden door creaked as he opened it. He turned, raising his hand in front of her. "Don't come in too far."

Inside the cinderblock chamber, a scrawny man with cuffs shackled around his ankles cowered in the corner. He blinked, twisting on a thin bed of blankets. The light permeating the shadows was as vivid as a room full of flashing cameras.

She gasped. Cerdo tossed the prisoner a handful of nuggets, as if feeding some feral animal. He ushered her back into the stone hallway and shut the door.

At the bottom of the stairs, she halted, gaping at him. "What are you doing with that man?"

He puffed his chest. "He's my prisoner."

"You're crazy. Wait until I tell Manuel."

Cerdo lips closed into a creepy smile. "He knows."

She flinched. How could Manuel allow this to go on in his house? "You're tormenting him!"

He burst out in a devious laugh. "This form of torture is more gratifying than murder."

Chapter Twelve

Mark arrived at his office and made dinner reservations for seven o'clock. He requested a bottle of red wine for the table and a violinist to serenade them during the meal. His pulse raced as he anticipated Hailey's reaction.

He opened the lid of a new box of Sherman's records and pulled out a file. It belonged to another drug dealer Sherman sent to prison. Mark's secretary Tamara McGuire interrupted through the intercom. "Owen would like to see you ASAP."

"Did he say what he wanted?"

"No, but he sounded bothered. He asked for Greg, also."

Mark laid the file on his desk and followed the sausage aroma down the hall to Owen's office. Greg sat in a side chair, eating a breakfast sandwich, while Owen paced the floor.

Mark tapped on the door. "What's up?"

Owen stopped pacing and placed a hand on each side of his waist. "Did you hear the morning news?"

"I caught some of it. Why?"

"Does Chicago ring a bell? Three groups of overdoses! Twenty dead around the city." Owen's voice grew louder as he spoke.

"I saw it. Anything on the drug?"

"The toxicology tests came up negative. The lab sent samples away for further analysis. If those results don't show anything, we're in deep shit."

Greg unwrapped another sandwich and took a bite. "Do you think it's a new drug?"

Owen crossed his arms. "It sure as hell isn't one we've seen before. I need you both to fly to Chicago and see what you can find. Talk to the Narcotics Department. Interview witnesses. Get some answers. If this is a new drug, we have to identify it. We need to warn Health and Human Services, DOJ, and DEA. The UN's Office on Drugs and Crime already called, breathing down my neck for information. We can't let it transport out of the country. What a foul mess." He paced again and took a breath. "Well? What the hell are you two standing here for? Don't you have a plane to catch?"

Mark hesitated. "Can we leave early tomorrow morning? I have something important going on at home this evening."

"I have something important going on," Owen mimicked in a shrill voice. "Dammit, no! Cancel your damn plans. I want you both in Chicago tonight. We can't lose another day. Make the airline and hotel reservations and go home and pack—and bring back some answers!"

Greg tossed his sandwich wrapper in the trash and stood. The corners of his eyes wrinkled as he saluted Owen. "Yes, sir."

Mark reluctantly followed Greg out of the office and prepared an apology. If this didn't give him an ulcer, he didn't know what would.

****

Hailey hummed all morning. Finally, they would celebrate their anniversary. She stayed busy, changing bed linens and washing four loads of dirty laundry. At one o'clock, she sat in the rocking chair, folding a basket of towels and sorting clothes into piles. She surveyed the living room and kitchen; they both needed a good cleaning. The inability to hide a messy room was one of the drawbacks of an open floor plan, although the design made it easier to look after the kids. The phone rang, and she hurried to the kitchen, carrying Anna's blouse in her hand. She glanced at the caller ID and picked up the phone. "Mark? What's wrong?"

"Honey, I'm sorry, but I have to cancel on tonight's dinner." His voice quavered.

She tightened her grip on the soft polyester fabric in her hand. Of course, she should have known.

"I know you're upset. I need to investigate an overdose in Chicago."

She remained silent.

"Hailey? Honey, please try to understand. You know this is the type of case the DTA investigates. I tried delaying it until tomorrow morning, but Owen wants us to leave this afternoon."

His voice sounded sincere. The change of plans didn't surprise her. The overdoses led the top headlines on the noon news.

"Hailey? Are you still there?"

There was no use in taking out her disappointment on him. "I watched the news. Are you coming home to pack?"

His voice became brighter. "I'm rearranging my schedule. I'll leave here in an hour. The flight leaves at five-thirty. I can see you a short time, and then I'll head out."

"Okay." Despite her disappointment about dinner, her heart swelled. "Mark?"

"Yes?"

"We'll do dinner another day."

"Thanks. I knew you'd understand. I love you."

She smiled. The appreciation in his voice resonated through her. "I love you, too."

Chapter Thirteen

The flight ran into turbulence, and Mark let out a huge breath when the plane landed safely in Chicago. He stepped off the plane, giving the flight attendant a half-hearted nod. He should be home celebrating with Hailey.

Greg had already picked up his luggage and was waiting at the car rental when Mark arrived. Mark volunteered and drove the rental car to the hotel, a short distance from the airport. He checked into his room and called Hailey. "Hi, honey. I landed."

"How was the flight?"

"Bumpy, but I made it. Are you and the kids okay?"

"Yeah. Everything's fine. I just put them to bed. Ethan finished his homework a little while ago. He scored a goal at his soccer game."

He smiled. "Tell him I said 'Way to go.' How's Anna?"

"Good. Her teacher started them practicing for the dance recital next month. Anna's going to be a fairy in the magic forest."

He ended the call. Mark leaned back in his chair and smiled. Hailey spoke as if everything was back to normal. He rode the elevator to the first floor where Greg was waiting for him in the lobby.

Greg folded the hotel flyer he was reading and slipped it into his pocket. "Where do you want to eat?"

"Let's check with the concierge. I'm not that hungry."

Greg chuckled. "My stomach's growling. I could eat anywhere."

The concierge listed several possibilities, but they opted for the restaurant adjoining the hotel. The host seated them right away and handed each of them a menu. The server set a basket of rolls on the table and took their order.

Mark unfolded a napkin on his lap. "Did you get a chance to call Sherman's wife?"

Greg chose a roll from the basket. "I called Kay this afternoon. She said Sherman had acted odd before he disappeared. He didn't tell her what was bothering him. He left for work one day and never returned."

"And that's all she told you?"

"Yes." Greg spread butter on the roll and took a bite.

"Did you ask her any more questions? To jog her memory?"

Greg stopped chewing. "Come on. Are you implying I don't know how to interrogate a witness?"

Why was he giving Greg a hard time? They were on the same side. "No, I'm sure you asked the right questions."

The server delivered their drinks and salads.

Lifting his glass of diet soda, Greg raised his brow. "I did."

"I'm sorry." Mark sipped his coffee. "I wish we knew what Sherman was investigating before he disappeared. Why isn't anything showing up in his documented accounts? No memos. Nothing. Even his personal calendar was empty."

Greg glanced up from eating his leafy greens. "Where did you find his calendar?"

Picking up his salad fork, Mark stabbed a crouton. "In the back of his desk drawer. I rummaged through his possessions again after I questioned his co-workers. I never noticed it before."

The server came with another basket of rolls. Greg chewed the last bite of his salad. "You make it sound like he's dead."

Mark shrugged and continued digging into his Caesar salad. "Let's face it. Sherman's been missing for over a month. There's a good chance someone knocked him off."

Pushing the salad plate away, Greg leaned back in his chair. His face twisted.

Mark stopped chewing. "What?"

"As far as I'm concerned, it wouldn't be a tremendous loss."

Mark set down his fork. "How well did you know Sherman?"

"Not too well, but from what I knew of the man, I wasn't impressed."

"What do you mean?"

Greg hesitated. "He was a womanizer. At the NNIC, he flirted with all the women in our unit. The man lacked any scruples."

"Were others aware of his behavior?"

"I'm sure they were. He was quite open about his conquests. Guys like him have a way with bragging." Greg shrugged. "Who knows? Maybe a scorned lover finished him."

Mark rubbed his eyes. "I didn't consider Sherman a Casanova. If that's the case, we may never find him."

The server delivered the meals, and the aroma whetted his appetite. Mark was glad he had ordered. Greg dived into his prime rib, and Mark savored his grilled salmon.

Mark finished his entrée and lowered his fork. "What did Sherman do in his free time?"

"We didn't associate much. He led his own life."

"Let's take a closer look at his personnel file when we fly back. We might find other contacts to interview."

Greg sipped his drink as the server cleared some dishes. "Okay. I'll work on that."

Mark waited until the server refilled his coffee. "I'll go through his desk again and look for a new lead."

When he finished the last bite of prime rib, Greg took out his oral diabetic medicine and belched. "Now I can order dessert."

Mark's phone vibrated, and he removed it from his pocket. Hailey had texted good night. "Shouldn't you watch the sweets—because of your diabetes, I mean?"

"I should, but I don't." Greg chuckled and settled his gaze on the dessert menu.

Chapter Fourteen

Hailey woke to sunlight streaming through the sheer bedroom curtains. Grabbing the alarm clock, she groaned. Thirty minutes past the hour. Darn. How could she forget to set the alarm? She raced into the shower. Keeping a normal school routine was important. The fewer disruptions she encountered while Mark was away, the better. She threw on a pair of gray sweats and a T-shirt, woke the kids, and ran downstairs. If she hurried, she could cook some hot oatmeal while they dressed.

The kids seemed fine at breakfast, but when Hailey walked them to the bus stop, Anna gripped her hand. "When's Daddy coming back?" Her soft voice wavered. "I'm scared."

"Daddy won't let anything happen to us." Ethan sounded confident in his big-brother voice. "He's a good daddy."

Hailey smiled at his self-assurance. Giving Anna and Ethan the same love and security she had growing up as a child warmed her heart. "Don't worry. Everything's okay." She squeezed Anna's hand. "Look! Here comes the school bus."

As she waved good-bye to Ethan and Anna, she frowned. Children grew so quickly.

Katherine waited at the bus stop and waved. "I turned on my coffeemaker. I have the day off. Are you free for a little break this morning?"

Hailey scratched her neck. Tough decision. Clean a messy house or talk with a grown-up? "I can make time for a small cup." She followed her friend inside the split-level home.

In no time at all, Katherine had arranged a plate of blueberry muffins and set out coffee cups on the table. Spoons and creamer completed the preparations.

The aroma awakened Hailey's appetite.

Katherine lifted the coffee pot and poured the coffee. "Ethan told Nate that Mark's away on business. Let me know if you need any help while he's away."

Managing a small smile, Hailey pulled the cup closer to her. "Thanks. I hope he won't be gone long."

Katherine splashed creamer into her cup and passed her the carton. "I always get anxious when Jake leaves town. Transporting the kids to school around my work schedule isn't easy."

Hailey stirred the creamer in the coffee. "How long is Jake away this time?"

"Six months. We'll see how soon he's here before he's deployed again."

"I don't know how you do it, working odd shifts at the hospital and taking care of the kids." Leaning an elbow on the table, Hailey propped her chin. "I'm glad I don't have to worry about that again for a while."

"Where did you work before?"

"The NIH."

"The National Institute of Health? No kidding! I didn't know you were in the medical field, too."

Savoring the aroma, Hailey sipped the coffee. "I carried out genetic studies. But I quit after Ethan was born. I didn't want to miss one milestone of his childhood."

Katherine laughed. "When I told Jake that after Nate was born, he told me to set up a video camera." She frowned. "Unfortunately, we need the money. The mortgage isn't going away anytime soon."

Hailey nodded and selected a muffin. "I loved having my career, but I wanted to stay home like my mother did for me." She shrugged. "Call me old-fashioned, I guess."

"I call it nice." Katherine smiled and sipped the coffee. "If Jake and I could swing our finances, I'd do the same."

Hailey removed the muffin paper and split a piece of muffin off the top. "Our family budget took a huge shock. No more big vacations for us. I spend my Sundays clipping coupons."

Katherine lifted a muffin from the plate. "How long have you lived here?"

"About five years. We moved a year after I had Anna. We wanted a place closer to Mark's work and his parents."

"Do you think you'll ever go back to work?"

"When the kids get older. I'm working on my master's."

Katherine's jaw dropped. "Good for you! I don't have the time or energy to go back to school."

"It's tough. But when we can save enough money, I take a class. I should finish in a few years. Glancing at the wall clock, Hailey picked up the cup and stood. "Speaking of time—I spent all my time the past few weeks studying for my final exam. My house is a wreck. I should go clean it."

A bright smile lit up Katherine's face. "Thanks for stopping over."

Hailey walked to the sink and rinsed her cup before leaving it. "We'll have to do it again sometime."

She strode back to the house and went through the front door, closed it, then turned the deadbolt, unlocked it, and rotated it again. She exhaled a sigh. Now the house was safe. Leaning down, she picked up the toys and socks scattered around the room. The house wasn't the same without Mark.

After twisting her thick hair in a high ponytail, she cleaned bathrooms, scrubbed floors, and made the beds. Her face warmed when another dozen roses arrived with a note: *Sorry. We'll try again. I promise. Mark*

Their sweet fragrance perfumed the air as she placed the bouquet in a vase next to the previous day's flowers. *Oh, Mark. I wish you were here.*

At eleven o'clock, she vacuumed the living room carpet, then walked into the kitchen and started cleaning. She washed the breakfast dishes, relaxing as the warm soapy water became a mini spa. From the corner of her eye, she glimpsed some movement at the window above the sink. Startled, she peered closer.

A dark-haired man with wide eyes stared at her.

She opened her mouth and closed it. The trespasser wasn't a stranger. The glass bowl she was holding slipped out of her hands.

The dish shattered on the floor. The crash transported Hailey out of her daze. She blinked twice. Her eyes weren't playing tricks on her. She leaped over the small glass pieces and hurried to the door, opening it. "Parker!" She greeted him with a hug. "Tom Parker! What are you doing here?"

"Hello, Hailey." She had forgotten how deep his voice was. "You look as adorable as ever." His face reddened. "Shit! You haven't changed a bit."

She grinned at the man she once had a major crush on and, standing back, gave him some space. "Come on. I've changed plenty." She looked down at her old sweats and worn T-shirt. "Maybe not for the better, though."

Someone behind him coughed. "Ahem. What am I? Chopped liver?"

Hailey regarded the aging man with the receding hairline and held out her arms. "Stefan?" She hugged him. "You're here, too? What a surprise!"

Stefan circled his arm around her shoulder. "Sorry if we scared you. We rang the doorbell, but the vacuum was running."

The two men waited in the kitchen as she swept up the broken dish. Warmth spread from her neck through her cheeks. Great way to look like a total klutz. She invited them into the living room and served them coffee. Still giddy, she seated herself on the rocking chair. "Gosh. It's mind-boggling to see you both. Why are you here?"

"What? We can't visit an old friend?" Stefan's tight lips broke into a grin. "I don't think I've ever seen you flustered."

She threw her head back and laughed. "It's been fifteen years. Of course I'm rattled!"

Parker's solemn eyes met hers. "It's only been fourteen."

His stare lasted a moment longer than necessary. She bit her lip and turned to Stefan. "You two are the last people I expected to see."

Stefan laughed. "That's pretty obvious."

"Why are you here? I'm sure you have more pressing issues than making a social call. You're still the director at the SCA, right?"

He nodded his head, and his smile faded. "We need your help."

"What do you mean?"

He set down his coffee cup on the end table. "A big drug case is going on in Chicago. Did it make the news here?"

"I watched the newscast yesterday." *And my husband's investigating it.* "So many young people died. It's terrible!"

Stefan raised his hand and gestured at Parker. "He tracked down the man responsible for the deaths. His name is Manuel de Mendoza."

"Mendoza? I've heard of him. He lives here in Washington." She scoffed. "He's reputed to be a high-class antique dealer."

Parker's lip curled. "I see you don't believe that either. Mendoza moved here from Colombia. Reports say he had a falling-out with his father."

Hailey nodded. "José de Mendoza."

"Yes. My hunch is the separation was a ruse to build up business connections in the States."

"Let me guess. Drugs." Hailey pursed her lips.

Parker's eyes grew cold. "Mendoza owns several properties around the District, but his main residence is here. In Great Falls."

"The photos of his place were all over the Internet when he bought it. It's a multi-million dollar mansion."

"He's behind the deaths. One of the researchers who created the drug was a doctor from Chicago. Dr. Charles Moulin."

"One? There are more?"

Parker nodded. "It's a good possibility."

"Why do you say that?"

"I searched Moulin's house yesterday. I found details of Moulin's meeting between Mendoza and someone called Cerdo. According to the airline manifest, Moulin never returned home. We found his car at O'Hare."

"How did he get the drug to the teens?"

"Moulin has contacts throughout the city. A lot of dealers. I tracked down one of them—Wendell Hautz. He admitted getting a package in the mail and selling it on his turf."

Hailey's voice softened. "Did you confiscate the drug from Hautz?"

Parker shook his head. "No. He sold everything. After I roughed him up, I drove to Moulin's place. He had exotic shrubs growing in his living room. The place looked like a tropical garden. Before I could collect samples, I got called for an emergency. When I returned to Moulin's place, the house had burned down."

"Arson?"

Parker nodded. "Looks like Mendoza didn't want any evidence left."

She sighed. "He must have other researchers if Moulin was expendable."

"From what I learned, Moulin was reckless. Considering all the deaths, he probably didn't test the drug. Though he was smart enough to expose it if he failed to return home."

"As a doctor, he should have known better." Hailey crossed her arms and looked at both men. "Animal testing and clinical studies are important protocols in pharmaceuticals. What class of drug is it?"

"We're not sure." Stefan frowned. "The toxicology drug panels are negative."

"What's showing up on the tests?"

"Benzene rings, amino groups, esters, and carboxylate groups." Parker read the list from his phone.

Hailey tapped her finger against her chin as she repeated the names.

"The doctors are waiting for results at a reference laboratory." Stefan leaned back into the sofa cushion. "I don't like wasting time."

She nodded. Any delay could slow the case. "What kind of symptoms did the kids have?"

Stefan frowned. "Irritability, delusions, hallucinations, loss of coordination, vomiting, dizziness…"

She narrowed her eyes. "Couldn't the doctors do anything?"

"The kids died before the ambulance came."

Parker set his coffee cup on the end table and leaned closer, jaw tight. "One teen, a seventeen year old, took a smaller dose. He's the only survivor. He's had multiple seizures, and now he's in a coma. It's baffling the doctors."

"I can't imagine what those parents are going through." She folded her hands on her lap and shook her head.

Parker walked over to the window and wiped his eyes.

Why was this case affecting him so deeply?

Stefan turned to her. "We need your help."

"What can I do?"

"Mendoza's hosting a dinner party at his mansion, and many prominent people are attending. We're certain he's entertaining some of the guests as potential contacts for the drug. He's probably hiding information at his place, but we need someone to interpret his files—someone who's familiar with toxicology. We're hopeful Parker can take the info to the doctors so they can treat the boy."

Hailey took a moment to absorb Stefan's request. She stammered. "But I haven't worked at the SCA in years." She turned her head toward the window. Parker gazed at her beseechingly, and a chill ran through her. She unfolded her arms and scratched her neck. "I don't do this type of work anymore."

Parker stepped toward her. "Please think about it. We only need you this one time. I resigned from the SCA four years ago, but the agency needs our help."

"He's right." Stefan nodded. "The SCA specializes in using electronic surveillance. We go after spies and terrorists. Our agents are experts in computer networking. They aren't well versed in pharmaceutical toxicology. You took a few courses at least." He paused. "You'd be away for three days max."

"Three days?" How could she just pick up and leave her family?

"You need to get briefed in Texas. We'll get you updated ear implants. You'll return home after the dinner party Saturday night."

An image of Mark flashed through her mind. "But there are *other* agencies with narcotic experts to handle this case. Can't another agency...?"

"No." Parker slapped his fist against his thigh. "We can't risk any mistakes."

She paced the floor. "I don't know. The ramifications for foiling a drug king are serious. Mark doesn't even know about my past. I have my own family now. What do I tell Mark and my kids? That I'm going away on a secret mission? That would raise a lot of questions—which I'm not prepared to answer."

"Hailey, please. It's critical or we wouldn't ask." Parker stood beside her, his eyes filled with tears.

She searched his face. "What's really going on? You're hiding something."

His voice cracked. "The kid in the coma is Justin."

Fighting for breath, she clutched his arm and sank onto the couch.

Parker held her arm, steadying her. "Hailey, are you all right?"

Stefan turned to him. "Get her some water."

Parker hurried to the kitchen and returned carrying a glass of water. "Here, take a drink."

Her skin tingled and a sudden coldness ran through her body. Finally, she pulled herself together. "Justin's in a coma?"

Taking the empty glass from her, Parker set it on the end table and collapsed beside her. "Yes. The doctors had to intubate him. God, Hailey, his arms have so many IVs running into him that he looks like a marionette. All they can do is monitor his chemistry levels. Grace told me to pray, but I stopped praying years ago."

Hailey cringed. She was to blame for that. "Is Grace with him?"

He nodded. "Justin's our only child." His voice caught. "If anything happens to him, I don't know how we'll get through it."

She rubbed her hand on his shoulder. "Oh, Parker, I'm so sorry."

"Justin's best friend, Ben Gerome, came into the ER with him. They played baseball together when we moved to Chicago. Ben told me about the drug deal that happened moments before the kids turned wild. He said they acted like crazy animals. They jumped off cars, ran in-between traffic, and tried flying like birds."

"Wait—that boy didn't take the drug?"

Parker shook his head. "No. He's the one who called 911. Ben said the other kids pressured Justin into buying the drug. According to Ben, Justin only bought a small hit. I bet that's why he didn't die."

Hailey lingered on the sofa, too shaky to stand on her own. "What was Justin thinking?"

He shrugged. "Drugs are a bigger problem than we realize. I didn't even know the kids he hung out with messed with drugs."

"He'll be okay, right?"

Parker drew in a long breath. "We don't know. It's bad. Something's causing him to stay in a coma. The doctors can't clear the drug from his system."

Stefan sat on the other side of her. "This is why we need your help—to identify it. The dinner party is Saturday evening. The agency has been monitoring

Mendoza's mail and gathering information for months. An agent intercepted the RSVP for a Dr. Frederick Lavoie and his fiancée from Canada. The couple sent their regrets. They're getting married in Quebec on Saturday, so they won't be at the party. We want you and Parker to become the couple. We'll send the RSVP confirming your arrival. As guests, you can search the mansion. You'll use a camera to take pictures of the files, like in the old days. Once you find the structural formula, you two can sneak out before anyone discovers what you're up to."

Parker stood and paced. The dark circles under his eyes emphasized his tired face. "Stefan kept tabs on your education. Of all the agents, you're the most experienced in this area. I wouldn't have a clue what I'd search for even if it jumped out in front of me."

Hailey raised her eyebrows at Stefan. "What will the agency say, sending in two former agents on the case?"

He gave a dismissive wave. "Don't worry about that. I'm still the director. I already called Parker's supervisor about pulling him for a week. I'll reinstate your security clearance for this case and take the heat when the assignment is over. The unit chief in personnel owes me a couple favors."

She shifted her gaze to Parker. His hazy gray eyes begged her to agree.

He squared his shoulders. "This plan will save Justin." His voice didn't sound convincing.

Hailey massaged her hands. Justin was a baby the last time she had seen him. How could she pull this off? She couldn't sit at home and do nothing. "Of course," she said at last. "I'll do whatever I can."

Stefan's face brightened. "Splendid! I told Parker you wouldn't let us down."

Parker's eyes met hers. "Thank you. I'll never forget this."

She sensed no trace of bitterness in his voice.

Chapter Fifteen

Mark punched his fist into another bed pillow and shoved it under his head. This one was lumpy, too. It was no use. All night, he had played musical pillows. How could anyone get a good night's sleep in a hotel room? He sighed. The room wasn't the problem. Sleeping wasn't the same without Hailey lying next to him. He peered at his watch. The plan for an early start was dwindling. He hadn't even showered yet. Reaching his arm across the mountain of rejected pillows, he clutched his phone. He had two text messages. Hailey had messaged good morning and pasted an emoji face blowing a kiss. Owen asked why he hadn't reported any new developments yet.

Yawning, Mark tossed the sheets aside and sat. He rubbed his forehead and stifled another yawn. Might as well begin the day. He texted Greg:

Running a little late. Let's meet in 30 min. Front desk.

He walked into the bathroom, opened the shower door, and turned on the water.

****

Mark rode the glass elevator down to the lobby. The doors opened to full-length mirrored walls and a marble tiled floor. The place would have mesmerized Hailey. On sleek white accent chairs, two guests sat and conversed, relaxing next to a three-story cascading waterfall. A mother walked by holding a wailing baby. He smiled as an image of Hailey calming Anna as a baby came to mind. Greg was by the breakfast bar, pouring coffee in a cup.

His partner looked up as Mark approached. He added creamer to his coffee and pushed a plastic lid on the cup. "Are you going to eat?"

Mark shook his head and continued walking. "No time. I'm still digesting last night's dinner." He frowned. He should have dined with Hailey.

Greg grabbed a donut and mini muffin from the pastry carousel and followed beside Mark. They stepped through the sliding door and walked to the parking lot. Greg plopped the muffin into his mouth. "Where do you want to begin?"

"Let's go to the police department first and see if there's any new information. We'll speak to the chief. Afterward, we can check out the hospital and talk to the doctors and family. We'll decide where to go from there."

Quickly, Greg took a bite of his donut and shoved the rest in his pocket. "Okay. I'll drive. I was at the station a couple of times. I still have some contacts in the narcotics division."

Mark got in on the passenger side and latched his seatbelt.

Greg pushed his coffee in the cup holder and drove out of the lot.

It smelled good. Darn it, he should've poured some coffee. "Did you travel much at the NNIC?"

"A fair amount." Greg maneuvered the car through the busy intersections with ease. "My family didn't mind. My wife and kids liked the area. The mountains were beautiful in Pennsylvania. Lots to do around the city. The town was relatively safe."

"You don't talk much about your kids."

"They don't live with me anymore. After the NNIC closed, I lost my job. My wife filed for divorce and got custody of the two boys. They moved out of state, and I got visitation on holidays and one month in the summer."

"That must have been tough."

"It was. They're older now, in college. Between their social lives and summer jobs, I see them on a holiday, if I'm lucky. We talk on the phone sometimes, but they're big on texting."

"I'm sorry." Mark stared out the window. It would crush him not to see Hailey and the kids every day.

Greg stopped at a red light. "My younger son has diabetes like me, but he has Type 1. His doctor diagnosed him when he was nine. He uses an insulin pump to regulate his blood sugar."

Mark glanced at him. "I'm sure you worry about him."

"Nah. He's a responsible kid. He takes care of himself now." They finished their ride to the police station in silence. Finally, Greg pulled into the lot and found a vacant parking space near the rear. "Let's see what we can find out and report to Owen."

Chapter Sixteen

Bella spent the morning evaluating Moulin's results. The laboratory was a modest two-story facility located at the outskirts of the city. Reagents, supplies, and state-of-the-art instrumentation filled the rooms. For years, she had worked in the lab and studied under the most kind but notorious researcher she had ever known. She assisted alongside his small team of talented researchers, learning from them. When they retired and moved on, she continued researching fields that appealed to her. It seemed as if she'd worked here all her life. She had conceived the idea for Euphoria years ago, but she needed the capital to fund the project. Manuel had the wealth and power to implement the venture.

She leaned over the wire rack of test tubes and pipetted the correct amount of reagent into each glass tube.

An arm wrapped around her waist. "*Hola chica linda.*"

She jumped, splaying her fingers against her chest. "Shit, you scared me." She good-naturedly punched Manuel in the arm.

Grinning, he removed her goggles and gazed at her. "The receptionist wasn't at her desk so I thought I'd come in and surprise you. I called your name twice, but you didn't hear me." His eyes sparkled. "You're adorable when you're flustered."

She smoothed her upswept hair and straightened the wrinkles in her lab coat. "What are you doing here?"

"My morning appointments finished early." He lowered his head and gave her a long kiss. Then standing back, he wrinkled his nose. "How do you deal with the smell around here?"

"It's not that bad. You get used to it." She laughed at his facial expression. Manuel could be so dramatic. She gently swirled the test tubes, returned them to the rack, and set a timer. "I don't even notice it when I'm working."

"Did you find the problem yet?"

"No." She ejected the pipette tip into the small biohazard bag next to the rack of test tubes and raised her head. "Before I left your place this morning, I reviewed Moulin's papers in your office. He sandwiched a sample of the drug into a thin layer between two pieces of lens paper and hid it in his notes." She lowered her hand, clamping it on top of Manuel's hand wandering above her waist. "I tested it on mice. They were energetic and played for a few minutes. I expected that since they experienced the euphoria from the drug. Before long, their movements became erratic. They grew sluggish and disorganized. Then they died."

Manuel grunted. "How could Moulin not test the drug? I gave him the information from the other scientist. All he needed to do was combine the compounds." He ran his hand through his hair. Bella grinned at him. "Did I say something wrong?"

She winked and gave him a kiss. "No. I like when you show an interest in my work." She patted a large white contraption sitting on the counter. "There was enough sample to run tests on this old dinosaur. I performed the maintenance this morning and got it operational."

"What is it?"

"It's a gas chromatography-mass spectrometer. Don't worry about the name. This is the gold standard in drug testing. It detects particular substances in a specimen. I ran some samples after testing the controls. This gives me the drug's exact composition. I can compare it to both researchers' formulas and find the discrepancy."

"How does it work?"

"I'll show you." Bella straightened her shoulders and pointed to the right-hand side of the analyzer. "The molecules in Euphoria will separate in this column. They come off the column at different times." She motioned to the instrument's left side. "The mass spectrometer over here ionizes the molecules. It captures and detects the chemical fragments. Once I run these samples, I'll compare them to known substances. Then I match the compounds to determine the discrepancy."

Manuel scratched his head. "Is this the machine hospitals use?"

She shook her head. "I knew you'd ask that. Usually they send out specialty testing to reference labs."

He leaned against the counter and crossed his arms. "We can't risk having Euphoria identified. It's too dangerous."

"It won't happen." She pressed a button on the front of the machine and gave him a sideways glance. "I still can't get my sample to give a specific result, and I know what the answer should be. The two chemicals break down so fast in the body it will be nearly impossible to isolate the compounds. Besides, if the reference lab does detect a small amount of dopamine, they won't make a connection. Dopamine is naturally produced in the body."

"What about aparistine? Can they identify it?"

"I doubt it."

His brows narrowed. "I'm not following."

"Aparistine isn't documented in the medical books. Charles Moulin and his father were the only scientists I know of who researched the compound. No one will connect it to the toxicology results."

"But what if someone does?"

"Don't worry. If someone does discover aparistine, I have a creative idea on how to hide the drug in the cargo. The idea came to me when I hopped in the shower this morning. I need you to find forty antique vases."

"Antiques?"

She grinned. "You're an antique dealer, right?"

"Supposedly."

"Then get something like the oriental urns around your place. Check with your contacts. They don't have to be expensive—only look it."

"You piqued my interest. I'll get right on it." Manuel smoothed her sleek hair and handed her the goggles. "I'm sorry you're assuming this extra work. I know you have other responsibilities. *Gracias.*" He leaned over and kissed her. "Let's plan to eat out for dinner. I'll see you this evening." He walked to the door and waved.

She hit her hand on her forehead. "Wait. I forgot to talk to you about Cerdo's houseguest."

Manuel turned. "We'll discuss him later. I have a meeting with Antonio. He finished that job in Chicago."

Chapter Seventeen

Mark parked the rental car in the hotel lot and slammed his fist against the steering wheel. The horn beeped as he banged it against each word. "One. Dead. End. After. Another."

Greg frowned and leaned back in the seat. "At least the boy's mother was cooperative."

"What puzzles me most is the father. You'd think the police would swarm around the hospital like gnats to support him, but he's AWOL."

"It's like he's hiding."

"If that was my son, you couldn't drag me away from that hospital bed. This is crazy. The father's nowhere around." Mark removed his phone from his slacks. "Let me contact the police department one more time." He dialed and put the call on speaker.

"Chicago Police Department. How may I direct your call?" a pleasant voice answered.

"This is Agent Mark Langley with the DTA in Washington. Can you connect me to Officer Tom Parker?"

"I'm sorry, sir. Detective Parker isn't here."

"He hasn't checked in?"

"Not since yesterday when he interviewed one of the dealers in the overdose case."

"He questioned a dealer? Where?"

"He found the scumbag at Turner's Pub. Didn't the detectives on the case give you the info? Wendell Hautz is a known dealer in the area. He's been in and out of jail for years."

"What did Hautz say?"

"Officer Parker hasn't turned in the report yet. He has a lot on his plate right now, with his son in the hospital and all."

"Can you tell me where Officer Parker went?"

"He didn't say. Can I forward you to his voicemail?"

"I've left three messages already. When you speak to him, please ask him to call me. I left my contact information with the chief earlier this morning."

"Of course, Mr. Langley. I'll pass along the information."

"Thank you." Mark disconnected the call. "Where the hell is he?"

"I don't know." Greg shook his head. "It's strange the department doesn't know the location of one of their men."

"He must know something...Tom Parker. Why does that name sound familiar? Let's run a check on him. Turn on the GPS and find Turner's Pub. If the dealer is still hanging out there, maybe we can get some answers from him." Mark honked the horn again and turned the key in the ignition. "Dammit! Parker has to know something."

****

GPS led Mark straight to Turner's Pub. He parked the car near a neglected brick building in the north side of town. He and Greg hurried to the main sidewalk and continued down the narrow cement steps to the lower entrance. A few small tables occupied the smoke-filled room and a television blared near the pool table. Mark flashed his ID.

The bartender pointed at Wendell Hautz drinking booze in a secluded corner of the bar.

Mark shook his head. Sleazebags always had the same mentality when it came to hiding from the police. Somehow, a bar made derelicts feel invisible.

The pub was nearly empty. Two other patrons sat at the counter. Didn't they have anything better to do than an afternoon routine of putting away a few drinks? One rested with his head down, tanked and half-asleep. The other munched on peanuts while nursing his drink.

Unbuttoning his sleeves at the wrist, Greg rolled them up and smirked. "I'll handle the guy. I have experience in this type of questioning." He threw a heavy punch and heaved Wendell up against a wall.

The customer eating peanuts rushed out the door.

Mark smirked.

Greg launched another punch. "You bastard. Where did you get the drugs?"

Wendell writhed, his thin frame unable to escape the agent's grasp. "What are you talkin' about?"

Greg shoved him harder, his jaw tightening. "The dope you sold the other night to those kids. Don't play dumb with me, you asshole."

Mark stood a foot away. Wendell's breath reeked of alcohol, and he smelled like he hadn't used soap in weeks.

"I already talked to the *po-lice*. I told the cop I ain't in the business of sellin' drugs no more."

Stepping closer, Mark folded his arms. "Is that so?"

Wendell's gaze followed him. "I'm cleaning myself up to be more respectable. My probation officer would throw my ass back in jail if I got caught dealing again."

"You bastard. I know you talked to the police." Greg smashed Wendell's head against the pub's nicotine-tarnished window. "Now where did you get those damn drugs?" When the man still didn't answer, Greg forced Wendell's face tight against the glass.

A loud thud echoed from the impact. Wendell turned his head. "I…I don't remember."

Greg shattered the window with a beer stein. From the bar, the bartender raised his head. "Hey, you have to pay for that. I don't care that you have a badge!" The short, bald-headed man wet his lips, waiting for an answer.

Mark's eye twitched as he met the bartender's stare. "No worries."

Grabbing a shard of glass, Greg pointed it at Wendell's weathered face. "How's your memory now?" He inched the shard closer, touching the man's bony cheek. "I'll ask you one more time. Where did you get those drugs?"

Wendell remained silent.

Surprised at Greg's style, Mark eyed him and nodded. Take no mercy.

Greg pressed the glass deeper, cutting Wendell's skin. "Answer me or I'll gouge your bloody eyeballs out!"

"Okay, okay. Don't stab me!" Wendell's body trembled.

"Start talking."

"I got them from a supplier. Moulin. His name's Moulin. Dr. Charles Moulin. He's an old doc here in Chicago. Does research in his spare time. I already told all this to the other cop."

Mark stepped next to Wendell. "Tell it again."

Sweat beaded on Wendell's forehead as he struggled. "He…he mailed the drug with a note telling me to sell it around my turf. Sss…said it was strong, but he never said it could kill. I-I swear. I didn't know those kids would die."

Mark glowered. This fellow couldn't get much slimier. "I have news for you, you asshole. All drugs can kill."

Greg kept a tight grip on Wendell's chest. "So you sold a drug you knew nothing about to twenty teens and killed them? Do you know what your probation officer is going to say about this?"

"But I didn't sell it to twenty kids."

"Twenty kids that died."

"No, it was a small group. Maybe six or seven. After I sold my delivery, my head started hurting so I went home."

"Do you expect us to believe someone else got hold of the same drug as you?"

Wendell's eyes grew wide. "Maybe two people."

Tilting his head, Mark stepped back. "Why do you say that?"

"There were three separate spots. Moulin has lots of contacts. I bet he mailed a bunch of envelopes. I sold everything I had to those kids in Lincoln Square, but you can't blame me for the other deaths. Those sections ain't my territory."

Mark studied Wendell's face. The bum was telling the truth.

Greg showed his teeth. "Where's Moulin now?"

"How would I know? It ain't my day to watch him." Greg thrust Wendell's face against the broken window and the crack deepened. A piece of glass slashed through his skin. Wendell's face turned white, and he screamed. "I...I don't know. I...I swear I don't. He's somewhere in Chicago. I'm not sure where."

For some strange reason, maybe it was the man's shrill voice, Mark believed him. The police department could locate Moulin's house. He nodded at Greg. "Let him go. We've gotten all we can from this loser."

Greg heaved Wendell to the floor and kicked him four times in the gut.

Mark turned and walked to the bartender. Shoving a hand in his jeans pocket, he pulled out his wallet and laid money on the counter. "This should cover the broken window." He followed Greg out to the car and called the police department.

Chapter Eighteen

Hailey spent the afternoon in her living room, strategizing the final details. For hours, they had planned. They called headquarters, made airline reservations, booked hotel rooms, and reserved rental cars. Could she pull the assignment off without telling Mark the truth?

"So, everything is settled. Tonight you'll fly to Texas, and we'll brief you at headquarters in the morning." Stefan paced around the contemporary living room furniture and returned to his seat next to Parker. "Bruce confirmed the implant is ready for tomorrow's surgery."

She tensed, gripping the sofa cushion. "Are you sure I need another update?"

Stefan nodded and looked at his phone. "It won't take long. Bruce is setting it up with the surgeon now. It's an outpatient procedure."

Her stomach twisted in a tight coil. "It seems unnecessary. The one I have works fine. And I hate hospitals."

Looking up from his phone, Stefan frowned. "I'm sorry if this ordeal brings back some painful memories. You need the implant. Bruce has made giant strides with his inventions. I want your ears updated with the best technology." Parker waved his hand in the air, and

Stefan's eyebrows knitted. "Did I forget something, Parker?"

"While you two are in Texas, do you mind if I fly to Chicago and see Justin?"

Stefan placed his hand on Parker's shoulder. "Spend the day. We won't need you until tomorrow night."

Hailey leaned forward, wringing her hands. "This breaks my heart. That sweet little boy…I'm so sorry, Parker."

He looked at her and nodded. He seldom showed emotion.

As Stefan continued scrolling through his messages, he glanced at them again. "Tomorrow evening, Hailey and I will meet you in D.C. We'll review the floor plans with SCA field agents at my office. Any questions?"

Hailey shook her head. "Not from me."

"You and Parker should brush up on your French since you're traveling from Quebec."

Hailey smiled. "We only need a few phrases. People there speak English."

"Good catch." Stefan nodded. "Saturday, we'll go over the strategy again and you two can dress in your disguises."

They reviewed the plans a third time. Hailey walked into the kitchen and dialed Mark's parents. She asked Peggy to babysit Anna and Ethan while she left town to visit a sick friend. Holding her breath, she called Mark. Her stomach muscles tightened into a quaternary knot. No doubt, the news would catch him off guard. The call connected to his voicemail. She exhaled and left him a message. She had never lied to him. Hidden the truth, maybe. But never flat-out lied. Technically, she did have a sick friend. Justin. The sweet little boy was three years old when she left the agency.

Hailey mused on the crush she once carried for Parker. Who could blame her? With his broad shoulders, muscular frame, and winning smile, he was quite a catch. Her heart fluttered. He had helped her through some tough times. It was only natural they had grown close. She owed him her life.

"You seem miles away."

The deep voice led her back to reality and she turned and found Parker standing at the doorway. She lowered her head, hiding her warm cheeks. How could his presence still cause this effect on her, after all this time? "I was thinking about the agency."

With confident movements, he inched closer and lifted her chin. His black hair was graying, and the defined lines on his face made him exceptionally handsome. He stared into her eyes. "This assignment might bring back some painful memories."

His attentiveness unnerved her. "No doubt. We have many unresolved issues." His parents' faces flashed through her mind. "Are you sure we can work this case? Our personal feelings got in the way of the last assignment."

His tone softened, and he brushed a wisp of hair from her face. "About that last case…"

Hailey dared to stare at his face. She regretted her mistake. His eyes were magnetic. She stammered, longing to run, unable to face the memory of where they left off. "We shouldn't talk about this now."

"But *I* need to discuss this. I want you to know—"

A cough rumbled from the doorway. Stefan gave them a stern look. "We need to keep on schedule. Hailey, why don't you go pack? A taxi will drive you to the airport. I emailed your boarding pass to your cell. Oh, and one more thing, don't eat after midnight. You'll have mild sedation for the ear implant procedure." He turned to Parker. "You're going to miss your flight if we don't head out now. Traffic around the Capital Beltway gets congested this time of day."

"You're right." Parker turned to her, his eyes full of tenderness. "We'll talk later. I'll see you tomorrow night. And Hailey…"

"Yes?"

"Thank you."

She forced a smile. "Send my love to Justin and Grace."

After they left, she went upstairs and dragged three suitcases out of the hall closet. Trembling, she opened Anna's dresser drawer and collapsed on the bed. What was she doing? Leaving the kids so she could help Justin. What would Mark say? Was she being reckless? She slid off the bed and sank to the floor. She said a prayer for Justin. Regret swelled her heart.

She walked to the bathroom and splashed water on her face. *Grow up.* She did what she had to do. She tossed the kids' clothes and toiletries in the suitcases and rushed to meet them at the bus stop.

Chapter Nineteen

Mark drove the rental car to the rear of the building and parked under the lamppost. He leaned back in the seat and unfastened his lap belt. "I bet one of the drug dealers killed him."

Greg's eyes narrowed. "Killed who?"

"Tom Parker."

"Are you still thinking about that detective?" Greg opened the passenger door and stood, stretching his arms over his head. "I'm sure he can take care of himself."

He pushed open his car door and walked alongside Greg into the hotel lobby. A heavy weight pushed down on Mark's stomach. "But I don't get it. Why wasn't he at the hospital?"

Greg shrugged. "He could've been following up on some leads. He's probably with his son right now."

"I think there's something more to it."

"I don't know, but I'm done for the day." Yawning, Greg pressed the elevator button, and they both entered the car. "Do you want to eat at that restaurant again?"

Mark shook his head and pressed the second and fourth floor buttons. "No, it's late. I'm taking a hot shower and going straight to bed. We have an early flight tomorrow."

"All right. Do you want to grab breakfast here or at the airport?"

"Let's eat at the airport, once we check in."

At the second floor, Greg exited the elevator, and Mark listened to his voicemail on the ride to the fourth level.

"Hi, hon. I'm leaving town for a few days. My friend Lily is very ill. I called your parents, and they'll take care of the kids until one of us comes home. My cell phone reception might be weak where I'm staying, but I'll call when I can. I love you."

He phoned Hailey, and the connection sent him to her voicemail. Instead of leaving a message, he hung up. The doors opened. Frowning, he walked down the hallway. What was she thinking, picking up and leaving? He unlocked his door with his room card. What a wasted day. The only thing he learned was Moulin's house had burnt to the ground the day before. He tossed the phone and room card on the comforter.

Opening his briefcase, he pulled out his flight itinerary. The return flight was 8:40 AM. He should pack. Picking up his room card, he slid it in his wallet. The scraps of paper from Sunday's to-do list were tucked behind two twenty-dollar bills. He plucked out the first paper. He blinked and looked again. Shaking his head, he blinked one more time, staring at the names. The tension mounted in his body like a volcano.

"Dammit!"

Jotted down on the paper were the names of Hailey's coworkers from the SCA. Stefan Bruno. Tom Parker. The name had to be a coincidence. He read it again. Tom Parker. It couldn't be. Tom Parker? *No, Hailey. He can't be the same man.*

128

Hailey was gone.

Tom Parker was missing.

Hailey's past was a mystery.

A cold knot formed in his gut. What the hell was going on? Sinking down on the mattress, he grabbed his cell phone and dialed. "Hi, David. It's me."

"Hey, buddy. It's been a while. What's causing you to call this time of night?"

Mark glanced at his watch and grimaced. "Sorry. I forgot about the time zones. I'm in Chicago working on a case. I need a favor."

"What kind of favor?"

"I need to know all you can dig up on Tom Parker. P-A-R-K-E-R. He worked at the Special Crimes Agency until four or five years ago. Then he got a job as a detective for the Chicago PD."

"SCA, huh? I'll get right on it. How soon do you want it?"

"Can you get me something first thing tomorrow morning?"

"Hell, Mark. I'm in bed. It's almost midnight. Some people actually sleep."

"This is important. I figured since you work at the Agency this wouldn't take long."

"I'll do my best, but I didn't plan on going in until noon. I took the morning off to get my oil changed."

"You don't do that yourself?"

David chuckled. "Not anymore. Don't tell your dad. He'll think he failed me."

Mark grinned. "Don't worry. I won't." He plunged backward on the bed and kicked off his shoes. Gripping the scrap of paper, he fell asleep.

****

At 5 AM, Mark crawled to the bathroom. Had he even slept at all? He studied his haggard appearance in the bathroom mirror and cringed. Deep lines carved his forehead. When did he get so old?

As he waited at the elevator, he glanced out the window at the sun beginning to rise. Vibrant magenta-and-pink swirls colored the sky. Too bad Hailey wasn't here to share this view. She loved sunrises. He rode the elevator down to the hotel lobby. The doors opened to reveal the sight of Greg standing by the front desk, clutching a half-eaten muffin. Mark pointed at the food. "What's this? A pre-breakfast snack?"

Greg's face reddened, and he shrugged. "I needed to eat something. My sugar was too low this morning. By the way, you look like shit."

Mark sighed. "Feel like it, too."

They walked outside. The airport shuttle bus would arrive soon. Greg sat on the metal bench, taking up the majority of the seat. "Still arguing with Hailey?"

Mark lowered his suitcase on the pavement. He clenched his jaw. "I don't want to talk about it."

"Women." Greg slapped him on the back. "There's no rule book for them."

He sighed. "That's for sure."

At the airport, Mark checked his voice mail. David had left a message. Mark excused himself and found a secluded spot at an adjacent gate.

His hand shook as he called David's number. "Thanks for getting back to me so fast. What did you find out?"

"Lots. You found a man with a loaded past."

Leaning forward in his seat, Mark pressed the phone closer to his ear. "What do you mean?"

"Tom Parker did work at the SCA until he resigned four years ago and began working at the Chicago PD. That SCA is even more secretive than the CIA." David laughed.

Mark tapped his foot. Now wasn't the time for David's jokes.

"He started college in pre-med and married a woman named Grace Calhoun. In 1997, they adopted a baby boy who'd be around seventeen years old now. Parker worked with a woman named Hailey Robinson, a victim of a high school abduction."

"Abduction?" His mind reeled with questions.

"According to the reports, a woman and two men shot a teacher and bus driver at a gas station near Sacramento. The bus was taking a group of kids back from a field trip. The killers stormed the bus and took four teens to a cabin in the mountains. Three classmates escaped, but Hailey didn't get away."

"My God, what happened to her?"

"This is where it gets tricky. The newspapers reported on the abduction, but not about her release, which is odd."

"How can that be? She couldn't have just disappeared."

"I did some more digging. The authorities transferred her to the SCA facility in Texas after her rescue. I couldn't access her medical records, but I stumbled upon a list of doctors on her case."

"Parker?"

"You got it. He was in residency at the agency's clinic and assigned to Hailey's care. She also had a psychologist assigned to her. But that's not unusual for kidnap victims."

"So she stayed in Texas instead of returning to California?"

"Yes. A year after the rescue, she began training as an agent for the SCA. The following year, Parker quit his residency and joined the agency, too—as her partner."

Mark stiffened and forced himself to swallow.

David continued. "With her emotional history, using her as an agent would be a difficult dilemma. The records I found showed she trained hard and was an exceptional worker. Her cases were important victories for the SCA. But in 2002, Hailey and Parker worked a case in New York, and she resigned within a week."

"What happened?

"I don't know. Hailey left Texas, but Parker ended up staying with the agency until he joined the Chicago PD. Four months into his new job, his wife Grace divorced him. She got custody of their son, citing Parker's work as a dangerous environment. Parker got weekend visitation. From what I examined in his records, he never missed a date. Ever. Now fast-forward to this week. Parker flew to National Airport yesterday morning and returned to O'Hare last night."

Mark closed his eyes. Parker had made contact with Hailey.

"There's one more thing. Parker made arrangements to come back to Washington tonight."

"Tonight?"

"Yep. And he's flying back to Chicago on Sunday morning."

He pressed the phone tighter against his ear. "Why?"

"I'm not positive, but I have a hunch." David hesitated. "No offense, Mark, but I'm going to be straight with you. It's odd that Hailey picked up and left her job. You don't resign from a prominent place like the SCA after two years unless something catastrophic happens. I'm assuming this Hailey Robinson is *your* Hailey. Is that correct?"

Mark struggled to control his voice. "You're the secret agent. You tell me."

"She is. And my guess is you weren't aware of her past. I had to sell my soul and a firstborn son, whom I don't even have, to get this information. The media's buzzing about a big drug deal that killed a large number of teens in Chicago. I'm sure that's why you were there last night. Out of nowhere, Parker shows up in D.C. yesterday instead of staying in Chicago with his son, who, by the way, was the single survivor in the incident. But I guess you know that."

He rubbed his forehead. "Yes."

"I found records of airline tickets for *your* Hailey going to Texas."

"Texas?"

"Yeah. I was surprised by that one, too. I thought she might have gone to Chicago."

"What's in Texas?" He groaned. "The SCA."

"You're catching on fast."

"What's their plan? Are they working for the SCA again?"

"I imagine Hailey is getting briefed as we speak."

"What are they working on?"

"Well, considering Parker's flight plans, I'd say something's going down Saturday."

"I wonder what they're plotting." Mark turned toward the passengers gathering in the boarding zone.

"I'm checking into that."

The airport's intercom system announced his flight number. "Hey, they're calling my plane to board. Keep me posted. Got to go. Thanks."

"No. Thank *you*. I used more detective skills on this case than in the past six months. I'll be in touch."

Chapter Twenty

Nightmares haunted Hailey through the night. Twice, she shot upright in bed, shouting for help. Parker's injured parents shrieked on the street. The noisy cars sped closer, firing gunshots. The sirens echoed in the distance. A tow truck circled around her, reversing. Beep. Beep. Beep. She covered her ears. Where did the tow truck come from? Beep. Beep. Beep. There was never a tow truck at the accident. Beep. Beep. Beep.

The alarm clock. Ugh! It couldn't be seven o'clock yet. Her eyelids refused to open. She swung her arm up and down over the nightstand until she pressed the snooze button. She turned on her side, sinking her head deeper in the soft feather pillow. Ten more minutes. Make them count.

What made her think she could ever come back to the SCA? Had Stefan forgotten how she ruined the last case? She had killed Parker's parents! No. She had stood there like a frightened child and watched them die. Watched. Killed. It was the same thing.

She peeked at the clock and rolled on her back, sighing. Six minutes. She squeezed her eyes tighter. The tragedy had played over and over in her mind for months. She had shirked her duties. Played hooky while

Parker stood guard for a suspected terrorist reported in the vicinity.

"Give me twenty minutes to show them the Empire State Building," she had told Parker. His parents were anxious to see the view. "I'll walk them back to the hotel once they see the cityscape." Parker was hesitant. But he gave in. He was a pushover when it came to her requests, and she took advantage of the soft spot he felt for her.

He stayed at the lookout point while she rode with his parents to the top of the building. She called. "We're on our way back. I told you it wouldn't take long. I'll be there as soon as I drop them off." While they walked on the crosswalk, two cars screeched from around the corner. The passengers fired at each other and passersby, killing Parker's parents in the gunfire.

Police arrested the gang members in the chase, but Parker had detested her after that day. Who could blame him? Other than Grace and Justin, his family was gone. He wouldn't even look at her. Beaten by heartache and guilt, she resigned from the agency and never spoke to him again. Until the previous day.

Saving Justin would make up for her blunder. She wouldn't let him down. Closing her eyes, she prayed. *Please give me a sign that everything's going to be okay.*

Beep. Beep. Beep.

Groaning, she sat and turned off the alarm. She picked up her phone and checked the messages. Mark and Ethan had each texted good morning. Anna had typed her smiling emoji faces and a sun. With the time difference, the kids were already in school. Her stomach twisted. Even before she stepped off the plane late last night, she had missed them. Missed Mark. She raked her hand through her hair. What was she doing here?

The shower rejuvenated her, and she dressed quickly. Glancing at the clock, she opened the suitcase. Hailey packed her nightgown and tucked in a travel bag filled with makeup and toiletries. Scratching her hands, she scanned the room and slipped on her shoes. She retrieved her purse from the dresser and grabbed her suitcase before riding the elevator to the main floor.

The doors opened and the aroma of sausage tempted her appetite. She checked out at the front desk and walked outside. Stefan stood next to his car by the bellhop. "Morning."

She smiled. "By the look of the magnificent sunrise earlier, it should be a great morning. No rain in sight."

He grasped her suitcase and laid it in the backseat. "We can keep your luggage here until we drive to the airport later." He turned the key in the ignition and merged onto the highway.

Stefan was quiet during the first part of the ride. He and Mark shared similar demeanors. Both men wore serious expressions when they concentrated. Stefan's wire-rimmed glasses gave him a more reserved look. She bit her lip, studying him more. "How's your family doing?"

He looked at her as if she had interrupted some deep thought, and he turned his head back to the road. "They're good. Robin is still teaching."

"Still?"

He nodded and glanced in the rearview mirror. "She says she'll retire when I do."

"What about the boys?"

"Sam got married last fall."

"Little Sammy?" She laughed. "He swore he'd never have a girlfriend."

He nodded. "Things change, I guess. He's twenty-six now."

"How's Erik?"

Stefan put on his turn signal and merged onto the exit. "He and his wife just had their second child. Another boy."

"What about Thomas?" Stefan's oldest son was three years younger than she was.

"He and his girlfriend moved to Arizona. He's working as a landscaper."

"Did any of them join the SCA?"

Stefan turned right at a stoplight. "Erik did. He didn't want any preferential treatment from me so he requested to work out of the San Francisco office."

"Oh, I miss seeing them. We had a lot of fun at your house."

Stefan nodded. "The boys still talk about the year you stayed with us. You were the closest they ever had to having a sister."

She warmed inside. "And they were like brothers to me."

As Stefan drove through the entrance gate, Hailey pulled out her driver's license and handed it to him. Stefan showed it to the guard, and they drove into the complex. "We scheduled your implant for early this morning. Bruce said he made some improvements."

She scratched her hand. "Will he be there during the procedure?"

"No. Your surgeon can handle the implant. Dr. Banks has been with us for three years."

Hailey took in the view and caught her breath. The brick complex had new wings and buildings. Signs at the entrance gate pointed to the various departments.

Stefan steered the car toward the right. "Does the place bring back memories?"

She continued staring out the window. "Yes. But it seems like yesterday."

He parked the car near the main door and left the engine idling. "I'll let you out here and meet you after the surgery." He grimaced. "Medical procedures still make me queasy. Ask the front desk to page Ernie Banks."

Within minutes, a curly blond-haired man walked down the corridor to the security desk. His charming smile shone through his tanned face. "Good morning, Mrs. Langley. I'm Dr. Banks. It sure is a pleasure to meet you."

She shook his hand. The young man's deep Texas accent made her smile. "Nice to meet you, too, Dr. Banks."

"Mrs. Langley, please call me Cubby. My friends enjoy callin' me that for some reason."

"Okay, Cubby." She smiled. "I bet you don't play baseball. And please, call me Hailey."

He extended his hand and guided her through an entryway. "The clinic is down this hallway. Stefan told me that you worked here a while back. Does the place look the same?"

She nodded and walked alongside him, passing a group of men and women dressed in white lab coats. "There are lots of changes. The clinic has moved."

"You have a good memory. We've added a new outpatient center for special surgeries, like the one you're having today. We've enlarged the research facility, too. Besides Bruce Hanover's other projects, he's busy inventing new spyware and implants for our agents."

"Do you work with him much?" She squeezed her hands. There was no reason to tremble.

"Only when he makes a new contraption for a patient. He's usually too engrossed with his creations to socialize. The staff leaves him alone." Ernie stopped at the doorway. "Before we start your procedure, I need to draw some pre-op blood work. If you'd like, we can visit Bruce while we wait for the results."

Hailey maintained a tight-lipped smile and nodded.

The phlebotomist drew the blood samples with ease and sent them to the on-site laboratory. Hailey tugged her sleeve over the taped bandage on her arm. She strolled with Cubby downstairs.

They chatted and turned down a hallway. "This is new."

Cubby nodded. "The expansion included a new wing for more modernized analyzers and supplies." He stopped at a door marked *Research Lab*. "This is Bruce's den." He opened the door. In the corner of the room, a man hunched over the counter, working on robotic equipment.

Her heart raced, betraying her.

"Bruce, you have a visitor."

The old man stood and hurried over to them. "Hailey, my dear. Stefan told me y'all might stop by this morning." His arms looped around her shoulders in a bear hug. When he stood back, his thick, black-framed glasses slid down his nose. "You sure are a looker. You haven't changed at all."

She smiled back at the thin man and disregarded his wrinkled face. "You look the same, too."

"Liar." He pointed to his head. "I'm gray now."

"But the beard matches. You're as handsome as ever." She struggled, hiding her bitterness. Time had aged him into a helpless old man.

"Stefan told me you're back for a secret mission with Parker." His tone grew more serious. "We miss you at the agency. I lost touch with you after you moved away. Things were a lot of fun when y'all worked here. Ah, to be young again…"

Hailey waited, but his face went blank, and his eyes became sad and distant. "Bruce? Are you okay?"

He blinked, as if trying to remember where he was.

"Bruce?" Hailey waved a hand in front of him and turned to Cubby. "Should we call someone?"

Cubby stepped closer and peered at his eyes. "Sit down, Bruce. I'll pour you a glass of water."

Shaking his head, Bruce lifted his hand and grasped his chest. "No need. I was caught in a memory. When you're old like me, you'll experience some of these…oh…what are they called—senior moments. Now where were we?" He rubbed his forehead. "Ah, yes, we were talkin' about how much fun we had with you and Parker here."

Hailey kept the conversation lighthearted while Cubby was in the room. She chatted in polite pleasantries as Bruce gave her a tour of his lab and she updated him on her new life. But she tapped her fingers against her thigh. When could they talk in private?

"So, you're fixin' to get an ear implant this morning?" He spoke as if the intervening years had never happened.

Didn't Bruce realize he had betrayed her? He had been like a father to her. Hailey forced herself to relax. "Cubby tells me you made a new and improved version."

"Yes, ma'am, I did. It's four times more sensitive than your original implant. I equipped it with a personal location device chip." He pretended to ring a lasso in the air. "I roped a winner with this one!"

"A GPS?"

His eyes gleamed when he spoke. "Global positioning system. This one's half the size and lighter than the current models. It recharges without any physical connection to the power source." He put the miniscule device in her hand. "Here's a prototype. I like to stay ahead of the technology curve. Even Stefan's not aware of this new adaptation yet."

She examined the tiny gadget. "I'm amazed how you spend your time."

"I'm always busy." He winked at her and laughed. "I don't leave the lab. It's a good thing I'm a bachelor."

Cubby's cell phone beeped, and he looked at the screen. "Your pre-op work is normal. We can begin the implant procedure."

Hailey gave Bruce a hug, but bitterness gnawed at her. Could she be wrong about him? "It was wonderful to see you."

"It's always a pleasure." He waved as they left the room. "Enjoy your new world of listening. You'll notice the sensitivity difference in the lower range."

Chapter Twenty-One

Mark strode through the terminal to the baggage claim area. His muscles were still tense from the turbulence on his flight back to Washington. Checking the nametag, he lifted his suitcase from the carousel. He walked to the other side of the revolving belt where Greg stood. "I'll head back to the office and give Owen an update." He stifled a yawn. Investigating Tom Parker demanded a higher priority than going home and sleeping.

Greg nodded. "I'll drive to work once I restock my diabetes medicine. My sugar's been high with all this stress."

"You might want to watch your junk food consumption, too." Mark pointed at the bag of cookies Greg had purchased after they exited the plane.

A smile spread across Greg's face. "That might make a difference."

"Take your time. I don't mind starting the travel report."

Greg wrenched his suitcase from underneath a bulky piece of luggage. "Thanks. I shouldn't be long."

****

Mark unlocked his office door and turned on the overhead lights. The phone rang as he set down his briefcase. Reaching over the desk, he lifted the receiver. "Mark Langley."

"Hello, Mark. This is Felicia Pratt from the Chicago PD Narcotics Division. I have an update on the overdose case."

He sat in his chair and grabbed a pen and notepad from the desk. "What is it?"

"The street name of the drug is Euphoria."

"That's a new one."

"Yes. Six more kids died last night in Detroit. It looks like the same drug. We questioned one of the dealers. He owned up to selling the drug. Said a physician mailed it to him."

"Moulin?"

"Yes. His house burned down two days ago."

"I drove past it yesterday."

"The fire marshal suspects arson."

"Any location on Moulin yet?"

"No. But they didn't find his body in the house. I'll keep you updated."

"Thanks."

Mark sat in his chair and leaned back. Euphoria. What a misnomer for something that kills people. He scratched his head. Where had he seen that name? The hairs stiffened on the back of his neck. He pulled out his wallet and opened the slip of paper he had copied from Elliot Sherman's notebook.

He scratched his head. "How the hell did Sherman know about Euphoria a month before it surfaced in Chicago?" He picked up the phone and dialed. "David, it's me again. Anything new?"

"No, but I have some hunches."

"Like what?"

"Well, we know that Parker's son was one of the victims from the drug incident in Chicago."

"Yes."

"I bet they're investigating the same case as you. I tracked down Parker and Hailey's hotel reservations for tonight—two separate rooms, by the way. I researched any and all known connections to drug dealers in the Washington D.C. area."

Mark snickered. "That would fill a phone book."

"Yes, but the *big* dealers, the slick ones who never get caught, would fill about half a page. One connection stands out from the rest. Manuel de Mendoza."

Mark started up his computer. "Why him?"

"Because he's up to something. His father's a well-known drug lord in Colombia. José was one of the leaders in a revolutionary movement twenty years ago. Mendoza claims he cut ties with his family. He opened a business collecting antiques and paintings, but we're sure it's a scam. We're keeping tabs on this one."

"Has he done anything yet?"

"Since he arrived in the United States, he's bought several commercial properties. He's set up different bank accounts and made hundreds of contacts with high-profile people."

"It sounds like he's definitely up to something." Mark typed in Mendoza's name in the computer's search bar.

"Lately, he's been wiring large sums of money into his accounts from South America."

Mark stroked his chin. "Even though he cut ties to his father?"

"Yeah. By a bizarre coincidence, he's hosting a huge dinner party Saturday night at his mansion. His guest list is full of powerful people from around the world." David paused, his voice growing excited. "Guess where Parker and Hailey made lodging reservations?"

Images of Mendoza and his stately house appeared on the computer screen. Mark let out a sigh. "Next to Mendoza's mansion."

"Close. Great Falls doesn't build many hotels. They're a couple miles away in Vienna."

"Shit." He massaged his temples.

"I bet Parker and Hailey plan to go undercover to investigate the Chicago overdoses."

"It looks that way. Thanks, David. You've been a huge help." He couldn't hide the frustration in his voice.

"Let me know if you need anything else, Mark. I wish I had better news."

"Me, too."

"Say hello to Hailey for me. I haven't seen her since your wedding. How many years has it been?"

"Ten. We recently had our anniversary." He closed his eyes at the reminder.

"Ten years and there's still so much mystery and intrigue in your marriage." David laughed. "How lucky can you get?"

"Smart ass," Mark mumbled and slammed down the phone. He hurried to Owen's office and told him about a lead on the case that required two dinner invitations.

Greg's door was open when Mark headed back to his office. He knocked and stepped inside the room. "Welcome back."

Greg unloaded folders from his briefcase and looked up. "Did I miss anything?"

"That depends. Do you have plans for tomorrow night?"

Greg's brow arched. "No, why?"

"Well, you do now. And you're going to need a tux. Grab your jacket, and I'll fill in the details over brunch. I'm starved." For the first time in weeks, he was in control.

Chapter Twenty-Two

Bella hunched over the countertop. She had spent the morning running tests and studying lab reports. The lab was home, and she managed it with confidence. Lifting her head, she breathed in a whiff of Manuel's cologne. "Don't even think about trying to scare me."

"Aw, how did you know I was here?" Manuel planted a few kisses on her neck and looped his arms around her waist. "Give me a kiss."

She sighed. There was no time for kisses. As she turned, her pulse raced at his presence. His sculpted jawline outlined his bronzed face and highlighted his adoring dark eyes. Damn. Why didn't she linger in bed this morning? "Okay. One kiss, but then I need to work." Lifting her chin, she let his lips capture hers. Umm. That kiss was addictive.

His gaze locked with hers. "I wanted to stop by and say good morning."

She wrapped her arms around his neck. "I'm glad you did. We need to discuss Cerdo's house guest."

"You preoccupy me." He kissed her once more and groaned. "Did you find anything on the Euphoria? We're losing time, and the drug needs to be shipped next week."

Yawning, she nodded. "I found a contaminant mixed in with Moulin's aparistine. It's a chemical that contains imidazole rings, structurally similar to aparistine."

"What is it?"

"Ranabine."

Manuel's brow wrinkled. "Ranawhat?"

She held back a smile. "Ranabine. It's a chemical found in the seeds of *Bixa aparra*. Inside the shrub's flowers. Moulin centered his research on the shrub's leaves and bark. Those have the highest concentrations of aparistine. When he combined his chemical with dopamine, he made two critical errors. The aparistine was too concentrated, and the ranabine contaminated the sample."

"Are aparistine and ranabine the same?"

"No, aparistine is a hallucinogenic. Ranabine is classified as a deliriant. It's a powerful anticholinergic that blocks the acetylcholine neurotransmitter receptor sites."

Manuel's eyes narrowed as he raked a hand through his thick hair. "*No tan rápido*. You're talking too fast. Acetylcholine?"

She stumbled at his expression. "I'm sorry, dear. Acetylcholine transmits signals from nerve cells to cardiac and skeletal muscle cells. Signals won't send if the receptor sites are blocked. The blockage leads to coma and death."

"Do you think Moulin contaminated the sample on purpose?"

She shrugged. "Sometimes a scientist tries to safeguard his research so others won't steal his work. I doubt Moulin did that. He performed extractions on live plants. He used that information to derive the synthetic formula. I think some seeds were minced in by mistake.

149

I can synthesize this in the lab and make pure aparistine without contaminants."

"So you think rabanine, or whatever its name is, could have caused those deaths in Chicago?"

"Definitely." She held up a report. "Even the tiniest amount of *ranabine* is lethal. It penetrates human skin and infiltrates across cellular tissue into the nervous system. At one time scientists linked chemicals like ranabine to poisonous tree frogs in the Amazon rainforest."

Manuel's brows arched. "Tree frogs make their poison by eating plants?"

"It's very possible. But since *Bixa aparra* is extinct, no one tests aparistine and ranabine anymore. Moulin discovered the root interferes with cognitive abilities and causes memory loss. He also speculated that the waxy flowers and seeds could benefit burn victims." She handed him the report. "Here, I made you a copy to take home and read."

He flipped through the pages and rolled the report in his hand. "Thanks. Did he ever confirm any of his hypotheses?"

"Not that I know of. With the deforestation of the rainforest over the past forty years, the plant has died out. Even if scientists wanted to study the plant, they couldn't."

"That's fortunate for us." Manuel put his arm around her and pulled her closer.

She pressed her hand across his chest, preventing another steamy kiss. "True. The plant disappeared before scientists focused any time on exploring the compounds. No one else propagates the plant."

"Charles mentioned his father still grows a shrub."

"But the man must be in his late eighties." She shrugged. Who knows if he even took care of it. As for Dr. Moulin, we know what happened to him and his house. His plants were the last of their kind." She shook her head. "I hate to see plants become extinct." A timer beeped, and she pressed the button on the gadget. "Stay right here. I'll return in a minute."

She loaded a tray of samples in the analyzer and returned, carrying a new tray. Picking up the pipette, she prepared another batch of samples in the mixing tray and set it aside. She looked at Manuel. "What's wrong?"

His frown deepened. "I've been thinking about your remark. *Bixa aparra* is extinct because of me. Now the world might never recognize the plant's worth."

"Don't beat yourself up over it." The analyzer beeped, and she loaded the tray. "How do you want me to proceed with the contaminants?"

He tapped his fingers on the counter. "Extract the ranabine contaminant from Moulin's sample. Then salvage the plant's raw aparistine to ship a sample to Colombia."

"You want to send it to your father?"

"Yes. I want a pure sample in case I need it later. Go ahead and dilute the aparistine concentration. Combine it with dopamine and produce mass quantities of Euphoria. Hanover's research is still connected to our database."

She narrowed her eyes. "Don't you think we should test the drug first?"

He shook his head. "When we sampled the shrub's leaves at Moulin's house a couple of years ago, we experienced the trip it gives. Bruce's dopamine has been ready for weeks. For some reason, he's delaying the report. I'm not worried about his component, though. He's very thorough."

Shaking her head, she crossed her arms. "I'd like to test the mixture of aparistine and dopamine. There could be synergistic effects from the interaction of the two chemicals. I don't recall Moulin running synergy trials."

Manuel winced. "My father will be livid if we delay the shipments. There's no time. Just dilute the aparistine."

"But—"

He touched his warm finger to her lips. "It'll be okay. You worry too much."

Bella yawned and covered her mouth. "Okay, if that's what you want. I'll start right away. It shouldn't take too long. Did you bring the urns?"

"Antonio will drop them off later." He traced a finger under her eyes then smoothed her hair with his hand. "You look tired. Why don't you take tomorrow off?"

Sleep sounded tempting. "There's no time."

"Nonsense. You've been working nonstop. There's still a week left. The dinner party's tomorrow night, and I want you to look your best. Get some sleep tonight. After we review the preparations tomorrow, I want you to pamper yourself at the spa. I can't wait to show you off to my guests."

She scoffed. "You don't think I look good enough now?"

"Bella." He gave a stern look.

"I'm sorry." She rubbed her temples. It wasn't fair to grouch at him. "I'm tired."

"You're beautiful all the time, but you deserve a break. Finish what you can tonight and do the rest after the party. One day isn't going to hurt us." He brushed a tender kiss on her lips and walked to the door.

"I still need to talk to you about Cerdo..."

"Later." Manuel waved and shut the door.

Chapter Twenty-Three

The implant procedure took less than an hour. While she waited for Cubby, Hailey browsed through the magazines on the table. She wiped her sweaty hands on her jeans. Was she nervous about the hearing test or edgy from seeing Bruce?

A tall nurse with curly brown hair brought in a tray.

Hailey's stomach turned a happy somersault when she saw the turkey sandwich.

"Dr. Banks was called out on an emergency. He'll bring the audiologist and check your hearing levels as soon as he returns."

Hailey devoured the lunch and waited. As she paced the floor, she glanced at the wall clock. The opportunity might not come again. She walked to the nurses' station. "Do you mind if I wait for Cubby in the courtyard? I've missed seeing the gorgeous views here."

The nurse gave a brilliant smile. "Not at all. Can I bring you anything else?"

"No, thanks. I'm good."

Her pulse quickened as she walked down the corridor. Instead of turning right toward the patio, she headed to the left and descended the stairwell. At the bottom floor, she straightened her shoulders and marched toward the lab. She yanked the door open and eyed Bruce who was standing next to a counter, connecting wires to a machine. The humming of the air conditioner was the only sound in the room. "Hello, Bruce."

Turning, he staggered backward, arching his eyebrows. "Hailey. You're back. Did you forget something?"

She stepped toward him, unable to control her shaking. "We need to talk."

He set down a tiny circuit on the counter. "About what?"

"About why you never mentioned you knew my father."

Bruce gave a quick laugh. "How would I know your father?"

For a brief moment, she doubted herself. "After I resigned, I flew to California and visited my parents' gravesite."

He nodded. "I figured you'd visit their grave when you were ready."

"I also went to see the executor of my parents' estate. The lawyer had a few loose ends to wrap up. When I sorted through the documents in the safe deposit box, I found bank records of a trust fund established in my name." Bruce's face turned white. Her heart stung at the betrayal. "Imagine my surprise when I learned *you* set up the account."

"Me?"

"Yes, you. The deposits stopped after I became a patient here."

Sweat beaded on his forehead. He reached toward a small box on the shelf above the counter and pulled out a tissue. His arms shook as he blotted his brow. "You made a mistake."

"I thought so, too. Until I found an old photo of my Papa and Uncle Henry playing baseball when they were younger. You were in the picture." She studied his face. "You never told me. I didn't even know you back then. Why would you send me money?" Bruce clutched his chest, but she ignored his distress. "I deserve some answers." She waited. She wouldn't back down.

Sighing, he pulled out a nearby stool and sat. "Your Uncle Henry was my best friend."

Hailey steadied herself against the counter. "What? How?"

"We went to med school together in Los Angeles. I moved there from Texas, but Henry grew up in Orange County. He and I would drive to his house on weekends and hang out with Xavier."

"Why didn't you tell me?"

He frowned. "What difference would it have made?"

"Papa said Uncle Henry got caught up with drugs." Did she really want to hear the ugly truth?

His frown softened. "I can promise you, Henry didn't use drugs. He was a good man who worked many odd jobs to make money for his family. I'm sure your father told you about their hard life."

She nodded. "Papa mentioned my grandmother's cancer, but he didn't like to talk about it."

"After Henry died, my colleague Andrew and I decided to help your family. Andrew came from wealth so he sent money each month. Once I got a job, I also contributed. The money helped take care of the family and pay your grandmother's medical bills."

Hailey shook her head. "Papa was a proud man. He'd never take your money."

"Ah, but your grandfather did. He cashed the checks each month, even after his wife died. When your grandfather passed, your father found out what Andrew and I had done. He was livid. We convinced him to put the money in a trust fund for you. Xavier didn't make a lot of money, but he loved you. He wanted to give you more opportunities."

She crossed her arms. "You should've told me. I was so furious, I threw away all the letters you sent me."

"I wondered why you shut me out of your life." Bruce removed his glasses and wiped his eyes with his hand. "You have to believe me, Hailey. I loved Henry and Xavier like brothers. Their deaths touched me, too."

She wrapped her arms around her waist. "Can you tell me how Uncle Henry died? The autopsy report cited possible cerebral hemorrhage. But Papa said there were rumors about drugs."

He massaged his chest again. "It's a long story. I can't go into that now."

"Can't or won't?"

"Does it matter?"

She clenched her fist. "Don't treat me like a child. I don't need you to protect me anymore."

The door swung open, and Cubby hurried in the room. "There you are. The nurse told me you walked to the courtyard. I figured you moseyed down here. I need to run some final tests before Stefan comes."

Hailey kept her gaze locked to Bruce's eyes. "Cubby, can you give us five more minutes, please?"

"I wish I could, but Stefan wanted to pick you up in time to catch your flight."

She could have screamed, but instead she glowered at Bruce. "We'll finish this conversation later." Turning, she followed Cubby out the door.

During the post evaluation, Cubby shot her curious looks. He recorded the results in the computer. "Your new hearing levels are extraordinary. Fortunately, I'm only checking your hearing. Your blood pressure would set off alarms. Let's take a walk before Stefan comes."

On the way back to the entrance, Cubby provided a brief tour of the complex's new wings. "Bruce hasn't experienced panic attacks since I've been here. Today he suffered two episodes. Do you mind telling me what you said to upset him?"

"I'd rather not." She avoided his stare as they waited at the front desk. It wasn't fair to take her bad mood out on him. "So, tell me, are you married? Any children?"

He blushed. "Real slick. No, I don't have time for either."

"Where are you from?"

"Right here. You didn't detect my accent?"

"I did, but it's not as strong as Bruce's. I thought you might have developed it after moving here."

Cubby shook his head. "No, ma'am. I don't leave the Lone Star State much. Though, I'm fixin' to leave tomorrow to attend a medical conference in Baltimore."

Hailey gasped. "Baltimore's only about an hour and a half away from where I live, depending on the traffic."

"It sure is a small world." He smiled, and a dimple appeared along the side of his lower lip. "I'm nervous about traveling. I heard the East Coast is mighty busy."

She raised her eyebrows and nodded. "I hear you. Moving to Maryland was quite an experience. The traffic is more congested and the people seem busier, but I'm sure you'll adjust to the hustle and bustle. Are you planning on seeing anything around Baltimore and Washington, D.C. when you're there?"

He scratched his chin. "I'm not sure I can. The conference has a lot of activities planned."

"If you find the time, rent a car and visit me. I'll give you a personal tour around D.C., and you could stay for dinner."

He hesitated. "I'd hate to impose."

"Nonsense. I'd love to show you the monuments and museums." Hailey stood and peered through the glass entrance. "Here comes Stefan."

Cubby held the door open for her. "I'll think about it. Thanks for the offer."

"I'll get your phone number from Stefan and text you my contact info. Give me a call or stop by, and we'll make plans. I'll tell my family you're an old friend."

"Okay, but I wouldn't come to see y'all until at least Tuesday." They walked to the car, and Cubby opened the car door.

She reached in her purse and pulled out her cell phone. "I'll put it on my calendar so I won't forget."

Chapter Twenty-Four

Bella stood with Manuel by the basement stairway. Cerdo needed to stop his sick game. What kind of vile person got his kicks from tormenting someone? Cerdo's breathing grew louder as he climbed the last step in the narrow passageway. With wide eyes, he nodded at them. "Manuel. Bella."

Manuel's neck and ears were a dark red. "Bella's concerned over your prisoner. How is he?"

Frowning, Cerdo crossed his arms. "He hasn't stirred today."

Bella gasped. "Kill him and get it over with."

"No! He needs to suffer more—like I've suffered."

The crimson coloring spread over Manuel's face. "When is this charade going to end?"

Cerdo lifted his chin and sneered. "When I'm ready."

Manuel bared his teeth. "I allowed you to use this place against my better judgment. I'm uncomfortable with this type of torture. When we transport the shipment and leave the country, I want him released."

"Why? He's not bothering anyone." Cerdo gave her a cold stare. "Did Bella put you up to this?"

Manuel lifted his arm and grabbed Cerdo's shirt, shoving him against the wall. "*Hijueputa*. You listen to me. I don't let Bella or you make my decisions. *I* run the show around here. Don't forget that. I want him out of here. You have one week."

Cerdo glared at Bella. "Fine."

"And don't ever include Antonio in your crazy plans again. You shouldn't have involved him with your scheme to kill Moulin. Antonio's *my* bodyguard, not yours, and he suffered my wrath for his insubordination." The muscles tensed in Manuel's neck. "Do not cross me again, or you will regret the day we met."

Cerdo yanked Manuel's hands off his shirt. "Don't threaten me, you dumb ass. You need me. And not that it matters, but I told Antonio you ordered the hit on Moulin."

Manuel glowered. "How dare you! You're nothing but a piece of shit with an insatiable desire to control people."

Giving a dismissive wave, Cerdo walked through the hallway. "I'll deal with my prisoner when I'm ready. Not when you or Bella tell me to."

Bella stayed a few feet behind Manuel, following Cerdo past the living room fireplace. Manuel shadowed him into the foyer. "I'm not in the mood for your brazen insolence. Vengeance is dangerous. It bites you in the ass when you're not looking. Get rid of him or I will."

The foyer mirror captured Cerdo's reflection, causing Bella to shudder.

He screeched an uncanny laugh and slammed the front door.

Chapter Twenty-Five

When they arrived at the airport, Hailey and Stefan maneuvered through the throng of travelers toting carry-on bags. The PA announced the latest arrival from Chicago. Hailey spotted Parker walking out of the terminal. His chiseled face gave him a rugged appearance. Her body warmed as she waved.

Parker met them and shifted the shoulder strap of his bag. "How did everything go?"

"Good." She lifted a finger to her ears. "My brain was on hyper drive at first, but it's adjusting to the increased number of sounds. Hailey searched his face. "How's Justin?"

"He's getting weaker." Parker choked on his words. "The doctors still can't identify the drug or figure out why it's affecting the nervous system."

"I'm so sorry," she whispered.

Parker blinked. "He looks so helpless. I *feel* helpless."

"Focus on the fact that he's alive." She held his hand and squeezed. "Before the weekend is over, we'll find the drug."

At the hotel, Parker checked in and wheeled his suitcase to his room. Hailey found a cushioned sofa next to a table of complimentary drinks in the atrium. When she finished texting Mark, she looked up.

Stefan walked toward her, typing on his cell phone, and collided with a hotel guest. He apologized and sat next to Hailey.

"Why are you so distracted?"

He stared at the guests walking by, but didn't seem to register their existence. "Four more people died today—Indianapolis."

"Oh, no." She shut her eyes. "I can't believe how many kids use drugs."

Stefan shrugged. "The problem keeps getting worse."

Parker stepped out of the elevator and she waved. He looked miserable. It couldn't be easy leaving Justin at the hospital. Taking slow steps, he approached them. "Did I miss anything?"

When Stefan shared the latest information about the fatalities, Parker's jaw clenched. "Let's get this son of a bitch."

****

As they drove to the satellite office in Washington, D.C., Hailey's adrenaline pumped full force. Strategizing was crucial in executing a solid plan. She hadn't worked a case in so long. Would she remember what to do? Stefan parked the car in the underground garage, and they rode the elevator to the third floor. The facility was smaller than the Austin complex. Hailey followed Stefan as he gave a brief tour. She passed the executive assistant's office and a cluster of smaller cubicles.

Stefan ushered them into a small conference room decorated with contemporary furnishings. A warm glow expanded through Hailey's body. She was back working again. She felt like she had never left. The

163

room had the smell of new furniture. Attached on the wall were an oil painting of the city's landscape and a portrait of Stefan as the SCA director. Two women and three men, ranging from their late-twenties to late-forties, sat around the table conversing with each other in low voices.

Hailey nodded at one of the men who turned and stopped speaking. He smiled, and a sense of well-being enveloped her. She hadn't seen George since she left the SCA. They had worked a few cases together. She and Parker padded to the table and took their seats in the cushioned chairs.

At the head of the table, Stefan scanned a stack of documents, tapping his pen as he reviewed the material. "Let's get started, shall we? Hailey, Parker, I'd like you to meet Jillian, Angel, Leroy, and Ramsey. You both should remember George." Stefan nodded at each of the agents. "Their info is in the packets I handed out earlier. George will lead the group tomorrow night and report back to me."

Stefan laid headshots on the table in front of Hailey and Parker and passed each of them a brown envelope. "These are the photos of some of the guests you'll meet. In the envelope are your bios for the couple you are impersonating. We'll review these extensively tonight." He opened a carton and unrolled the contents.

Hailey was relieved to see how prepared they were. "Are these the blueprints for Mendoza's mansion?"

"Yes." George nodded. "I procured a set from the builder and one from the county."

Hailey and Parker perused the documents. Hailey whistled. "This basement has everything. Two guest rooms, three bathrooms, and a wine cellar. It even has a sports entertainment area." She laughed. "Mark and the kids could live forever on the basketball court."

Stefan chuckled. "My boys wouldn't have moved out of the home theater. Basements this extravagant are great for entertaining. I doubt Mendoza would risk hiding paperwork downstairs. Assuming this party is on the main and bottom levels, the best chance for finding information is here." He tapped his pen on the upper level.

Hailey peered at the drawings. "Which room are you thinking?"

"Based on the floorplan, these six rooms are bedrooms with private baths. The master room is here." Using his pen, Stefan circled the largest area at the end of the north wing. "The county records show this room's dimension is thirty by forty feet. But the builder's floor plan indicates the room is thirty by sixty."

Smiling, she studied the paper more closely. "So we're dealing with a secret room in the master bedroom. I bet it's behind this bookcase." She pointed to a rectangular box on the drawing.

Stefan nodded. "I agree."

Hailey skimmed the plans again. "I imagine a house this size could accommodate several secret rooms. Parker, we'll need time to sneak upstairs and access the hidden space."

Parker moved his finger along the drawing. "We'll have to move quickly. Where are the agents stationed below, George?"

The agent leaned over the table and designated a window on the blueprint. "Use this window in the sitting area in case you need to get out. We'll post two agents on the ground below. If you're able, find out what else Mendoza is hiding. Schedules. Contacts." He opened his briefcase. "You'll need equipment. Here's a camera and a flash drive to download files. You can use your hacking skills again, Parker."

Parker nodded and gripped the flash drive.

Hailey dropped the camera into her purse and turned to Stefan. "Do you mind if I keep this floor plan with me? I'd like to study it closer."

He nodded. "Go right ahead. I ran off more copies." Hailey rolled up the plans. Stefan unrolled an aerial map and aimed his pen at a section near the main roadway. "George assigned Jillian and Leroy to cover the grounds near the mansion's front and east wing side doors."

George pointed to a group of sketched bushes in the landscape. "Angel and Ramsey will hide below the master bedroom sitting room. I'll have access to the grounds, as well."

"I've assigned two more agents near the road." Stefan gazed at Hailey and Parker. "The plan is solid."

Hailey picked up a rubber band from the table and twisted it around the blueprints. "It looks like you've taken into account every precaution."

Stefan reviewed the plan and escape route on the upper level several times. "That's all for tonight. Go home and get some sleep. Tomorrow we'll reconvene before heading out." He shook the other agents' hands as they left, and then he turned to Hailey and Parker. "I need to return some phone messages. Do you two mind taking a taxi back to the hotel?"

****

When she stepped on the hotel elevator, Parker pressed the button to the fifth floor. "Would you like to come to my room and talk?"

The day had been like a dream. Hailey had forgotten about the adrenaline rush before a case. "I'll come in for a while. I'm too excited to sleep. I forgot how stimulating this work is."

He ushered her to the sofa and closed the drapes. Whistling, he walked into the kitchenette and opened the mini fridge. "Can I get you something to drink? Coffee? Water?"

"Water's fine, thanks." She scratched her hand and glanced around the room. Maybe she shouldn't have come there.

Parker returned carrying two bottles of water and handed her one. "Enjoy the water—it's eight bucks a bottle here."

With a laugh, she leaned her head against the sofa. "This feels like old times, doesn't it?"

"I remember." He stared for a moment. "We'd stay up for hours talking over our cases." Sitting next to her, he looked down at his drink. "I hope tomorrow goes well."

She touched his arm. "Everything's going to work out okay. I can feel it."

"I hope you're right." He guzzled some water.

Her stomach wobbled. The time was right. She might not get another chance. "I'd like to see Justin."

His lips tightened in a firm line. "I don't think it's wise."

Why was he being difficult? She was helping him. "I wouldn't disturb him."

He turned the bottle around in his hand and set it on the end table. "Don't put me in this position. You know what would happen. Grace is his mother. She's the one who needs to stay with him."

Regret tugged at her heart. "I wouldn't take any time away from her."

Parker groaned. "Just you being there would make her feel uncomfortable."

"Why?"

"You know why."

"But I've stayed away for seventeen years," she whispered.

"That was the adoption arrangement."

She bit her lip. "I can't stay away any longer."

"You agreed to those terms in the contract. You terminated all parental rights." Parker stood and paced to the kitchen.

"But it's not fair!" She put down her water and began wringing her hands.

Straightening his arms, he leaned against the bar. "Hailey, please don't start. I know how you feel…"

"You couldn't possibly know how I feel. I need to see him." She fought to control the bitterness in her voice.

"No."

She rose, knocking over the water bottle. "He's my son!"

"Not anymore, he isn't."

The rebuke stung. "He'll always be my son!"

"When you gave him up, you promised to keep your distance."

"I have."

"Forever."

The reminder lanced her heart. "You're being unfair. He's dying."

He slammed his fist on the bar. "Don't say that. He can't die." Parker pushed himself up and stomped near the window, raising his hands to rest on top of his head as he faced the curtain.

A muscle twitched in her hand. Her knees buckled. She sat on the edge of the couch, wringing her hands. "I was young. I couldn't give Justin the life he deserved. I'm not asking to take him back. I only want to see him."

Rubbing his jaw, he walked back to the couch and sat. The hard lines on his face softened. "The adoption papers were clear. No contact." He placed his hands on top of hers and stilled them. "If the decision was mine, I would allow it, but Grace would lose it if she found out you're Justin's biological mother."

Her hands squeezed into tight fists. The urge was unbearable. "I wouldn't tell her."

Parker ran a hand through his hair. "Argh! Don't you understand? She'd take one look at your face and know the truth. Don't forget, you're the one who wanted us to protect him."

She stood. "Well, you did a hell of a fine job, didn't you? You divorced Grace and deserted him. Parenting takes sacrifice, Parker. You were too busy changing careers, and now he's messed up with drugs. How did that protect him?"

Standing, he reached for her.

"No. You stay away from me." She extended her hands and backed up a step. "Justin's dying! Dying, Parker! And I don't know him…You won't let me see my own son."

He wrapped his arms around her.

She pushed him, pummeling her fists against his chest with all her strength.

He silently took his beating.

"Why did I do it? Why did I ever give him up?" She searched his face. Finding no answers, she rested her head against him and let him hold her. A dozen daggers stabbed her core. "Oh, Parker. It hurts so much. I missed his whole life. What if I lose him forever?" With as much force as she could muster, she scraped her nails deep across her hands.

"I know. I'm scared, too, but you need to stay strong." Parker rocked her against him, smoothing her hair. He stiffened beneath her. "My God. You still don't cry, do you?"

She froze, and her heart thumped against her rib cage.

He stared into her eyes. "You haven't shed one tear since I've seen you." He pulled away. "After all this time, you haven't cried?"

Hailey shook her head. "Not since you told me about my parents."

His face paled. "Oh, Hailey, the therapists told you to cry. You can't bottle your emotions. It's not healthy."

She turned away. "It's not your problem anymore."

Sighing, he picked up her hands. "Look at these marks. You've got to stop hiding your feelings. What does Mark say?"

Her cheeks warmed. "He doesn't know."

"What do you mean, he doesn't know?"

She lowered her head. "I put up walls to protect myself."

"So you don't let him in?"

She didn't answer. He wouldn't understand the loneliness and despair weighing on her soul.

Parker exhaled and lifted her chin. "My God. How many walls are surrounding you?"

Hailey shrugged. "I'm more secure than Fort Knox."

He frowned and a muscle twitched in his neck.

She gathered up her courage. "Please let me see Justin. I'm begging you."

"I'm not doing this to hurt you. It's only natural you want to see him again." He gazed at her, pushing her hair behind her shoulder. "I know you're in pain." His voice softened. His fingers tenderly traced a path along her cheek. He groaned. "My God, after all these years, nothing's changed."

"What do you mean?"

"You still enchant me. Like a lei flower from a tropical island." He brushed the flyaway wisps from her face, held her hand, and inched closer. "God help me. I don't care that you're vulnerable." He pulled her closer and kissed her lips, crushing her against him.

She began to push him away, but her lips responded, meeting his passion. She was his lei flower, and he was a honeybee collecting his sweet pollen. The steamy kiss tantalized her, urging her to taste more. She fought for strength to escape his grasp. Finally, she pushed him and put a hand over her mouth. "What are you doing?"

Parker stood and rubbed his jaw. "I'm sorry. I got caught up in the moment."

She closed her eyes; heat burned up her neck into her cheeks. "Parker. I won't do this to Mark." She raced to the window and dragged her hands through her hair. "How did this happen?"

He stepped next to her, but she backed away. "No. That's close enough. You're too dangerous." Shaking, she scanned the room and held her hands against her head. "I can't think anymore."

Reaching over, he massaged her shoulders. "You're tired. You shouldn't be alone tonight. Do you want to stay here?" He nodded at the sofa. "I'll sleep on the couch. I promise nothing will go on."

She hesitated. His manly scent used to calm her. Now it terrified her. "No, I can't. I have to go." She ran to the door and slammed it.

"Hailey…"

Down the hall, she raced to her room, catching her breath as she lifted the room key against the lock. She dashed in and flung herself on the bed, clenching her hands. The urge was back, in greater intensity, begging relief. She scratched until she drew blood, corporeal pain numbing her sadness. *Don't cry. Crying's a sign of weakness. Stay strong. Don't go back to that dark place.*

She buried her face in the pillow and screamed, pounding the bed with her fists. Why did she give Justin away? How could she change Parker's mind? No. Stay away from him. He was too dangerous. Ugh! The kiss was intoxicating. Why did she let him get to her? She was married to Mark.

She grabbed her hair and yanked. What was happening to her? The previous day she had been a normal mother, washing dishes and sending her kids off to school. Now she was gallivanting in a tiny hotel room, kissing another man. If Mark kissed his old girlfriend, she'd fume. She shouldn't have agreed to save Parker's son. Her first-born.

Justin.

For over seventeen years, she had squeezed the harrowing memories into the deepest crevices of her being. It was a secret she couldn't share. A part of her died when she gave away her son. Parker had rescued her then. But being around him now was dangerous. She fell into that trap once, and it was hard to resist the attraction. *Stop insisting on seeing Justin. You'll ruin what's left of any relationship with Parker.* After she dressed in her nightgown, Hailey brushed her teeth and went to bed, tossing under the sheets until long after midnight.

Chapter Twenty-Six

Mark lay in bed, watching the numbers flip on the alarm clock each passing hour. Why hadn't Hailey called? He had left dozens of messages on her cell. He'd know she was okay by the sound of her voice.

Besides worrying about Hailey, the missing persons case gnawed at him. At four o'clock, he crept downstairs to the study and paced. The small area was only large enough for a desk, office chair, and bookcase, but it was the perfect place to mull over his problems. An idea came to him that was worth trying. He picked up the handset from the phone on his desk and dialed David's number. Mark stifled a yawn as he connected to the answering machine. "Hey, it's me. Sorry, it's late. I have another favor. I'm investigating the disappearance of an agent, Elliot Sherman. He worked at the NNIC in Pennsylvania for ten years. When the agency closed, he took a job working at the DTA. He disappeared a month ago, and I'm running into dead ends. I thought with your contacts, you might point me in the right direction. Call me at the office on Monday. I'll fill you in on the details."

He lowered the handset on the receiver, and his hand knocked over a picture of Hailey holding the kids. He gripped the whitewashed frame and set it upright on the desk. Squeezing his eyes shut, he whispered, "Honey, please call."

Instead of returning to bed, he opted for the recliner and dozed off. At six o'clock, Ethan and Anna woke. They scurried into the living room and climbed on his lap. Ethan grabbed the TV remote next to the chair and controlled the channels. The phone rang. Mark stretched his arm over Ethan's head and grabbed his cell on the end table. "Hello?"

"Mark? Hi. I bet you're watching cartoons. I've missed you." Hailey's voice was bright.

He drew in a long breath and shifted the chair upright. Finally. What a relief. "Me too. I'm glad you called."

"How are you and the kids?"

"We're doing okay, but they keep asking when you're coming home."

"They're sweet. I miss them. When did you get back?"

"Yesterday. What's going on?" Stay calm. He scooted the kids off his lap.

"I'm sorry I left on such short notice. My good friend Lily called last minute. She's sick. She's been getting chemo and feels awful. She wanted to see me."

"Where are you?"

"At Lily's place. Do you remember her? She was my friend when I moved to Texas. We send each other Christmas cards each year."

A knife slit his heart. "No, I don't remember her. How could you pick up and leave the kids without talking to me first?" His tone was harsher than he intended.

"You weren't here. I asked your parents to babysit them. I didn't think it was a big deal. I wouldn't have left if it weren't important. I'll tell you about it when I come home tomorrow. Things are busy today, but I wanted to call and say I love you. I needed to hear your voice."

He sighed. *Don't start an argument. She needs a clear head tonight.* "I'm sorry, hon. I miss you, too. The bed's not the same without you."

"Are the kids still there?"

He lowered his head. "They're on the floor. Mesmerized by the cartoons."

"Tell them to behave and give them my love. I should go. Lily's calling. Bye, Mark, I love you."

"I love you, too." Frowning, Mark ended the call and stared at the keypad. Hailey was adept at controlling her voice, but he caught snippets when she trembled. "Damn," he whispered. "Let tonight go well."

Chapter Twenty-Seven

Hailey tossed the phone on the comforter and brushed away the heaviness in her stomach. She collapsed backward onto the mattress and flung her arm on the pillow. Ugh! She hated lying. She had almost told him everything.

His voice was gruff. Naturally, he was irritated. She had left him. Twenty-four hours. That's all she needed. She'd patch things after she got home.

Calling him was a gamble. But talking to him, hearing his voice, still didn't help sort through her mixed emotions over the forbidden kiss the previous night. It confused her more. Dammit! How could she feel excited and guilty at the same time? She and Mark had ten years. How could Parker sail into town and tug at her heart again? Rubbing her eyes, she turned her head toward the nightstand. The clock displayed 7:10 AM. She slid back under the sheets.

****

Hailey was still in her pajamas when a knock tapped on her door at 10 AM. Parker probably wanted to go over some details about the night. She put on her robe and raked a hand through her hair. She unlocked the latch. "Parker, we need to—"

Stefan's smile extended across his face. He stood in the hall holding an emerald evening gown and carrying a shopping bag. "Good morning."

"Morning, Stefan. I thought you were Parker."

"I passed him in the hallway. He's meeting us downstairs for brunch."

She adjusted the tie of her robe. "Can you give me half an hour? I'll jump in the shower."

"Take your time. After we eat, we'll drive to the office and review tonight's strategy."

"Sounds good." She pointed to the gown. "Are you wearing dresses now?" She giggled as his ears reddened.

The sixty-year-old father of three sons glanced at the bag. "What? No! You're wearing this to the party tonight." He handed over the outfit and the shopping bag. "Here's your disguise. Ever consider switching to blonde?"

Chapter Twenty-Eight

Bella woke to sunlight streaming in her bedroom window. She stretched her hand on the unoccupied pillow next to her and sighed. Mornings weren't the same without Manuel. Combining Moulin's work and Hanover's data required longer hours in the lab than she had projected. The prior night she'd slept in her condo instead of driving farther into the city to the mansion. She missed Manuel's firm body pressed against her back and his strong arms secured around her waist. She missed his warm breath on her neck, stirring nerve endings down her spine.

Her cell phone chimed, and she reached under her pillow and grabbed it.

Manuel texted: *I missed you. Call when you wake up.*

She glided her fingers across the keypad and waited.

He answered on the first ring. "Late night? I thought you were taking off early."

"I finished some tests, and then I saw my dad. My place was closer."

"You should reconsider moving in with me."

Bella smiled. She loved staying at his place. "I can't."

"Why?"

"You know why."

"What if I'm never ready to make that commitment?

"Then I'll stay right here in my condo."

"You frustrate me."

She laughed at his husky voice.

"Can we meet for brunch?"

She pulled an extra pillow underneath her head and leaned against it. "I'd love that. What time?"

"Ten. I'll meet you at your favorite place. After we eat, would you like to come back here for a while before your spa appointment?"

"Sounds great. See you soon."

At the restaurant, she drew in a sharp breath when she spotted the bouquet of wild flowers Manuel held. He greeted her with a long drugging kiss and pulled out her chair at their private table. After they dined, they drove to the mansion. They walked hand in hand, meeting Antonio on the front lawn. The valet drivers had already roped off a parking area near the circular paver driveway.

Manuel greeted Antonio and observed the additional staff hired for the event. "The guests are coming in from all parts of the world. Make sure the valet attendants are insured."

Antonio nodded. "Already done. I spoke with your father last night. He's peeved you're hosting this party."

Manuel's face reddened, and his grip around her hand tightened. "You and I have both seen how angry my father gets. My mother's a saint for staying with him."

"Unfortunately, you experienced his wrath firsthand. Especially when you were younger."

Clenching his jaw, Manuel gestured at her. "Bella knows about my father's temper. I still bear the scars on my back. He's always run my life." A catering van whizzed past, and he paused until the noise subsided. "What else did my father say?"

Antonio shrugged. "Not much. He wants you concentrating on more important things."

He scoffed. "My father knows the purpose of this event." Manuel led them past the concrete steps to a small table with assorted stemware and beverages. He poured a glass of lemonade and passed her the drink. "Do you want anything, Antonio?"

"No, *gracias*. How many guests tonight are potential contacts?"

"About half. Some others are politicians involved with drug regulations." Manuel picked up another glass and poured himself a cold drink. They continued walking through the gardens, quieting their voices as a gardener rolled a cart of dahlias, asters, and daisies along the walkway. The short, robust man handed one to Bella and meandered down the path.

Antonio followed beside Manuel as they stepped onto a circular pavilion. "Any information on Detroit?"

Gesturing to Bella, Manuel waited until she sat on a curved bench, then he sat next to her. "Cerdo called. The police still can't identify the drug. Yesterday's incident in Indianapolis has spawned more doubt from our buyers. I'm getting tired of fielding the calls." He set down his glass and slid his arm around her waist. "Bella's still working out the kinks."

Antonio sat on a smaller bench across from them. "Did you get the urns I dropped off for you, Bella? When I stopped over late last night you were gone."

She finished the lemonade and set her tumbler next to Manuel's glass. "Thanks for delivering them. I haven't opened the containers yet. Manuel told me to take today off."

Manuel rubbed his thumb against her back. "She's been working non-stop, carrying the success of this deal. She needs a break."

"I agree." Antonio smiled. "Does your family know about you two yet?"

"*La quiero.*" Manuel lifted her hand and kissed it. "I'm taking her with me to meet my parents once the orders ship."

Antonio's face brightened. "I knew you were falling in love. I've seen the way you look at each other."

Manuel kissed her cheek, and she warmed. "I'm worried how his family will accept me, especially Manuel's father."

Antonio directed his attention to Manuel. "Your father didn't approve of your last girlfriend."

"Approve is an understatement." Manuel clenched his fist and pounded the wooden seat. "Transporting Selena to the Caribbean was unconscionable. Human trafficking. I will never forgive him for that."

"Selena's family won't either. They still can't find her." Bella gaped at the men, but Antonio shook his head. "Don't worry Bella, Manuel won't let that happen to you. His father will see that you love him."

"Sometimes I wonder if my father even cares that I'm happy. As he grows older, he's getting more out of control. His temper still terrifies me."

They waited as another gardener wheeled a pushcart and added pea gravel to a section of the walkway. Manuel turned to Antonio. "Did you complete the assignment I gave you in Illinois?"

Antonio nodded. "It was easy. I shipped the shrub to your father's manor this morning. Moulin's old man is deaf. He didn't know I was in the house."

Bella gazed at Manuel, and her skin tingled. He did care about saving the plant.

One of the servants strode across the gardens and handed Manuel an envelope.

Manuel opened it and pulled out a paper. "Ah, the finalized guest list." He waited until the attendant walked away, and then he offered the paper to Antonio. "The politicians on this list support me as long as they remain in the political spotlight. The relentless cockroaches feed off others. Remember this— corruption finds its niche in all facets of humankind. Politicians conduct their own private agendas."

Grinning, Antonio rose from the bench. "Like when you took down the NNIC a couple years ago?"

Manuel smirked and gestured to Bella. "That was her idea."

Her cheeks warmed at the praise. "That agency was a major concern. Luckily, it was in financial difficulty. Manuel made a few phone calls to the right people, and the funding dried up."

Gently, Manuel squeezed her shoulder. "We couldn't risk the NNIC tracking this drug. Closing that agency was critical to slow down any investigation. The government is clueless about the magnitude of the drug problem in the States."

She nodded. "The majority of Americans don't care about stopping illegal drugs. The problem's too big for anyone to make a difference."

Manuel squared his shoulders and stood. "People know the country has a drug problem, but they do nothing. Apathy rules. We stand to make a healthy profit spreading Euphoria throughout the world." He offered his hand as she stood. The trio turned toward the stone mansion and began walking. "It's funny, actually."

Antonio's brows knitted. "What is?"

"Americans are oblivious the country is ruining itself from within. Drugs. Crime. Riots. Corruption. Terrorism. Protests. Those who recognize the problems are powerless to prevent them."

"Careful. Your bitterness is showing." Antonio smirked.

Manuel squeezed Bella's hand. "I can't help it. I grew up around violence for thirty-three years. I hated living with a father who justified his murders. I had hoped the United States was different. But the longer I stay here, the more I see our countries are alike. Violence is everywhere. Drugs are only part of this country's corruption. Americans complain about terrorism from other countries, yet they suffer violence and hatred from citizens without ever stepping on international soil. Look at the random killings in schools. At the workplaces. In public arenas. Nothing makes headlines anymore unless twenty or more people die."

They stopped near a stone fountain in the rear lawn. Antonio dipped his finger in the water and blotted his neck. "You truly despise this place."

Manuel sneered. "My contempt for Americans gives me pardon for my crimes. They'll never win the war on drugs."

"Americans are so far down the slippery slope, they can't climb back." Antonio tossed his head back and laughed.

"The fatal blow is legalizing drugs. Marijuana is only the beginning." Manuel joined in the laughter and led the way up the capped stone steps near the front entrance. "Once Euphoria spreads, no one will stop the devastation."

"Your father is set up for production in Colombia."

"This venture will enable him to control more political arenas." Manuel grinned. "Euphoria will draw money into Colombia and help our economy. Though we are still a developing country, the U.S. will soon experience how it feels to be a poor nation."

Bella slowly pulled her hand away from Manuel's grip as he surveyed the property. She fought back tears. How could he hate this country so much? He never cared about the land's beauty when he bought the estate. He wanted the power that money carried—to rule others and secure his own personal freedom. She might have initiated this venture, but her motives were altruistic. She still loved her country and her fellow countrymen.

Antonio lowered his voice as they neared the manor. "Your father needs some samples and the formula so he can begin production."

"I'll send it when Bella finalizes the drug. The shipment you mailed today is our insurance in case we need it." Manuel's cell rang, and he drew it from his pocket. "It's Cerdo." He put the call on speaker. "Hello."

"Hey, it's me. Didn't Bella say the Canadian doctor couldn't come?"

Scratching her cheek, Bella leaned toward the phone. "Dr. Lavoie? I called him last week when I didn't receive his RSVP. He gave his regrets. He's on his honeymoon this weekend."

"Someone RSVP'd under his name. You should plan on some unexpected guests this evening." Manuel grinned as Cerdo relayed the information.

Bella wet her lips. "Get ready for an interesting night."

Chapter Twenty-Nine

The tightness in Mark's chest worsened throughout the afternoon. The kids had picked on each other all day. Bickering. Hitting. Name-calling. Tattling. Nothing he did improved their behavior. The final blow came when Anna cried, "Mommy doesn't cut my sandwich that way. I want Mommy!" He could have pulled his hair out.

On the drive to his parents' house, Ethan and Anna argued again in the backseat. Mark glanced in the rearview mirror. "What's the matter this time, Ethan?"

"Do you have lice, Daddy?"

"Lice?"

Ethan nodded. "Julie had it in my class. You keep scratching your head."

He started running his hand through his hair, stopped himself, and groaned.

"Now look what you did." Anna smacked Ethan's leg. "You gave Daddy a tummy ache."

Ethan slapped her arm. "I did not."

"I don't have a tummy ache, and I don't have lice." Mark groaned again.

Anna whispered. "Daddy growls like a bear."

Ethan laughed. "A grumpy grizzly bear."

He helped the kids unload their suitcases from the car. "Remember your manners. I expect a good report from Grandma and Grandpa." He followed them through the front door. Even the aroma of his mother's butterscotch oatmeal cookies didn't lift his mood. "Can't they get along?"

Peggy greeted each child with a kiss. "They're kids." She pointed to the luggage. "Are you planning on being out late?"

Mark plucked a warm cookie from the cooling rack. "I have a late meeting. Can the kids stay here tonight?"

Anna and Ethan each grabbed a cookie and dashed into the living room.

"The kids are welcome here anytime." His mother moved the suitcases away from the door. "How's Hailey?"

Mark paused. Mom loved Hailey like a daughter. "She's good. She called this morning and said she'll return home soon." He stacked three cookies on a napkin and kissed her cheek. "I'll call you later. Thanks, Mom. You're the best."

He strode to the car. On the way home, he called Owen and reviewed the plans.

"Did you get the invitations I left with Tamara?"

"Thanks for handling that. She gave them to me before I left."

"Let me know how the evening goes. I hope you find some dirt on Mendoza."

Back home, Mark quickly dressed in his disguise. Emotions of pride and anger swirled around his mind. Keeping this part of her life from him was huge. He would talk to Hailey when she returned home. The secrecy had to stop.

****

Mark drove into Great Falls and followed the GPS directions to the address he'd been given. He steered along the winding driveway until Mendoza's mansion came into view. The landscaping that welcomed him was exquisite. "Holy shit!" The words slipped out of his mouth. Lighted stone columns guided him to the parking attendants near the garages. He handed the key to the valet and started toward the grandiose manor.

Wearing a tuxedo and top hat, Greg waited near the steps in front of the archway entrance. He leaned on his crook cane and greeted Mark with a big grin. "Rather impressive, isn't it?"

"You or the house?" Mark lifted his head, taking in the full height of the building. "I'm glad I saw this place in the daylight. Otherwise, I wouldn't believe how the other half lives. The Internet images don't do this place justice."

"The inside will probably blow us away even more than the outside."

"What are the chances it's not as extravagant?"

With a laugh, Greg raised his arm around Mark's shoulder. "Zero to none."

Together they passed through the double doors. A string quartet played music near the entrance. Greg was spot-on. They entered the marble-floored foyer, where a crystal chandelier dangled from the ceiling. Mark glanced at his reflection in an eight-foot gilded French mirror on the wall.

Greg wore a gray toupee for his disguise as Wilhelm Worth, an elderly widower from England. Mark posed as Worth's personal assistant. His fake mustache and black-framed glasses covered his face. Gray-colored hairspray aged the sides of his hair.

They entered the great hall, and the butler announced their names. Mark did a quick sweep of the room. No sign of Hailey.

Each room was more dramatic than the last. The foyer paled in comparison to the great hall. The European influence was obvious, and Mark wrestled to keep from gaping. Two marble hearths stood sentry at opposite ends of the room. Alabaster sconces lit paintings by the Masters. They stopped near a trio of accent chairs, and Mark swept the area again.

Greg turned around the room. "You sure know how to pick a party."

"How old is this place?" Mark's sudden interest in historic houses surprised even himself.

Greg wrinkled his face. "My guess is the late 1800s." He pointed at the high ceiling and guided Mark to the far end of the room. "See the elaborate details in the molding?"

"It's impressive." Mark shot a look over the top of his glasses. "Actually, a bit overdone."

"Are you crazy?" Greg scoffed. "People would do anything for these moldings today."

"The man has taste. I bet he pays a hefty sum to his decorator." Mark perused the painted murals above him and shook his head. "It makes you wonder what the rest of the place is like."

"I'd love to find out." A server strolled past, offering a platter of stuffed mushrooms and parmesan-crusted crab cakes. Greg ogled the food. "This is going to be quite an evening. I'll return in a few minutes. I'm testing my sugar to see if I need my meds before the party kicks into full gear."

"When you come back, we can start monitoring Mendoza's movements."

Greg's forehead creased. "I still don't get why Owen thinks there's a connection between Mendoza and the Chicago drug case. I think that's a stretch."

Mark shrugged. "Owen has good instincts sometimes." He couldn't tell Greg or Owen his real motive for coming tonight. Keeping an eye on Hailey was *his* problem. When Greg left, Mark glanced around the room. Conversation animated the crowded mansion. Senator Davidson seemed to be in spirited conversation with Senator Thomas. On his left, Senator Marlin talked to Governor Hill from Maryland. Mendoza conversed with Senator Barkley and his trophy wife from New York.

A server offered wine. He took a glass and scanned the room again. Where was she? The entrance area would give him a better lookout spot. He set his drink on a table next to the chairs and mingled through the crowd.

The butler announced Dr. Frédéric Lavoie and his fiancée Antoinette Xavier. They entered the foyer, and Mark waited near a pair of velvet slipper chairs. The stunning blonde-haired woman turned more than a few heads. The couple stood close together with their arms entwined. Mark mused at their closeness. *I wish Hailey and I were that affectionate.*

When the butler introduced the governor from Delaware and his wife, Mark did a double take of the woman. For a moment, he mistook her for Hailey; the shorter woman sported the same hair coloring. Leaning against the chair, he searched the crowd. A hand squeezed his shoulder, and his muscles stiffened at a woman's voice. "Mark?"

Chapter Thirty

Hailey arrived at the mansion dressed to blend in with the cocktail attire of the crowd. Her gown exposed a bare shoulder and had a side slit to halfway up her thigh. The wig Stefan bought transformed her into a stunning blonde. Her makeup rivaled a professional model's. She didn't recognize herself. Even Parker had walked past her at the hotel.

She followed Parker's lead and they advanced to the hall. Wow. Compared to this house, her home was a shack.

They wandered into the ballroom where onlookers watched couples dance the tango. Parker leaned toward her. "You look stunning tonight."

Chills raced through her body. She couldn't stop the heat rising up her neck to her cheeks.

Soon Mendoza approached them. "Dr. Lavoie, let me introduce myself. I am Manuel de Mendoza. I'm glad you could come." He shook Parker's hand.

Parker was handsome in his tux. His thick brown glasses and goatee made him appear sophisticated and intellectual. He shifted into character. "*Bonsoir, Monsieur Mendoza.* Thank you for having us. Allow me to introduce my fiancée, Antoinette Xavier."

Hailey smiled and extended her hand. "*Bonsoir, Monsieur Mendoza. Enchantée.*" Her silver sandals boosted her height three inches, but he still towered her by a few inches.

He kissed her hand and brazenly stared; his dark eyes entranced her. The stylish man was striking in his black tux. *"Bonsoir, Mademoiselle Xavier.* Please, call me Manuel."

A young attendant dressed in a red vest and bow tie approached Mendoza and whispered in his ear. Mendoza scowled and turned to Hailey and Parker. "Pardon me, please. There's been an emergency." He followed the assistant into the foyer.

Hailey exhaled. "We fooled him."

"Did you catch what the man said?"

She nodded. "The implant's working well. There was an incident parking a Jaguar."

An elderly man approached them. "Dr. Lavoie? Excuse me." He spoke with a strong English accent. "I'm Dr. Jenner from Immuno-Bio Research Laboratory in Sheffield. I found your journal articles on chemicals influencing the brain quite informative. Could I speak to you more about your research?"

Parker curved his arm around Hailey's waist. "Oh, yes. The article on catecholamines."

Hailey smiled at the gentleman. His face was on a photograph Stefan had shown them.

His eyes sparkled with a curious glint. "And who is this charming young woman? Is this your daughter?"

"No, this is my fiancée, Miss Antoinette Xavier."

"Enchantée." Hailey smiled as he kissed her hand. "Please excuse me while I find a bathroom and freshen up."

She turned and walked through the crowd. Being back in this environment was surreal. Meeting the guests, observing their quirks and mannerisms, all increased the excitement. But her mission was upstairs. In the event Dr. Jenner was watching, she headed toward the bathrooms. With any luck, Parker would get away soon, and they could search the mansion together.

As she waited in line near the bathroom, she pulled a comb from her purse and swept it through her hair. An older woman collided with her, and Hailey let go of her purse. They exchanged apologies. She leaned down and collected her belongings, reclaiming the lipstick and mirror. The timing couldn't have worked out better. "This line is too long. There's got to be another bathroom," she mumbled to the woman behind her and climbed the curved staircase.

The décor on the second floor was equally as grand. A few couples talked quietly on settees in the hallway. At the master suite, she tried turning the knobs on the double wooden doors. Reaching in her hair, she pulled out a hairpin and picked the lock. Hailey made a fist and shook it. "Yes!" After all these years, she still had it. She opened the door and slipped inside the dark room. She fumbled in her purse and clutched her cellphone. The heavy door creaked.

Chapter Thirty-One

"Mark? Mark Langley? What a pleasant surprise!"

Colleen? He froze at the woman's smooth sexy voice calling out to him. How did she recognize him after all these years? Shit. His cover was blown. He turned, and she eyed him with a flirtatious stare.

"Mark! I'd recognize your stance anywhere. You look the same...except your hair is gray...and you wear glasses...and a mustache."

He hesitated, concealing his surprise and confusion. This wasn't the time or place to chastise her. Even though she'd dumped him and never called or apologized. "Colleen? Is it really you? You haven't changed, either." He stepped back and checked her up and down. The red diamanté-studded gown she wore was hot. She still had her act together.

"Liar." She adjusted his tie and dusted off imaginary lint from his lapel. "I look even better. Our younger years were so taxing from all the cramming we did."

"How could I forget? You excelled in high school, but when you started college you decided partying was more fun." Mark studied her. Did she detect the hostility in his voice? How could he stay angry when he couldn't keep his eyes off her?

"After I switched schools, I cracked open the books again." She slid a finger across his cheek, ignoring the insult when he turned away. "And you were no saint either when we dated. You had your share of fun, too." She studied the guests in the room and lowered her voice. "Why are you here? This isn't your crowd."

"My friend invited me. His date canceled on him last minute." Why was he explaining this to her? He didn't owe her any explanations. A cough sounded behind him, and he turned.

"This oyster tartare is delicious. You should try some." Greg munched on a plate of hors d'oeuvres. "Are you going to introduce me, or are you going to keep this attractive woman all to yourself?"

"Excuse me. Colleen, this is Wilhelm Worth." Mark turned to Greg. "Wilhelm, this is Colleen Toole. Or isn't it Toole anymore?"

"It was Mansfield for a while, but I'm back to Toole." She winked. "My husband didn't last six months before he strayed."

"I'm sorry." His mind flashed back to the last time he saw her. Did she end up marrying a womanizer like the one she was with at her last college party? *Don't be callous. People change.*

She shrugged. "Some marriages work out and some don't. What about you? Are you married? Still single, perhaps?" Her eyebrows arched.

He laughed. She still had a brash personality. Total flirt. He was better off that she left him. Hailey was a devoted wife. "I'm married. Ten years now."

"Ten years? I'm impressed. If anything changes, darling, let me know."

Mark coughed. He shouldn't talk about his personal life. He couldn't trust her anymore. Never could. "How are your parents doing?"

"Mom died a few years back—cancer. Daddy has Parkinson's."

"I'm sorry."

She smiled, but her face revealed her sadness. "Mom's illness was hard on him. He wouldn't see a doctor until after she died. By then he had lost much of his motor control."

"How is he now?"

"His cognitive abilities are hit and miss. He has good days and bad days, but his tremors are terrible. One of his old associates invited me here tonight."

"I always liked your father. A.C. is one of a kind. He's a very bright man."

She blushed. "He had quite a few articles published in the medical journals in his day."

"I read about his research and award in the newspaper. Andrew Cecil Toole. Even thinking about his achievements makes my head spin." Mark grinned. "Plus, he's the only man I know who named a daughter after a biochemical receptor."

Colleen giggled. "Yes, my own eccentric legacy from my dad, the bio geek. But actually, the receptor is a combination of his and my name. I can't believe you remembered. You were never one for science."

"Acetylcholine. That's the extent of my science background." Mark's shoulders relaxed. She was still perceptive and sensitive. Qualities he liked. She didn't seem self-absorbed anymore.

Greg forced a cough again, and Colleen appeared to take the hint. "Sorry, Mr. Worth, but I haven't talked to Mark in years. We were close until I transferred to Harvard." She shifted back to Mark. "What did you end up majoring in college?"

"I flip-flopped between business and criminology. Then I settled on criminology—with the government."

"Fighting crimes. You were always one to do the right thing." She stared at him as if she expected him to rebut her.

His anger diminished. She was still a beautiful woman. Carefree. Perhaps Colleen didn't realize how she had hurt him.

She tugged at her diamond drop earring. "So you're with the government now?"

"Yes."

"What agency?"

She was only making small talk. He'd fake it. "I work downtown." He made his voice sound official. "If I tell you anything more, I'll have to send you to an undisclosed location in Eastern Europe."

"Very funny. All right, I can take the hint." She turned to Greg and took his arm, welcoming him like an old friend. "Mr. Worth, can I call you Wilhelm? Let's get a drink so I can fill you in on my younger days with Mark…"

Chapter Thirty-Two

The door creaked, opening wider, and Hailey grabbed a candlestick from the nightstand.

"Anyone in here?"

She exhaled and held up the phone. "Psst. Over here."

Parker maneuvered around an antique French clock set on a side table. "Sorry I'm late. The doctor kept asking me questions about my journal article."

"I figured you'd come once you had the chance. I got here right before you came." She squinted, waving her phone light. "This light isn't too bright."

"Here." Parker pulled a light from his suit pocket, flicked it on, and the room brightened.

She scanned the area. The bedroom was as impressive as the rest of the mansion. Stepping past the king-size mahogany bed, she started right to work in the sitting room. She unlatched the windows and lifted the glass a few inches. Passing the granite fireplace, she shuddered. Thankfully, there was no fire.

Hailey strode back to Parker and gaped at the candle chandelier. "This place is the definition of opulence. I bet Mendoza has quite the ego." She pointed to the left side of the room where built-in bookcases lined the walls. "According to the blueprints, the entrance is over here."

They hurried to the wall and began sliding books across the shelf. One of the books would open the latch, but which one? She worked swiftly.

A whiff of his aftershave stirred her senses. It was an earthy scent. Their gazes met, but she broke it off. She tested another section of books across the shelf and felt him studying her. Her heart fluttered. *Focus, Hailey*. Why had he kissed her the previous night? She was a married woman. "We need to work fast. Security cameras are all over this place."

A soft click sounded near Parker and she rushed over, following him through the doorway.

He turned on a light. "Hurry."

The small chamber smelled like leather and cigars. A computer rested on top of a writing desk. Parker headed straight to the computer and turned it on. He began rifling through the files in the filing cabinet next to the desk. "It's booting. Find what you can. We'll only have a few minutes."

Hailey hurried to the rear of the room and rummaged through a pile of letters spread across a cherry wood desk.

Parker turned back to the computer and typed on the keyboard. "I'm in!" He shoved a hand in his pants pocket and pulled out a jump drive.

"Already?" She glanced up. "How did you figure out the password?"

He inserted the jump drive in the computer. "I took a shot at Euphoria."

She searched through a stack of files. A large desk calendar shifted, exposing a tan envelope. "This might be what we're searching for." She pulled a packet from the envelope. On the top corner of the cover page was the word EUPHORIA. The page below had an image of a chemical structure. "Bingo!"

"What did you find? Can you identify the drug?"

"Give me a minute." Hailey flipped through the packet. "I need to study this."

"There's not much time."

She opened her purse. "Stefan gave me a camera. I'll take some photos of the...Oh, shit."

"What?"

"The camera's missing!"

"What do you mean?"

"It must have fallen out while I was in line for the bathroom."

"Dammit!"

"It's okay. I'll use my cell phone." She took out her phone and pressed the button.

"Keep snapping." Parker typed on the keypad. "The files are downloading."

Quickly, she worked, turning page after page of the packet. Her phone beeped. A text message appeared on the screen: ABORT MISSION.

"Oh, no. Parker, we have to get out of here."

"I need a couple more minutes."

She tilted her head. Footsteps thudded down the hall. "Now! They're coming."

Dammit! Parker jerked the drive from the computer and shoved it in his pocket. He grabbed Hailey's arm, and they darted from the room. With his free hand, he drew a semiautomatic from his pants.

"Hurry. They're almost here," she whispered.

They raced to the sitting room window. Parker climbed out the opening and stepped on the stone ledge. He offered a hand to Hailey. "Careful."

She lifted the bottom of her dress and swung around. As she grabbed his hand, the cell phone dropped. "My phone!"

"Leave it. They're coming!"

Ignoring him, she leaned over and stretched her fingers. The door swung open, and she raised her head. Two men bolted into the room. She left the phone on the floor and turned. A strong hand grabbed her arm and threw her on the floor. She kicked as a wet cloth pressed over her face. Gunshots blasted, and the darkness consumed her.

Chapter Thirty-Three

From the great hall, Mark chatted with Colleen and Greg while he monitored the foyer entrance. Colleen's phone chimed, and she turned away. Mark eavesdropped on part of the conversation. A nurse from the nursing home was discussing A.C.

She ended the call. "I should go. Daddy's giving the nurses a hard time. He's asking for me. I usually check on him during the week when I get the chance. Since my mother passed away, he misses the companionship."

He nodded. "You're a devoted daughter." Too bad she wasn't a devoted girlfriend. Shit. Why did he care anymore? He loved Hailey.

"I'm all he has left. Now it's my turn to take care of him." She gave Mark a hug. "It was good seeing you. If you ever get the time, let's have lunch and catch up."

Smiling, he studied her. She was only being polite. "I'd like that."

"I'll give you a call later." Colleen opened her clutch and handed him two business cards. He wrote his work number on one and passed it back. She turned to Greg who was holding a fresh plate of stuffed mushrooms. "It's been a pleasure meeting you, also, Mr. Worth."

They stared as she sauntered to the door. Greg shoved the last mushroom in his mouth and licked his finger. "Now that is *one sumptuous lady.*"

Mark didn't reply. He searched the room again. Where was she? It was getting late. He forced himself to engage in polite conversation about the mysterious Wilhelm Worth. Greg played the part of a philanthropist, creating stories about his successful bank ventures.

An hour later, Dr. Jenner approached him and Greg and asked if they had seen Dr. Lavoie and his fiancée. The couple flashed through Mark's mind. "Pardon me. What did you say her name was?"

Dr. Jenner tilted his head in thought. "Antoinette. Antoinette Xavier, I believe."

He blinked. The names of Hailey's parents. Dammit! "When was the last time you talked to them?"

"Maybe an hour and a half ago. I introduced myself earlier. Antoinette left in search of a lavatory. When she didn't come back, Dr. Lavoie went to find her."

His mouth went dry. "We'll help you. Greg, why don't you search this floor? I'll check upstairs."

Dr. Jenner tipped his chin. "I appreciate your help."

Up the stairs he dashed, running down the hallway, searching each room. The door at the end of the hall was ajar. He pulled out the gun secured at his waist and flipped the light switch. The bedroom was vacant. He followed the sound of crickets chirping through an open window in the sitting area. A blonde wig and cell phone lay on the floor next to the chaise. He put the gun back in his pants and picked up the phone. Trembling, he typed in Hailey's password. *Don't turn on. Please don't turn on.*

The password permitted him access.

"Damn!" Hailey wouldn't recklessly drop her phone. His heart convulsed against his chest as he read the last text:

ABORT MISSION

He gripped the phone hard, as if he could squeeze out more information. Please, God, no…

****

Mark slid the phone in his tuxedo jacket. He raced down the staircase; the partygoers were still dancing and chattering. Greg stood with Dr. Jenner at the bottom of the stairs, questioning one of the wait staff. Mark couldn't control his shaking. He tapped Greg's shoulder. "Family emergency. I need to leave."

Greg called after him. "What's wrong?"

He didn't reply. Outside, the guests formed a line at the parking entrance, and he gave the valet his ticket. He ripped off his tie and unbuttoned his top shirt button. The guests around him spun faster and faster. He gasped for breath. Grabbing his own cell phone from his pants, he dialed. "Hi, Mom."

"Mark, what's wrong?"

"Nothing." He struggled to control the panic in his voice.

"You sound agitated. How's the meeting?"

"Running late. Did Hailey call?"

"No. This isn't like her. She always texts or calls before the kids go to sleep. I bet she lost track of time."

His fingers curled into a fist. "Hailey said her connection was awful." His shrill voice cracked. "I'm sure she'll call. Gotta go. I'll call you in the morning."

"All right. Get some sleep tonight."

Staring into the darkness, he clutched the phone and cursed. What did Hailey get herself into? A vivid image of a bullet in her head flashed across his mind, and his entire body quaked. He raised his arm and hurled the phone against the pavement. "Nooo!" The phone shattered.

The valet drove up with his car and handed him the keys. Mark took the keys and picked up the broken phone. He yanked the spectacles from his face and tore off his jacket, tossing them both in the passenger seat. Sleep was definitely not in the picture tonight.

Chapter Thirty-Four

Mark flung the door open at the SCA field office. Rage fueled his frenzy. Despite the late hour, a dozen staff members sat in chairs, absorbed on their phones and computers. A middle-aged woman with auburn hair lifted her head as he barreled past. She stood and blocked the entrance to the double doors behind her.

"Is Stefan in there?"

"Sir, you can't go in there."

"I can go wherever I damn well please!" Raising his arms above her head, Mark pushed the doors and stomped into the room.

He recognized both men from the background report David had sent two days earlier. Stefan Bruno, the SCA director, sat at the desk, and Tom Parker paced the floor by the side window.

"Where the hell is she?"

Stefan shot Parker a fleeting look. "Who's *she*?"

"You son of a bitch!" Mark lunged across Stefan's desk, his muscles tense and shaking. "You know damn well who! Where's Hailey?"

Stefan jumped from his seat and backed up against the wall. "She's probably home with your kids."

Mark charged at him, but Parker stepped between them. "Let's calm down and discuss this rationally."

Snarling, he bolted at Parker. "You bastard!"

Parker raised his arms, his clenched hands guarding his chest. "Oh, cut the shit. You're not the only one worried about Hailey."

The two glowered at each other. Mark fought the intense desire to murder him. "Tom Parker. You got Hailey in this mess. Where the hell is she?"

Parker puffed his chest, ready for battle.

Mark prepared to take a round with him. He'd take great enjoyment destroying the man's contentious attitude and beating him to a pulp.

"We don't know." Parker's voice quieted.

"What the hell do you mean, you don't know?" Mark's jaw clenched. "You were with her!"

"Dammit!" Stefan slammed his fist on the desk. "We have no idea where she is."

Mark kicked a chair across the room. "This is preposterous. What kind of agency are you operating?"

"Let's get one thing straight, son. I don't appreciate outsiders criticizing my tactics." Stefan took a step toward him, his nostrils flaring. "I don't tolerate accusations and threats. So calm down." He pointed to a TV screen mounted on the wall. "We checked the surveillance tapes. Someone tipped Mendoza off. We warned them to leave. Parker climbed through the window first, but Hailey didn't make it out."

He glared at Stefan. "Who tipped them off?"

"Hell if I know. This was a covert mission, and no one—I mean *no one*—knew about it."

"Well, your security is a joke. Even I figured out she was there, so God only knows who else knew about your shitty plans." A chill hung in the room, and Mark gnashed his teeth. "Let me tell you this—I want my wife back! By God, if she's not returned alive in one piece, there will be hell to pay." He gestured sharply and walked out the door.

Chapter Thirty-Five

Hailey woke up in a fog. The throbbing in her head was unbearable. She sat on a hard chair and tried lifting her hand, but she couldn't budge. Something covered her eyes. A gag over her mouth made it hard to breathe. Her body tensed. Mark…Mark…Oh, no. The window. Parker? Did he make it out? She strained, pulling her hands apart. Dread spread through her body. The twine cut into her skin. The place was quiet. Musty air hinted a faint odor of smoke. Was there a fire? Where am I? She focused on muffled voices.

"How's your shoulder?" a woman asked.

"It's only a graze," a man with a Spanish accent said. "Did you talk to Manuel yet, Bella?"

"I told him that we caught the female impersonator, but not the man. Manuel wants to see us later," the woman replied. "Do you know who she is?"

"We're not sure yet."

"Is she a spy?"

"Probably."

"Why are we holding her? Why don't we kill her now?"

"Manuel was specific. He doesn't want her harmed."

"Why? What does it matter?"

"He has his reasons," the man answered.

"Do you think she can hear us?"

"Nah, she's in the other room." A new masculine voice with an imposing tone spoke. "But keep your voices down. She'll wake up soon."

"Antonio, you need your arm looked at. Go see Dr. Fernando. He doesn't live too far away. He's discreet," the woman said.

"I'll stay here overnight," the domineering man said. "What are we supposed to do when she wakes?"

"Don't worry," the woman said. "I'll give her a sedative. It'll keep her knocked out tonight."

Sweat dripped down her forehead. How could this happen again? *Focus.* So far, she could hear three kidnappers. Bella. Antonio. An overbearing man. She pulled her wrists, reaching for the ropes. Footsteps came closer, and she froze. Could they hear her heart thumping? A flowery fragrance hit her nose. Then a whiff of antiseptic filled her senses. A cold sensation tingled on her skin, scrubbing back and forth. She braced her limb, not flinching when a stinging sensation pricked her arm. If she could only stop the icy fluid coursing through her body. *Stay awake.* She was too groggy to fight.

Chapter Thirty-Six

Mark threw up twice after he walked out of Stefan's office. He searched during the night, driving a two-mile radius around the mansion and vacant lots. Finally, he headed back to his office and searched the agency's files on Mendoza. By six o'clock, he called Greg and Owen. He needed help. Lots of it. The pain in his chest gripped him as he paced the room and waited. They arrived, and he gave them the details of Hailey's abduction.

"So, let me understand this." Greg's brow furrowed. "Your *wife* is involved with the drug case from Chicago? The same woman who does nothing but stay home all day and take care of your two kids?"

Mark tightened his lips. "That's correct."

"How's that possible? She's only a housewife."

"Hey. You're talking about Hailey."

Owen turned to Greg. "Hailey's a retired agent from the SCA. Her former partner works for the Chicago PD. His kid's the one in a coma."

"How did you know all that?" Mark narrowed his eyes.

Leaning forward in his chair, Owen straightened his shoulders. "I did my own investigation after you requested tickets to Mendoza's party. I figured something fishy was going on. Your five-year

213

reinvestigation form gave me a headache. Much of your wife's background is sealed, but I got the essentials of her training."

Greg's eyes widened. "This is absurd. What are the chances she's connected with a drug case halfway across the country?" He patted Mark on his back. "I'm sorry, pal. We'll find her."

Owen nodded. "We'll use all our resources, Mark."

Greg turned to Owen. "Should we alert the other agencies?"

Mark shook his head. "I don't want my family knowing what's going on. This needs to be kept under the radar."

Using his cell phone, Owen jotted notes. "I'll ask the director to notify the other agencies. We'll call some agents on the case and keep the investigation under wraps while we wait. In the meantime, we'll set up surveillance, make some calls, and put out an APB. We'll post extra personnel at the airports and transportation depots. And we can distribute interagency flyers. Somebody out there may have seen her. They won't get far."

Mark wrapped his arms around himself. *Why couldn't he stop shaking?* "What if you're wrong? What if they flew her out of the country already?"

"The FBI handles kidnapping cases all the time. Let them do their job." Owen stood and strode to the door. "Why don't you sleep for a few hours while Greg and I put things in motion? You look horrible."

The fatigue drifted his focus. "I can't rest until Hailey's found. By the way, I need another cell phone. Mine broke. I'll submit a request for a new one." He should have listened to Hailey when she put a protective case on her cellphone. Why didn't he buy one, too?

"Let's go to work." Owen walked into the hallway, and Greg followed, closing the door behind him.

The office phone rang. Mark picked up the handset. "Langley."

"This is Tom Parker. We need to talk. Can you meet me?"

Mark's fist tightened. He fought the desire to reach through the phone line and strangle the man. "Where?"

"Fourteenth Street. The food court inside the Reagan Building. I'm sure you could use a decent meal if nothing else."

He contemplated his options. Killing the smug bastard was top on his list. "I'll be there in thirty minutes."

****

Mark marched through the food court, past the queues of shoppers shuffling bags of food. The aroma of coffee and cinnamon rolls made his stomach rumble. Food wouldn't seduce him today. Hailey was missing. Closing his eyes, he sighed. He should be home with her. He scanned the area lined with popular food franchises and looked twice at the man standing by the stairs. Even from a distance, Parker looked haggard. Mark scowled. Like he himself looked any different. He tried not to snarl as Parker approached.

Parker extended his hand. "We got off on the wrong foot last night. I accept full responsibility."

Mark scoffed at the gesture. "She's your partner. Why did you leave her?"

"I replayed the scene a thousand times in my head. If I'd stayed, we'd both be prisoners or dead. I fired shots, but they outnumbered me. I couldn't risk hurting Hailey in the crossfire."

Parker's excuse sounded sincere. "How did they get there so fast?"

"I don't know." Parker raked his hand through his hair. "It was a setup. The men wore masks. They moved like cheetahs. I tried to go after her, but they shot back. I scaled down the wall where our agents waited in the bushes, and we ran to the side passageways, but we were too late. A white van bolted from the premises and sped down the lane."

"Didn't you try to follow them?"

"Of course I did. I alerted the operatives near the entrance. We chased them through the city, but their vehicle outmaneuvered us." Parker rubbed his hand over his unshaven chin. "I know I screwed up."

"You're damn right, you did."

"Can we please focus on Hailey?" Parker snapped. "The SCA's used all its manpower. We need to pool our resources."

Mark crossed his hands over his chest. The proposal was reasonable, but he wouldn't cave. "You've done enough damage."

"We can cover more territory if we join forces."

"I don't want you anywhere near this case."

"You need us."

"True. But I don't like you, and I sure as hell don't trust you."

"I understand your frustration, believe me."

Mark balled up his fists. "You have some nerve, coming back after fourteen years, asking Hailey for help. She's not an agent anymore. You put her life in danger. Hell, did you consider how crazy this idea was? What idiot approved it? Was it even sanctioned?"

"Give her some credit. Hailey's worked these cases all the time. I didn't force her into this."

"She's *my* wife."

Parker's face reddened. "You're an ass. She has more to offer than staying at home catering to you. Didn't you wonder why she kept this case from you?"

"What do you mean?"

"I read the notes on the roses you sent. The flowers are all over the house. You two are having problems."

Clenching his fists even tighter, Mark straightened. "Stay out of our life. You don't know anything about us."

"By the way, how did you find out she was gone?"

"I went to the party last night."

Parker's eyes narrowed. "Hailey didn't tell me you were there."

"She didn't know. I stayed in the other room. I didn't recognize her until after I looked for her upstairs."

Parker laughed. "You didn't notice your own wife right under—"

Mark swung his right arm and caught him in the face. People gathered around them, and nearby, a woman pointed.

Staggering backward, Parker touched his nose. Blood trickled over his lip. "Hailey's a compassionate woman, and if you don't appreciate her—"

Mark cocked his arm again, but Parker ducked and grasped his wrist. Wrapping his other arm around Mark's neck, Parker hissed, breathing heavily. "I gave you one hit. You won't get another one." He plowed Mark into a table.

Amid the stares and gasps of neighboring customers, someone shouted, "Call security!"

Mark got on his feet, feeling like a bull ready to charge. "What are you saying?"

Parker stood as if taunting him. "Hailey was full of life. She doesn't have that spark anymore. She's dying with you."

"Let me guess. *You* could make her happy."

"You don't know her."

Mark stared, ready to land another punch. "And you do?"

"I know why she doesn't cry."

"What do you mean? Of course she cries."

"No, she doesn't." Smug satisfaction settled on Parker's face. "You never noticed. Like I said, you don't know her."

"You bastard." Mark's voice shook. "I love Hailey and she…she believes in us." His voice faltered.

Parker jammed his hands in his back jeans pockets. "Are you willing to work together to save her?"

Mark's stare remained fixed on Parker as he deliberated. At last, he swallowed. "Okay. Let's get her back."

Chapter Thirty-Seven

Hailey couldn't control her shaking. Straps restrained her to a wooden chair. When would Sam and the others send help? She quivered at the woman standing in front of her in the small cabin. "You little bitch. You cost me a fortune!" Madge's rancid cigarette breath was inches from Hailey's face.

She turned her head, but Madge grabbed her jaw and jerked her face closer. "Don't like the smell of me, bitch?" Madge's bony hand lashed out, catching Hailey hard on the cheek. The blow jarred her. Tears streamed down her cheeks.

"What're we gonna do with her?" one of the men asked.

Madge yanked her hair. "I'll teach this hussy a lesson. She don't like my smokin'." She stomped behind Hailey. There was a 'chink' of a lighter opening and then a long draw. The woman wrenched Hailey's blouse away from the back of her neck, and pressed the cigarette there. The burn seared deep in her skin.

Hailey screamed, not familiar with the high pitch of her voice. "Stop! Please stop! The pain burrowed through her flesh as she cried.

"You're about to learn a real hard lesson, brat." Madge howled.

Hailey slumped forward, whimpering. The woman burned her three more times before she left Hailey alone in the cold room.

They came later, untying her from the chair and throwing her on the rug, flames raging in the fireplace. The men pinned her to the floor and ripped off her clothes. The more she struggled, the more they berated and beat her. Madge stood at the side of the room, like some watchful stone demon.

Afterward, Hailey barely heard their voices. The blood dripped down her face, and her swollen eyes obscured her vision. "Stop." She whimpered. She wanted the fire to leap out and burn them. Burn her. Consume her. Let her die. The assault and laughter had persisted until smoky darkness devoured her.

There was no laughter now. This time a potent aroma choked her. Someone breathed on her, hovering over her, kissing her neck. *Mark, help!* A rough, unshaven face scraped against her skin. Her stomach clamped in a tight ball. *Stay still. It's the only way.* Struggling would encourage the abuse.

Warm fingers touched her chin, and the hand lowered, lingering on her breasts.

Hailey squeezed her hands, the nails cutting her palms. *Mark! Why aren't you finding me? Oh, God. He thinks I'm in Texas!*

The hands shifted down past her navel, and she prayed. She tried to kick, but her legs rubbed against the coarse rope. *Please someone—help me.* A moment later long fingers slithered lower, sliding her dress up over her thighs. *Breathe, Hailey. Don't show any reaction.* She swallowed the sour vomit rising in her throat.

The man untied her gag and pressed his hand over her lips. Something cold crushed against her neck. He whispered in her ear, "Don't scream or I'll slit your throat." He kissed her again.

She forced herself to open her mouth. Then she bit down on his lips.

"You bitch!" He smacked her face.

Hailey gulped. "Help! Someone help me!"

He punched her lower jaw, snapping her head back. She staved off the darkness enveloping her and managed one shriek. He slapped her cheek and secured the gag. *Not again. God, let me die this time.* Her hope vanished.

A door screeched, and a scuffle ensued.

"What the hell are you doing?" That was Antonio's voice.

"Aw. I'm only having fun," the creep said.

"You want to piss off Manuel?" The anger in Antonio's voice was unmistakable.

"Let him watch her. How can you expect me to spend hours with this girl and not get aroused?"

"Be careful. Manuel's in charge. He will not tolerate rape."

"A little petting won't hurt."

"Get out!"

The door slammed and the scent of deodorant soap filled the air. She held her breath. Antonio was standing over her. Would he take a turn?

She tensed her muscles, preparing for round two.

He removed the gag and nudged a straw against her cracked lips. "Drink the water."

She emptied the glass and swallowed.

He loosened the ropes around her hands and feet.

Her chafed wrists stung as the ropes shifted across her skin.

"I'll leave the gag off for a while," Antonio said. "No one can hear you. If you yelp one word, I'll make it tighter. Do you understand?"

She swallowed and nodded.

Antonio closed the door and soon a game show played on the television in another room.

She exhaled. *Please God, get me out of here.*

Chapter Thirty-Eight

Bella packed Manuel's clothes and favorite books in a suitcase and started down the stairs.

Cerdo entered the mansion through the secret entrance and walked behind the kitchen. He turned his head to the right and left and stole downstairs.

She hurried, skulking a safe distance behind. The dark hallway didn't seem as spooky or long today. She stooped behind the open door and peered through the crack near the hinges. The room reeked of urine, sweat, and decay.

Cerdo hummed as he threw food scraps on the floor.

The thin man huddling in the corner scampered off the blanket and snatched some crumbs. The man picked something out of his scraggly beard and ate it. "How long do you plan on keeping me here?"

Cerdo snickered. "Are you tired of this place?" He tossed a water bottle at him. "It's been one month, and no one knows where you are. It's time I pay your wife a visit. She might want a man's affection."

The prisoner charged, even in his weakened state, but the length of the thick metal chain held him out of range. He hissed. "You leave her alone."

Cerdo cackled.

"You bastard! It's just a matter of time before you're caught." The man's gruff voice wavered.

Laughing harder, Cerdo spat at the prisoner. "No one will catch me. When the project is over, I'll be long gone—and wealthy. You'll die with nothing, and I'll have everything."

The prisoner glared. "The world isn't about money."

Cerdo scowled. "Everything's about money."

Bella turned and crept up the stairs. After this weekend's shipment, she would investigate the prisoner. There was more to this abduction than Cerdo let on.

Chapter Thirty-Nine

Mark pulled his car into the garage and dropped his head on the steering wheel. Why did he think they would rescue Hailey today?

Thirty agents were working on the case and there wasn't one solid lead. They had scouted Mendoza's properties and tapped into his emails and phone. Nothing helped.

He rubbed his eyes. When was the last time he'd slept? Damn Parker for involving her. And to suggest they were having marital problems. How dare he!

Even so, Parker had seeded a germ of doubt. Was Hailey unhappy? She never complained about staying home with the kids. She was active in the school organizations and the kids' activities. She *seemed* happy. Oh, how would he know? Work kept him busy. Their sex life was lacking. But didn't all couples drift apart from time to time? A shiver inched up his spine at the missed anniversary dinner. He had hurt her. And she didn't cry. Parker said she never cried. Why didn't he notice that? Everyone cried.

All Hailey wanted was to have him at home more. Why didn't he treat her better? She was his wife, not a nanny. *Please, God. Give me one more chance to make things right.*

He shuddered. Did she still love him? Or would she prefer Parker instead? He got out and unlocked the door to the house.

The place was quiet with toys still scattered across the living room carpet. Mark had often teased Hailey of being a science geek when she argued a messy house was proof of entropy in the world. "It takes more energy to keep things in order," she always said. That was the truth. People could say the same about relationships. He walked to the study. The red light on the answering machine blinked in triplicate. His finger pressed the button.

Mark. What time did you want to get the kids today? Beep.

Hi. Mark. You must be working. Adam and I plan on taking the kids to the zoo. We'll come home by dinnertime. Call me when you can. Beep.

Hi, Mark. It's Mom. If you get this message, call me. We plan on stopping somewhere to eat on the way home from the zoo. If you're not home, we can keep the kids overnight and drive them to school in the morning. Call me. Beep.

He smacked his forehead. Oh, God. The kids. He pressed the button again and listened to Hailey's announcement.

Hi. You've reached the Langleys. Sorry we missed you. Please leave a message.

He replayed the message over and over.

In the chair by his desk, he rested his head between his hands. Would he hear her voice in person again? How did others deal with the heartache? His world was a vortex, spiraling out of control, stripping away everything important.

Chapter Forty

Colleen parked her car outside the Oakwood Nursing Home and steeled herself. Visits with Daddy were always difficult. They were sad reminders of lost times. She should have insisted he see a doctor when the hand tremors first appeared.

A nurse with sandy-colored hair glanced up from the computer screen at the desk and smiled. "Two nights in a row. A.C. will be happy to see you again. He always asks for you."

A warm glow expanded through her body. "I wanted to see him again. Daddy wasn't himself last night."

"The doctor is working on different meds to find relief from his symptoms."

Colleen sighed and waited as an orderly wheeled an elderly resident past. "The L-Dopa and trial meds aren't working."

The middle-aged woman shook her head. "He balks at taking them. Some days he's more confused. We're still running tests to determine the cause of his dementia."

She crinkled her nose, holding her breath as she walked down the corridor. The hall reeked of bleach, but it didn't mask the bitter odors permeating the air. She paused at the doorway. His Spartan room lacked the amenities of her childhood house. In the beginning, A.C. grumbled at his primitive room. Over time, he adjusted to the twin bed, small dresser, and wooden table. He developed a liking for TV game shows.

The fragrant fresh-cut tulips on the table filled her senses. She had hired a nursery to deliver flowers twice a week as reminders of the beautiful love he'd shared with her mother.

He was napping, as he did so often these days. Who was this frail man? His thinning pearl-white hair had receded, leaving soft curls on the sides of his head. At least he still grew bushy eyebrows.

She pasted on a smile. "Hi, Daddy."

He wakened upon hearing her voice. "Colleen." A smile slowly spread across his face. "I'm glad you came."

She bent and kissed his cheek. He needed a shave. "I left work early. I can stay for a while."

His lips formed a tight line. "I missed you last night. I kept asking the nurse to call you."

"I came, but you were asleep. I was at a dinner party."

"With Jake?"

"No, Daddy, We divorced years ago. Remember?"

"You're right." He wrinkled his eyebrows. "Who was the boy you dated in high school?"

She blinked. "Mark?"

"Yes. What happened to him? He was a nice young fellow."

She struggled for patience. That split was the biggest regret of her life. "We went our separate ways. I was older than he was. You transferred me to a different college. We grew apart."

"You need someone to love like I love your mother."

Colleen's face warmed. She had a boyfriend. Their relationship was different from her past flings, but he still wasn't like the one who got away. After Mark, she had dated too many married men with their share of problems. Men addicted to drugs and alcohol. She never mentioned any of their names. No one paralleled Mark. When he married, she reciprocated. Said *I do* to a gorgeous scholar from Harvard. He lacked Mark's charismatic personality and fidelity.

She debated on telling A.C. about her newest interest. No. Wait and see where it went. She propped him on his bed pillow and took a seat. "I hear you're giving the nurses a hard time about taking your medication. You need to listen to them. I want you to get well."

He scoffed. "Ta! I'm not going to get any better."

She bit her lower lip. "Don't say that."

"Did you speak to Bruce about his research? He's studied that damn dopamine neurotransmitter for over forty years now. What's taking him so long?"

"We talked about this. I visited him a few months ago. His work needs to go through clinical testing first and that's years away."

A.C. threw a pillow off the bed. "Did you tell him I have Parkinson's?"

She picked up the cushion and wrapped her arms around it. "Yes, I told him the doctors gave you dopamine agonists to activate your receptors. Bruce wants to help, but his hands are tied until he confirms there aren't any long-term effects."

"Like what?"

229

"You know the drill. They test for tumorigenesis, psychosis, mood changes, dependency…"

His arms crossed in defiance. "Bullshit. I'm sixty-eight years old. What do I care about dependency and mood changes? I'm allowed to act cranky. I'm old!"

She smiled at his spirit. "You're not old. Besides, I found a way to monitor Bruce's computer system. Anything he discovers, I can show you."

"Is that a fact? Where did you learn about computers?"

"In college." It was so lovely when her father flattered her.

He wrinkled his face. "What school did you go to?"

"Daddy, you paid my tuition bills to the University of Maryland and Harvard."

"I did?"

"Yes, you did." She put the pillow behind his head and wrestled to keep her smile. How could he forget these significant details?

"Wow, I guess your old man has been good to you."

She raised her head and kissed his wrinkled forehead. "You're the best. So was Mom."

Sniffling, he wiped his nose with his sleeve. "I miss her…Millie was everything…She was the first movement of my symphony."

Colleen got misty-eyed. "I miss her, too."

He held out his hands and touched her face. The tremors were prominent this night. "I want to be with her. Sometimes I think if I pray hard enough, God will take me so we can be together."

"Things will happen according to God's time. We can't rush them. Besides, I want you here. With me."

"Hogwash! You should take care of a husband and kids. You don't need to spend your time here with me. I'm too much trouble."

She lifted her chin. "You're no trouble. I'm always here for you."

He patted her hand, and his face clouded. "You're such a dear friend. Did you meet my daughter Colleen?"

She let out a long sigh. "Daddy?"

His eyes closed, and he mumbled, "Millie should come soon. I'm eating dinner with her before I meet Bruce at the lab. I know she's the one."

Chapter Forty-One

In the morning, Mark drove to Mendoza's mansion and slowed at the estate's secluded entranceway. By some fluke, he might see Hailey scrambling down the driveway, running for her life. The idea was ridiculous. Still, the hope kept his sanity.

Two undercover agents posted in an unmarked car waved as he stopped his SUV at the end of the road. He'd worked with Frank on several occasions. The other agent, Louie, had finished his second tour in Afghanistan the previous fall. Frank opened his car door and walked toward him. Mark rolled down the window. "Morning, Frank."

Frank gave a short nod with his head and leaned against the door. "Any news on your wife?"

He choked up. "No."

Frank raised an eyebrow. "No ransom request yet?"

"Not yet."

"How did the search warrant go yesterday?"

Mark turned his head toward the driveway. Hailey wasn't coming. "The place was clean. The housekeeper said Mendoza left town on business. The other staff didn't know anything."

"Who helped with the search?"

"Greg and an agent from the SCA. Tom Parker."

"I met Parker. He set up the team to check on portable satellites. He's organizing the electronic surveillance. He seems to know what he was doing. A few of the agents are assigned to it." Frank straightened and tapped the car door. "We'll get your wife back, Mark. Don't you worry."

He rolled up his window and shut his eyes. Worry was the only thing he could do.

****

Mark arrived back at his office, unable to shake his mood. Tamara handed him phone messages as he passed her desk. He clutched the notes and closed his door. Sitting on the chair at his desk, he skimmed each memo and tossed them on the floor. What if he never saw her again? Dammit! Where was she? Was she still alive?

Groaning, he stared out the window. He should've protected her better. Why didn't he listen when she wanted him home more?

Surely she understood. Why did he discount the sadness in her eyes when she smiled? God, he missed that smile. And how her eyes glimmered when she laughed. She was his rock. He lowered his face in his palms and let the sobs choke him.

When Mark raised his head, thunder rumbled in the distance. What would he tell the kids? How would he explain their mother was gone? Dammit. Why was he worrying about this? All that mattered was finding Hailey.

He scrunched his face and breathed in. Concentrate. Feel if she's alive. Her coconut-scented hair teased his senses. He'd cuddle with her on the sofa at night, kissing her earlobe, pretending they were in

233

the Bahamas. He clenched his sweaty hands. *Wherever you are, honey, I swear I'll find you.*

Rubbing his eyes, he leaned his head back against the chair. What was he missing? The FBI surveillance on the mansion and transportation terminals showed no activity. Owen was checking into other properties: businesses, rentals, vacation homes. Greg and the SCA monitored the staff's actions and researched Mendoza's associates. The case was a blank slate. Mendoza was missing, and Hailey had disappeared along with him. Why couldn't he find her? Dammit, Mendoza. Call!

Buzz. Buzz. He looked at the office phone lighting up with a caller. The caller ID number was unfamiliar. Hailey! His hand shook as he lifted the handset. "Langley."

"Hi, Mark. How are you?"

"Colleen?" He leaned back in his seat.

"Yes. I kept your number the other night. I'm sorry I had to leave the party early. Would you like to meet for lunch sometime so we can catch up more?"

"What? No!" You stupid ass. This isn't her fault. "What I meant to say is I'm busy today."

"It sounds like you certainly are." Her voice teetered on rudeness.

"I'm sorry. Work is…rather tense and involved right now."

"Sounds like it." She paused. "Mark?"

He tapped his fingers on the desk. "Yes?"

"Is everything okay?"

"What do you mean?"

"Excuse me if I'm out of line here, but I noticed you weren't wearing your wedding ring the other night." Her voice softened.

He shook his head. Colleen had some nerve. "My personal life is none of your business. Why do you care, anyway? You left *me*. Remember?"

"I knew the gibe was coming. That's why I want to have lunch—to explain."

"That's not necessary."

"Look, I know you're busy, but you've been on my mind. You seemed preoccupied the other night. You attended the dinner party without your wife. I'm not judging, but I can tell something's going on. I went through a painful divorce. The breakup is hard, but once it's over, you feel like you can breathe again."

"I've got to go." Mark replaced the receiver and paced. His vision blurred and drifted out of focus until he buckled on the floor. His hands clutched the sides of his head, and he leaned back and sobbed.

Chapter Forty-Two

Hailey tilted her head and listened. From time to time, kids squealed and muffled voices came from her left. She heard broken English and fragments of Spanish, but some languages were unfamiliar. Where was she? Was she even in the country? How would the SCA know where to look for her?

She stretched her fingers over the ropes. The cords carved into her skin, deeper, as pain jolted through her body. Soon she would untangle the knots around her wrists. Her muscles pulled at her shoulders and a dull ache had set in. Her whole body hurt. Dammit! She had to get out of here.

The floor creaked and she stiffened. Which one was it this time? A hand stroked her shoulder, inching toward her breasts. Using every reserve, she remained still. God, help her. If she ever got loose, she would castrate this bastard. Grab a scalpel, and dissect him into tiny pieces. She gagged at his strong-smelling breath, but forced herself not to react. He flattened his lips to her neck and licked her, slobbering kisses along her skin. His heavy breathing showed his arousal. She could grab that tongue from his mouth and wrap it around his neck. Squeeze her thumbs into his neck until his eyes bulged. Make him gasp for breath as she choked away his life.

A door screeched. Someone jerked her tormentor away, and the room became silent. She tilted her head again.

"Stop touching her, you pervert. Live out your fantasies on someone else's time."

Antonio.

"Maybe it's the only way he can get a woman— through some disgusting delusion."

Bella.

"You want to talk about fantasies, *Bella*?"

"Manuel likes the name. In this world we all play our roles, don't we, Cerdo?"

The creep's name is Cerdo.

"Your life is crazier than mine," Cerdo answered. "What are you two doing here so soon?"

Antonio coughed. "Manuel's furious. He doesn't want you alone with her. He sent me to drive you back."

"Damn you, Bella. You squealer. You should mind your own business." Cerdo's voice dripped with disdain.

"Antonio's been Manuel's right-hand man for years. Don't start imagining yourself any higher in this operation," Bella said. "Did you find out who the woman is?"

"Her name's Hailey Langley," Cerdo said. "She's working undercover trying to get the lowdown on Manuel. She's—"

"Mommy!" A child wailed, blocking out Cerdo's conversation.

Hailey worked the knot against her wrists as the mother calmed the upset child. A few minutes passed, and the crying faded.

"Fine, I'll go," the creep said.

Footfalls scuffed across the carpet, and a door opened. Voices chatted outside, and a siren echoed in the distance. The door slammed, and her world was silent again. Did anyone know she was here? Lighter steps neared. Sweet magnolias drifted above. *Please God, help me.*

Hands stretched behind the chair, pulling the ropes tighter around her wrists. Damn!

"Tsk. Tsk." Bella jeered. "Stop trying to get loose. It won't happen."

Hailey controlled her breathing until footsteps padded in the distance. The tightness of the rope numbed her fingers. Her raw skin seeped fluid, but she refused to cry. *Don't you dare give up!*

In the next room, the TV turned on.

She could only pick up snippets about the Chicago drug deaths. Surely, her kidnapping made headlines. A lump formed in her throat. No. The SCA wouldn't leak any news. She twisted her arms, tearing off the scabs. Arrgh! The pain cut into her bones. What was taking Parker and Stefan so long? They knew Mendoza was behind this. What was happening with Justin? Was Parker able to help the doctors?

Mark had to be freaking out. She hadn't called him at all. And the kids. What were Anna and Ethan doing without her? *Please, God, let me get home…I have to get home.*

A newfound sense of purpose galvanized her. Clenching her teeth, she pulled against the ropes. She twisted her wrists, wincing as the strands cut deeper into her skin. She worked her fingers on the knots again. *Push through the pain.* Somehow, she would escape. Her family needed her. And she needed them.

Chapter Forty-Three

Mark was in an oversized cage. He leapt across the ground, thrashing against the metal frame. His fists yanked the bars back and forth. "Let me out!"

Nearby, Mendoza stood with his hand gripped around Hailey's arm, mocking him.

She writhed, swinging her free arm at Mendoza's chest. "Mark! Help me!"

"Hailey!" He sprang upright in bed and peered through the darkness, his clothes drenched in sweat. He held a palm against his head, waiting as his breathing slowed.

Tossing the sheets aside, he rolled out of bed and stepped into the bathroom. He wouldn't bother showering today. He studied his reflection in the bathroom mirror and groaned. "I'm pathetic."

He glanced at his clothes. What was the use in changing? He opened his top drawer, grabbed his gun, and trudged downstairs. The fridge contained an orange juice carton and a gallon of expired milk. Shaking the container, he drank the last drops of juice and tossed the box, missing the garbage can. In the living room, he picked up a tennis shoe lying against the sofa. Its mate hid under the rocking chair. He tied the laces and clutched his car keys.

He drove to Mendoza's mansion again and parked near the entrance. Frank and Louie sat in their car and waved. Mark patted the side of his pants, his Glock accessible. Perhaps today he would see Hailey racing down the driveway, screaming for help. And Mendoza right behind, chasing her. Mark would pull out his gun and shoot Mendoza's face and chest into a minced pile of ground flesh. Then he'd run and scoop Hailey in his arms, and hold her close against him.

He leaned his head against the seat. Why did he allow himself to hope?

****

When Mark arrived at his office, he listened to his voice mail on his office phone:

Hey, Mark, it's David. You hooked me on another interesting case. I interviewed Elliot Sherman's wife in Silver Spring. The poor woman is beside herself. I'm heading to North Carolina in the morning to talk to her son. I'll keep you posted on what I find out. Beep.

Mark. This is Pam in Technology. Your new phone is ready. Beep.

Hey. It's Parker. Give me a call when you get in. It's important. Beep.

Mark looked at the time on the display. Parker had sent the message an hour ago. He grabbed the phone on his desk and dialed. "What's going on?"

"Mendoza has multiple land holdings listed under aliases. We got warrants to search his properties." Parker's voice was taut. "Two of our agents searched a warehouse in the District and found blood on the floor."

He jumped up, overturning his chair. "How much blood?"

"Calm down. We don't know if it's Hailey's. The place is vacant. I'll call you as soon as I find out more. The lab's here. I have to go."

Mark slammed the phone and took a step back. Trembling, he gripped his hair and looked around the office. He swayed sideways as the images blurred together. With one full sweep, he bulldozed everything off his desk.

A gasp came from behind him, and he turned. Tamara stood in the doorway, holding a cup of coffee in her hand. "Ahem." She handed him the mug. "Owen would like to speak with you. I already told Greg to meet in his office." She motioned her head toward the hall. "Go. I'll clean this up."

"Leave it."

Tamara stretched her arm out and touched his shoulder. "Are you all right?"

He took the drink and stepped past her, walking in jerky movements. "I don't know how that feels anymore."

Trying to compose himself, Mark walked to the end of the hall. Greg sat across from Owen, eating a donut and talking about the Nationals baseball game. He entered the room, and they both stood.

Owen grimaced. "You look terrible."

"I'll take that as a compliment." He forced a small sip of coffee into his mouth.

"Couldn't find a razor?"

Mark ignored the taunt and stifled a yawn. "Tamara said you wanted to see me?"

"The FBI thinks there's still a possibility we'll hear from the kidnappers." Owen leaned back against his desk. "They might want to cut a deal. Some kind of trade. Meanwhile, I want you and Greg to continue working on the Sherman case."

He stiffened and his jaw dropped. Was this a bad joke? Owen's expression didn't waver. "No disrespect, sir, but I'd rather search for Hailey."

Owen shook his head. "I disagree. Right now, we're defenseless. We can't sit on our asses and wait. It's been two days and no one's contacted you. You need to keep busy. Besides, we appear incompetent the longer Sherman's case lingers."

Mark threw his coffee cup across the room. "Are you shitting me? I don't give a damn about Sherman. My wife's missing!"

Greg popped a donut hole in his mouth and rubbed a hand over his jaw. "Is it possible she wasn't kidnapped?"

Mark flinched and stepped closer toward Greg. "What kind of question is that?"

Wiping his mouth with the back of his hand, Greg shrugged. "No one but the SCA guy saw her captured. Can you trust him? For all we know, the two of them scammed you. Maybe she had the hots for him and decided to spend a week away."

Mark swung his fist, but Greg ducked.

"Now hold on a damn minute!" Owen stepped between them as Mark lobbed a second punch. "Mark, you're way out of line."

"You son of a bitch!" He lunged at Greg again, but Owen held him off.

Owen turned to Greg. "You should go."

Mark couldn't stop shaking. "I'll save you the trouble. I'm taking the rest of the day off." His vision blurred as he tramped past a stream of spilled coffee to the door and turned. "What the hell is wrong with you two? I've worked here for ten years. I've earned more respect than you suggesting Hailey planned some elaborate scheme to leave me."

He slammed the door and plodded down the hall. Tamara sat at her desk reading a report. She seemed engrossed with the paper, but she had to have heard the conversation. Hell, the whole unit heard it. Grabbing his briefcase and jacket, he dashed to the elevator. He slammed his hand against the buttons, activating four floors. His chest tightened as the elevator stopped on each floor. Finally, the door opened on the ground level. Hot tears ran down his face as he made his way to his car.

The garage attendant studied him and activated the gate arm. "Have a good day, sir."

Mark sped through the gate. The tires squealed, and he peeled out in the street.

****

Somehow, Mark arrived at Toole Biomedical Research Laboratory without concentrating on his driving. He stared at the business card Colleen had given him at the dinner party. Should he go in? They hadn't talked in years. And now she was giving him marital advice. Yawning, he rubbed his temples. He glanced over at the tuxedo jacket he'd worn the other night. "I forgot to return the tux." As he picked up the jacket and moved it to the back seat, Hailey's cell phone fell out of the pocket and landed next to the phony eyeglasses on the passenger seat. He had forgotten about the phone. He could use hers until he picked up his replacement. Clutching the phone, he turned it on.

He typed in her password. Eight missed calls—from home and his parents' house. Those must be the kids trying to call. A calendar reminder displayed on the screen: *Ernie "Cubby" Banks.* He scratched his head. That's funny. She'd never mentioned that she had known a Cubs player. Of course, there were a lot of things she hadn't mentioned. There was the entry for the past Sunday night. *Tenth anniversary dinner.* His heart squeezed. Why didn't he come home that night? He flipped to the previous Tuesday. *Tenth anniversary dinner.* The day he flew to Chicago. He was such a fool. He scrolled through the rest of the dates. The calendar was blank until the current day: *Spend day in D.C. & dinner with Ernie Banks.*

A sudden coldness ran through him. Ernie Banks died the previous year. This was a different Banks. What the hell? He scrolled through the dates, unable to stop his hands from trembling. There were no prior meetings. He slammed his fists on the steering wheel. She did leave him!

He tapped his fingers against the phone and glanced around the parking lot. He needed to get a grip. Hailey was his wife. She wasn't fooling around. He put her phone in his jacket pocket and stepped out of the car. Why would she have dinner with another guy?

Mark opened the glass door and plodded into the lobby. An attractive receptionist with a low-cut dress showing bounteous cleavage greeted him. "May I help you?"

Tears clouded his vision as he forced a smile and skimmed the tiny reception area. "Is Colleen Toole available?"

"May I have your name?"

"Mark Langley."

She reached for the desk phone. "I'll call her for you. Please take a seat."

He chose a chair by the window and grabbed a gardening magazine from the side table.

"Ms. Toole will arrive shortly." She replaced the handset and gestured to the coffeemaker on the counter. "Please help yourself."

Without reading the articles, he flipped through the pages of the magazine, his hands shaking. Think. Hailey was an agent. It was natural she worked with men. She had worn a disguise. He had picked up her wig. She was on an assignment, not skipping town. He rubbed his eyes.

Heels clicked against the floor, and he raised his head, fixing his gaze on Colleen. The taupe dress she wore extended below her lab coat and accentuated her shapely legs.

"Mark?"

He greeted her with a hug. She seemed the same. Confident. Chipper. Secure. "Hi. Thanks for seeing me."

"What a surprise. After our last phone call, I didn't expect to see you again." She studied his face. "Are you okay?"

He hesitated. He could use a woman's perspective. Colleen had experienced her own share of hardships.

"Can we talk?" He motioned to the young receptionist at the front desk. Her gaze ping-ponged between paperwork and him. "Somewhere private?"

She nodded and placed her hand on his shoulder. "You look like you need a friend. Let me take you to lunch."

Colleen drove him to Kali Orexi, a quaint, family-owned Greek restaurant. Paintings of iconic Greek landmarks decorated the interior stucco walls. An older woman greeted them and escorted them to a small table in a secluded corner where an oil of the Parthenon hung on the wall. Colleen removed her sweater and draped it over her chair.

Mark lifted his head and eyed the spherical pendant lights, which added a quaint ambiance to the inside. The place was like the pizzeria he'd taken Hailey to on their first date. Where she had charmed him with her lustrous eyes. He glanced around the room. Did the customers think he and Colleen were a couple? He hung his jacket over the back of the chair, and a server came and offered drinks.

"I'll have a glass of red wine." Colleen's eyebrow lifted. "Do you want anything?"

"Just a coke."

She smiled, and a dimple formed on the left side of her mouth. "Still the same guy." They chatted about the string of thunderstorms pummeling the city. Colleen sipped the wine and lowered her drink. "Now tell me what's going on. You didn't talk the entire ride here. Did you shower today? You look horrible."

"I have a lot on my mind." He twisted the glass in his hand.

She leaned closer, her tone softening. "I used to distract you when we dated. I could try that, or you can tell me what's troubling you."

Mark's face warmed. She still remembered after all this time. He searched for the right words. "Have you ever thought you knew someone and realized later they were different?"

Colleen laughed. "Yes, my ex-husband." Her smile faded. She stretched her fingers across the table and touched his hand. "I don't think we ever know anyone completely. We all have a past. Even you. Look at us. We dated over a year. But we didn't know each other. We didn't know ourselves. I wanted to party and experience freedom. You wanted a commitment. That's where we went wrong. You had a vision of your future. I needed to find myself. Maybe the person you're talking about is still searching."

Mark circled the rim of the glass with his finger. "Perhaps you're right."

She leaned back in her chair and gave a smile that extended across her face. "Hey, women are always right."

"My sisters tell me that all the time."

"You're lucky you have sisters. I always wanted someone to play with when I grew up. Share clothes, have girl talk. And torment." She paused, smoothing the napkin on her lap. "Did I ever tell you I once thought I had a sister?"

He raised an eyebrow. "What do you mean?"

"One night when I was in high school, I overheard my parents talking about a car accident. My dad sounded upset. He said his friend Bruce promised to 'take care of the girl.' Said he didn't need to send money to California anymore." Colleen shrugged. "I think my dad had another kid somewhere."

He rubbed his chin. "That's strange."

"I hinted to Daddy about having a sister. He stared at me as if I had two heads and asked if I was pretending with my imaginary friend." She shrugged and laid her napkin on the table. "I don't get it. Why wouldn't he tell me about her?"

"He was probably embarrassed."

She shook her head. "It doesn't make sense. My parents fell in love during college. They were in love until Mom died. How could he have an affair?"

The server delivered coffee and baklava. They reminisced over the drive-in movies they had watched during their first summer together. He forgot about Hailey and listened to stories of Colleen's life after college. When they dated, Mark thought Colleen was the one. She was playful, mischievous, bold, and wicked. How had she charmed him? He grew quiet and stirred his soda with a straw.

She frowned. "It's obvious something's still bothering you."

"Why do you say that?"

"You just poured creamer in your soda glass."

He pushed his glass away and glanced at his watch. God. What was he doing here?

"Do you want to tell me what's going on?" Her eyes were shiny spotlights, blinding him.

He looked down at the table and shook his head. "I wish I could, but I'm unsure myself."

"See? That's my point. You don't know yourself as well as you think."

His shoulders slumped. "Right now I don't know anyone at all. It's so complicated." He fumbled in his pocket, pulled money from his wallet, and placed it on the table. Looking up at her, he managed a weak smile. "How did you get so smart? You weren't this worldly when we dated."

Her face glowed. "Age makes you wise. But life experiences make you wiser. I shouldered more of those experiences than you." She put her hand on his sleeve and squeezed. His body reacted uncomfortably to the sensation. She stroked her thumb on his arm, and he studied her gaze with steadfast attention. Was he reading too much into that look?

What was Colleen offering? The perfume she wore stirred his senses, eroding his resolve. He fell for her tricks when he was younger. He used to love the scent when he kissed her body. Back when they were lovers. She had a way of grasping his attention, manipulating him. She still wore flowery perfume. He shouldn't do anything he'd regret later. He pulled away from her hand. "We should go."

She pursed her lips. "If you ever want to talk, or want anything else, I'm here." She leaned forward and hugged him.

Chapter Forty-Four

Hailey jerked her head back. She must have fallen asleep again. There was no longer a period of disorientation when she woke. She raised her arms and thighs slightly and stretched the muscles. Her stiff neck and shoulders ached. Her legs tingled, her body was numb. Even her stomach gurgled. She twisted her slender wrists, wriggling as fast as the pain would allow. The ropes ground deeper until blood seeped over her hands. How many days had she been there? What was taking so long? Surely Stefan had agreed to the ransom request. She gulped. Was there a ransom? A chill flowed through her spine. *God, don't let me die.* She sucked in a quick breath.

"Did anything happen during your shift? You look flushed."

Bella's voice. Who was she talking to?

"No. How was Manuel last night?"

Antonio had come back. She exhaled.

"He was quiet. He thinks they're closing in on him. The authorities searched one of his warehouses this morning. They found Moulin's blood on the floor and called in forensics. I say we kill the woman now. If we wait too long, she'll identify us."

"Manuel is firm with his decision."

"I don't understand. What's the point of holding her?"

"She's a distraction." Antonio spoke in a labored voice. "The agencies are focusing on her—not finding Euphoria. The longer they're preoccupied, the easier we can transfer the drug."

"But she's distracting me, too. I spend so much time here I can't get my work done. I hope I can get the drug ready by this weekend."

"I'll try to help you more."

"Thanks, Antonio. Has she stirred much?"

"She doesn't respond when I talk to her. I always check on the ropes. Sometimes they get loose. I know she picks at them."

"I noticed it too. I'll sedate her for the night. We can't risk her escaping."

"I know this isn't easy, but once Euphoria gets shipped, Manuel won't be as stressed." Antonio's voice grew softer as he spoke.

"I want this over with." Bella paused. "Are you sure you're okay? You're sweating like you ran a marathon."

"My shoulder's been hurting."

"Let me see."

"I'm okay."

"Let me see it...Oh, Antonio, it's infected. Didn't you see Dr. Fernando?"

"I hate doctors."

"You're going to have a date with a mortician if you don't get your ass to Fernando's office." Bella spoke in a shrill voice. "He'll put you on an antibiotic. I'll call and tell him you're coming. I can stay here until you come back."

A door closed, and the heavy footfalls faded. Lighter footsteps neared, and Bella's voice cackled. The woman grabbed Hailey's arm, and pierced the skin with a needle. Hailey stiffened, tightening her fists. *They won't defeat you. Stay strong...Mark!*

Chapter Forty-Five

After lunch with Colleen had ended and they returned to her workplace, Mark drove straight home. He steeled himself to visit the kids after he showered. How could he prevent his face from betraying his fears? When he had called earlier, his mother sounded suspicious. She could always tell when something was wrong. That night, he would have to tell his parents the shocking truth.

He collapsed on the sofa and stared at the wall. Did it hold some hidden clues that would lead him to Hailey? The place was quiet without her. He'd do anything to hear her squeal and laugh with the kids on the floor.

She had the cutest dimple on her chin when she smiled at his jokes. Even though most of them were corny. She'd giggle when he folded the laundry, and he'd laugh at her animated voice when she read bedtime stories.

He inhaled. He loved the vanilla-scented hand lotion she used before bed. The glint of gold in her iridescent eyes. Her honey lips on his. His insides would thump at her sweet, gentle kisses. They had been so happy. Somehow he lost focus on loving her, appreciating her. A week ago, his life was complete, and now everything was gone. He should have treated her better. He couldn't lose her.

Mark walked upstairs to the master bedroom. A heavy ache compressed in his chest. In an exhausted trance, he turned on the faucet and stepped into the shower.

The cold water pelted his skin and became hotter. He stared into nothingness, letting the scalding water hammer his body. The soap slipped from his hands, and he fell to his knees as the pain exploded inside him. He wasn't worthy to stand. *Please God, bring her home.*

In slow motion, he turned off the water and grabbed a towel, drying his body. As he buttoned his Oxford shirt, the doorbell chimed. Grabbing his jacket, he rushed down the stairs and cracked open the door. A young man in his late twenties, sporting a perky smile, greeted him.

Great. A salesman. Mark tucked his shirt in his jeans. "Yes?"

"Howdy, sir. Is Hailey available?"

"No, she's not. And you are?"

The man's smiled faded. "Do you know when she'll come back?"

"No." Mark put on his jacket and glanced at his watch. His mother expected him five minutes ago. Why wasn't the man budging? "Can I give her a message?"

The caller scratched his cheek. "I thought she'd be home by now. Are you her husband?"

Mark studied him closer. "How do you know Hailey?"

"I met her last week. She told me to stop over after my conference so we could have supper together."

A surge of hope ran down his spine, renewing him. "Are you with the SCA?"

"I'm sorry. I can't divulge that. I'm Ernie Banks." He stressed his name as if Mark should recognize him.

Mark dropped his jaw. The man was much younger than he'd envisioned. "You're Cubby?"

"Yes, sir. I am. Do you know where I can find her?"

Could he trust this man? "She's been away for a few days."

Ernie frowned. "I'm sorry I missed her. I did a procedure on her the other day. She planned on giving me a tour of Washington, D.C. if I found the time."

"You're a doctor?"

"Yes, sir, I'm sorry. I thought she told you about me."

"You work at the SCA?"

"Well, I…"

Mark clenched his hands. Would he have to shake the answers from him? "Hailey's missing. If you know anything, you've got to tell me."

The color drained from Ernie's face. "She's missing? I didn't know. Where's Parker?"

"Something went wrong with the assignment. He got away, but we don't know where Hailey is."

Ernie scratched his head. "Why aren't y'all using the GPS?"

"She dropped her phone when she tried to escape. The GPS is useless."

"No, the GPS in her cochlear implants. The ones I…"

"The what?"

"The implants for her ears. She's deaf without them. Last week I inserted a more sensitive model. Ones restructured with a GPS system."

He shook his head. "Wait a second. You can track her?"

Ernie nodded. "I'll need to log my laptop into the SCA network, but yes, I can pin down her position. I'll call Stefan and tell him. We can use the satellite office."

A spark of hope lit inside Mark. He grabbed his keys, turned the lock on the doorknob, and closed the front door. "What are we waiting for? Let's go!"

Chapter Forty-Six

The voice on the phone was frantic. "Bella, listen. Agents are on their way. Thirty minutes, tops. Ditch whatever you can and get out."

She clenched her hands and screeched. "No! I need more time." She hurried around the room, wiping fingerprints. It wasn't perfect, but she got most of the prints or smeared them.

Hailey was still out cold. Bella loosened the ropes around her wrists and ankles. She opened her bag and pulled out a long syringe, injecting the contents into Hailey's arm. This would counteract the sedative's effects. She had been anticipating this moment. Bella would let the woman enjoy one freaked-out high before she died. But Hailey had to die. Why should this woman and her husband stay together when Bella didn't have her *happily ever after* yet?

Bella scanned the room, double-checking she hadn't overlooked some telltale evidence. Satisfied, she grabbed her bag and closed the door.

Chapter Forty-Seven

Using Hailey's phone, Mark called Owen from the car as he drove Ernie into SCA headquarters. "Dispatch a rescue team to the SCA ASAP. I texted Parker and Greg. They'll meet me there." He filled Owen in on the latest events.

When Mark and Ernie stepped off the elevator, Greg and six agents from the DTA waited in Stefan's office. An agent from IT assisted Ernie at the computer while Stefan organized his men for the rescue.

Mark hovered as Ernie logged on the laptop. "Why is the computer so slow?"

Ernie lifted his head. "It's searching for the signal. While I wait, hand me your cell phone and I'll install the GPS software on it. You can monitor Hailey on the phone once we locate her."

He pulled Hailey's phone from his jacket. Ernie connected a cable to the device; his fingers glided around the keyboard as he began the download.

A loud knock pounded on the door, and Parker rushed in, scanning the room. He nodded at Mark. "Thanks for the text. Did you get the location yet?"

Mark paced the floor and shook his head.

From his desk, Stefan set down the phone, and Parker neared him. "Stefan, how many agents do you have available?"

"Four plus you. They're mobilized downstairs."

Ernie looked up from the screen. "The signal's working. Hailey's here in the District. Better notify the police."

Stefan picked up the handset. "I'll alert them."

The group gathered closer behind Ernie, waiting, until at last he jumped from his seat. "Got it!"

Mark dashed over to him. "You found her?"

"Yes." Ernie pointed to the screen. "Here's the address. She's not too far."

The agents typed the address into their phones as Stefan issued specific orders about the rescue. "Okay. We're set."

Disconnecting the computer cable, Ernie handed the cell phone back to Mark. "It's downloaded. She's the yellow blip on the screen. Can I come along?"

Frowning, Mark tightened his grip around the phone. "I'd rather you didn't. I can't risk you getting hurt in any crossfire. I'll call you once we find her." He clutched his car keys from his pocket and turned to the group. "Let's head out."

On the ground floor, they rushed out of the elevator and raced toward their cars. Greg plucked the keys from him. "I'll drive. You'll kill us before we get there." Mark opened the passenger side door and narrowed his eyes as Parker jumped in the backseat.

The car sped through the city as Mark called Owen with an update and monitored Hailey's location. When Greg stopped behind a line of cars at a red light, Mark slammed his fist on the dash. "Dammit! Use the siren and run the lights."

Greg glanced sideways at him. "Let me do the driving. You'll get us in an accident. Hailey's going to be all right."

"You're damn right, or I'll kill those assholes with my bare hands." He pointed at the changing light. "Step on it."

Chapter Forty-Eight

Hailey's brain fog lifted, and a tingling electric charge surged through her body. She was alert with a clear mind, though her heart thumped out of control. Lifting her arm, she tore off the blindfold in a hard tug and blinked, allowing her vision to adjust to the dim room. Moisture dripped from her brows as she slipped off the ropes dangling around her hands. Her evening dress covered her, but it was now wrinkled, stained, and torn. The room spun around her like a centrifuge. She wiggled the ropes off her ankles, and they transformed into snakes.

Slivers of light punched through the window blinds, highlighting a path to a door. She steadied herself against the wall, trying to stay vertical on her wobbly legs. The gateway to the door called her. She inched her way closer. Hurry. Her hand touched the smooth lever and she opened the door.

A blast of sunlight blinded her, and spots floated across her eyes. A sharp pain throbbed across her head as if a sledgehammer hit her. Squinting, she fumbled on the wrought-iron railing outside her door, and it melted in her palms. Something was wrong. Was she hallucinating? The sensations were so real.

A circus tent with walled off rooms encircled her, each with its own colorful door. Wherever she turned, costumed clowns gawked. The kidnappers from her youth stood beside her in clown masks, grabbing at her. Madge's voice rang with laughter. She shrank back at the distorted figures. They looked like images reflected in a funhouse mirror. The clowns eyed her and approached, ripping newborn babies from their abdomens.

She spun around again. A horror show with grotesque aliens surrounded her. Hailey bumped into one and squawked. The alien spoke in a garbled language. She lost her balance and fell, but she pushed herself upright and hobbled away. A strange creature brandishing a syringe raced toward her. Faster and faster, she hurried. She looked back. Hairy beasts stretched their arms, chasing her. They wanted her blood! They were collecting her DNA! The mother spaceship with lights above in the sky harbored the alien's genetic material. She could sabotage their DNA. She stumbled to the double helix rising over a pool of fluorescent blue cytoplasm slime. Her hand tightened around a nucleotide.

Chapter Forty-Nine

Mark's heart pummeled inside his chest as he stared at the blip on the screen. This was his one link to Hailey. He glanced at the neglected apartment buildings with broken windows and clenched his jaw. His wife was a hostage among these thugs. "Hurry! We're almost there."

Greg honked, maneuvering the wheel around a group of teens wearing dark hooded sweatshirts loitering on the sidewalk. He stomped on the brakes and screeched the car's tires as he turned a hard left into the Sunrise Motel parking lot. The other patrol cars followed.

Mark bolted from the car, racing past the delinquents hanging around the street. He checked the screen. "She's moving!" Parker caught up and ran beside him. They followed the signal to the rear of the building. Mark lifted his head and skimmed the vicinity. "Where is she?"

Parker pointed to a group next to the motel pool. "There."

It was near dusk. A figure in green scrambled up a pool ladder. The guests massed together, buzzing among themselves, pointing, and speculating.

Waving his arms, Mark hastened toward her, tears brimming his eyes. "Hailey!"

"Adenine. Thymine." She twisted her torso and glanced down. "Get away from me!" Her speech was slurred. Wavering, she climbed faster, glancing at the crowd. "Guanine, Cytosine…"

"Hailey! Stop!" Mark grabbed the first rung of the ladder and turned his head. "I can't make out what she's saying."

Parker slowed his steps. "Oh, God. She doesn't recognize us."

Mark climbed, following her movements. He could save her.

Hailey grabbed the top rung. The bottom of her dress tangled between a step and the rails. She ripped her gown free and crawled on the diving board. She stood, her legs quavering.

"Mark! Don't startle her. She'll fall."

Hailey advanced forward on the platform. She tripped on her tattered gown and spread her arms, grasping the air. Mark's hand clung to the sixth rung, powerless to stop her as she plummeted into the water. The guests' screams masked her cry. Parker dove into the pool and disappeared below the surface.

"Hailey!" Mark hurried down the ladder and raced to the pool's edge. Parker broke the surface. His arms looped around Hailey's waist as he swam toward Mark, performing rescue breathing. Parker raised her in the air.

Mark's arms shook as he clutched Hailey's limp body. He laid her down on the cement surface and brushed the tangled hair off her face. "Call 911!" Blood dripped from her nose. Leaning over, he placed his ear next to her mouth. No air brushed his cheeks. Her chest didn't rise. "Hailey!" He placed his fingers on her neck.

Oh, God, no. He knelt over her abdomen and started chest compressions. The rhythm of each squeeze transmitted his plea. "Come on, come on, come on…"

The agents held back the crowd as Greg ushered the paramedics to the pool's deck. Greg placed a hand on Mark's shoulder. "Move back. Let the paramedics work." When he wouldn't leave, Greg and Parker wrapped their arms around Mark and dragged him off Hailey.

Mark's gaze remained glued to her. The rescue workers attached electrodes to her chest, and he moaned, bearing her pain. Her body jolted in the air. He flinched and started running to her, but Parker held him back. Losing hope, he buckled to the ground. *Please, God, no. No…Don't let her die…*The minutes passed like sand stuck in an hourglass.

Finally, her arms flailed, and she vomited.

Chapter Fifty

Mark tapped his foot and peered at the clock on the waiting room wall. Hailey had been in the ER for three hours and twenty-one minutes. He looked at Parker sitting next to him, holding a cup of coffee. "What's taking so long?"

Parker shrugged. "These things take time. The doctors have to examine her."

The doors had swooshed open throughout the night. Mark leaped from his chair each time an attendant walked past. Now their faces blurred together. A brown-haired nurse dressed in scrubs scurried by, not even glancing at him. He started chasing her. "Dammit! Someone talk to me. What's going on with my wife?"

Standing, Parker patted his shoulder. "Let's take a walk. The fresh air will do you good."

"But—"

"Don't worry. The nurses will find us."

Parker led the way outside as another ambulance entered the ambulance bay. He handed Mark the coffee, shouting over the high-pitched siren. "Here, this might help."

Mark took the cup. "Thanks."

"What happened in the ambulance?"

"It was awful." He rubbed his forehead, trying to stop his body from shaking. "She climbed off the stretcher while they were putting in the IV. I held her hand and tried to calm her, but it was useless."

"Did she say anything?"

"Nothing coherent. She looked at me and screamed. She begged the paramedics to let her die before the alien took her. Then she threw up and had a seizure." Mark's voice trembled. "I've never seen anything like it."

Parker's lips tightened into a thin line. "This place has an excellent trauma center. She's in good hands." His phone rang. He pulled it out of his pocket and looked at the screen. "Do you mind if I take this call?"

Mark shook his head. "No, go ahead."

Parker turned his back and lowered his voice. "Grace, how's Justin?"

"No change since we talked this afternoon. Where are you?" Mark recognized Grace from their conversation in Chicago. Her shrill voice echoed through the phone.

Parker put a hand up next to his ear. "I'm still tracking down the drug Justin took."

"Forget the drug. This is insane. How could you pick up and leave us?" Grace's voice rose even louder. "Your son needs you."

He stretched his neck left and right. "If I find the drug, the doctor can treat him."

"You need to come home. Dr. Buchanan said Justin's getting weaker every day." Her voice broke. "Damn you. Justin needs you. I need you."

"All right. I'll get a flight out tomorrow." Parker's voice cracked. "Keep talking to him. Tell Justin I love him." The phone disconnected with a sharp click. He wiped his eyes and turned. "Ahem. Sorry about that."

"It's okay. I forgot that you're going through the same thing as me."

Parker patted his shoulder. "Hailey's a fighter. She's going to make it."

Mark raised his arm and wiped his eyes on his jacket sleeve. "I can't lose her."

"You're not going to lose her."

Overcome by emotion, Mark closed his eyes and brushed a hand across his runny nose. He inhaled a deep breath and opened his eyes. Parker stood watching him.

"Do you need anything?"

Mark shook his head. "No…Yeah. Can you call Owen? Tell him what happened."

Parker nodded. "I already did. And I've talked to Greg. He and the other agents are staying back. They're sealing off the hotel room. They want to run interviews before the guests check out in the morning. Greg said he'll stop by later if it's not too late."

"I'm sure he'll be busy tonight."

"I imagine."

"Would you mind calling Ernie Banks and updating him on the rescue?"

"I did that, too. He took a cab here and rushed into the exam room while you were pacing the hallway. He'll come out and talk to us when he can."

"Thank you." Mark took a gulp from the coffee cup and spit it on the ground. "Ew. This is awful."

Parker chuckled. "I know."

"Then why did you give it to me?"

"I hated to waste it. I thought it would wake you up." Parker patted his shoulder. "Come on. Let's go back in."

When they sat down in the waiting area chairs, a physician clad in bloodstained scrubs entered the room. Mark raced to him. "How's Hailey?"

"Are you her husband?"

Trembling, he nodded. "Yes, I'm Mark Langley. How is she?"

The doctor shook his hand. "I'm Dr. Gewant. I'm the Chief of Emergency Medicine. Your wife's condition is critical. She's getting fluids for her dehydration. Our primary concern is her nervous system. I'm waiting on her blood work. We're treating her symptoms until we know more. Fortunately, she received immediate medical attention.

"Can I see her?"

Dr. Gewant nodded. "Once she moves to ICU. The nurses are preparing her room now." His expression turned more solemn. "Unfortunately, there's something else."

"What?"

"Your wife's in a coma."

"A coma?"

"She's on a respirator, and she's on a defibrillator to stabilize her heart. The nerve receptors that stimulate muscle impulses are blocked. It's affecting the vagus nerve. We're monitoring her, but her condition is grave."

A chill went through Mark. "She's going to live, isn't she?"

Dr. Gewant's lips drew taut. "We're doing everything we can. We need to identify what's causing the problem."

Parker stood. "It's got to be Euphoria."

Mark jerked his head. "You're crazy."

Parker's eyes widened. "No, I'm not. She behaved like the kids who overdosed in Chicago. Didn't you hear what she said when she climbed the ladder? She was stoned."

"She was confused. How would you act if someone shanghaied you for three days?"

"Confused?" Parker's jaw dropped. "She was naming the DNA base pairs! She was hallucinating."

"Euphoria?" Dr. Gewant furrowed his brow. "Isn't that the new drug from Chicago?"

Parker nodded.

Frowning, Ernie walked into the waiting room and nodded at Mark. He handed a paper to Dr. Gewant. "The labs are in."

Dr. Gewant took the report and scratched his head. "This isn't good. We'll have a hard time treating her until we know the drug's classification."

Parker waited as a nurse walked past carrying an IV bag. "We tried to get info on the drug. Hailey took pictures of the structural formula. But she dropped the phone when they kidnapped her."

Mark patted his pocket. "Wait. I found Hailey's phone on the floor that night." He removed it from his jacket and pulled up the photos.

Parker grasped the phone. "Dammit! The answer's been here the whole time." He showed the pictures to the two doctors. "Here's the chemical structure of Euphoria."

Clutching the phone, Ernie looked at the picture. "Euphoria? That's the drug Bruce is working on."

"Say again?" Parker's eyes grew wide.

Ernie nodded. "I overheard him talking on the phone a few times. I'm sure that's what he called it."

He passed Hailey's cell phone to Dr. Gewant, swapping it for the lab report.

"Send me the image and I'll make some phone calls." Dr. Gewant handed the phone back to Mark. "One of the nurses can give you my email."

Mark rubbed his unshaven chin. "Who's Bruce?"

Ernie looked up from studying the lab results. "Bruce Hanover. He's the Chief of Staff at the SCA. He specializes in technology innovations."

A sudden coldness spread through Mark. "What's he doing with Euphoria?"

Parker reached in his pants pocket and pulled out a phone. "I don't know, but I'm damn well going to find out."

Ernie crossed his arms and waited as Parker searched his contacts. "Try using video chat. Bruce has it on his phone."

Mark stood near Parker as he made the call. An image of an elderly man appeared on the screen. "Parker? Howdy! I was ready to leave for the night. What's going on? You look upset."

"Cubby and I are at the hospital. We need your help. Hailey's in bad shape."

"What? Why?"

"Someone gave her the drug Euphoria."

"Euphoria?" Bruce stammered. "That's impossible."

"Bullshit!" Parker clenched his fists. "It's on the streets."

Mark grabbed for the phone. "Hasn't he seen the news?"

Stepping away, Parker raised the phone from Mark's reach.

"I-I-I don't watch TV. I barely leave this place." Bruce clutched his chest.

Parker's eyes narrowed. "Then get your head out of the lab and read the newspaper. Almost thirty people have died already."

Mark stood behind Parker and waited as Bruce scratched his head. "It can't be." The elderly man stuttered as he spoke. "Euphoria's experimental. It's not a street drug." He lowered his head and mumbled, "How did it get out?"

Parker shrugged. "It doesn't matter now. I need you to focus. Can you help? Justin's been in the hospital since last week and Hailey's in critical condition. The doctors are at a loss."

"Oh, no." Bruce looked up, his voice shaky. "I added an anticholinergic as a safeguard so people can't steal the drug. It inhibits the nerve impulses. Blocks acetylcholine from binding to nerve cell receptors. Anyone using Euphoria will suffer neurological effects, become comatose, and die."

"Die?" Mark gulped and grabbed for the phone again.

Parker held the phone away from Mark. "Hailey's already in a coma." He choked. "The doctors can't stabilize her."

"And Justin?"

"He's been in a coma since last week—and growing weaker. Are you saying there's no hope…no cure for them?"

"I didn't say that. I'd never create a drug without a remedy. Both Justin and Hailey need the antidote to pull off the anticholinergic." Bruce leaned toward the screen. "Is Cubby still there?"

Ernie moved in front of Mark. "I'm here, Bruce."

"Hailey needs the antidote right quick and then she should be infused with an acetylcholine supplement. Watch her for seizures. I'll text you specifics now on the supplement and the dosages for the antidote's formula."

"Okay. Can the pharmacy make the solution?"

"Yes, they should have it on hand. Once it binds the inhibitor, the symptoms should begin to clear." Bruce paused. "Where's Justin admitted? I'll call the hospital and consult with his doctors."

Parker gave him the information. "Thanks. I'll take the next flight out to Chicago."

Anxiously hoping for a miracle, Mark turned to Parker and blinked back tears.

****

A friendly blonde-haired nurse escorted Mark to the ICU after midnight. His skin turned cold at the sight of the tubes running around Hailey's head and chest. The machines connected to her body sputtered strange pumping noises. Mark rocked side to side, staring at Hailey until his knees buckled. He collapsed on the chair next to the bed. Her chest movements matched the beeps on one of the contraptions.

Up. Down. Up. Down.

He caught the sympathetic looks on the nurses' faces. Helpless, he stared at the machines keeping her alive. His chest tightened, and he struggled to breathe. Finally, he inhaled and smelled the disinfectant. The room felt like a holding zone, waiting for her frail body to die. *Dear God, how did this happen?*

A breathing tube sealed her mouth. He leaned over and let his finger brush her cheek, her warmth the only sign of life. He sat in silence, unable to take his gaze from her ethereal appearance, and his fists tightened. What hell had she gone through? Someone would pay for this! He sighed. Revenge didn't matter now. *Open your eyes, Hailey.*

Scabs and welts formed a bracelet around her bruised wrist. He winced and picked up her limp hand. Tiny scars tracked her delicate skin. Scars from her scratching. He had never registered the significance of the marks. What was she hiding from him?

Trembling, he held her slender fingers against his cheek, and a sob rose in his chest. *Stay strong. For Hailey.* If he could do things over, he wouldn't waste time dwelling on her past. He would surprise her with more gifts. Tell her how beautiful she was. How much he loved her. He would make more family time. Leave work early to see Ethan's soccer games. He wouldn't forget their anniversary. Would they get a chance at another year?

He rubbed his arms, but the shivering persisted. His chest was heavy, his insides caving in. A tear slid down his cheek. "Hailey. I'm here. I'm not going anywhere." Another tear fell. "I love you. Why didn't I tell you more often? You're everything to me. I can't lose you."

As the tears spilled down his cheeks, Mark rubbed them away. "Fight, honey. You've got to fight," he whispered. "I love you. I'll make things up to you. Please, come back." He laid his forehead against her palm and inhaled her skin. "Don't leave me...I love you...I can't live without you." He cried, letting exhaustion overtake him. Then he slept.

Chapter Fifty-One

"Bella!"

She dropped the beaker and froze. Shit. The receptionist must have taken an early lunch. Where could she hide? The supply closet was too full. The office was an option, but she had to face him sooner or later.

"Dammit, Bella! Where are you?" His voice was getting louder. She ducked behind the counter and peered out.

The lab door swung open, and Manuel stomped through the lab, his face crimson. "You gave her the drug, didn't you? I know you're here. Don't try to hide from me."

Inhaling, she stood from behind a counter and shrugged. "We needed to buy more time. I couldn't risk anyone finding you. By the time she dies, Euphoria will be on its way."

Manuel tramped closer and raised his hand. "I told you not to hurt the girl—and Antonio reminded you. Several times."

Garnering courage, she bent down and read the meniscus from a graduated cylinder. Manuel's temper had become sharper over the past few days, but this was still her lab. Her territory. She recorded the value on a clipboard and raised her head. "I did you a favor. You always make Antonio do your dirty work. Well, I'm not afraid to do it, either."

"We're better than that, Bella. Why do you think I use Antonio?"

"We couldn't risk witnesses."

Manuel slammed his fist against the counter. "Dammit! There wasn't any evidence linking this project to her."

She rolled her eyes and walked past him. "You're so naive."

His hand shot out and grabbed her arm, hard. "You'd better change your attitude, missy." His stare emitted hot lava.

She flinched and dropped the clipboard. "Or what?" She shook her arm from his grasp. "You'll hurt me? Kill me? Who's going to do your research then?" She threw a disposable pipette in the biohazard bag and rubbed her arm. "Don't threaten me. You seem to forget who gave you the idea for this venture in the first place."

"Bella." He lifted her chin to meet his gaze.

She tried desperately to stop the water pooling in her eyes. This was the biggest argument they ever had. He had never harmed her before now.

Manuel stared at her arm and recoiled at the red blotch. "I'm sorry. I didn't mean to hurt you. I have a lot on my mind. Between the operation and my father, I'm stressed." He kissed her arm. "I'm so sorry."

Shaking, she jutted her lips and picked up the clipboard, collapsing in the closest chair.

He touched her hair. "Darling, I know you're upset. But after we ship the drugs, I want us to fly to Colombia and start our own family."

Her mouth opened, but no words came.

Manuel knelt on one knee, and his expression softened. "Why do you think I want you to meet my parents? *Te amo mucho.* I want to marry you. To make love to you every night and watch you sleep in my arms." His finger caressed under her chin. "I want you to have my babies."

Her hands trembled again. "Manuel. Do you mean it?"

He nodded. "My father's a harsh man, but my mother is different. Family is everything to me. I bought the airline tickets already. I was going to surprise you at dinner tomorrow. We leave Saturday night."

Bella lowered her head. "I'm sorry I doubted you. I didn't want…" She stopped. He wouldn't understand the real reason she injected Euphoria into Hailey. She leaned over and kissed him. "Forgive me. I promise it won't happen again."

A faint smile lit his smoldering eyes. "I can't stay angry at you." He kissed her, more passionately, held it long. Slowly, he pulled away. Manuel stood and gestured at the papers scattered across the counter. "What's the status of Euphoria?"

She brushed back stray hairs falling around her face and stood next to him. "I'm behind schedule because of all the interruptions, but I'd feel better running synergy studies."

Manuel waved a dismissive hand. "Do what you want. Something is still wrong. Antonio said the girl is in a coma. Find out what the problem is and fix it. The shipment needs to be picked up Saturday afternoon at the mansion. We can use the old cargo van in the garage to transport the drug. Antonio will help you. Our buyers are waiting."

She nodded. At least he consented to further testing. "I'll have everything ready. Are you coming over to my place again tonight?"

"No, it's too risky. I'll stay with Antonio. The vacation house is more secluded. Cerdo said the agents found the hidden entrance at the mansion. We shouldn't use our phones either." He bent down and gave her a gentle kiss. "I won't rest until this is over. I'll leave your plane ticket with the receptionist and meet you Saturday at the airport."

"Thanks." She blew him a kiss as he left. Smiling, she picked up the clipboard and began working. She would have to hurry. Colombia. Wow! Somehow, between the hubbub, she needed to pack.

Chapter Fifty-Two

Mark spent the day at Hailey's bedside. He stared at her frail body, hoping for an eyelid to twitch or a finger to move. Anything to show she would pull through this nightmare. The ICU nurses stole into the private room and performed their quiet routine. Beside the bed, the IV bag dripped with the antidote. Hailey seemed at peace, but he longed to hold her. No. He wanted to grab her arms and shake her until she woke. *"Please, God. Let her live. I promise I'll come home more. Give us a second chance. I'll be a better husband. Please...Take me instead. Don't let her die!"*

Cubby supervised the administration of the antidote. He stayed with Mark most of the day and left in the evening to catch his flight back to Texas. Stefan stopped by before he flew out to San Francisco on another case. Mark had been alone for an hour when the phone rang. "Hello?"

"Mark, it's Tamara. I heard what happened. I'm so sorry. Do you need anything?"

He blinked hard, unable to control his emotions. "No."

"I'll stop by later. I'm sure you could use a friend."

"Thanks. That means a lot."

"I know this is the last thing on your mind, but your friend David called. He's left several messages for you to call him back. He went to Duke and spoke with Kay Sherman's son. He said he learned some info on the Sherman case you might find interesting."

"Did you tell him about Hailey?"

"No, I didn't want to give out any of your personal information."

"If he calls again, tell him I'm at the hospital with Hailey. Give Greg the messages—he knows about the case."

"Okay. Owen notified the unit yesterday that Greg was handling your cases. Greg's been working nonstop, searching for clues on Hailey's kidnappers. I should go. I'll talk to you soon."

An hour later, a knock drummed on the door, and Greg peeked in the room. "You up for visitors?"

Mark nodded, but couldn't speak. Greg and Owen walked in the room, carrying a paper bag and a foam cup.

"How's she doing?" Greg whispered.

"She's still getting the antidote. We have to wait and see." Misty-eyed, he choked back a sob. "The doctors said they're doing their best…all they can, but…" He lowered his head.

Greg patted his shoulder. "She'll pull through. Hailey's tough."

Owen set the paper bag and cup on the overbed tray. "We brought you some sandwiches and coffee. Figured you might need them."

Mark wiped his cheeks. "Thanks. Maybe later."

"Greg and I can sit here if you need a break. Why don't you lie down in the lounge and try to get some sleep?"

"No, I want to stay in case she wakes."

"Then we'll keep you company." Greg pulled two chairs closer to the bed. "I never apologized for the other day. I was wrong to say those things about Hailey. I should've trusted your instincts."

Owen nodded. "We were asses."

Mark had forgotten about the argument. "Don't worry about it. She's here. Nothing else matters." He rubbed his temples. "How's the case going?"

Greg's expression soured. "Not well. We worked all day and still can't get a description of the kidnappers. The desk clerk doesn't remember who rented the room."

"What about the payment? Did they use a credit card?"

"They paid two weeks upfront. Cash. No prints showed up in the room."

"No fingerprints?"

"None." Owen folded his arms over his chest. "Motel guests come and go daily. Other than Hailey's prints on the doorknob, we found nothing. It's absurd that the alarm clock, TV remote, *and* phone were clean. Hell, there wasn't even a fingerprint on the damn toilet handle! Either the motel employs the most competent housekeeping staff on the planet or the room was wiped clean."

Heat rose along Mark's neck to his face. "Someone tipped them off."

Greg nodded. "It looks that way."

"Dammit!" Mark ran a hand through his hair. "How did they learn the news so fast? We didn't pin down Hailey's location until right before we drove to the motel."

"I agree. But it took time to connect into the computer. And we fought traffic when we rode across town."

"Still, that was half an hour."

Greg's brows narrowed. "Do you think the doctor from Texas leaked something?"

Mark blinked hard. "Ernie? No. He was shocked when I told him about Hailey."

"You're right." Greg frowned. "He wouldn't suggest using the GPS if he was in on it."

Owen stood and paced the floor. "Who else knew about the rescue besides Parker?"

As if on cue, the door opened, and Parker stepped in the room. Mark curled his lips. Parker nodded at him and strode to the foot of Hailey's bed. "How's she doing?"

Mark squeezed his eyes shut. The wave of emotion passed. "The same. The antidote's been dripping for hours. All we can do is wait."

"That's promising, isn't it?" Parker spoke in a thick voice. The gray skin on his face stretched tight, and his eyes sank in dark caves. None of the men looked good. As they stared at Hailey, the tension in the room simmered and thickened.

Owen stood first, breaking the awkwardness. "Greg and I should go. We have work in the morning. Call if we can do anything. We'll check in again tomorrow." The two men shook Mark's hand and left.

Parker dragged an empty chair closer to the bed and sat. "She looks...pale."

He grunted. "What do you expect? She's been missing for days."

"Oh, give me a break. I haven't seen Hailey since I pulled her out of the pool."

Mark studied him. He shouldn't pass judgement when Parker had his own troubles. "Sorry. I'm tired. I didn't mean to take out my frustrations on you."

Parker flashed a mirthless smile. "It's all right. This isn't easy on anyone."

Turning to his wife, Mark pressed his face against Hailey's hand. *Please, God. Kindle the embers inside her. Give her the strength to fight.* He glanced at Parker, who seemed lost in his own world, and turned his attention back to Hailey. "Did you ever love someone so deeply a part of you died inside when they got hurt?" Mark hadn't intended to say that aloud.

"Yes," Parker whispered.

Mark glared at him. "Hailey's *my* wife."

Parker's eyes went cold. He folded his arms and straightened in the chair. "Look. I didn't come here to pick a fight. I'm aware you're married, but I'm not talking about Hailey."

"Oh." His voice softened. "Who are you talking about?"

"My son."

Mark looked at him. "It's been so crazy here I forgot to ask about him."

"My problem. You have your own. I tried not to bring him up."

"How old is he?"

"He was seventeen."

"Was?"

"He died…late last night."

"What?" Mark stared, searching Parker's face for some type of emotion.

Parker lowered his gaze to the tiled floor. "Damn drugs." He drew in a breath. "I flew...to Chicago to see him...but he died before I arrived."

"I'm sorry."

"Yeah. Life sucks." Parker glanced up. A hushed fury filled his voice. "I fucking hate this world...so unfair. My God, Justin was only a boy. He'd just started living. A stupid mistake. One stupid, stupid mistake. Now, no graduation. No college. No girlfriend...no living...nothing. A big...fat...zippo." His voice grew angrier, louder. "He was cheated out of life. All because of the fucking drugs. How can we protect our kids when drugs are everywhere? This is so...damn...unfair." Parker stood, and the chair slid away, as if it, too, was trying to escape the room.

Mark walked over to him and put his arm around Parker's shoulder, struggling to find the right words. "Man, I'm really sorry."

Parker's eyes flickered with sadness, and he lowered his head to his chest. "Why did this have to happen to him? He was a good kid. Why him?" He furiously wiped his face with his sleeve. "God, I'd do anything to have him back. He'll be...Funeral is the day after tomorrow. We made the arrangements."

"Why didn't you stay? You should go back."

"I'm flying back tomorrow. I came here to make sure the antidote helped Hailey...even though it was too late for Justin."

A pall of silence hovered over the room. Mark offered Parker the coffee on the table and said a prayer for him. For some reason, God had brought them together. They were an ill-suited pair, linked together by a common love.

Chapter Fifty-Three

Mark woke to the gentle knock on the door. He must have drifted off in his chair. Parker was still sleeping, his head bowed down onto his chest. The door opened a crack and an old man poked his head through the doorway. Mark recognized him from the video call. He nudged Parker. "Bruce is here."

Parker rushed to the door, and he followed.

"I got a flight as soon as I could." Bruce stood at the doorway, his hands fidgeting with the black trilby hat he gripped. "I flew to Chicago first, but you had already left. I'm so sorry about Justin."

Parker nodded and blinked. "I keep thinking this is a bad dream—that I'll wake up and find Justin recuperating in the hospital bed."

Tears welled in Bruce's eyes. The feeble man was much older than Mark imagined. "I'm sorry about Hailey, too. I know you're both heartbroken. I don't understand how this happened."

Parker thrust Bruce against the door. "Damn you. How did you get mixed up with a drug lord?"

Mark wrapped his arms around Parker's shoulders and pulled him off Bruce. "I know you're upset, but this isn't the place, Parker."

Bruce's hands quivered as he folded the hat in his coat pocket. "Let me explain."

"Explain? Your drug killed my son!"

A nurse walking past gave them a stern look. Bruce's face turned red. "Can we talk someplace private?"

Mark closed the door and led them to the elevator.

They found an empty corner in the cafeteria, away from the groups of nurses and staff taking a morning break. Parker took a seat across the table from Bruce and crossed his arms over his chest. "Okay. Start talking."

Bruce rubbed his eyes and took a deep breath. "Three years ago, a man named Manuel de Mendoza approached me, asked me to investigate dopamine. He said he owned a pharmaceutical company and needed scientists to work on his project. He offered me a grant to do his research. Said it would be a huge advancement for medicine."

Parker straightened in his chair. "You know it's illegal to conduct personal experiments on government property?"

"I know, but I couldn't pass up the offer."

Mark leaned toward the table. "Why dopamine?"

"There's a lot more to dopamine than we once believed." Bruce's voice filled with excitement. "We knew it masked pain and controlled behavior. But it's linked to other disorders, too—autism, OCD, schizophrenia, and depression. For years, I've worked to prove there are distinct subtypes of receptors and I've mapped gene locations. When the research became too expensive, I had to stop. Then Mendoza came along with his grant."

"How much money did he offer?"

"Ten million."

Mark gasped. "Seriously?"

Bruce spread his arms wide. "I made huge strides. Injections of dopamine only work to some degree in the peripheral nervous system. It hasn't infiltrated the central nervous system where the brain's pleasure center is—until now. I created a way for dopamine to cross the blood-brain barrier."

Parker gave a quick laugh and unfolded his arms. "That's impossible."

"No, it isn't." Bruce grabbed a napkin from the table and reached his hand into a shirt pocket. He removed a pen and sketched out structural formulas. "I found a protein to act as a transporter. When I bind the amine group in dopamine to the carrier protein, the structure of the benzene ring alters. It crosses into the central nervous system. I tagged my injections with fluorescent labels to prove it."

Parker's jaw dropped. "Bruce, this is big."

A glow spread across Bruce's face, and he nudged the eyeglasses higher on his nose. "I knew you'd appreciate the significance of this finding, Parker. But I'm running into a problem. The dopamine is fragile. The bonds linking the complex pop like a tightly wound spring. Once the compound crosses the blood brain barrier, it breaks down. The euphoric feeling doesn't last long. I need to find a way to make the transmitter stay intact longer."

Parker's face showed concern. "But is it worth subjecting patients to the side effects? Hemorrhaging, vomiting, hallucina—"

"The dopamine isn't stable long enough to cause those reactions." Bruce wrinkled his brow and turned to Mark. "Do you have a picture of the drug?"

"Yes." Mark turned on Hailey's cell phone and showed him the formula.

"Aparistine." Bruce banged his hand against the table.

"What's wrong?"

"The image is different from my dopamine." Bruce sketched the figure from Mark's phone on the napkin next to the original. "Look"—he pointed at the napkin—"there's another compound attached here. I haven't seen it in years. Where did you get this?"

"From a researcher in Chicago. A man named Charles Moulin. We think Mendoza killed him last week. We found his blood in Mendoza's abandoned warehouse."

Bruce's smile disappeared. "Chuck's dead?" He stood and paced around the table. "I can't imagine someone outfoxed that arrogant jerk."

Mark narrowed his eyes. "You know him?"

"We went to med school together."

Parker's phone buzzed. "It's Grace. I have to get this. She wanted to talk about the funeral arrangements." He walked to the rear door and stood outside in the hallway.

Bruce removed his glasses. "This is beginning to make sense."

"What do you mean?" Mark couldn't figure out the old man's reasoning.

"During school, four of us students tested the impact of aparistine on the brain. We had hoped the project would launch our medical careers."

"Aparistine? I never heard of it."

"It's rare. It's in the plant *Bixa aparra*. Chuck, er…Charles came across the shrub in the Amazon."

"Why was he in the Amazon?"

"He and his father traveled there one summer before college." Bruce sat in a chair next to Mark. "They noticed the aborigines using the shrub. When Chuck and his father tried it, the high seemed harmless. They smuggled some saplings on the plane back to the States. Chuck started a little greenhouse. He developed a method to extract aparistine from the leaves and refine it into a powder."

"Wasn't that prohibited—testing drugs at the university?"

Bruce's cheeks turned red. "Technically aparistine wasn't classified as an illegal drug since no one knew it existed. The loophole allowed us to stay within university policy. We wanted to test something no one else had. The data helped us map dopamine pathways. The other projects in the class didn't come close."

Mark rubbed his temple. "You've worked on dopamine all these years?"

"My entire life." Bruce's face brightened. "I've always wondered how people experience euphoria when neurotransmitters activate. Now we can help patients with mental illnesses and Parkinson's."

Mark shook his head. "This is too much medical lingo for me."

Parker walked toward them and sat in a chair, his red eyes wet with tears. "What did I miss?"

He and Bruce filled Parker in on *Bixa aparra* and aparistine. Mark scratched his bristly stubble. "How did the college project turn out?"

Bruce's face paled. "It was a disaster. My best friend died after he inhaled aparistine. Henry bled from the inside out. It was the cruelest, most gruesome death

I've ever seen." He pulled the last napkin from the table's napkin holder and wiped his eyes.

Turning to the table behind him, Mark plucked more napkins from a holder and handed them to Bruce. "Were you expelled?"

Bruce took the napkin and blew his nose. "No. The university never found out the truth."

Goosebumps tingled on his arms. "Why?"

"Our careers would have ended." Bruce sniffled. "I know it's inexcusable. I think about Henry every day. He was the brother I never had...His younger brother was Hailey's father."

Parker gasped. "That's why you were adamant about helping her years ago."

Bruce nodded. "I promised Henry I'd look after his family. When Hailey arrived at the clinic and I learned about her parents' deaths, I had to help her."

Mark exhaled in disbelief. "Does Hailey know?"

"She figured out that Henry and I were friends in college, but she doesn't know how he died. Sometimes it's best to leave things alone." Stretching his arm across the table, Bruce picked up his glasses and put them on his face. "Another classmate and I made Chuck swear we'd each do something in Henry's memory one day. Back then, the notion seemed impossible. Now we're in our sixties, and time is running out. I never thought any of us would ever create something so extraordinary. But when I made dopamine cross the blood brain barrier, I had to name it Euphoria."

A shiver ran up Mark's spine. "Moulin called his drug Euphoria, too."

Parker's brows knitted. "Why did Moulin spend so much time with this drug?"

Bruce shrugged. "Everyone experimented with drugs in the 70s. Chuck got caught up in the craze. He discovered that aparistine stimulated dopamine reactions similar to cocaine and heroin. Once scientists recognized dopamine was a neurotransmitter, they raced to map brain activity. Research consumed the medical communities."

Parker chewed on his bottom lip. "Do you think Mendoza contacted everyone in your group?"

Bruce shook his head. "There was only Chuck, Andrew, and me. Andrew has Parkinson's and lives in a nursing home."

A woman in blue scrubs emptied her food tray and walked near them, toward the exit. Mark held off speaking until she was out of earshot. "How did Charles gain access to your data?"

"I assume Mendoza passed it to him. At my first meeting with Mendoza, he wanted me to map the structural formula of aparistine from the shrub. I told him the drug was too dangerous."

Mark slid his chair up against the table. "Didn't you think it was strange when he asked you to research aparistine?"

"No." Bruce shrugged. "Mendoza grew up in South America. The plant was indigenous to that area."

"Do you think Mendoza hired Charles Moulin to do the job after you refused?"

"Chuck's the only person I know who's familiar with the plant. It makes sense Mendoza approached him."

Mark rubbed his jaw. "So he combined your dopamine with Charles's plant and created some super drug?"

"It looks that way."

Parker clenched his teeth. "He can create a potent street drug and use your dopamine for pharmaceuticals."

A service employee stepped near them and cleaned tables. They lowered their voices. "It's a clever concept." Bruce scratched his head. "Mendoza's spearheading research for two different venues."

Parker let out a long breath. "He's using the euphoric effects of dopamine. And he's exploiting the multitude of psychosomatic properties in aparistine."

Bruce's eyebrows arched. "Together, he's masterminding an extremely powerful drug. I hope he's aware the interaction of the two chemicals could be synergistic."

Mark narrowed his eyes. "What does that mean?"

The expression on Parker's face revealed his concern. "You think the combination of both drugs could produce a more intense euphoria?"

Bruce massaged his temples and nodded. "Stronger than we could ever imagine."

Parker sneered. "Shit. The two chemicals aren't on the government list for controlled substances. They can easily be transported out of the country."

"And Mendoza can make millions in trafficking," Bruce added.

Parker pulled out his phone. "We've got to put aparistine on the list and nail Mendoza. I'll tell Stefan to contact the DEA. This will turn into a disaster if we can't stop him."

"No, it won't. The formula he stole from my files is erroneous." Bruce touched a finger to his head. "Only I know the correct formula."

Mark rose from his chair. He was on brain overload. "You two make the phone calls. I'll check on Hailey."

****

When he walked back into Hailey's room, the nurse was adding more antidote solution in the IV bag. Mark waited by the door, allowing the older woman to finish her work.

She tugged the IV stand behind the bed and skirted around the portable monitors. Removing the stethoscope around her neck, she positioned the round silver end on Hailey's chest and listened. Then she turned and dimmed the lights, smiling at him as she walked out.

Mark collapsed in the chair and kissed Hailey's hand. He leaned over and whispered, "Please, honey, open your eyes."

Parker returned with Bruce, and they updated Mark with the latest developments. By mid-morning, Dr. Gewant came in the room and conferred with Bruce on Hailey's treatment.

When Dr. Gewant left, Bruce pulled out his hat and phone from his pocket and checked for messages. He adjusted his hat on his head. "I'll be back in a few hours. I need to visit an old friend before I fly back to Texas. Call me if she wakes."

Mark squeezed Hailey's hand, trying to transfer his energy into her body. An hour passed, and she let out a small groan. He jerked from his seat. "She's waking up."

Parker dashed to the door. "Get a doctor in here!"

Dr. Gewant and three nurses hurried into the room. One of the nurses halted as she passed in front of them. "Wait in the hall."

Mark's heart raced at the flurry of activity surrounding Hailey. He queried any staff who rushed past him, "Is she okay?"

"Let them do their job. How about we grab some coffee?" Placing his hand on Mark's shoulder, Parker led him to the waiting room and put money in the coffee machine. "Here." He handed Mark a cup. "We could be in for a long day."

Taking the drink, Mark allowed a smile. "Thanks."

"Let's not mention Justin's death to Hailey yet. It would only upset her."

Mark sipped the hot beverage and nodded. "You don't have to convince me."

At last, Dr. Gewant walked into the room. "The antidote's working. We removed the breathing tube. She's sleeping now. Hailey will be groggy for a while, but she's turned a corner."

The doctor's encouraging words cracked Mark's brave pretense. He bowed his head and wept.

Chapter Fifty-Four

The waves rocked Hailey back and forth, towing her wooden raft from the shore. Her parents paddled a kayak toward her and continued onward. A crying baby on a sailboat cruised through the water. Parker rode past on a jet ski with his arms extended. "Join me." He kissed her, and she tasted the desire on his lips. She extended her arm, but he shoved her. "You killed my parents. I can't stand to look at you." As he sped away, she clung to the twine securing the logs, the rough water jouncing the raft from all sides. When she turned around, everyone had disappeared in the waves.

The emptiness choked her. She had lost much in her life. Mama. Papa. Justin. Parker. Why did she keep so many secrets? Her vision drifted out of focus. Through her turmoil, one person constantly fought for her. Mark. Why did she hide her pain from him?

The waves grew turbulent, and great white sharks circled around her, baring their razor-sharp teeth. She gripped an oar, pulling it through the water to escape, but the sharks gnawed relentlessly on the wooden planks. Moving to the center of the craft, she shouted for help.

Mark swam nearer, fighting against the waves and pummeling the sharks. "Hailey!" He extended his arm and held out his hand, his bloody arm mangled.

She couldn't let him risk his life for her. "Go. Save yourself!"

His head dipped under the water, and seconds later, he reappeared, choking. "I'm not leaving without you. Take my hand."

She hesitated. Why was he so stubborn?

A shark bit his shoulder. He clenched his teeth and waited. "Trust me."

What was she doing? Mark wasn't the problem in their relationship. Trust him. Love him. Don't keep driving him away. Let him in.

The raft broke apart. She fought the waves, and her head bobbed under the water.

Mark called to her again, his fingers straining across the water. "Hailey."

He risked his life for her. He loved her. He truly loved her. Mark! If she loved him, she would need to trust him. Treading the choppy water, she stretched her arm, extending her fingertips. Desperately trying to grip his hand, she plunged below the surface.

He grasped under her arms and lifted her above the water, crushing her to him.

"Hailey."

With an effort, she forced open her eyes. She blinked. Mark. His face came into focus. The gentleness in his gaze contrasted with his tangled hair and scraggly beard. With his head tilted, he gazed at her. His smile made her feel alive again. "Mark." Was her voice garbled from the water?

She wasn't drowning. She lay in a bed with machines around her. Where was she? "Hi." The word came out of her mouth as a mumble; the mucus smothered her voice.

297

He squeezed her hand and wiped his eyes with his shirtsleeve. "Thank God you're okay."

His warm voice wrapped her in a velvety blanket. A shadow moved on her other side. She slowly turned her head.

Parker grinned. Was he crying, too? "Hello, Hailey."

She turned her head back to Mark. Then to Parker. And back again to her husband. Her mouth opened, and she gasped. "You two…?"

A slow smile spread across Mark's face. "Yeah, we've met."

Closing her eyes, she pulled the sheets over her heated face, and muttered, "Oh, shit."

Mark and Parker laughed.

Hailey lowered the sheet and joined them.

Chapter Fifty-Five

Colleen sat in the chair, waiting for her father to finish chewing his tuna salad sandwich. A quick knock tapped on the door. She handed A.C. a napkin and helped wipe his face. "Come in."

With shoulders sagging, Bruce walked into the room as if a four-ton beam weighed him down. "Howdy, friend."

A.C. sat taller in bed and crooked his head, a broad smile forming across his face. "Well, I'll be. I just pissed my pants." He held out his hand. "It's good to see you."

Bruce shook his hand. "This visit's long overdue." He cast an apologetic glance her way. "I'm sorry, Colleen. I should've called."

Smiling, she piled the napkins and silverware on the food tray. A.C. hadn't been this ecstatic in weeks. "Nonsense. It's good to see you again. Daddy loves visitors."

"I'm sorry if I'm interrupting."

"No, you're good. I'm leaving in a few minutes to go back to work anyway."

Bruce pulled a chair from the table and straddled it. "You're looking well, A.C."

Frowning, A.C. folded his arms over his blanket. "Bullshit! I'm miserable. I'm living out my dying days alone."

"I'm sorry about Millie. The funeral doesn't seem that long ago." Bruce sighed. "I feel alone, too. All I do is work in the lab. At least you get a bed and cooked meals."

"I'm sure you eat better than the slop I get." A.C. chuckled.

Bruce locked eyes with Colleen. "You're lucky your daughter visits."

A.C. scoffed. "She doesn't come as often as I'd like. She's always busy."

Her cheeks warmed. "Daddy, please. You know I visit when I can."

"Where did we go wrong?" A.C. took off his reading glasses and blinked back tears. "We were once on the top of our game. What was the meaning of it?"

"I don't know." Bruce shook his head. "Sometimes I wonder the same thing."

"Thank God for Millie. Without her, I wouldn't have known what happiness was. Now I sit here and wait to die."

Deep down, Colleen moaned. She couldn't let him go. She patted his hand. "Daddy, don't talk like that. I'm still here." She lifted the lavender cardigan from the back of her chair and put her arms through the sleeves.

"Something better is out there waiting for us." A.C. gave a blank expression.

"I hope so." Bruce shook his head and frowned. "Lately, I find myself questioning the meaning of my existence. I've tried so hard to run from my past. To prove I meant something. In the end, it didn't matter. Life is full of wins and losses."

A.C. reset his glasses on his nose. "Enough blubbering. What brings you here? This place is a long way from Texas."

"I came to catch up on some visits. I decided to put my research on hold—indefinitely."

Her stomach lurched, and she stopped buttoning the sweater. "What about your work on dopamine? We were counting on you to help Daddy."

A.C. frowned. "I thought your work was going well."

Bruce gave a cheerless smile. "Not any more. Things changed."

An awkward silence followed. Bruce glanced at her and waited. She could take the hint. She looped the purse strap over her shoulder.

"Leaving already?" A.C. made a poor attempt of acting disappointed.

She nodded. "I wish I could stay longer."

"Can you stop by again tonight?"

Colleen sighed. She could visit for a week, and he would want her to stay longer. "I'll see. Work keeps me pretty busy." Leaning over, she kissed him and then turned to Bruce. "It's good to see you again. Your visit made Daddy's day."

She lingered in the hallway outside the room and strained to hear the conversation. She smiled at the camaraderie. Rarely did Daddy receive visitors. Seeing him interact with his former colleague gave her a different perspective.

"Colleen's a beautiful woman."

"Takes after Millie."

"She has your drive, though."

"Oh, hell, cut the chit-chat. You've worked on that project for forty years. You would never give up on your dream. What happened?"

"I screwed up." Bruce's voice cracked. "I hoped after all this time, I'd finally done it—created something in Henry's memory. Now it feels wrong. I wanted to experience the euphoria Henry felt before he died."

Colleen closed her eyes. Daddy had mentioned Henry's name a few times.

A.C.'s voice softened. "We were so jealous of him that brief moment when he looked so happy—before all hell let loose."

"I spent my life trying to make restitution. Now Henry's niece is in the hospital, and Xavier's grandchild is dead." Bruce blew his nose. "Are we cursed because of Henry?"

Colleen leaned closer to the door. Who was Henry?

A.C. chuckled. "Blame it on Charles. It was his damn shrub."

"Remember when we both swiped one of his saplings?"

"Yep. He had so many he never noticed."

"Mine died. I don't think I watered it enough."

Bruce laughed. "Mine's four feet tall. By the way, Chuck is gone, too. He got mixed up with a drug lord."

"I'll be damned. After all these years, the crazy S.O.B. met his match."

A nurse carrying a tray with a medicine cup walked toward her, and Colleen pretended to search her purse. "Ms. Toole, did you forget anything?"

She plucked the keys from her bag and turned down the hallway. "No, I was just leaving."

Chapter Fifty-Six

"No, Mom, we didn't have a fight. Everything's fine." Mark closed his eyes and bent his head. His brain squawked, "Weasel." What kind of lowlife lied to his mother?

"Are you sure you didn't say something to her?" Peggy was hard to deceive.

"I'm sure. Hailey didn't leave me."

"Okay, if you say so. But—"

"Mom. She'll be back in a couple days. I swear."

"Don't tell her about the kids acting up. It will make her worry more. Tell Hailey that Anna and Ethan miss her."

When Peggy had told him stories of the kids' behavior, he cringed. How did Hailey manage all the tattling and nitpicking? "I'll tell her. She misses them, too. Don't worry. I'm sure she'll call today." An elderly nurse frowned as she walked past, and Mark stepped across the hall into a supply closet.

"Okay. I worry about both of you."

"You don't need to. Tell the kids to behave if they want to go to the amusement park next week. I promise I'll drive over before they go to bed tonight. Last night I had an emergency at work. Thanks for all your help." He tucked the phone in his pants pocket and chuckled.

If his mom found out Hailey worked as an undercover agent, she'd flip.

From the hallway, he peeked inside Hailey's room. The nursing assistant was giving her a sponge bath. He turned and walked toward the hospital chapel. On his way, he jumped and clicked his heels. His wife was alive. Life was great.

****

On his way back, Mark stopped by the vending machine and emptied his wallet. His arms overflowed with cookies, chips, nuts, and snack bars. Hailey hadn't eaten in almost a week, and his stomach had convulsed for days. He pushed the door handle to Hailey's room and halted. A deep voice came from inside.

"Can't you remember anything?"

He frowned. Dammit. Couldn't Parker let her rest? He thrust the door open and walked in.

"No, my memory's a blur." Hailey was sitting up, her thin, bony frame propped against the pillows in the bed. Regret tugged at his heart.

Scowling, he stepped closer to the bed and dumped the snacks on the tray table. Couldn't Parker register the exhaustion on her pale face? He controlled his voice, but gave Parker a hard stare. "Let's keep the questions for later."

Parker reddened and stood. "He's right. I'll leave you two alone while I hunt down some strong coffee. I'm glad you're okay." He leaned in and kissed her forehead.

The door closed, and Mark continued scowling. Now that they had been given a second chance, he wouldn't risk anything happening to her.

Hailey shook her head. "Oh, Mark, give him a break."

He jerked at her sharp tone. "What did I do?"

"I saw the frown. Can't you be nice to him?"

"I'm trying." His neck tensed. "Sometimes he gets to me. Why did he have to kiss you?"

"We're friends." She patted a spot next to her on the bed, and he sat. She took his hand and caressed it with her thumb. "Don't get angry at Parker. It's my fault I'm here."

He stiffened. "How can you say that? He talked you into helping him. He's the reason you're in here."

"He's trying to save his son. Try to see him the way I do. He's a good man." Her shimmering eyes entranced him.

Mark squared his shoulders. "You're right. You're back safe and sound. Nothing else matters."

She yawned. "I know you're hurt. I should've told you about my past. I'm really sorry."

He pulled the bedsheet over her and held her hands. "Don't dwell on that now. The important thing is you're okay."

"I wanted to put that part of my life behind me. During the past week, I thought a lot about us…about our relationship." Hailey leaned over and coughed. She held a hand against her throat. He gripped the pitcher, poured water in a cup, and handed it to her. Her arms quivered as she emptied the cup and set it on the tray. A bright smile spread across her face. "Thanks."

"Shh. No more talking. You're exhausted." A loose strand of long hair fell in her face, and he tucked it behind her ear, his fingers lingering against her cheek.

Shaking her head, she scratched her hands. "Mark, we need to talk. You and I both know something hasn't been right in our marriage. I'm not the person you think I am."

He smoothed her hair and stared at her hands. "Later. Get some rest." Why hadn't he questioned her earlier about her fidgeting? He stood and walked to the window. "I thought about us, too." As he stared through the glass pane, he rubbed his clammy hands on his jeans. "I wasn't fair to you...I put work before our family. I missed our anniversary dinner, and I made you feel underappreciated." He paused, bowing his head. This apology wasn't heartfelt enough. "Dammit! You're everything to me. I don't deserve a second chance, but I'm begging you for one."

His lip trembled as he waited for her answer. Whoever said silence was golden definitely wasn't married. Her silence ticked away, and his hope began to dwindle. How would he live without her? Turning to face the inevitable, he jumped.

She lay on the bed, slumped to the side, with her eyes closed.

"Hailey?" He dashed to the bed and lifted her head back on the pillow.

The monitor beside her beeped a steady rhythm. She breathed out a soft snore, and he exhaled.

He leaned over and kissed her cheek. "Sweet dreams, honey."

****

In the afternoon, Dr. Gewant transferred Hailey to the progressive care unit. The wing on the fourth floor was a little more peaceful than the ICU, but the nurses seemed stricter, monitoring the noise level and the number of visitors in the patient rooms.

Although she was on the road to recovery, Mark wouldn't risk sleeping yet.

Parker lingered a while longer in the room. "I'm heading out for a bit. I'll stop back before I fly out."

When Parker left, Mark crawled in bed next to Hailey and looped his arm around her waist. As he updated her about the kids, a tap knocked on the door. Greg peeked in the room, carrying a bouquet of roses. "Am I disturbing you? Owen said your wife was awake."

Mark made a wry face at Hailey. "So much for alone time." He lifted himself out of bed. "Honey, this is my partner Greg."

She flattened her uncombed hair and smiled. "Hello. It's nice to finally put a name to the face. Mark talks a lot about you."

"Same here. Everyone at the office has been worried about you. Mark hasn't slept in days." He arched his eyebrows and swayed his head toward Mark. "I thought he was using the bags under his eyes to pack clothes for a vacation."

Mark sat in a chair and slid an empty chair beside him. "Ha, ha. You look bushed, too."

Greg took the seat and coughed. "Stress is wreaking havoc on my body. There's no time to sleep—or eat. I must be coming down with some bug. We're working around the clock on this case. Which is one of the reasons I'm here." He turned to Hailey and pulled out a security device from his pocket. "Do you mind if I record this?"

Hailey lifted a hand to her neck and scratched. "Why?"

"We're trying to find some fresh leads. Owen sent me here to check if you remember anything about the kidnapping."

"I don't think now is a good time." Mark stood from his chair and stepped beside Hailey. He would speak to Owen about this.

"It shouldn't take long. Do you mind, Hailey? I'll stop when you say so."

She shook her head. "I wish I could help, but everything is blank."

"Don't worry. It's normal in traumas like yours." Greg sat back in the chair and turned on the device. "Can you tell me how many kidnappers there were? Were there more than one?"

She wrapped her arms around herself, and her forehead creased. "I'm sorry. My memory's blurry."

"Can you recall anything the kidnapper said? Did they talk about Mendoza or the drug?"

"I'm not sure...There were voices so there must have been more than one...Everything else is foggy."

While Mark massaged his wife's shoulder, he glared at Greg. "It's okay, honey. It will take time."

Greg seemed oblivious to Mark's eye signals. "Did the person have a dialect, an accent, or any distinct quality to their voice?"

"I..." She twisted her hands together and glanced at Mark.

"That's enough." Mark huffed. "Can't you see she's not ready? Let her strength come back before you grill her."

Greg turned off the recorder and lifted his head. "I'm sorry, Hailey. I didn't mean to upset you. Owen insisted I come." He turned to Mark. "I told him we should wait, but you know Owen. There's no stopping him when he gets something in his head."

Mark tensed and tightened his lips together. "Yes, I'm all too familiar with his methods."

"I should go and let you both rest." Greg glanced at the flowers on his lap as he rose from the chair. "Oh, I forgot. The office got these for you." Leaning over, he turned away and coughed. He handed Hailey the bouquet.

She inhaled the flowers. "Roses, my favorite. Thanks."

"I put my card in there in case you remember anything. I'll be in touch."

She rubbed her finger over one of the pink petals. "Thank you."

Greg straightened and slapped Mark on the back. "Hang in there, pal. Get some sleep. You look like you need it." He walked to the door and turned. "If you remember anything—anything at all—call. You have my number."

She nodded. "I'll do that."

A short time later, Hailey insisted on getting out of bed. She walked beside Mark down the hallway as he wheeled the IV stand.

Tears blurred his eyes at Hailey's persistence.

The nurses praised her progress, commenting how strong her legs had become.

Hailey smiled at their admiration. She seemed happy, but she was hiding something.

Mark walked her back to her room. "What's wrong?"

She rested her head on the pillow and sighed. "I can't pinpoint it. Something's bothering me about the kidnapping."

A bubbly young nurse wearing a twisted ponytail came into the room and checked Hailey's vitals. She replaced the IV bag on the stand and left.

An hour later, Parker knocked on the door, sporting a bright smile, shaved face, and new clothes. "How's the patient?"

Mark crossed his arms and frowned. The shower had restored Parker's entire appearance. "Hailey's on the verge of remembering something."

Parker rushed toward them. "What? The kidnapper?"

She shook her head. "No, not that...I know this sounds strange, but I remember a smell."

Chapter Fifty-Seven

Hailey sat up against the pillows on her bed and sighed. Greg's business card was still in the bouquet he had delivered. She picked up the handset from the phone on the nightstand and dialed.

"Tremblay, Division of Investigations."

"Yes, this is Hailey Langley. Mark's wife. I'm sorry to bother you."

"You're fine. I was working through my stack of paperwork. What can I do for you?"

"You told me to call if I thought of anything." She scratched her hand. Was she ready to do this?

"Yes, I did."

"A few details have flashed in my mind. I didn't tell Mark. He's too distracted right now."

"Of course. Do you want me to come to your room?"

"Can we meet in the hospital courtyard? This room's making me claustrophobic. There's a patio right outside the cafeteria for patients and visitors. I'll sneak away from the nurses."

He chuckled. "Sure. Whatever's easier. What time?"

"Is five-thirty too soon?"

"Perfect. See you then."

****

Hailey wheeled herself to the outside courtyard where the air was considerably hotter and muggier. A gust of wind wobbled her IV stand, and she grabbed it. She chose a small table near the rear and waited. Dark clouds drifted in her direction. She should have checked the forecast before setting up the meeting. A hundred yards away was the parking lot for staff, patients, and visitors. Today, only a handful of people gathered at the tables, braving the brewing storm.

Tall arborvitae bushes and Leland cypress trees landscaped the yard. Hedges and vibrant-colored lilies and petunias added warmth near the entrance. Two middle-aged men sat to her left and chatted with a bald man. To Hailey's right, a younger woman wearing a lab coat conversed with a man carrying a food tray. At another table, an orderly dressed in green scrubs read the newspaper.

A strong gust lifted her robe, and she gripped the threadbare fabric against her leg. She hated hospitals. Even the faintest whiff of the antiseptic cleaner brought back painful memories.

Through the trees, a white van pulled into the visitor lot. Greg opened the door and strode to the upper entrance. A few minutes later, he opened the glass door leading into the courtyard. He motioned to the sky. "Are you sure you want to talk here? A storm's coming."

She brushed the loose hair from her face. "This shouldn't take long."

Greg took a seat across from her. "How are you feeling?"

"Better."

"You look better."

"Thank you. I'm still a little weak, though."

He nodded. "I appreciate your call. Where's Mark?"

"I sent him home. He needs a shower and some sleep. I don't want him worrying about anything else."

"I imagine his stress level is maxed. Is Parker still here?"

She shook her head. "He flew back to Chicago a while ago."

Greg removed a notepad and pen from his shirt pocket. "Let's get started before it rains. What did you want to tell me?"

"I don't know if this is important, but I remember a smell."

His eyebrow arched. "A smell?"

"Yes."

"What kind of smell?"

"It was more of a fruity smell."

He laughed. "A *fruity* smell?"

"Yes. Like the kind from ketoacidosis."

His face tensed.

"You have diabetes, don't you, Mr. Tremblay?"

"Why do you ask?"

"Diabetics with uncontrolled blood sugar can go into diabetic ketoacidosis."

Greg straightened his back. "What does that have to do with me?"

She propped her elbow on the table. "I think you were one of my abductors."

He stared. "You're joking."

"I'm not laughing. When I was tied to a chair, a sick man with fruity breath hovered around me."

His face reddened. "I don't see how this relates to me."

She narrowed her eyes. "There was a man called Cerdo. A fitting name. The pig couldn't keep his hands off me. I'll never forget how helpless I felt being groped with that horrible odor near my face. It took every effort not to throw up. When you handed me the flowers today and coughed, I smelled it again."

He curled his lip. "You're reaching. My diabetes doesn't prove anything. There are thousands of diabetics around here."

She shook her head. "No, but your breath has a fruity odor. You're in ketoacidosis. There aren't many people in this town walking around in your condition." She leaned toward the table, studying his body language. "It all makes sense. As my kidnapper, you were busy guarding me while keeping up the ruse at work. I'm sure you're under a lot of stress, not eating right or taking care of yourself." She stretched her neck to the side. His cheeks were turning red. "I bet your phone records would raise some eyebrows."

His nostrils flared. "You can't prove anything."

"Maybe not, but I can tell Mark and Parker what I know. You'd be their top suspect."

"Don't be ridiculous. Why the accusations? Are you wired? Do you think you can trick me into confessing to something?" Greg screeched in a high-pitched voice, his crimson coloring spreading down his neck.

"No. But I'm trying to understand why you did it. Mark trusted you. How can you look your family in the eye after what you did?"

"You don't know anything about me." He rasped the words.

"Then enlighten me."

He looked away and then glared at her. "Not everyone has a perfect little life like you and Mark. After the NNIC closed, the bank repossessed my house. My wife had an affair with my coworker and left me. She filed for custody of my kids and I got nothing. I rarely saw my boys."

She frowned. "I'm sorry to hear that."

"You're sorry? Sorry doesn't cut it. I lost my insurance. All the stress made my diabetes worse. Do you know how demoralizing it is not to have health coverage when you're sick?"

"Surely the personnel office would help you—"

Greg hit his hand on the table and glowered. "They didn't give a damn about me! Congress plays God. They act so high and mighty, cutting budgets and slashing jobs. They don't give a second thought to people who devote their lives serving this country. Politicians are self-serving. I hate them all. They don't care about me or my health. Did you know they even have their own health plan? No wonder they don't care about getting decent insurance for the common people."

She slid her hand down her leg and touched the metal object taped to her thigh. "Don't try to rationalize your actions. You kidnapped me, you pervert!"

He shrugged. "I didn't intend it that way. The French couple you impersonated RSVP'd their regrets a week earlier. When their name appeared on the guest list, Mendoza and I were suspicious. We made plans to catch the impostors at the party. After your abduction, I realized who you were." Greg glanced at the sky. "It's ironic. Mark was there that night."

"What are you talking about?"

"He asked me to attend Mendoza's party with him. Mark didn't admit it until afterward, but he went there to keep an eye on you."

Hailey jerked her head.

"Oh, don't act so shocked." He waved his hand, dismissing her reaction. "He talks about you all the time."

She choked. Mark came for her?

"While he searched for you, Owen put me in charge of the Chicago case and Sherman's disappearance." He smirked. "Those were two cases where I overlooked many leads."

"You're insane."

He coughed. "Owen assumed I was out in the field, investigating clues. Meanwhile, I babysat you at the motel and got contacts lined up for this weekend's delivery."

"You bastard. Who's helping you?" His smug expression gnawed at her.

"We had three scientists, but now we're down to two. You might know one of them—Bruce Hanover."

She crossed her arms. "Bruce would never help you."

Greg's hand brushed a small wave. "He doesn't have a clue what's going on. He's stuck in his own little world."

"How did you persuade him?"

"We didn't. Bruce thinks he's working on a new pharmaceutical. We needed his dopamine to combine with Moulin's drug. We're marketing Euphoria as a natural drug that stimulates feelings of ecstasy."

A sudden coldness ran through her body. "Bruce will be furious."

"Probably. He must suspect something. He hasn't responded to emails or phone calls lately." Greg shrugged. "It doesn't matter now. Our deliveries will go public in two days."

"But the drug isn't ready. Look what happened to me."

He leaned back and shifted his hands behind his head. "Moulin handed over his data without testing it first. His carelessness cost us millions of dollars. Luckily, another scientist found the error. We've lined up orders for twelve countries. Other buyers are waiting to confirm the drug's worth, and we'll transport that batch at a higher price next week."

Dust and leaves swirled around him, and his eyes took on a crazed look. "I liked you. I hoped you and I could build a…more meaningful relationship. He extended his fingers close to her cheek, but she recoiled. "You're an attractive woman and I have needs. I enjoyed getting acquainted with you during your captivity."

Hailey clenched her teeth. "You make me sick."

His face hardened. "It's a shame you figured this out. Now I don't have a choice."

She leaned forward and touched her hand against her thigh. "What are you going to do? Kill me in front of everyone?"

Greg scoffed. "Give me some credit. Do you see the orderly at the table over there reading the paper?" She looked at the dark-haired man wearing the scrubs.

"Meet Antonio. He's a bit of a prude. Didn't like me touching you. When I text him, he'll come to this table and push your wheelchair to my van." He pointed to the parking lot. "Your partner shot him, so he's trigger happy. If you cause a scene, innocent people will die. Get ready for your final ride." He pulled the phone out of his pocket and glanced at the sky. "The timing's perfect. Looks like we'll beat the storm. I'd hate to get my suit wet."

Hailey leaned an elbow on the table. "Before you send the text, check around the tables to the left and right of Antonio—at the people in disguises." Greg shifted his gaze to the table of men. "And to the table on your right." She gloated as his eyes blazed. "Did you think I wouldn't tell Mark and Parker about you? Any second they'll come over and arrest you and Antonio."

The agents rose from their seats, and she smiled. She'd beaten Greg at his own game. Two agents rushed behind Antonio, and the other four sped to her table. Mark led the group, revealing his clenched teeth as he charged.

Hailey stood and grasped the firearm from her thigh, but Greg heaved the table, knocking the gun out of her hand. He grabbed her arm with one hand and pulled a Glock 22 from his trousers with the other. He aimed the gun at her head, positioning her in front of him. "Freeze!"

Mark stopped and signaled the others to halt. Antonio drew a handgun from his scrubs and pointed it at the group. He hastened behind Greg and Hailey near a tree.

Greg squeezed her arm tighter. "Unload your guns and toss them."

"Give it up." Mark shook his head, keeping his gaze on them. "It's over."

"It's not over until I say it is."

In precise movements, Mark stepped toward him. "Let her go. We'll hunt you down until we find you."

"Not as long as Hailey's my hostage." He stepped back, dragging her with him. "Now throw down your guns!"

Mark remained resolute. Hailey eyed the sniper at the third-floor window. If she could pull away, he might get a good shot. Greg shoved his gun against her temple. "Drop your weapons." No one budged.

Boom.

A shot came from Antonio's gun. The agent standing next to Parker clutched his leg. Antonio aimed the gun at Hailey. "The next one goes through your wife."

The blast rang like a bell tower in her ears. It had been a wise move, clearing the area of civilians. He might kill everyone.

Greg pressed his weapon firmer against her head. "Drop your weapons or she dies."

She tried to copy Mark's stoic face. How could he remain so calm?

"You know we can't do that." Mark's voice was steady. "If you kill her, there's nothing stopping us from killing you. You'll lose your leverage."

Her arm went numb. She tried not to move with the cold metal pushing against her skin, but her legs wobbled. She couldn't endure a long standoff.

A few seconds passed, and Mark spoke again. "You have other options. Put the gun down and release her. We can discuss it after you let her go."

Greg squeezed her limb until she winced. "Are you shitting me? She's my ticket out of here."

"You can't run from us." Parker glowered at him. "We know what you did. It's on tape."

Greg shook her arm, his stare burning. "I knew it! You sneaky bitch, you *were* wired."

She didn't dare swallow. She tried not to breathe. This landmine might explode any moment.

"You're surrounded. Release her. Don't make things harder." Mark stood motionless, his gaze on her and Greg.

"Go to hell! If I'm going to get out of here alive, I need her." Greg lowered his head and snarled in her ear. "You'll pay for duping me." He kicked the IV stand to the ground, ripping the tubing from her hand. Blood spilled from the opening. He burst out in a demented laugh. "Mark, your wife is trembling."

She held back a cry and pressed the back of her hand against her thigh. *Just kill the son of a bitch.*

Antonio shrieked and braced his right arm. He stooped behind the tree and stared at the window where the sniper was hiding. Greg looked up and aimed his gun at the sharpshooter. He fired twice, and clamped his free arm under Hailey's breasts, wavering backward. "Don't move a muscle or she dies." He zigzagged through the grass while she kicked and thrashed.

Antonio brandished his weapon at the agents. He meandered around the evergreen trees, working his way to the parking lot. The wind grew more intense and large raindrops hammered Hailey's head. The blustery weather would make the sniper's aim difficult. Greg rushed faster to the van, dragging her as she continued kicking. Antonio followed a short distance behind. Mark and the others trailed, shooting at Antonio. He fired back, striking two. She turned her head. Mark!

The rain fell at a steadier pace as Greg wrenched her closer to the van's rear door. "You sure are a feisty one." She swung her feet and kicked him in the groin. He tightened an arm around her torso, lowered his gun to the bumper, and opened the door. Hailey looked inside and jumped.

"Don't move!" A burly man hiding in the van aimed his Glock straight at them.

Greg grabbed for his weapon.

"Don't even think of it," the stranger said.

Struggling against Greg's grip, she caught another glimpse of the man inside. Where had she seen him before? Footfalls sounded behind her. She turned. Antonio was behind her, grimacing, his arm covered in blood.

He raised his handgun and pointed it at the mysterious man, but the man shot first.

Antonio fell to the ground, blood spurting from his rib cage.

Without hesitation, Hailey snatched Greg's firearm from the bumper. She pulled the trigger. The bullet struck Greg in the arm. She squeezed the trigger again, hitting him square in his chest. A surprised expression suspended on his face as he stumbled backward. He collapsed, pulling her down with him. A hoarse cry resonated from her mouth. She lifted herself a few inches above his body and met his cold gaze as the light faded from his eyes.

Chapter Fifty-Eight

The rain hit Mark like pellets striking his skin as he ran. His legs couldn't push him fast enough. Like dominos, Hailey, Antonio, and Greg had toppled to the ground. He was powerless to save his own wife. His heart squeezed, hampering his breathing. Hailey!

When he arrived at the van, Hailey was standing there shaking. Mark wrapped his arms around her and kissed her forehead. "Thank God you're okay."

She hugged him and collapsed in his arms.

As if on cue, the storm clouds ruptured, and the rain dumped on them. Mark lifted Hailey and peered inside the van. "David! How did you sneak in there?"

A wide grin spread across David's face. "Give the credit to your dad. He taught us a lot about breaking into cars when we hung out at his garage."

"Your timing's perfect. What the hell are you doing here anyway?" Mark extended his arm and gripped David's hand as he climbed out.

David secured his handgun back in its holster. "I worried when you didn't return my phone calls on the Sherman case so I called your secretary. She told me Greg took over your assignments while Hailey recuperated in the hospital."

Mark's mind reeled. "You came because you were uneasy with Greg carrying my workload?"

"No." David blinked through the downpour. "I came because I found out his wife divorced him to marry your missing person Elliot Sherman."

Water dripped from his hair as Mark shook his head. "If you continue solving my cases, I'm going to request you transfer to my agency."

"Are you kidding me?" David laughed, slapping his hand on Mark's shoulder. "I wouldn't get a break from all the action."

Chapter Fifty-Nine

Colleen checked in at the nurses' station on the way to her father's room. A middle-aged nurse looked up from the computer screen. "Andrew keeps asking for you. He's getting ready for bed."

"How was he today?"

"He had a better day than yesterday."

When she reached his room, A.C. was resting in a chair, watching the evening news. She tapped on the doorframe. "Hello, Daddy."

He gasped. "Millie!"

She forced herself to keep smiling. "No, it's me. Colleen."

He studied her. "Yes, Colleen...my beautiful daughter."

She kissed his cheek. Then sliding a chair across from him, she sat. "I can't stay long. I want to show you something. I got it from Bruce Hanover. Tell me what you see."

His eyebrows knitted together.

She couldn't fault his confusion. He had dementia. Why would she put faith in his judgment? But she needed him. It was impossible to save him without his help. She lacked his expertise. Following chemical formulas and creating synthetic drugs was easy. Molecular interactions were more complicated. She couldn't predict how functional groups reacted with hydrocarbon chains. A.C. could interpret reactions of amides, alcohols, esters, and aldehydes. She removed a drawing from her purse.

"Look at the picture." She waited as he put on his reading glasses.

He looked at the ringed structure with letters branching from it. A.C. had spent years investigating the compound. He'd recognize it.

He glanced at the picture. "It's dopamine."

She smiled. "I knew you'd recognize it. Now look closer. Is anything wrong with the configuration? Does it contain something that doesn't belong?"

A.C. peered at the picture again. "Where did you get this?"

"Why?"

"There's a second drug in here—aparistine. I once knew a man who studied this compound. Bruce and I warned him never to use it."

"I got it from Bruce's files. I told you that I installed software on his hard drive when I visited him. I track his progress." She leaned closer. "Do you see anything else?"

He readjusted his glasses higher on his nose and viewed the structure again. "The dopamine links to a short hydrocarbon chain."

"Why did Bruce do that?"

He shrugged. "Probably to act as a carrier protein to transport the dopamine."

She leaned over and pointed. "What's the purpose of the lipophilic wall he integrated?"

"It slows the enzymes from decomposing dopamine." A.C. clamped his hands to his head. "Oh my God! How ingenious!"

"What?" He hadn't been this excited since he bought his research lab fifteen years ago.

"These alterations will allow dopamine to cross the blood-brain barrier." He lowered his eyelids and exhaled. "Bruce did it. He found a way to get to the central nervous system."

She fought the urge to jump on the bed. "Daddy, do you know what this means?"

"Of course I do." A.C. chortled like a kid surprised at a birthday party. "Some scientists spend their lives uncovering the massive cosmoses of the solar system. But this...this achievement is just as significant. He's penetrated the minute crevices of the human brain."

"Why doesn't he want to share his research? He can help patients with Parkinson's."

"I don't know. He's very upset." A.C. scratched his head and studied the structure again. His eyes widened, and his smile turned. He lay back on the pillow.

"Daddy, what's wrong?"

"Nothing."

"But you're white as a ghost."

He stared at the ceiling. "Did Bruce start any trial studies?"

"No, I told you. He didn't intend to reveal the findings until he completed the preliminary testing. And now he plans on holding it off forever."

A.C. licked his lips. "Let me try it."

"What?"

"Let me take the dopamine—without the aparistine. I don't want to hallucinate and squander any sense of reality I have left. Why would Bruce add aparistine anyway? It adds no value to dopamine."

Colleen shrugged. "I don't know."

He stared into her eyes. "I want to try the dopamine."

"Are you sure it's safe? I need to—"

"Yes. I'm certain. Can you make it?"

His excitement warmed her heart. "Give me a day or so, and I'll bring you a sample." She folded the paper and placed it back in her purse.

He picked up the remote and powered it off. "I'll let you get back to work. Good night."

She blinked her eyes. "Are you tired already?"

He tugged the blanket and covered his chest. "You need to start making the medicine—tonight."

She could barely hold back a laugh. "Well, okay, Daddy. I'll make it right away. This is the miracle we're hoping for." She bent over and kissed him. "I'll see you soon. I love you."

A.C. closed his eyes and smiled. "I love you, too."

As she turned at the door and checked on him, she caught his gaze following her. He never hurried her visits. What was he plotting?

Chapter Sixty

When Mark walked back from the gift shop, he met Parker in the corridor outside Hailey's room. With a laugh, Parker pointed to the magazine in Mark's hand. "Buying Hailey reading material?"

He chuckled. "I have to do something to keep her busy. She's getting stir-crazy in here. Are you leaving now?"

Parker nodded. "It's time. The funeral's tomorrow. Grace needs me. I already told Hailey good-bye. She's getting color in her cheeks again."

"Thanks for all your help. I imagine you're due for a long sleep."

"We've all had quite a day. Remember, don't mention anything about Justin. Hailey would chase the next flight to Chicago."

Mark stifled a yawn. "Don't worry. She won't find out from me. Do you intend on flying back after the funeral?"

A slow smile formed across Parker's face. "Checking to make sure I stay away?"

Mark ignored the taunt and thrust his hands in his pockets. "I know you have a lot going on, but there's still a drug shipment set to ship out in two days and…"

"And we still need to find those bastards responsible for Justin's death." Parker's lips pressed in a tight line. "I'll see what I can do. But I won't make any promises."

He shook Parker's hand. "Have a safe flight. We've had our differences, but I'll keep you and your family in my prayers."

Parker grinned.

"What?"

"This sendoff is entirely different from the night we first met—when you stormed into Stefan's office."

The night was still fresh in Mark's mind. He couldn't contain his smile. "Then let me come full circle and tell you to go to hell if you ever involve Hailey again on a case."

****

Mark was sitting in the shadows of the room watching Hailey sleep when David poked his head through the doorway.

"Why are you hiding over here in the dark?" David whispered.

"I'm steering clear of the nurses. They've given me the evil eye since I wheeled Hailey inside after the shootout."

David laughed. "You're being paranoid."

"No, I'm not. The one with the silver-gray hair in a bun chewed me out. Anyone within a five mile radius could hear her war cries."

David tilted his head toward Hailey. "How's she doing?"

Mark gazed at her. "She fell asleep an hour ago. She refused a sedative earlier, but she's calmed down."

"She's an amazing woman."

Unable to look away, Mark nodded. "She certainly is."

David grinned. "Look at you. You're blushing. You're as smitten with her as the day you first met."

"I know." Surely his heart would burst with so much love. "She means more to me than anything."

"And the fact she didn't tell you she was an agent?"

Mark shrugged and turned to David. "It doesn't matter. All I care about is having her back. I love her."

David's smile widened. "I'm glad you realize it. I always liked Hailey. She's the best thing that happened to you. She creates turmoil in your neat and tidy world."

"Very funny." He glanced again at Hailey and lowered his voice. "Seriously, I don't know what I would've done if Greg had succeeded in taking her."

"The van wouldn't have gotten far." David grinned. He reached in his pocket and pulled out two spark plugs.

He laughed. "How did you figure out Greg was in on this?"

"When I flew to North Carolina, Kay Sherman's son Jeremy pointed out Sherman was his step-dad. His real father was Greg Tremblay."

"I wish I'd known that sooner."

"I left at least a dozen messages with your secretary, but you didn't get them."

"I told Tamara to pass everything to Greg."

"Jeremy mentioned he had visited Greg over Christmas. He saw his dad's papers about a new drug called Euphoria. Greg claimed the drug was part of a clinical study for his diabetes. Jeremy asked his stepfather to find out if Euphoria was legit. My guess is Sherman started nosing around, and Greg killed him."

"If we found Sherman's body, we could wrap up the case."

"I don't think Sherman's dead," Hailey said in a soft voice.

Mark walked to the bed and kissed her forehead. The dark circles beneath her eyes emphasized her pale coloring. "How are you feeling, honey?"

"Still shaky." She fluffed her pillow and leaned back. "It's not every day I kill a man." Her eyes shifted to David.

"Honey, you remember David."

She nodded and held out her slender arm. "Yes. I recognize you from our wedding. It's nice to see you again."

He shook her hand. "Same here. You held your own out there today. I was proud that Mark's wife could handle a gun as well as he can."

"I'm relieved everything's over." Scarlet stains coursed over her cheeks as she smoothed her hospital gown. "Thank you for saving me this afternoon."

David gestured his hand toward Mark. "No problem. Covering this guy's back is my job requirement as his best man."

Mark rolled his eyes. "How did I ever tolerate you as a roommate?" He sat down on the edge of the bed. "Honey, why do you think Sherman's alive?"

She shrugged. "Just a feeling I have. Today, when Greg talked about Sherman, he never mentioned killing him."

He turned to David. "Is it possible he's still alive?"

"I don't know. Where would he be?"

"Who knows? Greg was a deranged man. We were lucky to find Hailey in that rundown motel."

David's eyes narrowed. "Why did Mendoza keep her in a motel? Why didn't he hide her at the mansion? There's plenty of space. Perhaps Sherman's there."

Mark shrugged and held Hailey's hand. "I don't know. We searched the mansion the day after she disappeared. We would have seen Sherman."

Hailey rubbed her eyes. "Did you go through all the rooms?"

He stared at her. "Yeah. Parker showed me the study in Mendoza's bedroom."

"Did Greg help?"

"Of course."

She raised an eyebrow. "And you think he actually did a thorough job?"

Mark scratched his neck. "Okay, Hailey, what did we miss?"

"There are three secret rooms in the mansion. The study was one. Maybe Greg hid Sherman in one of the other two places."

Nodding, David turned to Mark. "She could be right."

Hailey cast a skeptical eye. "Did you find the other rooms?"

He scowled. "No. Where are they?"

"Based on the blueprints I'm certain there's a hidden space behind the huge mirror on the foyer wall."

Mark covered his mouth. Hopefully, she didn't see his jaw drop. When he entered the mansion the night of the party, he'd glanced at his reflection in that mirror.

Hailey squeezed her eyes. "In the basement floor blueprint there was a spacious area behind the wine cellar. I doubt Mendoza has that much space devoted for his vintage collections."

David grinned. "You'd be surprised."

"True." She nodded. "But I bet there's another room behind there."

The door opened and light streamed from the hallway. An older woman dressed in a white uniform stomped into the room, her glare reducing Mark to a third grader. He banged his leg against the bedside table as he scuttled to the other side of the room.

The woman took Hailey's vitals and gave him another hard stare. "Your wife had a difficult day. She needs her rest."

Hailey leaned back against the pillow. "Give me five more minutes and I'll go back to sleep. I promise."

The nurse strutted over to Mark, her lips pressed into a thin line. "I won't let your wife disappear from her bed under *my* shift."

When she left, David leaned his head back and laughed.

Mark returned to the bed and jabbed David's side. "Don't give her reason to come back in. I'm already on her hit list."

"That old lady *really* looks intimidating." David turned. "You know, I think Hailey's on to something about the wine cellar. Greg's son Jeremy was taking a summer class at Duke. Greg sent him a book on Poe to help with his English class. Greg said Poe was his favorite writer. Jeremy thought it was odd since he wasn't even taking literature. I read Poe's stories a long time ago in high school. One story was about a man who sealed his enemy behind a brick wall."

Hailey's face brightened. "I remember the story. He wanted revenge on someone who insulted him."

David let out a small gasp. "Was Greg deranged enough to do something like that?"

Hailey nodded, and her eyes widened. "Greg felt betrayed after his wife left him. He blamed the separation on Sherman. I bet Greg locked him in the basement." She grabbed her robe near the bottom of the bed. "Mark and I will go with you."

Mark clutched the robe from her hand. "No, we won't. You're staying here."

David chuckled at their tug of war as he detached the phone from his belt. "You both can stay here. I'll get someone to help me check it out."

****

Mark drove home and packed Hailey a small travel bag of clothes and necessities. He danced on the way back to the car. Pulling Hailey's cell phone from his pocket, he dialed. "Mom, are the kids still up?"

"Hi, Mark. They're eating a bedtime snack now. Do you want to say hello?"

He tossed the valise in the trunk and turned on his ignition. "No. I'll be over in twenty minutes. I'll read them a story tonight and tuck them in bed."

Due to the traffic, he arrived ten minutes late. He parked the car in his parents' driveway and walked up the porch steps. Anna beamed at him through the window. She opened the front door, hopping like a kangaroo. "Daddy! You're here! You're here!"

Ethan ran down the stairs wearing his superhero pajamas and pounced on him. "We missed you!"

Mark scooped them into his arms and squeezed. "Boy, aren't you a sight for sore eyes."

"Did somebody hit you?" Anna squinted at him.

He narrowed his brows at his mother, but Peggy only laughed.

Anna leaned forward and peered closer at his face. "How did you get sore eyes, Daddy? Did someone punch you?"

He chuckled. These moments were priceless.

Ethan stepped back from the group hug and crossed his arms. "He didn't get hit in the face, silly. He forgot his sunglasses today, and the sun was too bright." The boy's face grew stern. "Mommy's going to yell if you didn't put on sunscreen."

Mark winked. "Don't worry. My eyes are better now. Guess what? I have exciting news."

Anna jumped, clapping her hands. "What is it?"

"Mommy's coming home soon. Three days at the most."

"Yeah!" Ethan said. He clasped Anna's hands, and they kicked their heels, dancing around Mark.

"Kids. Let your father come in and sit a while." They followed Peggy into the living room and the kids crowded him on the sofa.

Mark looked around the room. The kids' backpacks and sneakers lined the wall near the front door and board games were scattered across the carpet. "Where's Dad?"

"Outside in the garage. He'll come in shortly." Peggy picked up the remote from the rocking chair and powered off the television. "How's Hailey?"

The dark circles under his mother's eyes concerned him. "She's doing well. She's excited to come home. Are you and Dad okay?"

The garage door opened. Adam hurried in from the kitchen carrying an oatmeal cookie in his hand and clasped Mark's shoulder. "I thought I heard voices. I'm surprised you remembered where we live."

Peggy shook her head as he sat in the recliner. "Adam, you know Mark can't talk about his work." She turned to Mark. "We figured something top secret was going on. Do you want anything to eat? You've lost a little weight."

****

Mark had ample parking spaces to choose from when he drove back to the hospital. He stepped into the garage elevator and rode to Hailey's floor. The energy leaked out of the day, and the gravity of what had transpired made him want to crumple on the floor. He could sleep for a week.

Finding Hailey asleep, he checked her cell. David had promised to call when he learned any information. There was only one text: *Back at the Windy City. Hope you're feeling better.* Gazing at her, he touched her bruised hand and sighed. He shouldn't have given Parker a hard time involving Hailey. If Ethan or Anna were in danger, he would do the same thing.

He made a mental note to pick up his replacement phone at the office, a new task on his 'to do' list. As he waited for David's message, he sat back and breathed, finally allowing himself to relax. So much had happened since the afternoon. Thank goodness Parker had been there to help decipher the clues that his astute wife gave them.

"I remember a smell," Hailey said. "A fruity smell. I thought of it when Greg handed me the flowers."

"What kind of fruit?"

"I don't know. Sweet."

"The roses reminded you of that?" Parker asked.

"No, not that." She hesitated. "I smelled it when he said good-bye. He had the same odor my grandfather had on his breath."

Parker's eyebrow arched. "Any chance your grandfather was a diabetic?"

"How did you know?"

"The fruity scent is a sign of ketoacidosis. It happens in diabetics with out-of-control blood sugar." Parker's gaze shifted to Mark.

His eye twitched. "I'm going to kill him."

"He's the mole." Parker agreed.

"Who?" Hailey said.

"It all fits." Parker paced the room. "At the dinner party. He was your guest. During Hailey's rescue—he helped organize the operation. Now he's snooping to see what she remembers."

Mark clenched his teeth. "I'm going to kill him."

Hailey put her hands on her hips. "Will somebody please tell me what's going on?"

A blistering anger choked him just thinking about how Greg had duped him. He had been so blind. If Greg weren't already dead, Mark would rip open his chest, tear out his heart, and let the scavengers feast on his guts.

At midnight, a light tap sounded on Hailey's door, and Mark slipped into the hallway. David beamed. "We found Sherman."

Mark blinked twice. "How is he?"

"Weak. Delusional. He wouldn't have lasted much longer."

"Where is he?"

"Here. The paramedics said this has the best trauma center around. He's in the ER now. He'll stay here for a few days, but he should recover. His wife arrived thirty minutes ago."

A chill spread through Mark. "That was close. You saved his life."

David laughed. "Give Hailey the credit. You better watch it. She's sharp."

Mark stared into the distance. "I'm finding that out." He rubbed his eyes. "How did you dig up so much on this case? I sorted through Sherman's files for weeks."

"Simple. I talked to his family."

"But Greg told me he interviewed them last...Oh, shit."

"I'm sure he helped a lot." David smirked, his eyes widening. "I bet he also offered to conduct all the interviews. Fortunately, the news broadcasted the Chicago overdoses every day. All I did was put it together." He yawned and slapped Mark's shoulder. "It's late. Some of us have to work in the morning. Call if I can do anything more."

Mark shook David's hand, blinking away the tears blurring his sight. "Thanks for everything."

"You got a second chance with Hailey. Don't blow it." David took two steps and halted. "Oh, I almost forgot. I saw something tonight that might interest you."

"What?"

"Mendoza's mansion was empty."

"What do you mean?"

"The housekeeping staff's gone. Sherman was the only one there."

Chapter Sixty-One

Colleen worked long days in the lab, completing the dopamine for her father. She drove to the nursing home, imagining his excitement. The game room near the lobby was full of eager residents playing bingo with a group of high school teenagers. She looked inside for him and continued onward to A.C.'s room. A male attendant was helping A.C. put on his slippers. "Hi, Daddy." Wrinkles formed on his forehead as he looked at her. Sometimes he felt like a stranger, too.

The attendant stood. "Your daughter's here. Do you need anything before I leave?"

A.C shook his head. "No, I'm fine."

"I'll check on you later, Andrew." The attendant turned and gave her a reassuring smile. "He's had a hard day." He picked up A.C.'s dinner tray and left.

A.C. extended his arm. The tremors were lessening, but his movements seemed more rigid.

Holding his hand, Colleen gave a gentle squeeze and kissed his cheek. The fresh scent of deodorant soap masked the odors of his bedding. She pulled a ladder-back chair from the table and sat. "The tulips are pretty today." Smiling, she opened her purse on the table and took out a small box. "I have a surprise. I made the dopamine." This was as exciting as opening a gift on

Christmas. She unscrewed the plastic container and showed him.

He inspected the pill. "This is dopamine?"

Her smile turned sour. "I came the other day. I showed you the formula Bruce made."

His eyebrows knitted together. "Is he still working on his research? I thought he quit." A.C. eyed her suspiciously. "Did you tell him I have Parkinson's?"

She blinked, but a tear escaped. How could he forget so much? "I made a sample for you." She put the tablet in his hand. "Here, take it. I can't wait to see how this makes you feel."

He grumbled. "Another damn pill. I'm tired of taking pills."

"Please, Daddy."

"Leave it." He folded his arms over his chest.

Arguing was futile. She could only stay a few minutes. She opened the top drawer of the nightstand and pointed to the tiny compartment near the front. "Okay, I'll leave it in here so the nurses won't see it. I'll bring more next time I come."

"I'll take it later."

She sat back in her chair. "So what did you do today? Did you mingle with any of the other residents?"

He scratched the stubble on his chin. "Bruce came today. We talked about our project. Henry couldn't make it."

There was that name again. Henry. She slid her chair in a little closer. "Who's Henry?"

His nose crinkled, and he sniffled. "We didn't know. We couldn't help him."

She patted his hand. "Know what?"

A.C. wrapped his arms around his sides and swayed. "Millie knows it was an accident. She believes me. I love her."

Colleen bit her lip. Prying for information might confuse him more. "I loved her, too."

He took a shaky, deep breath. "You look like her. Beautiful. She had more freckles on her nose, but you have her eyes."

She sighed. How could her father, a genius in his time, remember so many details about his past, but not what he ate for breakfast? "It's getting late. When I come back, I want to tell you about a man I met."

"A boyfriend?"

"You could say that. I've been dating him for a while. I want you to meet him."

"Do you like him?"

"Yes. He makes me feel special. He spoils me." Her face warmed, and she rubbed his arm. "We'll talk more next time I come."

Colleen tucked him in bed and fluffed his pillow. "Can I get you anything before I go?"

"No. Everything I want is right here." He touched her hand, his face content.

She bent over and kissed him. "I love you, Daddy."

He pulled the cotton blanket to his neck and closed his eyes. "I love you, too."

Chapter Sixty-Two

Hailey woke to the sunlight pouring through the window and stared at her husband. Mark was sleeping in a contorted position on the pullout sleeper chair. At least he was getting some sleep. Who could rest when the nurses paraded in the room all night checking vitals? She plucked the comb from the travel bag Mark had brought and pulled it through her tangled hair. The sponge bath the previous day had helped her disposition, but if she could get a real shower, she'd feel brand new.

The TV remote hung next to her bed control. She pressed the power button and adjusted the volume. The meteorologist reported the weather around the country. An attendant knocked on the door and walked in. "I have your breakfast tray."

Hailey looked at the food—eggs, cornflakes, black coffee, wheat toast, and grapefruit juice. The assortment of food seemed like overkill, but her rumbling stomach was eager. She spread butter on the toast, poured milk in the cereal bowl, and began eating.

Mark turned, stretched, and shot upright, his eyes enormous. "What time is it?"

"Almost eight o'clock." She lifted the glass from the tray and drank the grapefruit juice. "How'd you sleep?"

"Not bad, considering it wasn't our bed." He rubbed his eyes. "How long have you been up?"

She yawned. "For a while." A long while.

He leaned on his chair and peered at the food tray. "The food doesn't look too bad. Are you hungry?"

"Starved. Do you want anything?" Hailey inched the tray toward him and glanced at the TV. "Shhh. I want to hear this." She increased the volume.

"What's on?"

"The news. There's going to be an update on the Chicago overdoses after the commercial. I want to hear what they're saying."

Bolting from his chair, Mark grabbed the remote and turned off the TV. "You shouldn't watch the news today." He set the remote on the ventilator next to the window.

"Why?" She yawned again. "I want to hear about the latest updates on Euphoria. The reporter is covering another funeral."

"Why do you want to hear about that? It's depressing." He picked up the pillow he had slept on and positioned it under Hailey's head. "Focus on getting rest. You should take a nap after you eat. You look exhausted."

"But, I—"

"No." He reached over and helped himself to a piece of toast. "Trust me on this. Dr. Gewant will never let you come home if you're not well. Besides, I want to enjoy us today, not worry about the rest of the world."

When she finished eating, a nurse with short chestnut hair walked into the room and gave Mark a nasty look. Hailey laughed.

The nurse would have made a great mother hen. She took Hailey's temperature and pulse. "Would you like help with your shower now? The doctor will come in later this morning."

Hailey pushed her empty food tray away from the bed. "Definitely."

Mark kissed her forehead and tucked in his shirt. "I'll come back after you shower. I want to check on Sherman."

Pulling some clothes from her bag, she grinned. "You want an excuse to stay away from the nurses."

He winked and ruffled her hair. "That, too."

****

Hailey finished her shower and texted Ethan and Anna short messages before school. Dr. Gewant tapped on the door, carrying his laptop. "Knock. Knock. How are you feeling today, Hailey?"

"Good." She smiled. "A lot better than yesterday."

He peered at the laptop screen and typed on the keyboard. "The last round of lab results look great. Your chemistries are almost all back in the normal range."

Hailey cheered. "When can I go home?"

He stopped typing and lifted his head. "Let's not push it. I'll stop back again later to check how your therapy is going. The nurses told me that you've been walking the halls. Keep up the good work."

When Mark returned from Sherman's room, she updated him about the latest on her lab results. Mark's secretary phoned and arrived later in the morning with a bag of magazines, puzzle books, and a photo of Anna and Ethan. "Mark asked me to pack the picture from his desk. In case you get homesick."

Hailey lifted the frame to her breast. Her heart contracted in a spasm. "Thank you. I miss them so much. We talk on the phone, but it's not the same."

"I'm sure they can't wait to see you, too." Tamara turned and gave Mark a broad smile. "We've missed you at the office. The news about Greg has everyone in a dither. Owen swears he'll throw the book at him posthumously."

Mark's face turned crimson. "I hope they nab Mendoza and all his cronies. Hailey could've died if we didn't find her when we did. It was only by some miracle that she took those pictures on her cell phone. Without them, we wouldn't have known about the antidote."

Awed by his attentive concern, an electric sensation surged through Hailey.

Tamara stood and grabbed her purse next to the chair. "I should go. I want to visit Elliot before I head back to the office. How's he doing?"

"I saw him earlier this morning. He's very weak."

"He's lucky to be alive." She adjusted her purse strap over her shoulder and walked to the door. "You must have caused quite a commotion yesterday. You're the topic of conversation at the nurses' station."

When Tamara left, Hailey patted her hand on the sheet, and Mark sat next to her. She warmed at his new protective side. Her skin tingled as he wrapped his arms around her waist and breathed in her hair. "Mmm. Gardenias."

"Can I ask a favor?"

He took another deep breath and kissed her forehead. "Anything."

"Take me home." She held her breath, anticipating resistance.

His hold relaxed, and he shook his head. "You know I'd do anything for you, but you almost died."

She rubbed his arm in a reassuring way. "But I didn't."

"But you could have. I can't risk you getting hurt again."

"This whole ordeal has been a wake-up call. I want to go home. I need a place to sleep without interruptions." She smiled. "Besides, it's time we celebrate our anniversary."

He held her hands, his warm fingers caressing her skin. "Let's wait another day."

Raising her chin, she pressed her hands to her waist. "Mark Langley, I'm going home today one way or another. Even if I need to hail a cab."

"Why do you have to be so stubborn?" Mark shook his head. "The kidnapping obviously didn't affect your determination."

"No, it didn't." She kept her hands to her sides. Waiting. He had no idea how headstrong she could be.

Tilting his head, he exhaled a long sigh. "There's no stopping you, is there?"

"No." She laughed. "Plus, leaving early will make the insurance company happy."

He grinned and walked to the door. "Okay. I'll speak with Dr. Gewant about getting you released."

"Yes!" She jumped off the bed and clapped her hands. "Let's pick up the kids on the way home."

Mark halted at the door and turned. "No. I want one night alone with you without them sneaking into our bed. You'll see them tomorrow, after you get a good night's sleep."

Hailey remained optimistic while Mark tracked down Dr. Gewant. When the nurse picked up the empty dinner tray, the doctor entered the room, scowling. "I'd like you to stay at least another day."

She walked around the bed, gathering her belongings. "I'll leave against medical advice."

Mark's eyebrows arched. "I think she means it."

They quibbled back and forth. Finally, the doctor massaged his temples. "Okay. You win, but you have to promise you'll rest in bed and return to the clinic for a check-up in two days."

"But—"

Mark pressed his hand on her shoulder and gently squeezed. "She'll be a model patient."

Dr. Gewant began discharge paperwork at the nurses' station.

Hailey jumped in the air and picked up the small bag Mark had packed the day before.

He grasped the items Hailey had collected. "I'll pack, hon. You might have fooled the nurses, but I know you're tired."

By the time the car merged on the highway, Hailey had rested her head against the window and drifted to sleep. When she woke, Mark was pulling the car into the garage.

He turned the car off. "Give me a minute to get the house ready."

A few minutes later, he returned and helped her from the car. A warm glow coursed through her body as she stepped inside the house and scanned the living room. Aside from a video controller next to the television, the place was immaculate. She hugged him. "I'm impressed. It feels good to be home."

Mark set down her travel bag and took her hand. "It's wonderful to have you back." Gazing into her eyes, he kissed her tenderly on the lips and led her to the stairs. "Can I make you something to eat before I tuck you in bed?"

She shook her head. She could melt with this affection. "No, thanks."

As they walked up the steps, he followed behind and mumbled, "I'm hungry, but not for food."

Hailey held back a giggle. She'd update him later about the improved hearing implants.

When he opened the bedroom door, she gasped. Vanilla-scented candles on the dresser lit the room. A trail of rose petals led from the floor to the bed. A bottle of Cabernet Sauvignon chilled in an ice bucket on the nightstand. Her eyes widened. "You did this?"

He tilted his head, seeming to enjoy her astonishment. "You're not the only one who reads those magazines you buy."

She pointed to the rose petals scattered across the comforter. "This is so romantic."

He grinned. "We had a bunch of them around the house."

"Everything's perfect." The smile on his face made her fall in love all over again.

Mark choked up as he lifted her in his arms. "Happy anniversary, honey. I love you." He bumped his shoulder against the door and closed it.

****

Hailey wrapped her arms around Mark's neck as he stepped inside the room. "Honey, I'm perfectly capable of walking." Her heart fluttered as he stepped to the bed and lowered her onto the mattress.

He pulled the covers over her waist, staring with unwavering attention. "I promised Dr. Gewant you would rest."

"A good-night kiss will help me rest better." A warm glow expanded through her body as he bent down and kissed her. She leaned up and kissed him in return. She had missed him so much. As he guided her head back on the pillow, her mouth opened over his lips. An image of Greg groping her flashed through her mind. Her body stiffened.

Mark leaned back. "Oh, God, I'm sorry." He stood and raked a hand through his hair. "I'm such an idiot. This is too soon. You just got home."

She sat, wringing her hands back and forth on her lap. "No, I'm sorry. I don't know why I did that."

He groaned. "We can't keep pretending everything's all right." She turned her head, but he sat next to her. "Why do you tense up? Talk to me. Please."

She couldn't let him in her prison. "You wouldn't understand."

"Try me." No anger came from his voice, only a sad helplessness. "What are you keeping from me?" he whispered. "Don't you realize I love you? What goes through your mind when we make love that causes you to pull away?"

Hailey closed her eyes. Dammit. He *had* noticed. For the first time in years, tears rushed to her eyes. Unable to bear the hurt in his voice, she scraped her hands. *Don't cry.*

"Don't you want that special connection between us?" His voice was raw. He took her hands into his grasp. "Let me help you stop scratching." He kissed the tiny scars. Shivers soared through her body. "I can't pretend anymore. Tell me what's going on. Sometimes being strong means taking a chance."

The tenderness in his voice chipped away at her resolve. She didn't deserve his loving attention. *Don't lose control.* She scratched harder.

Mark waited. He placed one hand on top of hers and caressed her arm with his other hand. "Please...Trust me."

Didn't she want this? She avoided his eyes. At last, she inhaled a deep breath and waited for the right words. "I was kidnapped." A weight lifted from her chest. She raised her eyes. In the dim light, his stare fixed on her, waiting. "It happened a long time ago when I lived in California. The others escaped, but I didn't get away." She shuddered. The kidnappers had dragged her by the hair into the cabin. Mark looped his arm around her waist. She bit her lip to keep control. "They tortured me."

He cursed. "The bastards."

She stared into the night; the darkness made it easier to hide. "They beat me. Burned me with cigarettes. Twisted my bones until they snapped." She closed her eyes. "They threatened to shoot me. Two of them fired rounds of ammunition over and over until I couldn't hear." Her voice was barely audible. "And then they raped me."

Mark pulled her close to his chest and buried his face in her hair. "Oh, my God. No."

Her eyes blurred as the viciousness flashed through her mind. She had never wanted him to know. "I pleaded with them to stop. At some point, I passed out.

When the authorities found me, they flew me to the SCA facility in Austin."

"Why the SCA?"

She met his gaze briefly and lowered her face against his chest. "The agency had collaborated with the FBI on tracing the kidnappers."

"Were they able to arrest your abductors?"

She nodded. "The FBI found them hiding out in an abandoned cabin. They shot the woman as she tried to escape. The two men died in prison."

He tightened his grasp around her. "I can't imagine what you went through."

"Bruce Hanover was the head doctor. He said I suffered some kind of mental breakdown."

"Is that where you met Parker?"

She nodded. "He was an intern. We felt a connection. He encouraged me to build a new life for myself and helped me progress in rehab. Because of Parker, I began speaking again. After I learned about my parents' deaths, he led me through my darkest times."

"I'm so sorry, honey." He kissed her forehead. "Who took care of you after you left the hospital?"

"Stefan Bruno was my guardian. He was the director of the SCA. I lived with his family until I turned eighteen. He arranged my psychological care and tutors so I could finish high school. After months of intense counseling, I made up my mind to work at the agency. Stefan was wary at first. But I convinced him I could handle it. I worked hard. I trained for over a year before he agreed. I was good at my job. People didn't suspect a young woman like me working as a secret agent." She shivered.

He wrapped a blanket over her shoulders. "Why did you leave?"

She closed her eyes, shaking at the memory of Parker's parents lying murdered in the street. "When Parker became an agent, we worked together. Then one day a case went horribly wrong. I resigned and traveled east to go to school. That's where I met you."

Mark brushed away the wisps of hair on her face, but she couldn't look at him.

"Tell me the rest."

Slowly, she raised her eyes. He waited, as if he knew she was still hiding something. She inhaled a few breaths, garnering more courage. "I got pregnant from the rape."

Mark inhaled, his jaw tightening.

Hailey forced herself to continue. "It was a hard decision, but I carried the baby and put him up for adoption. I couldn't take care of a newborn in my condition. Parker and his wife had been trying to have a baby for years, but they couldn't conceive. They adopted my baby. Justin's my son."

Mark wrapped his arms around her. His heart pounded against her chest and provided her strength. "Giving birth to Justin and then saying good-bye was the hardest thing I've ever done. I couldn't eat. I couldn't sleep. I couldn't even see Parker at first. I didn't want to live."

"Then what happened?"

"Stefan kept me busy, but nothing worked. He made me meet another therapist. I learned coping mechanisms to control my feelings. The counselor told me I wouldn't be happy until I let go of the past and forgave myself, but I only needed one thing."

"What was that?"

"Time."

"Time?"

"Time to mourn. To heal." She lowered her head. "Time to face what I did to Justin."

"What do you mean what you *did* to him?"

She shook her head, blinking hard. "I gave him away. What kind of mother does that?"

He leaned back. "Don't say that. You wanted a better life for him."

She lowered her head and picked at her hands. "I'm a horrible mother."

Mark lifted her chin with his fingers and locked her eyes with his. "You're an incredible mother."

She wrestled with the warmth in his husky voice. "Not a day goes by that I don't think about him, wondering what he's like, what he's doing." A hot tear stung her cheek. It surprised her. Crying was a sign of weakness. "Parker asked for my help while you were in Chicago. His son—my son—overdosed on Euphoria. I didn't want to lie to you, but I didn't know what else to do. I couldn't abandon him again. Can you ever forgive me?" Holding her breath, she searched his face. Would he give her absolution?

His compassion was too much.

Her body shattered with sadness. She leaned forward and sobbed in his arms.

Chapter Sixty-Three

Mark's mind spun like a gyroscope. The pain she had bottled up, refusing to forgive herself, oppressed her. He clutched her tighter as the crying intensified. Struggling to say the right words, he closed his eyes, helpless to erase the torment. Was there no limit to her suffering? Dammit! Why didn't Parker tell him that the boy laid to rest in Chicago was her son?

Helpless, he smoothed her hair. "Shh. Don't apologize. You had to help Justin." He pressed his lips tight. He should have figured this out sooner. The signs were there. Concentrating on work was easier than upsetting her with questions. He buried his face in her hair and wept.

"I'm sorry I never told you." She sniffled. "When I look at Ethan and Anna, I wonder how I could've given up a child. What I did was unforgiveable."

"No." He touched her quivering lip and brushed her cheek with his finger. He couldn't love her more than he did at this moment. "You need to forgive yourself. You did what was best. Your sacrifice makes me cherish you more." Mark wiped his own eyes as she drew a tissue from the nightstand and blew her nose. She reclined back into his arms, and he caressed her hand with his thumb. "I'm glad you told me. We're going to get through this together. I promise."

Time stopped as they held each other and cried again. Mark smoothed Hailey's hair, and her body relaxed. He kissed her forehead, and his lips grazed the tip of her nose. He caressed her cheeks. At last, his lips found hers.

Chapter Sixty-Four

With the burden of her secret lifted, passion flowed through her body. Hailey kissed back, timidly at first. Her lips parted. She teased his tongue with hers until the kisses became hotter, fiercer. An ember deep inside reignited. She slid her fingers over his chest. She wanted him. Needed him. Her cheeks heated, and she unabashedly met his stare. "I'm feeling better now."

His eyes roved over her body, and he raised an eyebrow. "How much better?"

Leaning over, she whispered in his ear, "A *lot* better."

Mark swallowed. "You need rest."

She lowered her gaze to the bulge in his pants and grinned. "Looks like neither of us wants to sleep."

He shook his head. "Not tonight."

Her arms curved around his neck, and she kissed him hard, emboldened by her revived confidence. "Nonsense." She unbuttoned his shirt and tossed it. "You won't need this." Hailey lifted her blouse over her head and simpered. "Can you help with my bra?"

Mark groaned. "You're a vixen." He unfastened the back and slid the straps off her shoulders.

Hailey flung the lacy garment on the carpet and pulled him closer, tugging at the button on his jeans. "You'll be more comfortable without these." The corners of his mouth turned upward. Unzipping his jeans, she lifted her eyes to stare into his and slid the denim over his knees. "Don't try to be a saint."

"You're making that impossible." His breathing quickened. "Are you sure you're ready?"

She wrapped her arms around his neck and kissed him again, tracing her fingers down the spine of his back. She had never felt more ready. "I'm sure."

He held her tightly and eased her down onto the pillow, whispering in her ear, "I want you to remember this night forever." Cupping her breast, he brushed her taut bud and leaned closer, gently tugging the peak in his mouth, teasing her until she gasped.

He stopped, but she pulled him closer, and the exploration continued; his moist tongue cooled her burning skin. As she squirmed against his strong, hard body, she smiled as he grew more aroused, and he rasped hungrily over her midriff, "I love to see you burn under my touch." He tugged at her panties. "I don't think you need these either." Running a hand through her long hair, he recaptured her lips. Her tongue danced with his. Then slowly his warm hands slid down her back, settling on her buttocks.

Hailey rolled on top of him; his engorged manhood pounded against her as she traced the muscular contours of his broad chest. She giggled. "I need to investigate a little." Flattening her breasts against him, she slid down his lean torso.

Finding his erection, she raised her eyebrows and grinned. "What's this?" His hot swollen flesh throbbed in her hand. His masculinity was at her mercy.

Drawing in a deep breath, he gazed at her. "You've enjoying this, aren't you?"

She nodded and stroked him. "Hon, I'm just getting started."

He groaned in protest. "We need to slow down. I'm going to lose control." He rolled her on the sheet and shifted on top, his firm hands caressing her legs. "Two can play at this game." His fingers toyed with her triangular mound of curly hair below her navel. "What's this button?"

His coy smile was adorable. She squirmed, his hot touch teasing her receptive body. "I think you need to investigate more." She breathed out the words.

He advanced toward her inner thighs and probed her.

She struggled to lay still. When his exploration ended, she was more than ready for him. Hailey's lips parted under his kiss as he slid inside her.

"Hon, did you lock the door?"

Mark took a moment to register her question. "What?"

"The door. Did you lock it? What if your parents drive the kids back tonight?"

He stammered. "For crying out loud. It's the middle of the night."

"Can you lock it anyway? Please?"

He grunted as he walked to the door and rotated the lock. He turned and leaped on the mattress, wrapping his arms around her.

Hailey laughed. "You look cute when you run." A strange sensation spread through her. Happiness? No, it was more like carefree bliss. Making love was different now. In ten years of marriage, she had never surrendered like this. Tonight, she would give herself to him—her whole heart and soul.

He pulled back the sheets. "Where were we?"

It had been a long time, but their bodies found a rhythm and moved together in perfect unison. He buried himself deep inside her as she bucked beneath him, her fingernails digging into his shoulders. Her legs tensed, and her breath came out in shaky puffs. "I'm on fire."

"Let it come, honey."

She clung to him, unsure what to expect. The determination on his face intrigued her. He leaned on his arms. She arched her back as he drove into her. At last, the intimacy consumed her whole body. "Mark!" She trembled beneath him, her body tingling. Deep inside, her spasms tightened around him. She pressed her thighs together, but the pulsation continued. She locked eyes with him. "I love you."

With one final thrust, he buried his face in her hair, and they soared together.

He collapsed onto the bed next to her. They held each other in silence as their breathing slowed.

She sniffled as a tear rolled down her cheek. "That was amazing."

"You're amazing." He leaned on his elbow and kissed the perspiration from her forehead. He tilted his head when her tears continued. "What's the matter?"

"That hasn't happened before...not in ten years...not ever."

He wiped her cheek and nestled her closer against him. "I sort of figured. Happy anniversary, honey."

"I'm glad your parents watched the kids tonight."

His eyebrows arched. "I can arrange another day or two if you want."

Hailey gave him a playful grin and ran a finger down his chest. "That's okay. We'll have to get more creative with our time. You realize this was only for the first year. We have nine more to celebrate."

Mark swallowed hard. "Tell me you're kidding."

She yawned. "Of course, I'm kidding." She gave him a long, passionate kiss and snuggled closer. "We'll celebrate the other years during the night."

Chapter Sixty-Five

Hailey woke to Mark's lips pecking a path along her shoulders. Their passion had burned long into the night and her entire body tingled inside. Mark's warm arms wrapped around her, and he kissed her as the morning sun shone through the window. This was the definition of ecstasy.

"I love having you back home." Mark's voice trailed off as he nuzzled her neck, the stubble from his chin tickling against her skin.

With her fingers, she traced a line across his broad chest, wandering lower until she found her target. She lifted an eyebrow. "Can you stay home today? It's Saturday."

A smile spread across his face. "Rest this morning and we'll rendezvous tonight. I need to check in at the office before the kids come."

"The office? Why?"

"I need to pick up my new phone. And see what's going on with your case. One of Mendoza's men is still out there."

Hailey frowned. "Who?"

He fell back on the pillow and rubbed his eyes. "Greg said Mendoza hired three scientists. One was Bruce. And we found Moulin's blood in an abandoned building. But there's one more."

"So we need to find the other researcher?"

"Not we—me. You're staying in bed." She scowled, and Mark shook his head. "Yesterday, Greg mentioned the third scientist decreased the concentration of aparistine. What worries me is he didn't say anything about removing the other chemical Bruce added as a safeguard."

"What chemical?"

"He attached a neurotransmitter that blocks a receptor site from working." Mark shrugged as she stared at him. "I might have mixed up some of that. Bruce's explanation confused me."

Grinning, she twisted on her side, aware his stare lingered on her breasts. "I'm surprised you remembered that much."

He pulled her on top of him and ruffled her hair. "I would've become a doctor if it meant saving you." He massaged her shoulders. "Maybe I'll sign-up for a class next semester."

"Ha. Ha. We can be study buddies. Mark and the Science Geek." She tapped a finger against her lip and forced herself to stay focused. "So you're looking for a researcher who worked with Bruce and Moulin?"

Mark's eyes widened. He shifted her off his chest and grabbed her cell from the nightstand. "I wonder…"

"Who are you calling?"

"I'm texting Bruce." His fingers skated across the keypad. "He and Moulin were classmates in med school. Bruce mentioned another colleague helped with their research project. I can't remember his name."

The phone buzzed, and Mark read the text. "Son of a bitch!" He jumped out of bed and grabbed his jeans from the floor.

Hailey sat and clutched her robe. "What's wrong?"

"I was duped." He took the garment from her. "You're staying here and resting. Dr. Gewant's orders."

"Where are you going?"

"Checking out a hunch." He opened his top dresser drawer and picked up his gun. "I won't be gone long."

Hailey's insides turned a somersault. She clutched her chest.

Mark looked at her. He turned, staring at the firearm in his hand, and halted. "When will I learn?" Shaking his head, he laid the gun in the drawer. He unzipped his jeans, slid back under the covers, and wrapped his arms around her.

She narrowed her eyes. "What just happened?"

"Work can wait. I'm sure everything's fine." He planted kisses on her neck. "I want to munch on you instead."

She touched his cheek and frowned. "Now I feel guilty. How long will it take you to check out the lead?"

He shrugged and caressed her breasts. "An hour. Maybe two. I'll go later."

Sighing, she threw back the sheets. "Go. Now."

"No." He slid his hand across her abdomen and settled on her hips. "We still have two more years to celebrate on our anniversary."

His flustered expression excited her. She giggled and brushed her nose across his chest. "We have more than that. Sleep deprivation is affecting your memory."

He cuddled closer against her, his growing erection pressing against her thigh. He wasn't playing fairly.

"Okay, let's enjoy one more year, and then you can go."

"Promise me you'll stay and nap afterward. I'll call Mom before I leave and tell her I'll pick up the kids at two."

She nodded. "I'll wait here until you return. But don't take long. I'd like to shower together before they come. We haven't done that in a while."

****

Hailey lay in bed, still basking in the memory of the frenzied explosions during her intense lovemaking with Mark. She didn't want to wash his scent from her skin and let the memories end. The doorbell chimed, and she hesitated. She pulled on her cotton robe and peeked through the window blinds. Whose car was in the driveway? The doorbell continued buzzing as she slid on her jeans and t-shirt and walked downstairs. She peeped through the eyehole and opened the door. "Parker!"

He greeted her with a bright smile. "How are you feeling?"

"Better." She stared at his bloodshot eyes and haggard appearance. What could have happened to him? "Come in. Can I get you anything? Coffee? Breakfast?" She stepped aside as he entered the house.

"No, thanks, I'm good."

"How did you know I was home?"

He flashed an impish grin and scratched his unshaven chin. "I stopped by the hospital this morning. Dr. Gewant told me you are one very persuasive young woman."

She grinned. "It took some coaxing, but he caved."

Parker followed her to the living room and they sat on the sofa. "Where is everyone?"

"Mark left a while ago. The kids are still at their grandparents. They're coming home in a few hours."

He leaned forward. "Are you sure you're okay? You look exhausted."

Hailey's cheeks burned. "I'm fantastic." He studied her a little too long. She had seen that gaze before. "Parker, we never talked about what happened that night in the hotel."

He gave a dismissive wave. "Skip it. I was out of line."

Her insides twisted. Why did she feel sorry for him? "I don't think I ever thanked you for raising Justin. I owe you a lot. I wouldn't have recovered without your help."

"I'll always care about you."

She rubbed the back of his hand. "When I was younger, I wanted the type of marriage you and Grace had."

Parker bowed his head, sinking it into his hands. When he looked at her again, sadness filled his eyes. "I was miserable with Grace. At one point she wanted me to leave."

Hailey blinked hard. "What? Why didn't you say something?"

"You were my patient. I couldn't burden you with my problems. When Grace found out we could adopt a baby, she asked me to stay."

"I had no idea."

"We tried hard to make things work, but a baby couldn't fix our problems. I had feelings for you."

She gasped. "Did Grace know?"

His mouth formed a tight line. "She sensed something. She never liked it when we worked together. She threatened to take Justin to Chicago. That was around the time you and I worked the terrorist case in London—when we first kissed."

She lowered her chin. How could she forget that night? After the mission, Parker's lips tasted hers, and his strong hands roamed her body. She burned for him, but it took every ounce of her strength to push him away—for Justin's sake. "I remember."

"I kept my loneliness inside. After my parents died, I needed to blame someone for my lousy life and loveless marriage, so I lashed out at you. I was angry with myself. Their deaths weren't your fault." His eye twitched and he avoided her gaze.

She placed her hand over his. "We don't have to talk about this."

"Yes, we do. I put the guilt trip on you when they died. I should've taken them around the city. They flew the whole way from Connecticut to see me and I had to act like the big shot and pretend I was too busy for them. They adored you. Don't you see, Hailey? You were the best thing in my life. I treated you terribly, and I pushed you away." His voice became brittle. "You quit the SCA, and I ruined any chance with you. Can you forgive me?"

Hailey's hand quivered as she covered her mouth. Fifteen years she had waited to hear these words. "I...I don't know what to say. Of course I forgive you."

Parker turned away and wiped his eyes. "Do you mind if I ask you a personal question?"

She narrowed her eyes. "It depends."

"Are you and Mark happy?"

Her lips parted, waiting for the words to form. "That isn't any of your business."

Parker's face reddened. "I'm sorry. I saw flowers around your house with notes attached. From all the apologies, I gathered you were having problems."

"What goes on between us is private. You had no right to snoop around my house. You're not responsible for me anymore. I can take care of myself."

"You're right. But I told Mark he doesn't appreciate you."

"You said that?" Hailey shook her head. "How did he take it?"

"Like swallowing cod liver oil." He rubbed his chin. "Why did you have to marry a man with a strong right hook?"

She covered her mouth and laughed. "Oh, Parker, I love him. Sure, we have spats. All married couples do. But Mark makes me feel special. He gets me. He respects and loves me more than I could ever imagine. We share two remarkable children. He's a fine man and a devoted husband." She took in the disappointment in his face. "I'll always cherish those times we had together. But it wouldn't have lasted. I needed to grow. My life is with Mark."

Parker sighed, sadness swelling his eyes. "He's one hell of a lucky guy."

She reached over and touched his hand. Despite their painful parting, he was still a special friend. "Are we okay?"

She held her breath as he eyed her up and down. Finally, he nodded. "We're good."

Exhaling, she shifted in her seat. "Now tell me about your trip. How's Justin?" She waited, but he didn't answer. Something preoccupied him. "Parker did you hear me?"

He blinked hard and looked around the room. "He's stable. Still no change."

"I'm sorry. Why isn't the antidote working?"

"I don't know." His eyes teared up, and he turned away. He pointed to the cell phone on the end table. "I thought you said Mark wasn't home."

She stretched her arm over his legs and picked up her cell. "I bet he forgot it after he called his mother this morning. He uncovered a tip on another researcher."

"Who?"

She shrugged. "I didn't see. He texted Bruce and asked him about his other colleague from med school."

"Can you show me, please?"

Hailey typed in her code. "Andrew Cecil Toole. Toole?" She scratched her head. "Where have I heard that name before?"

Parker read the text and looked up the name on his cell. "There's a business associated with A.C. Toole a few exits north. I'll try to catch Mark."

"What's going on?" She couldn't control the trembling in her voice.

"I'm sure it's nothing, but I want to check it out." He stood and lowered his cell in his pocket.

Hailey shot up from her seat like a rocket. She dropped the phone on the couch and grabbed his arm. "What aren't you telling me?"

"Nothing, I swear. I'll know more after I catch up with him." Parker walked to the door.

She hurried after him. "Wait. I'm coming with you."

He shook his head. "No. Mark would kill me."

"Then I'll find him myself."

"Dammit." He raked his hand through his hair. "Why are you so stubborn? You just got out of the hospital. For once in your life, let someone else handle it."

She grabbed his arm. "Swear you won't let anything happen to him."

His hand rested on the door handle. "You truly love him, don't you?"

A tear spilled from her eye. "More than anything in this world."

Parker wiped her cheek. "Then I promise."

When he left, Hailey paced the floor. She leaned over the sofa and picked up the cell phone. Searching on the phone's browser, she found Andrew Cecil Toole's business address. She shoved the phone in her front jeans pocket. Pulling her shoes from the closet, she slipped them on, grabbed the car keys, and hurried out the door.

Chapter Sixty-Six

Mark took the freeway exit and turned right toward Toole Biomedical Research Laboratory. The facility was two miles away, but the traffic was heavy. A.C.'s involvement would turn Colleen's world upside down when she learned the truth. He thrust a hand into his pocket. "Shit. I forgot the cell phone—and my gun." *Of all times not to have backup.*

He tapped his fingertips on the steering wheel. A.C. was well over sixty. The old guy wouldn't be hard to handle. He'd peek inside the building and return with backup if anything looked suspicious. If Euphoria got out, the drug would spread like a nuclear chain reaction.

The brick building was a modernized two-story structure. He parked under the signpost advertising the facility. Why was the lot empty? Racing to the main entrance, he tested the handle. A sign on the door posted the hours. Crap. The facility was closed on weekends. A keypad hung on the brick wall next to the door. Smiling, he shook his head and punched in the one code A.C. always used: C7H16NO2. When he had dated Colleen, he good-humoredly memorized the molecular formula for acetylcholine. The lock clicked.

Mark walked past the reception desk where the nosy secretary had sat when he visited Colleen a few days earlier. If only he had looked around the building then. He hurried down the corridor.

He entered a room full of supplies and gas cylinders arranged around a fireproof cabinet. On the ledge, a glass bottle set next to a container labeled HBr. Mark peered at the name. Hydrogen bromide. Hmm. He should have studied harder in high school.

Manuals and books lined the shelves of the office in the second room. He rifled through the letters on an oak desk and found a calendar underneath a stack of mail. He scratched his head. How odd. The calendar was from five years prior.

He sped down the hall to the next room. Scattered on one counter were glassware and test tubes. A bulky analyzer stood in the corner with papers strewn across the adjoining table. He picked up the report and his jaw dropped. The word "Euphoria" was on the cover along with its chemical structure. He flipped through the pages and stopped at the synergistic studies. Bruce had mentioned this. The results were incomplete. Under the reports, newspaper clippings recounted the Chicago drug deaths. Mark shook his head. Damn. He had wanted to be wrong about A.C.

He searched the adjacent room. A claw hammer sat beside an empty crate with a pile of nails spilled over the floor. Crates stacked on pallets filled the side of the room. The shipping labels were for Afghanistan, Thailand, Canada, Burma, Venezuela, and Bolivia. He shifted the cartons and revealed more destinations—Colombia, India, China, Laos, and Mexico. He grabbed the hammer and pried off the top slats from a crate.

Once the lid detached, he tossed the hammer on the floor. Little packages of cushioned air pillows filled the box. He fished through the pouches and pulled out a heavy container wrapped in brown paper. Unrolling the covering, he frowned. An urn? He reached into the ancient vessel and swirled his fingers around the smooth sides. Maybe Euphoria was secured inside. He turned the piece of pottery upside down and shook it. Nothing. Mark kicked the crate. Where the hell was the drug?

He laid the container back in the crate and grabbed a section of cushioned packaging. He couldn't resist the stress reliever. He braced his ears for a loud pop and squished. A milky white powder sprayed in the air. "Hot damn!"

A metallic clank sounded behind him. Mark turned. His eyes zoomed in on the hammer heading toward him. Whaam.

****

Mark moaned. His head ached as if someone squeezed it in a vise. He struggled to lift his hands, but they wouldn't budge. The wooden chair he sat on wobbled as he wriggled his legs. Someone had secured his feet together. A blurred image moved in front of him.

A woman pounded a hammer against the crate he had opened. When he moaned again, she turned and stepped toward him. "I can't believe you remembered the code."

He twisted his arms and blinked as his eyes adjusted. "Colleen?" His speech was garbled.

"You shouldn't have come. I have a lot to do." Her eyes were pools of liquid nitrogen, ready to freeze him on contact. She busied herself, wheeling a crate to the door.

"What are...when did...how did you get involved in this?"

She snapped. "This is Daddy's dream. He spent his entire life researching ways to block his patients' pain."

Mark groaned. "Your father doesn't want this."

She waved her hand, dismissing him. "He doesn't know what he wants now. I need Euphoria to help his Parkinson's."

"Don't...you're not helping him. You're—"

"Stop it!" She covered both hands over her ears. "I'm doing this for Daddy. You don't understand the benefits of coupling these chemicals. Daddy's life is meaningless if this doesn't work."

"He's made lots of contributions in medicine."

"But they weren't his *dream*." She pointed at the crates. "This is his vision, and I'm so close to making it a reality."

"Bullshit." A sharp pain shot through his head, and he winced. "That's your dream, not his."

Her eyes darted back and forth. "Euphoria is better than he imagined."

"It kills people. You almost killed Hailey."

She threw her head back and snickered. The magnolia-scented perfume filled his senses. "She should have died. Damn those medics for coming! I purposely didn't dilute her dose."

"You bitch." He yanked his wrists hard. The zip ties cut into his skin like a razor blade. "Why would you try to kill Hailey?"

She bent down, her breath warming his ear. "Don't you get it, darling? If I can't have you, she won't either."

His mouth dropped as he stared. "You're insane."

She paced on the floor, raking her hands through her long hair. "We made an adorable couple—you and I. But you chose to marry that sophomoric girl. She isn't right for you. She can't love you the way I did. I waited for you after Harvard." Colleen stepped back, her body shaking. "Can't you see? I loved you!"

"So you tried to kill her?" He strained against his seat. Hailey went through hell because of her. "Why do you think Euphoria is safe to use now?"

She wiped her eyes. "I'm wasting time on this nonsense."

"Did you find the chemical Bruce linked to his dopamine?"

Her head snapped up. "What are you talking about?"

"Check the formulas yourself."

Colleen hesitated and stepped toward the boxes in the corner of the room. "You're lying. I need to load these crates."

He jerked his hands; the ties cut his skin deeper. "Yeow! Dammit! You're going to kill a lot more people. Are you listening to me? Bruce added an anticholinergic."

She dropped a box and turned. Her icy stare penetrated him. "You're wrong."

"No, I'm not. The high aparistine concentration killed the kids with a larger dose. But the boy who took a smaller amount went into a coma—because of the anticholinergic."

"Daddy reviewed the structure."

"You trust a man who can't remember his own daughter? How stupid can you get? Hell, you might as well give him the drug, too."

Colleen slapped his face. "How dare you. He approved the formula."

His muscles stiffened at the glint of madness in her glassy eyes. "Perhaps you're right. Maybe he didn't catch the anticholinergic."

She turned and attached a shipping label to a crate. "Daddy would have told me if it was wrong. He's worked with these receptors his entire life."

"Then why didn't he tell you about the antagonist Bruce hid in his dopamine? He had to know Bruce sabotaged it." Mark didn't know what else he could say to convince her. Surely, she would realize his argument made sense.

Colleen stepped back and massaged her temples. Slowly, she scanned the room. Her frenzied face transformed into determination. Lifting her chin, she marched out the doorway.

Mark's chest tensed. What was she up to? She reappeared and pushed his chair into a tiny office off the main lab. She ignored his stare and disappeared again. With his head throbbing, he twisted his hands against the nylon zip ties. Warm fluid spread across his wrists. Colleen returned with a platform truck. He peered through the open doorway as she arranged six crates on the cart. She rolled the cart into the hall and came back, loading more boxes.

Maintaining a steady pace, she moved all the crates. Next, she wheeled tall gas cylinders into the lab. Mark fought through the pain as he worked on slipping his hands through the plastic ties. He paused a moment as she carried a Bunsen burner into the office and set it on the counter. Twisting the rubber tubing, she connected the burner to the gas outlet along the wall.

His heart shuddered as she rotated the valve handle. Glancing at Mark, she smirked and ignited the burner. She left and returned, hauling in another cylinder and placing it beside the burner. She rotated the handle counterclockwise.

"What are you doing?"

"Opening the valves. I turned them in all the rooms. When the place blows, everything will explode."

He yanked against the ties. "No, Colleen! This isn't you."

She hissed. "How would you know?"

His face chilled as she glared at him. She could actually pull off her scheme. "If you kill me, you'll spend your life looking over your shoulder. Agents don't forget when someone kills their own. Untie me. We'll figure this out together."

"No. Manuel's my life now." She stooped down and tested the tautness of the ties around his wrists and ankles. "The tank's full. When it empties, the gas in this room will cause a substantial explosion." She sniggered. "I see the fear in your eyes. Soon this whole building will blow. Good-bye, Mark." Cackling, she swung the door open and sashayed away.

The clicking of heeled shoes faded. A faint hiss leaked from the tank. He would feel the effects soon. Blood ran from his wrists as he wrenched his arms behind his back. The nylon ties sliced deeper into his wrists.

He twisted his torso from side to side. The chair tipped over and his head banged hard against the floor. "Yeow!" White stars floated around him. *Stay conscious.* He raised his head. The pain vibrated through his body. The open door taunted him. Freedom was three feet away. He shouted for help. *Don't let me die. God, I need more time. Please...*

Sweat dripped from his face. The walls spun around him. His vision blurred. The gas choked him; he couldn't gulp air into his lungs. A primitive fear gripped him as the gas slowed his reactions. He was losing feeling in his arms. Still bound to the chair, Mark slid along the floor and inched his way to the opening, quickening his movements. His listless legs moved aimlessly and bumped against the door. The door moved, and the latch clicked. Damn.

The room would blow any minute. He shouted one last time, and fell into a spasm of coughing. *Please, God. Give me a second chance with Hailey.* He groaned. *Okay, give me a third chance.* Using all his strength, he kept his eyes open. So this was how life ended? *God, no!* He would close his eyes for just a moment...

Chapter Sixty-Seven

Hailey spotted Parker's sedan on the interstate. Traffic was heavy, but she managed to get two cars behind his rental car. She pushed on the gas pedal, but the vehicles in front of him slowed to a stop. She depressed the button on the steering wheel. "Call Tom Parker."

"Hello?"

"Parker. What's the holdup ahead?"

"Hailey? Where are you?"

"Look in your rearview mirror." She gripped the steering wheel, steeling herself for his reaction.

"Hailey, Dammit! Turn around at the next exit and go home."

"No. I need to make sure Mark's okay." A horn beeped and sirens sounded behind her.

"Mark's going to kill me if you show up."

"I'll tell him it was my idea. Besides, you might need some backup." An ambulance flashed its lights a short distance ahead. "Can you see what's causing the delay?"

"A police car is pulled over on the berm. It looks like two cars were in an accident. The exit is in four miles."

A motorcyclist revved his engine as he drove between two lanes of vehicles and made his way past

Hailey's car. Crazy driver. No wonder there were so many collisions. "Does Mark suspect the man from the text—Andrew Toole?"

"I don't know. I doubt he's dangerous, though. Bruce mentioned he lived in a nursing home."

"I wish Mark had taken my phone." She sighed and looked in the mirror. "Is that another ambulance?"

"Yeah."

The siren echoed from behind and passed Hailey's car. "The tow truck's here, too."

"It shouldn't take long now." Parker's voice was tense. "The police are directing traffic."

****

Hailey's tires screeched as she jumped on the brakes and made a quick turn into the parking lot. She had tailed Parker's car, anticipating he'd try to lose her. Parker planted his rental next to Mark's SUV. She pulled up next to him and hurried out of the car. "Don't try to stop me." She didn't wait for a reply.

They dashed to the building, and Hailey yanked on the door's handle. A platform truck blocked the entrance to the lobby, and Parker shoved it down the hall. They raced into the first room. Hailey glanced at the reagents and supplies in the cramped space. "Mark! Are you here?"

She followed Parker down the hall as they searched each room. A pungent stench filled the air, choking her. She had smelled it before, but wasted no time mulling over it.

With erratic strides, they entered the last room on the first floor. "Mark! Where are you?" Scattered glassware covered the counter. The same smell filled her senses. She covered her nose with her arm and held her breath. "Gosh, that smell." The place was like a construction scene, nails and wood chunks spread over the floor.

"Where the hell is he?" Parker mumbled.

"Let's try upstairs." She turned toward the door. Four Bunsen burners were lit on the counter. "What the...?"

Parker pointed to the rear office door with an illuminated window. "There's a light on." They rushed to the door. Parker drew his gun from his belt, and Hailey turned the handle. Inside the room was a study in chaos. Mark lay unconscious or dead on the floor.

"Mark!" She stooped down, flattening her fingers against his neck. "His pulse is weak. Oh, God, no!"

He moaned.

"Mark!" Hailey slapped his face. "Wake up!" Blood coated the zip ties binding his hands. She lifted her head. "Find something to cut the ties. We can't drag him out with the seat tied to him."

Parker slipped the gun back in his pants. He searched the countertop and rummaged through the drawers. "Got it." He held up a pair of scissors and cut one of the ties.

Hailey shook Mark's shoulders. "Come on! Snap out of it."

Listlessly, he raised his eyelids. "Gas."

"What?" Hailey leaned back and gasped. The foul odor. She looked at Parker. His face revealed his horror.

"Shit!" Parker worked faster, cutting the remaining ties around Mark's arms and legs.

She slid her hands under Mark's head, and snapped them back. Something slippery oozed on her skin. She looked at her palms coated in blood. "Oh, my God!"

She patted his cheeks a little gentler and propped him on her knees. "Dammit. Wake up!"

"Get…out…"

Parker finished cutting the last tie. He hoisted Mark's limp body against his chest. "We need to hurry. Try to stand."

Mark mumbled and slumped backward. Hailey braced her hands to steady his torso. "He'll never make it out."

Positioning himself, Parker shifted his arms beneath Mark's shoulders. "Stay awake. Work with me." He lugged Mark out of the office and dragged him across the floor into the hall.

She searched for an escape nearby. "Look!" She pointed to an exit sign hanging from the ceiling near the rear of the building.

Taking a breath, Parker hauled Mark across his shoulders in a fireman's carry and ran. "Open the door!"

The noxious fumes twisted her stomach. She tightened her lips and sped past him toward the exit. Her palms rammed against the steel door. She launched into the bright sunlight and took a deep lungful of fresh air.

Parker raced through the door. "Keep running!"

They advanced a few feet. *Boom!* The loud blast echoed behind them. Hailey looked back as Parker stumbled. *Sssshblamm!* The second explosion roared, and the shock wave hit Hailey hard. The punch of the explosion propelled them through the air. They landed in a cluster of prickly barberry bushes. The side of the building exploded. Windows shattered and shrapnel shot in different directions. A hurricane of hot temperatures twisted around them. Hailey's skin tightened and blistered. Another huge bang followed, throwing intense heat toward them. She turned as the flames erupted through the rooftop.

Parker looked at the flames. "Holy shit!"

Hailey helped him carry Mark behind a row of boxwoods and collapsed. Acrid smoke rolled out of the building in waves. Ash covered them like polluted snow.

Wheezing, she struggled to breathe and waited for her heart to slow. Her dry throat burned when she coughed. When the coughing spell ended, she found Mark lying on the ground next to Parker. "Mark!" She crawled closer toward them and slapped Mark's face. "Mark! Wake up!"

The fumes from burning rubber and chemicals nauseated her. The flashes subsided, and Hailey sat in the grass, sweat dripping down her forehead. A sudden coldness ran through her as she stared at the fire.

Mark groaned and began moving. As he hunched over, she wrapped her arms around his shoulders and steadied him.

Between spasms of coughing, Parker sat in the grass and rubbed his eyes. "Now he wakes up."

"Honey, are you all right?" She kneaded Mark's back as he hacked.

Mark held a fist over his mouth while he coughed. He stared at the blazing fire and black smoke. "I don't…Will let you know as soon as I…" He stopped as another coughing fit hit him. "As soon as I can breathe." He stared at the inferno. "What happened?"

Parker wiped the sweat from his brow. "Oh, Hailey and I were in the neighborhood. We found you half-dead on the floor so we decided to carry you outside to chug a few beers with us."

Mark gave him a blank look. Parker seemed to struggle to keep a straight face.

She continued rubbing his back. "Don't listen to him. Someone tried to kill you."

A high-pitched blast popped, shooting another flame through the roof. Mark touched his hand behind his head and flinched. Blood trickled down his forearm. "Colleen. She was packing the drug. She did this."

Parker tugged off his undershirt and ripped the material into thin strips. "Hold these." He gave the pieces of cloth to Hailey and turned to Mark. "Who's Colleen?"

Mark clutched his head and swayed to the side. "A.C.'s daughter. Mendoza's other partner."

Sirens whirred in the distance as Parker limped behind him and inspected Mark's head. "Was A.C. involved?"

As Parker touched one of the cloths to Mark's scalp, Mark winced. "No. He's in a nursing home. Colleen was trying to find a treatment for his Parkinson's."

A scowl formed on Parker's face. "If I were her father, I'd pass on her help."

Hailey's hand shook as she handed Parker strips of fabric. "Is the wound deep?"

Parker skillfully wrapped the fabric around Mark's matted hair. "Yep. This should stop the bleeding, but he needs stitches. Make sure an ambulance takes him to the ER. He could have a concussion, too."

A smaller explosion erupted, and flames splayed the building. Mark turned and watched. "Colleen opened the valves on the gas lines. She wanted to destroy the evidence."

Hailey stared at him, her body shaking all over. "And you." Didn't Mark comprehend the gravity of what happened?

Parker secured the last strip around Mark's head. "What did you do to upset her?"

Mark's gaze settled on the inferno. "I don't have a clue. I guess she was all fired up about something."

"Fired up?" Hailey snickered. Her stomach lurched. Colleen Toole. The girl Laura had warned her about. "That crazy woman was mad as hell."

Chapter Sixty-Eight

Mark's head pounded like a jackhammer was jouncing it. The enormity of the situation began to sink in and he trembled. "You're right. Colleen wanted to kill me. You two saved my life."

Parker shrugged and sat on the ground across from him. "I was only doing my job."

Mark extended his arm and shook Parker's hand between coughing spells. "You could've died in there along with me. Thanks. I'll never forget what you did."

Hailey leaned beside him and kissed his forehead. "Oh, Mark! Thank God you're okay." She continued rubbing his back between his coughs. "Are you feeling any better?"

"My lungs feel raw. And my parched throat is killing me." He pressed a bloody hand against his head and flinched. "How did you find me? You promised to stay in bed and rest."

Parker tilted his head toward Hailey. "She helped me find this address. I told her not to come, but she wouldn't listen."

Mark gazed at her. Their eyes locked in shared understanding. How did he get so lucky? He couldn't help but smile at her. She meant everything to him. "No one can stop Hailey from doing what she wants. I learned that years ago. She's worse than the kids."

Another loud pop exploded from the building. "The kids! We have to call my mom and tell her I'll be late."

Hailey reached in her pocket and removed her phone. "I'll call. You stay here with Parker. I'll walk down the block so your mother won't hear the explosions."

When she left, Parker shook his head.

Mark touched the serum weeping from his wrist and grimaced. "What?"

"Next time, take a phone and call your partner for backup."

"It wouldn't have helped." His voice was still hoarse. "My partner died—the lousy weasel."

"You could've called me."

Mark stared a moment. "I didn't think you were coming back."

"What? And leave you and your wimpy agency alone to fend off drug smugglers?" Parker coughed. He lowered his head and cursed. "These past two weeks have been pure hell." The sirens grew louder. Parker stood and shouted a string of expletives over the crackling inferno. He stepped toward the street.

"Wait. Where are you going?" Mark used every ounce of stamina and stood.

Parker turned. A small stream of blood dripped from a gash on his cheek. "People are gathering. After the day I had, I'm not sticking around for long hours of police questioning. You both can enjoy that pleasure. Alert the authorities about A.C.'s daughter." Another round of flames belched from the building. "I'm sure our cars are totaled. Tell Owen to settle the matter."

Mark scratched his head. "You're not making any sense. You're going to leave?"

"I came back to help you finish the case. You have it under control." Parker stretched his neck. "Besides, it's time to go. I have some unfinished business in Chicago. A promise I made to a drug dealer last week."

Mark drew his eyebrows together. "But what about Hailey?"

"She doesn't need me. She has you."

He blinked. The fog in his head made thinking difficult. "But she'll want to thank you. She'll be disappointed if you don't say good-bye."

"She'll get over it." Parker stared, his voice hard.

"Dammit! Why are you being such an ass?"

Parker's jaw muscles twitched. "Damn you. Don't you think I want to stay? I've lost everything. My son's dead. My family's gone. I have nothing left."

He instantly regretted upsetting Parker. The man just buried his son. "But you and Hailey are friends. She told me how you helped her years ago. Your relationship has to count for something. Hell, you and I are even getting along."

Parker shook his head. "I can't do this now."

"But—"

"She wants *you*. Don't you get it?"

Mark scowled. What did Parker expect him to do? At last, he raked his hand through his matted hair and sighed. "What do you want me to tell her?"

Parker turned to the direction of the sirens. "Tell her I need some time alone." His face was as hollow as his voice. "She'll understand. When you get home, break the news to her about Justin. I don't want her to read about his death on the Internet. Be gentle. She's going to need you." He turned and limped down the street, disappearing in the crowd of onlookers. A parade of police cars, fire trucks, and ambulances whizzed down the block.

Mark settled back to the ground and held his head. The headache was relentless. The last thing he wanted was to spend the afternoon fielding questions. He turned his head and spotted Hailey escorting a pair of EMTs toward him.

Chapter Sixty-Nine

Somehow, Colleen arrived at Manuel's mansion without wrecking the cargo van. She couldn't stop thinking about Mark's conversation. His argument made sense. But if the formula was wrong, her father would have noticed the mistake. He wouldn't have tricked her into making a drug that would kill him. Oh, dear God. Maybe he did.

The bile rose in her throat. She squeezed her hands, but the shaking wouldn't stop. *Please, Daddy. Don't look in the nightstand.* She looked around, unable to move her legs. She had to pull herself together. He didn't remember anything anymore. The likelihood of him finding the pill in the nightstand was slim.

She would visit him at the nursing home that afternoon anyway. She couldn't hold off on telling him about her trip any longer. No doubt, a month would seem like a long time to him, but she could return sooner, if necessary. No one had connected Toole Biomedical to Euphoria—until now. She squeezed her eyes and sniffed. What she did to Mark was reprehensible. But there was no other way. A part of her had hoped they would get back together someday. Mark was the first guy who didn't sleep with her on the first date. Even her current beau didn't give her that consideration.

Working at a fast pace, she stacked crates by the guesthouse and stowed the other load in the garage. Colleen checked her phone. There was plenty of time to see A.C. Check-in was in three hours. A weight anchored in her stomach. Leaving him was risky. This might be their last time together. As she put the keys in the ignition, her cell phone rang.

"Hello?"

"Ms. Toole? This is Sarah Underwood—the administrator at Oakwood Nursing Home."

A sudden, cold chill of panic gripped her. "Is something wrong?"

"I'm sorry to tell you this over the phone, but your father passed away in his sleep this afternoon."

Colleen gasped and gripped the steering wheel. "What? No!"

"He had a good day. He didn't complain of any pain. In fact, before he took his customary nap, Andrew said he was feeling better. The therapist found him when she came for his treatment."

The rest of the conversation was a mumbled blur. Sobbing, she climbed the stairs to the empty bedroom and buckled on the edge of the bed. Finally, she floundered to the bathroom, leaned over the sink, and splashed water on her face. What would A.C. think about her latest actions?

****

At the nursing home, the supervisor escorted her to the room. "Take all the time you need. I'm sorry for your loss." She squeezed Colleen's hand. "The staff knew you were close."

When Colleen was alone, she found herself crying again. She studied her father's face. He looked happy.

Her hand trembled as she opened the drawer. The pill was gone. She sat next to him and sobbed. "Daddy. Why, Daddy? Why?"

The nurse came in the room and checked on her. "Your father requested that his body be left for science. This is a difficult time, but we should contact the agency. If you'd like, the social worker can help you with a memorial service."

Colleen talked between her sobs. "Thank you. I'll need a few days. Is that all right?"

"Take your time. Some families delay the service for a couple of weeks."

When she walked out of the facility, her soul was a hollow vessel. The only happiness she had left was with Manuel. She glanced at the time. She could still make her flight if she hurried. Grieving could wait.

At the airport terminal, she found two vacant seats. Manuel had planned to drive in from his summer house in Maryland and meet her. She hadn't seen him since Antonio died. She longed for his comforting touch. When he didn't show, she tapped her fingers on her phone and texted him.

The shipment is packaged and ready. Where are you?

She had missed Manuel. Preparing the drug during the past few days had consumed all her time. Colleen smiled. She had captivated him the first time they met. "Why do you call me Bella?" she had asked. "You know that's not my real name."

"I know, but in my country, *Bella* means 'beautiful,' and you are a gorgeous woman." Her heart had warmed at Manuel's reply. He had insisted everyone call her Bella. She sometimes forgot Colleen was her name. With her father dead, she wouldn't have a reason to stay in the States anymore.

A beep alerted her of an incoming text:

My dearest Bella, I am sorry, but I took an earlier flight. After much consideration, I don't think my family will approve of me seeing an American woman. Even one as lovely as you. I can't risk hurting you. I will stay in Colombia indefinitely. The US Govt has begun probing my businesses and domestic properties. It will be difficult for me to return. Thank you for changing my life. You showed me how to love. I will forever cherish our time. Siempre te amare. *You will always be my beautiful Bella.* Besos. ~ *Manuel*

Colleen read the text three times, each time hoping the message would change. Tears rolled down her cheeks. So many betrayals. Mark. Daddy. And now Manuel. The drops spilled on her phone as she shook her head. Chasing her father's dream had monopolized her life, and now she would pay for the sacrifice. When airport security and the police approached, she jumped. An officer read her the Miranda rights, but she barely listened. Around her, people gawked. She lowered her head as the police handcuffed her and escorted her out of the terminal.

Chapter Seventy

Mark leaned back in his chair, content to have his family home. The living room was full of life again.

Ethan shuffled into the kitchen and stood beside Hailey at the sink. He held a hand against his abdomen. "My tummy's growling. When's dinner?"

She shook the colander filled with strawberries and tossed them in the spinach salad. "Ten more minutes."

"But I'm starved. Can't you hear my stomach? Listen. Grrrr."

Grinning, she handed him a berry. "Here. This will tide you over a few minutes. Go finish your game with Grandma and Grandpa. Dinner shouldn't be long."

The juice dribbled down his chin, and he grabbed a napkin from the counter. "They're awful at video games. You're even a better player than Grandpa. Anna's playing with him now."

She tousled his hair. "You could ask them to play cards instead. They like Go Fish."

Mark held back a laugh. Hailey had been home a week and seemed much better, though she still struggled at times.

"Are you sure Hailey's feeling well enough to cook?" Peggy had been watching her daughter-in-law from a seat on the living room sofa and she stood. "I'll go in and help her."

"Mom, she's fine. This is her way to thank you and Dad. She made me promise to keep you in the living room."

"She's exhausted. Look at her." Peggy's brows narrowed. "You both need rest. I don't understand what's going on. Hailey comes home ten pounds lighter, and you managed a concussion and two stitches in your head."

"Dear, he can't talk about his work." Adam glanced up from the TV screen. "When do you go back to the office, son?"

Mark regarded Hailey as his mother sat on the sofa again. "In another week. The doctor put me on medical leave through next Friday."

"What did your supervisor say about you being out so long?"

Mark chuckled. Work didn't stress him anymore. "He's miffed. Especially since I'm taking vacation in three weeks. Did I tell you that Hailey's friend Cubby Banks is coming to visit? We're giving him a special tour of D.C. and bringing him to a Nationals game."

Adam laughed. "Too bad the Chicago Cubs aren't in town."

Mark turned his head toward the dining room as Hailey set the table. After the explosion, he had told her about Justin's death. For two days, she cried and refused to leave the bedroom, heartbroken. "I failed him again. I lost him forever." They talked at night when the kids went to bed. Although she was still despondent at times, she was finally opening up more about the kidnapping. She rarely scratched her hands anymore.

Mark told the kids that Hailey's sick friend from Texas had passed away. She was in higher spirits around Anna and Ethan, and they didn't let her out of their sight.

When Hailey cried, Anna picked up a baby doll and climbed next to her. She wrapped her tiny arms around Hailey and squeezed. "We'll make you feel better." Ethan even curled up next to his mother and read stories to her instead of playing video games.

Hailey remained Mark's primary concern. "I'll take you to Justin's grave when you're ready," he'd offered.

"Wait until the pain subsides," she told him.

Anna was sitting next to his father. She hopped up and threw the controller, waving her arms in the air. "I won."

"Want to play again, Grandpa?" Ethan grabbed the gadget from the floor. "Mom! Is ten minutes up? I'm hungry."

The aroma of roasted chicken and baked rolls wafted through the living room. Mark stood as Peggy started toward the kitchen again. "I'll help Hailey finish up, Mom. Stay here and keep an eye on Dad."

Chapter Seventy-One

Hailey removed a cookie sheet filled with homemade rolls from the oven. She smiled at Mark when he moseyed into the kitchen, and she smeared a light coat of butter over the rolls.

"What can I do?"

She turned on the faucet and began filling a water pitcher. It was nice that Mark helped prepare the meals now. "Give me a minute and you can pour water in the glasses."

He bit into a hot roll while he waited. "I got an email from Owen. Some agents seized the remaining boxes from Mendoza's mansion. Owen said the DEA fast-tracked aparistine to the Schedule 1 list. The government is deciding whether to add Bruce's dopamine to the list or keep his discovery private."

She handed him the pitcher and gathered warm rolls in a basket. "I can't believe Stefan let Bruce go. Research was his whole life."

"I forgot to tell you. Cubby texted me yesterday that a private company in Georgia hired Bruce. He'll continue his research there. Looks like the old guy will be all right."

"That's wonderful. I'm glad his career isn't ruined." She followed him into the dining room. "So Euphoria didn't slip out of the country?"

He filled the glasses, spilling water as he rotated around the table. "Unfortunately, some did. Owen said the Colombian government hid reports of a dozen deaths from a 'drug incident' last week. I bet Mendoza smuggled some samples back. I'm sure the government there isn't happy."

"I guess now the jerk realizes he has a tainted drug. I doubt he'll find anyone in Colombia to continue the venture, especially since no one has the shrub anymore."

"Our people will keep an eye on him." Mark set the pitcher on the table.

Sighing at the spills on the tablecloth, she walked into the kitchen and grabbed a dishtowel. Their life was finally getting back to normal.

Giggles came from Ethan and Anna in the living room as she returned. Mark took the towel and blotted the spills. "Dad sure does enjoy playing with the kids."

She smiled. She had missed the gaiety while she was away. "He just said, 'How do you work these damn controls?' "

Mark grinned and handed her back the towel. "He did?"

She nodded. "And your mom told him to watch his language around the kids."

"I guess you're going to keep your ear implants?"

She shrugged. The range in her new hearing tickled her. "I'm undecided. Stefan told me Cubby could insert a less sensitive pair." She swung the dishtowel behind his neck and drew him closer. "Until I decide, you and the kids better beware what you say about me."

"So you're okay not going back to the SCA?"

A wave of pleasure rushed through her as his gaze locked with hers. His dreamy blue eyes still entranced her after all these years. "I might go back someday, but not now. I want to take care of you and the kids."

Smiling, he tilted his head and drew her close. "Is that what you want? You don't need to prove anything to me. I want you to be happy."

Hailey caressed the nape of his neck and kissed him. "You're what I want." He wrapped his arms around her so tightly she could barely breathe. "Mark," she whispered as he lowered his head and returned the kiss. Her cheeks warmed. "What's that for?"

He leaned closer. "I'm glad you're here."

She nibbled his lower lip and slid her tongue across it. A shiver shook her body. "It's good to be home."

Epilogue

October 1, 2016, Illinois

Hailey held her breath as Mark slowed the car and passed through the wrought-iron gate of the cemetery. Her gaze followed the leaves whirling through the air when the wind gusted.

Mark pulled off the narrow road onto the gravel berm. He stopped the car next to a maple tree and turned off the ignition.

She stared out the window. Maybe after today she would see bright colors again. The wind picked up speed, and she shuddered. Too bad she hadn't worn warmer clothes.

"Here we are." Mark placed a hand on her shoulder. "If you're not ready we can come back another time."

She sighed. "No, I want to see my son. Especially today." As he unlatched his door and walked to the passenger side, she prayed she'd make it through the day.

He opened her door and offered his hand.

Shifting the bouquet of wildflowers on her lap, she clasped his reassuring grip.

They hiked down the pathway and her stomach churned. How could she say hello and good-bye to her child? The granite, marble, and fieldstone markers marched in the distance. Haphazard rows of stiff soldiers. Rows of people—strangers—who left a loved one behind. Some lives fulfilled. Others cut short. Like Justin. Death snatched them too soon.

A strong breeze caught her breath and she shivered. Mark gripped her hand tighter, and they continued searching the headstones. He had been a huge comfort over the past months. She couldn't stand there without his support.

"Justin should be around here. Over there." He pointed at a seraph sculpture embracing a heart-shaped headstone. Next to the marker, a container of fresh chrysanthemums lay on the grass. She read the granite marker:

Justin Thomas Parker
October 1, 1998 to June 15, 2016
Our Precious Child
Now God's Special Angel

Air froze inside her. The flowers in her hand dropped, and her legs wobbled as Mark helped her to the ground. Unable to breathe, she wrestled, until at last, air poured into her lungs. She leaned against his thighs as if he could shield her from the pain. The sky pressed down, crushing her like a heavy weight.

All the memories flooded her at once. The baby moving in her womb. The excruciating labor. The awe of seeing her precious son. His tiny fingers wrapped around her finger.

A twig snapped, and she raised her head. A teenage boy wearing a black-and-gray hooded sweat jacket stood behind them. His red hair complemented a face full of freckles.

"Excuse me. I didn't realize anyone was here. I...I'll come back later."

"Wait." She stretched her arm out to stop him. "Did you know my son?"

Mark jerked his head, but it was too late. She couldn't retract her question.

"He was my best friend." The boy's eyes grew large. "You're Justin's mother?"

She froze a moment and nodded. What did he know?

"My name's Ben. Justin told me about the adoption."

Hailey gasped. "How did he find out?" Parker and Grace wouldn't have told him.

Ben shuffled his feet and jammed his hands into his jacket. "Justin and I hung out a lot after he moved here from Texas. He lived two houses down. We played baseball together. One day a big moving van came. When he unpacked some of the boxes, he discovered the papers underneath Mr. Parker's will. He found out his birth mother was seventeen when she gave him up."

Emotion surged within her chest. "Was he upset?"

Ben nodded. "Oh, he was mad, all right."

"He was?"

"Heck, yeah. He said his parents lied to him. He thought you didn't love him."

Mark squeezed her hand, and she bit her lip.

"But my ma talked to him one day. I told her to stay out of it, but Justin was so angry she stepped in. Ma told him there could be a million reasons why his mother put him up for adoption—reasons we never considered. She said unless he walked a day in her shoes, he shouldn't judge her. Ma said nothing was harder than giving away your own child."

A tingling chill ran down her arm. "Your mother said that?"

"Yessum. I was there when she talked to him. She said a young girl faced hard choices. Like putting his well-being before her own happiness. She said his birth mother must be a strong, kind woman. Then she told him how a mother feels a certain love for her child. Said he should show respect by loving her back—even without ever meeting her. Ma reminded him that he was lucky to have two sets of parents who loved him."

"And?"

"His attitude changed. Especially about his birth mother—ah, you. He also stopped being angry at Mr. and Mrs. Parker."

Tears trickled down her face. "So he didn't hate me?"

He shook his head. "No. In fact, he considered you his guardian angel. You protected Justin. You gave him a better life."

"Did he say anything else?"

Ben rubbed the back of his neck. "Not too much. But we were going to search for you."

Hailey crooked her head. "What?"

"When he turned eighteen, we planned on flying to Texas." The teen stared at the headstone and wiped his eyes with his sweatshirt. "He'd be eighteen today."

Her eyes misted. "That's why we came."

"Mr. and Mrs. Parker called this morning. They asked if I wanted to put flowers on Justin's grave." He pointed to the globe of yellow mums on the ground.

"They must've stopped earlier, so you can hang out as long as you like."

Hailey touched his shoulder. "Can you stay a while?"

He hesitated. "Wouldn't you rather be alone?"

"I'd like to know my son better. Can you tell me more about him?"

His face brightened. "Sure. Where should I begin? He was a huge Chicago Bears fan. And he was an expert playing video games. He won a tournament two summers ago…" Ben continued talking. "He tricked his mother our freshman year. The tattoo was one of those good ones. It stayed on for days. Mrs. Parker kicked him out of the house. She thought it was real." They all laughed. "Justin was the bomb at soccer, too. He played goalie. I couldn't ask for a better friend."

Hailey listened as he related every detail. "What did he like to eat?"

Ben kicked his foot in the grass. "Chocolate milkshakes." His voice quivered. "We obsessed over them. We'd sneak out in the evenings and go through the drive-thru."

"What about school? Did he do well?"

Ben's eyes glimmered. "History was his favorite. He almost failed chemistry, though. I helped him a lot. He wanted to be a vet, but Mr. Parker said he needed to raise his grades."

Hailey beamed as the afternoon ended. "Thank you." She shook his hand. "Justin was an incredible young man. Parker and Grace did a superb job raising him. I'm happy you were his friend, Ben."

The teen nodded and brushed a tear from his eye. "Yessum. We all loved him."

Ben fumbled in his pocket and withdrew a silver pin. "Here. Ma gave this to Justin the day she spoke to him. Mr. Parker gave it back to me after the funeral."

She traced her fingers over the little angel carrying a gold heart. "I can't take your pin. You need something to remind you of him, too."

His cheeks reddened. "I kept his baseball mitt." He placed his hands in the hoodie's pouch. "Besides, he planned to give it to you. He wanted you to have a guardian angel, too."

When Ben left, Hailey and Mark stayed a while longer. She sat on the grass and plucked a daisy from the bouquet, inhaling the honeyed fragrance. "I'm glad we came. I used to think I failed him, but I made the right decision. Justin was a gift—not only to me, but to many people."

Mark touched her shoulder. "Life is full of regrets. We can't change our past, but we can cherish the gifts."

"You're right." She wiped her eyes and brushed her finger over the cherub pinned on her sweater. "Justin will always hold a special place in my heart."

When they walked back to the car, Hailey shivered again. Mark draped his jacket over her back and squeezed her hand. "Are you sure you're ready to leave?"

His concern warmed her heart. "I've been riding a roller coaster all day. Now I want to move forward and enjoy life. Someday, I'll tell Ethan and Anna about their brother."

Admiration filled his voice. "I'm sure the kids would appreciate hearing about him." He wrapped his arm around her. "Time to go home?"

Home.

An image of her parents rushed into her mind. Now the love from her own family warmed her.

Hailey breathed in the cold autumn air. She welcomed its chill as it awakened her senses. She leaned closer, pressing her lips to his, and drank in the sweetness of a kiss.

"Nothing would make me happier."

A word about the author...

A native of western Pennsylvania, C. Becker earned a B.S. degree in Medical Technology and MT (ASCP) certification. She has worked in clinical settings analyzing body fluids and testing drugs of abuse.

As an author, C. Becker has published multiple stories in various genres.